Blackbird,
Farewell

Blackbird, Farewell

Robert Greer

Frog Books
Berkeley, California

Published by Frog Books

Frog Books' publications are distributed by
North Atlantic Books
P.O. Box 12327
Berkeley, California 94712

Cover photo by Brian Erickson / istockphoto.com
Cover and book design by Brad Greene
Printed in the United States of America

Blackbird, Farewell is sponsored by the Society for the Study of Native Arts and Sciences, a nonprofit educational corporation whose goals are to develop an educational and cross-cultural perspective linking various scientific, social, and artistic fields; to nurture a holistic view of arts, sciences, humanities, and healing; and to publish and distribute literature on the relationship of mind, body, and nature.

North Atlantic Books' publications are available through most bookstores. For further information, call 800-733-3000 or visit our website at www.northatlanticbooks.com.

Library of Congress Cataloging-in-Publication Data
Greer, Robert O.
    Blackbird, farewell / Robert Greer.
        p. cm.
    ISBN-13: 978-1-58394-250-5
    1. Floyd, C. J. (Fictitious character)—Fiction. 2. African American bail bond agents—Fiction. 3. Bounty hunters—Fiction. 4. Doping in sports—Fiction. 5. Professional sports—Fiction. I. Title.
    PS3557.R3997B63 2008
    813'.54—dc22
                                                                2008016360
                                                                        CIP

1 2 3 4 5 6 7 8 9 SHERIDAN 14 13 12 11 10 09 08

Dedication

For Phyllis.
My heavenly darling, forever.

—◀○▶—

Acknowledgments

Special thanks to Kathy Woodley and Connie Blanchard, who did their usual yeoman's job, providing astute, much needed secretarial support during the gestation of *Blackbird, Farewell*. I would like to thank my editor at North Atlantic Books, Emily Boyd, for her thoughtfulness and keen editorial eye, especially as it relates to the novel's eye-catching cover art. As always, the copyediting skills of Connie Oehring and Adrienne Armstrong helped bring *Blackbird, Farewell* to its final form.

Author's Note

The characters, events, and places that are depicted in *Blackbird, Farewell* are spawned from the author's imagination. Certain Denver and Western locales are used fictitiously, and any resemblance between the novel's fictional inhabitants and actual persons living or dead is purely coincidental.

"Pack up all my care and woe,
Here I go,
Singing low,
Bye bye blackbird."

—*Ray Henderson and Mort Dixon*

Chapter 1

The $4 million Nike athletic-shoe contract in Shandell Bird's shirt pocket wasn't about to solve his problem—couldn't even put a dent in it—and neither would the $3.2 million he expected to start drawing in October, once the NBA season started. All that money, more money than he suspected any human being was worth, would only add to his problem. Somehow, deep down, he'd always known that.

Months removed from being one of the nation's elite college basketball players, he was now a big-money pro and celebrity, and there seemed to be no way to step away from the limelight. In a sense, he was fortunate that he had to worry about only $7 million and change, not three or four times that, like an NFL draftee. In the NFL the sky was the limit, and salaries weren't limited as they were in the NBA by a rookie scale that was pegged to where a player had been picked in the draft. Although the money tied to his contract wouldn't begin to roll in until he arrived at training camp in October, six and a half weeks down the road, he knew there was no way he'd be trouble free by then. Training camp would only serve to magnify his problems.

Amid NBA draft-day pomp and circumstance, the Denver Nuggets had made him the second overall pick in the draft, assuring him that once the ink was dry on his rookie-year contract, which he'd signed only weeks earlier, the dream he'd been chasing since fourth grade would be his.

Jittery and sweating, "Blackbird," as he was known throughout the sports world, found himself thinking, *Money don't buy you love,* as he uncoiled his six-foot-eight-inch, 250-pound frame from behind the steering wheel of the $93,000 Range Rover he'd bought just days earlier. He was about to make the bank deposit of a lifetime.

The shoe-contract money in his pocket, small potatoes in the professional athlete endorsement game, which he'd requested (much to the chagrin of his agent) be issued as a cashier's check rather than by wire transfer so it could be photocopied and savored for posterity, hadn't yet arrived when he'd bought the Range Rover. But no one at the dealership where he'd purchased the car—not the salesman, the manager, nor the head of the financial department—had batted an eye at letting him walk out the door a few minutes before closing time into gathering darkness and drive off in the options-loaded SUV. He'd bought the car on the strength of a handshake and the single word "Blackbird" scrawled near the bottom of a hastily drawn-up contract.

For years he'd wanted a white Range Rover, had even salivated at the idea, but his girlfriend, Connie Eastland, had insisted he'd look better in black. "Fits your image better," she'd claimed. "Gets to the heart of who you are on the court." Armed with Connie's advice and the endorsement of his best friend since grade school and his former Colorado State University teammate, Damion Madrid, he'd left the dealership in an ebony metallic Range Rover that screamed to the world, *Blackbird here! I'm soaring!*

Nike was already well on its corporate way to selling the public the branding package it had developed for him. The image of a soaring raven was emblazoned high on the outside ankle wall of every one of the $180 pairs of sneakers it sold under his name. He was

"Blackbird" now, the corporate suits he lunched with never missed reminding him. He was no longer, nor could he ever return to being, the lanky, introverted black kid from Denver's Five Points neighborhood. It was time for him to play the part, shoulder his share of the load, and walk the walk he'd been paid $7.2 million for. He was destined to become a household name, an eye-level product on Nike and the NBA's supermarket shelf. He was an energy drink in the offing, a high-end vehicle endorsement—hell, he'd even heard some of the suits whisper that his name could one day be as recognizable as the Coca-Cola brand.

The Nike suits and their NBA counterparts also seemed to enjoy reminding him, and never in a whisper, that they expected him to stay in character at all times. His image, and by inference theirs, would be reflected to the world by his behavior, he'd been told over and over at his Nuggets and his endorsement contract signings. With his head bent low over the signature pages as Julie Madrid, his attorney and Damion Madrid's mother, and his own mother, Aretha, looked on, he'd never looked up at those signings, thinking that he was selling a piece of his soul. Only Damion, who'd watched from across the room, recognized that what most people would have perceived as a festive occasion was causing Shandell pain.

Stretching and glancing skyward before walking away from the Range Rover, Shandell moved quickly across the always crowded parking lot of the Guaranty Bank in Denver's trendy Cherry Creek shopping district.

"Got Blackbird in the house," the guard sitting inside at one side of the revolving door called across the lobby to a line of four instantly attentive tellers as Shandell strolled in.

Shandell nodded at the moonlighting Denver cop, smiled, and

tapped his left fist against the bank guard's. "Ready for training camp?" the cop asked excitedly.

"Yeah," Shandell responded, heading for the nearest teller.

"Well, give 'em what for. Time to let folks on the coasts know we play basketball out here in the Rockies too."

"Sure will." Shandell stepped up to the closest teller and smiled. "Need to deposit this." He nudged the deposit slip and check across a marble countertop. The thin-faced teller, a dark-haired woman who'd emigrated from Russia five years earlier, eyed Shandell, a bank regular, and smiled back. She'd always liked the aloof African American giant with the shaved head, Dumbo ears, and fuzzy growth of mustache that never seemed to fully take hold. He was always polite in a refreshingly un-American way. He also seemed always frustrated, even sad, as if he were chasing something he couldn't quite catch, whenever he visited her window. As Shandell leaned down to meet her gaze, she suddenly had the distinct feeling that he was about to confide in her. When, however, he remained silent, she checked the endorsement on the back of the check and, unfazed by the amount, logged in the deposit.

"Thank you," she said softly, handing Shandell a receipt. Watching Shandell stuff the receipt into his shirt pocket, she asked sheepishly, "How long before your basketball games start?"

"A couple of months." His response was mechanical.

"You'll do good," the teller said reassuringly as Shandell flashed her a parting smile and pivoted to leave. On his way out, he gave the bank guard a halfhearted high five before stepping out into the bright noonday sun. It was a picture-postcard Mile High City late-summer day, but the undeniable crispness in the air announced that autumn, always a time of renewal for Shandell, and his favorite time of the year, was on the way. For him, fall had always meant a return to school and friends after a summer filled with loneliness, save for his friendship with Damion Madrid and his recent romance with Connie Eastland.

Now, instead of returning to the security of high school or a college campus, he was headed for a grueling job that started in October and, depending on how the Nuggets' season fared, might not end until the NBA playoffs the following June. A job in which his every action would be scrutinized and his deepest thoughts dissected. He would be talked about and written about, idolized and put down, and regardless of what he'd told Nike and the Nuggets, he wasn't at all certain how he'd react to that kind of scrutiny. All he could do, as his mother so often put it, was go with the flow. He'd spent most of his twenty-two years climbing a mountain that would have been insurmountable for most human beings, and now that he was at the top, he wasn't sure he wanted to be in a place where the whole world could see him, and only him.

As he slipped into the Range Rover to head home, he had the feeling that Damion, who'd passed on the NBA to head for medical school and a life away from the limelight, might have chosen the better path. Without Damion there to offer him guidance, he knew that for the first time in a very long while, he'd pretty much be on his own.

Moments after he started the engine, his cell phone chirped out its Connie Eastland–programmed aviary ring tone. "Bird here," he said, responding quickly.

The person on the other end of the line chuckled. "See you're at the bank. Puttin' in or takin' out?"

"Who's this?"

"You know who it is, Blackbird. Your guardian angel—and we need to talk."

Shandell opened his door, stepped out of the vehicle, and looked around only to hear the person he was talking to laugh. "Too late for looking, friend. You should've done that long ago." Still chuckling, the caller added in the singsong voice of a tattletale child, "I know something you don't know. So when do we talk, Mr. Number-Two Draft Choice?"

With his cell phone pressed to his ear as he continued to scan the parking lot's perimeter, Shandell weakly asked, "This evening?"

"What time?"

"Seven." Shandell's response was a nervous half-whisper.

"Where?"

"The Glendale courts," Shandell said without hesitation. "Across from the post office."

"I know where they are, friend. Seven o'clock, then. See you there."

The line went dead as Shandell stared into the distance, looking flustered. Several heart-pounding moments later, he sighed, gritted his teeth, and slipped back into his vehicle. Almost as an afterthought, he plucked the bank-deposit slip out of his shirt pocket and eyed it briefly before wadding it into a ball and tossing it onto the floor. Backing out of his parking space, he drove out of the parking lot, slipped his cell phone's earpiece into his ear, and hastily dialed a number. When the person on the other end answered, sounding groggy and half asleep, Shandell said, "It's showtime. Seven o'clock. The Glendale courts. Don't be late." He hung up and sped east on First Avenue, his back to the snow-capped Rockies.

Chapter 2

Rosie's Garage, a legendary Denver landmark, had been located at the corner of Twenty-sixth and Welton Streets in Denver's historically black Five Points community since 1972. Roosevelt Weeks and his wife, Etta Lee, had started their gas station and automotive repair business three months after Roosevelt, known simply as Rosie to his friends, had finished his training at the Denver Diesel Mechanics School. At the time, there was nothing on the premises but two aging Conoco gas pumps, an unpaved gravel drive, and a lean-to service hut for oil changes and lubes. A few locals maintained that the business had succeeded on the strength of Etta Lee's brains and Roosevelt's back, and when you came right down to it, there was more than a little truth to that statement. But no one, especially Rosie and Etta Lee, was keeping score, and over the years Rosie's Garage had grown from a run-down eyesore into a substantial enterprise. The now spotless concrete drives sported three service islands with six tall, stately looking 1940s-vintage Conoco pumps identical to those that had come with the place when Rosie and Etta Lee had originally signed on. The original lean-to hut with its grease-monkey pit had been replaced by a modern garage with three service bays, a gymnasium-sized storage facility, and a small business office. Whenever Denver politicians wanted to catalog the black community's business successes, they never failed to single out Rosie's Garage.

Every pump at Rosie's featured full attendant service from a bygone era. At Rosie's uniformed local high school students or college kids from the University of Colorado at Denver or Metro State still cleaned your windshield, checked the oil, and made sure the pressure in your tires was even all the way around. If they didn't, they knew they'd have Rosie or Etta Lee to contend with, and although Rosie, six-foot-four with no appreciable neck and massive shoulders that made him appear as if he was always wearing football pads, was generally even-tempered and slow to anger, he could intimidate almost anyone if crossed.

During Rosie's ownership, the garage had become more than a tourist attraction and community gathering place. Its back storage room, known throughout much of Denver simply as "the den," was a place for locals to not only hang out and shoot the breeze but gamble, play the numbers, and buy liquor on Sundays, a transaction that was still against Colorado law. Rosie didn't mind folks hanging out, since they accounted for a large amount of his business, but if he caught anyone cursing in front of a female customer, or if a poker game turned sour and ended in a fight, he'd send them all packing, often with a lot more than a simple nudge. Although local politicians, prosecutors, and cops knew what went on in Rosie's back room, it rarely got a mention at the precinct station, in the newspapers, or at City Hall, largely because Etta Lee knew the right palms to grease— and as she'd once commented boldly during a radio interview, "White folks ain't interested in black-on-black crime."

The morning had been slow, and Rosie had his head under the hood of a Jeep Cherokee in the first bay, socket wrench in hand, doing what he did best, as the SUV's owner, Damion Madrid, looked on. Looking perturbed, Rosie stepped back from the vehicle he'd kept in running condition during Damion's college years at CSU, set the wrench on a shop table, shook his head, and said, "If you're gonna keep this struggle buggy runnin' another four years, Damion, you're gonna have to treat it with a little more tender lovin' care. Hell, you coulda been drivin' yourself a brand-new Range Rover like Shandell's, ya know."

"Don't start, Rosie," Damion said, sounding irritated. "I hear enough about my stupidity from strangers. No need hearing it from family." Although Rosie and Damion weren't related by blood, they were indeed family, united by their common bond to CJ Floyd, Rosie's lifelong friend, and Damion's mother, who'd once been CJ's secretary. Julie Madrid had spent three years working her way through law school at night while working days on Denver's famed Bail Bondsman's Row as CJ's secretary. Now she was a successful criminal defense attorney and in large measure the person who kept Rosie, and more importantly the den, out of the newspapers and the limelight.

"I ain't startin' nothin', Damion. Just reflectin' on the truth. Hell, the Trailblazers were ready to snatch you up like a hot biscuit right after Blackbird if you'da decided to go on playin' basketball instead of wantin' to become a doctor. Their GM said so."

"I know, Rosie. I know." Damion sounded exasperated. He'd heard the same comments scores of times. He'd heard the Five Points trash talk—the claim that he didn't have a champion's heart—and he'd put up with the criticism of people he respected, people he'd known and looked up to all his life, as they were quick to remind him in supermarkets and 7-11s that he was crazy to pass up a sure $3 million for an MD.

"People gotta do what's best for 'em, I guess," Rosie grumbled as he grabbed one of the six quarts of oil he'd lined up on a workbench earlier. "Shit, CJ and Mavis just proved that," he added with a smile. "The two of 'em smokin' outta here for Hawaii and gettin' hitched without so much as a peep to none of us. You can't top that."

"Have you heard from them?" Damion asked, hoping to steer the conversation in a new direction. Hours earlier, just like Rosie, he had learned that CJ and Mavis Sundee, the soft spot of feminine sweetness in CJ's otherwise hard-edged life, had run off to the Big Island of Hawaii and gotten married, and he too was sorry he'd missed the chance to celebrate with them.

"Nothin' but a phone call from CJ yesterday sayin' they were married and they'd be gone for the next few days. You know, Etta Lee's really pissed." Rosie broke into a toothy grin. "The woman's been lookin' forward to bein' maid of honor in that weddin' for years."

Sympathetic to Etta Lee's disappointment, Damion nonetheless found himself thinking, *Good for them*. He was thrilled that CJ, after two tours of Vietnam and more than a three-decade career as a bondsman and bounty hunter, and the woman who'd stood by him all that time had tied the knot—happy that they'd finally made their vows before some disgruntled bond skipper or deranged cokehead ended up taking CJ out for good.

"Your mom knows all about it, don't she?" asked Rosie.

"Yeah. She's the one who told me."

Rosie shook his head and grinned. "Guess this could get CJ off the streets for good, 'cause Mavis, now that she's Mrs. Floyd, ain't about to let him risk life and limb runnin' down a bunch of bond-skipping pond scum. Hell, he needs to slow down anyway," Rosie said with a snicker. "The brother's damn near fifty-five years old."

Damion nodded in agreement. "And it's not like he doesn't have Flora Jean to take up the slack," he said, aware that CJ's partner, Flora

Jean Benson, a six-foot-one-inch Las Vegas showgirl–sized former marine, had been trying to get CJ to cut back for the past five years.

"I wouldn't mention nothin' to CJ about slowin' down, though." Rosie crossed his lips with a forefinger. "He might take it the wrong way. Besides, you'd be surprised how quick us old men can be," added the 260-pound onetime college football prospect who'd been forced to choose mechanics school over the University of Nebraska's football program the summer after finishing high school because he'd blown out his right knee in a motorcycle accident.

Damion simply nodded and smiled. Although he was an inch taller than Rosie, he was a good twenty-five pounds lighter. He'd seen Rosie and CJ toss knife-wielding drunks, gang-bangers, and disgruntled gamblers out the back door of the den into the adjoining alley more than once. There was no question in his mind that even five years hence, both men would still be able to do the same thing.

Securing a quart of oil into place to let it drain down into the engine, Rosie dusted off his hands. "Your boy Blackbird ready to start the season?"

"He says he is." Damion glanced across the garage bay toward the gas pumps outside to see a high school kid race toward a waiting car. Smiling and thinking that he'd made hundreds of similar runs as a high schooler, he was about to ask Rosie the kid's name when he realized who the car that had pulled in belonged to. "Shit! Old man Wilhite just drove up."

Rosie slipped his head out from under the hood and tossed the now empty quart of oil into an open 90-weight oil drum. Looking at Damion and shaking his head, he said, "Uh-oh. This should be good. You runnin' or stickin'?"

"Stickin'," Damion said defiantly.

Seconds later, Theo Wilhite strolled into the garage. He paused just inside the middle bay and scanned the place, looking as if he expected anyone within earshot to run for cover. A well-chewed two-inch cigar stub poked from the right corner of his mouth as, grinning ear to ear, he continued walking toward Damion and Rosie. Seventy years old and amazingly fit, with only the barest hint of a paunch, Wilhite, at just under five-foot-six, had spent a lifetime using his booming baritone voice and unbridled pushiness to make up for his diminutive stature.

"Well, well, well." Wilhite's words echoed off the walls as he slipped the cigar stub out of his mouth and stopped a few feet short of Damion. "If it isn't the wonder boy they call Blood and his faithful auto-mechanic companion. Hell, I decide to stop in for some gas, and lookie here, got me a twofer. Never figured on strikin' gold." He looked at Damion and chuckled. "No Blackbird here with you two boys to make it a triumphant kinda day?"

Damion, whose nickname (short for Blood Brother) had been bestowed on him in high school as a badge of honor by a cadre of black friends despite his Latino roots, remained silent.

"Hell, I'm surprised. No Blackbird!" Wilhite shook his head in mock amazement. "But then again, why would Shandell be here? No reason for a future NBA superstar to be hangin' out with a spark-plug jockey and a would-be doctor." He flashed Damion a sly, toothy grin. "How's life been treatin' you, Blood?"

"Fine," Damion said, starting as Rosie slammed the Jeep's hood and flashed Wilhite a look of pure disdain.

"And that's as it should be, son. *Fine*. Especially with you bein' all primed to head off to medical school here shortly and your sidekick Blackbird financially set for life. Things couldn't be nothin' but fine."

Wilhite eyed his cigar stub. Wet with saliva, the stub came close to matching the mocha color of his skin. "Now, as for ol' Theo here, things aren't quite so rosy."

Damion, who'd heard Wilhite's long-standing gripe about losing a good sized bet he'd placed on CSU to win the final game of the NCAA basketball tournament the previous March, only to see them lose in the final seconds, tried to ignore the comment. Turning to Rosie, he asked, "We done here?"

Rosie nodded. "Yep."

Wilhite, who normally let things go after issuing a backhanded swipe or two about either Damion's or Shandell's play in the championship game, seemed more bent on confrontation than usual. "Ignore me if you want, *Dr.* Madrid, or should I say *Dr. Choke*, but . . ."

Before Rosie, who was hoping to put a quick damper on things, had a chance to respond, Damion stepped to within inches of Wilhite. Hovering over the smaller man with his jaw clenched and his eyes narrowed in anger, Damion said, "You're pushing your luck, old man."

"Yeah, yeah, yeah."

Sensing that if things continued to escalate, Damion, known to be hot-tempered in the face of confrontation, might do something he'd be sorry for, Rosie stepped between the two men.

Shaking his head in protest, Wilhite eyed Damion. "Choker."

Seething, Damion cocked his arm and launched a right cross at Wilhite's chin. The punch was halfway home when Rosie hooked his own right arm under Damion's left shoulder and yanked him back into the Cherokee's fender as if Damion were anything but a six-foot-five-inch, 235-pound man. Pushing Wilhite, whose eyes were suddenly silver-dollar-sized, aside as if he were a rag doll, Rosie yelled, "Get the hell out of here, Theo!"

Surprised by Damion's reaction, Wilhite began backpedaling. "Touched a nerve there, did I?" he said, beaming from ear to ear as he increased the space between him and the angry-looking Damion. "Ain't good for a doctor to come all unglued like that, Madrid. No way losin' your cool like that could ever be good for a patient. I'd say you need to practice up on your bedside manner some, son."

Still locked in Rosie's grasp, with his upper lip quivering and his right arm still cocked, Damion had the uneasy feeling that Wilhite might be right. Maybe he did need to practice grinning and bearing it. Perhaps he did need to slap a governor on his often overly competitive spirit. He was still second-guessing his actions when Wilhite erupted with a booming laugh, pivoted, and walked out of the garage.

"Don't give Wilhite no never-mind, Damion," Rosie said, watching Wilhite swagger across the service drive toward his car. "You did good just to keep from cold-cockin' him. I woulda sure enough kicked the little runt's ass when I was your age. But ain't no way a doctor can do that."

"You would've, and I still might," Damion said, twisting out of Rosie's grasp. Boiling with anger and shaking his head, he walked across the bay to watch Wilhite slip into his car. As the self-satisfied-looking Theo Wilhite drove away, Damion shook his head, wondering what Shandell would have to say about Wilhite's comments when they met for their weekly three o'clock scrimmage at the Glendale basketball courts.

The Holiday Inn Express just off Pena Boulevard, six miles west of Denver International Airport, was several steps up from the kinds of places Leon Bird usually found himself staying in. So, as he lay stretched out in his underwear on a king-sized bed in a room he was shelling out $109 a night for, he planned to enjoy every second of his stay. He was in town, after all, to do a little extra father-son bonding with his future NBA superstar son and further cement the relationship he'd worked so hard at fostering the past year.

It hadn't been hard to get inside Shandell's head during that year, or to convince him on visit after persistent visit that what he needed was for his long-absent and worldly wise father to run interference for him in the treacherous world of superstardom. Shandell had been a docile, willing recipient of Leon's scheming and scamming, even in the face of Aretha Bird's protests.

Leon knew he had to be vigilant and above all careful if he expected things to play out his way. He'd have to milk the father-son reunion for all it was worth and uncork his bunco-artist best if he expected to finesse the whole rebonding con down a road that would reap him the ultimate payday. One false step and things could turn on a dime. Shandell would almost certainly recognize him for what he was, and the two overly protective she-devils who ran interference for Shandell—Aretha, whom Leon had left behind to fend for herself sixteen years earlier without so much as a "fuck you," and Shandell's big-titted piece of white pussy, Connie Eastland—would surely finish him off. Aretha he could deal with. He'd whipped her ass scores of times before. The Eastland woman was another story. One he was currently working on solving.

Personally, he'd never seen any percentage in screwing around with a white woman. Getting tangled up with them was the equivalent of giving some redneck cop an excuse to crack open your head. Or a reason for a car full of tanked-up white boys, out looking for trouble, to kick in your teeth. He understood his son's infatuation with the Miss Annes of this world, but he couldn't fathom why Shandell would take such a risk.

He'd often wondered how much Shandell had told the big-titted shrew about him. Wondered if Shandell had ever spilled his guts to her about his worthless, wife-beating, son-abandoning father. He had no real way of knowing whether he had, but he had Connie Eastland pegged. The dollar signs in her eyes when he'd had occasion to talk to her told him everything he needed to know. They also told him that if worse came to worst, he and Connie might be better off as partners than adversaries.

He'd made it a point during his last two visits from the Midwest to let Connie know he was onto her game. He'd clued her in on the fact that blood was thicker than water and that he would be the one to milk this cow. She'd seemed unfazed by him, however, standing her ground, even telling him once in a guarded telephone conversation that if push came to shove, Shandell would stand by her.

The air of certainty in her statement had grabbed his full attention, causing him to wonder what she had on Shandell and whether she really could derail his gravy train. But in the end, he'd decided that she was simply a passing fancy. The kind of fancy he might have to negotiate with or maybe even cancel out in the end, but a fancy nonetheless. He, on the other hand, was blood, the man who'd passed Shandell's athletic gifts on to him by virtue of his semen. There was no way he intended to let either his ex-wife or Connie Eastland stop him from reaping what was rightfully his.

Chapter 3

Damion and Shandell had been playing their weekly one-on-ones at the Glendale basketball courts, courts long favored by high-profile college and high school ballplayers, since the fifth grade. Over the years, Glendale, surrounded by an ever-enlarging Mile High City, had defied encroachment to remain an independent village, known for having a lower sales tax than Denver and for being home to the notorious Colorado Boulevard strip joint Shotgun Willie's. Glendale and the courts that pro basketball scouts often frequented seemed to chug along in a surreal zone of their own.

Years earlier, as grade schoolers, Damion and Shandell had sneaked onto the brightly lit courts at night after the big-time ballplayers had left to spend an hour or two with the courts all to themselves. They'd practice their ball-handling skills—bounce pass, shovel pass, pick and roll—or engage in a round robin of perimeter shooting until one or both of them gave out, it got so late they figured they'd better head home, or the big boys returned for a late-night scrimmage and ran them off. Now, instead of watching the big boys and waiting for court time, the courts were theirs for the taking and folks, big and small, gathered to watch them.

A crowd of nearly forty people, aware of Damion and Shandell's weekly ritual and unfazed by ominous-looking thunderheads to the west, stood behind the chain-link fence that surrounded the main Glendale court, prepared to take in a dose of Blood and Bird. Shandell stood at midcourt with a basketball tucked under his right arm. Looking briefly to the east toward Glendale's two most prominent municipal structures, the post office and the police headquarters building, he winked at Damion and put the ball into play. Bursting from the top of the free-throw circle with a high left-hand dribble, he powered to the right baseline before methodically working his way back toward the right side of the key. Fifteen pounds lighter and three inches shorter than Shandell, Damion stuck with him on every move. Each time the ball bounced off the court, its high-pitched ring seemed to announce to the onlookers that they were privileged to be watching. Stopping his dribble and leaning into Damion, Shandell pushed off Damion's right shoulder, faded back, and released an off-balance eighteen-foot jumper into the air, popping the net.

Damion shook his head as the crowd chanted, "Bird, Bird, Bird." Still shaking his head, he chased down the ball, grabbed it just before it rolled to the edge of the court and into the fence, and tossed it back into play. Moving swiftly across the court and seeming to glide on air, he dribbled straight to the free-throw line and fired up a jump shot. The ball bounced high off the front of the rim as Damion, a step quicker than Shandell, skied for the basket and slammed the errant shot home. The response from the crowd was a lingering *Aaahhh*.

"Dr. Blood," Shandell yelled in admiration as the ball slowly rolled back toward them, "nasty!"

"Ball's all yours, Mr. Blackbird," Damion said, tipping the ball up into his right hand with the toe of his sneaker and handing it to Shandell.

Shandell palmed the ball but suddenly appeared to Damion to be daydreaming. It was a transitory habit he'd never been able to kick even when the game was on the line. When Damion yelled, "Get your head back in the game, Blackbird," Shandell began a slow waist-high dribble toward the basket. On this day, his mind was on more than mere daydreams.

With Damion glued to his side and storm clouds gathering, Shandell was thinking not about the millions of dollars he'd soon be earning, or even his meeting later that evening with the person who'd called him as he'd sat in his SUV in the bank parking lot that morning. What he found himself thinking about, of all things, was his father—a man who had caved in to his drinking and gambling urges before Shandell was four, and who'd deserted him and his mother to head for Chicago and fail in the record industry when he had a family in Denver to feed.

Not wanting to end up like the father he'd basically never known, Shandell had given himself over completely to his mother's stern, God-fearing guidance at an early age. In many ways he'd become her obvious reflection, and the scores of greedy sports agents, money-grubbing women, and out-and-out ne'er-do-wells she'd shooed away from him over the years had earned Aretha Bird the nickname "Scarecrow." Shandell's perseverance had emanated from her, and it was largely because of her that he'd always been a loner, an introverted giant who was clumsy with words, slow to make friends, and distrustful of relationships. Only Damion had been able to break through Shandell's protective coat of armor to become a lifelong friend.

With thunder rumbling in the distance, the game seesawed back and forth until, with Damion leading 38 to 30, the sky opened up. As everyone, including Damion and Shandell, raced for cover to escape the downpour, Damion yelled, "What the hell was up with your game out there, Shandell? Half the time you seemed to be sleepwalking. You should've been killing me, man. Hell, you're on your way to training camp in a few weeks, and I'm out of shape. What gives?"

"Nothing." Shandell flipped his sweatshirt hood over his head. "Just thinking through a problem."

"Must be a doozy. Anything I can help with?"

"Nope."

"You sure? No problem with Connie, is there?" Damion asked, aware that Shandell and Connie Eastland's relationship was often volatile.

"'Course not."

All but drenched as they jogged toward their cars, and still confused over Shandell's lackadaisical play, Damion called out, "I'll meet you at Mae's."

"I'll be right behind you," Shandell yelled back, sounding strangely dismissive.

As he slipped into his Jeep to head for Mae's Louisiana Kitchen, the Five Points soul-food restaurant that had been owned by CJ Floyd's new bride, Mavis Sundee, and her family for more than a half century, Damion peered through the Jeep's rain-splattered rear window to see Shandell standing in the pouring rain next to his Range Rover, looking less like a future NBA superstar than a lost, frightened child. When Shandell realized that Damion was staring, he ducked his head and slipped into the vehicle. As he cranked the engine and pulled away from the curb, knifing ahead into pelting rain, Shandell had the strange sudden sense that he was trapped inside a chunk of black granite that was starting to sink at sea.

Shandell and Damion's dinner at Mae's turned out to be a heartbeat above morbid, and an hour after the meal of fried catfish, collard greens, sweet corn, and buttermilk biscuits, Shandell found himself saddled with a severe case of indigestion. His gastric distress was brought on not by the heavy meal or the feeling that he'd somehow strained the bond of friendship between him and Damion but rather by the knowledge that his 7 p.m. meeting at the Glendale basketball courts, which he'd been dreading all day along with being dogged by thoughts of his father, was at hand.

As he pulled his Range Rover to a stop on Kentucky Avenue just west of the Glendale main court, he thought about the strangely awkward meal he and Damion had shared. There'd been the usual small talk at first, and they'd even briefly slipped into their familiar banter about who had the best perimeter jumper and which of them was the better rebounder. But things had soon turned silent, and when he'd stared blankly into space after Damion had asked him for the fourth time if anything was wrong, the dinner and the evening had disintegrated.

Their only other real conversation during their meal had come when Connie Eastland had called his cell phone. His responses to her questions, responses he now regretted, had been terse. A mere "Yep," "Nope," and "We've already discussed that" were all he'd said before hanging up. As he'd slipped his cell phone back onto his belt, he'd eyed Damion and said with a shake of his head, "Women. Can't live without 'em; can't live with 'em. What kinda choice is that?"

Damion's response had been a noncommittal half-nod. Moments later, they'd each packed up generous slices of sweet-potato pie, Mae's signature dessert, scooted from behind the table, and, tapping clenched fists together as had been their custom since their early teens, headed for the exit.

When Damion had indicated that he was heading across town to his girlfriend, Niki Estaban's, apartment to spend the night, Shandell had sighed and said, "Like I said. With 'em or without 'em," before adding with a hesitant shrug, "Guess I should go over to Connie's and patch things up."

They'd said their good-byes with Damion convinced that the reason for Shandell's meal-time despondency and earlier lack of effort on the court had been initiated by Connie Eastland and Shandell trying his best to remember the last time he'd flat-out lied to his best friend.

Twilight was fading when a jittery Shandell slipped out of his Range Rover and punched the door-lock button on the keyless remote. The remote's chirp seemed to further unsettle him. The forlorn-looking courts, still wet from the earlier rain, were empty, and there was no one in sight. Taking that as a good sign, Shandell walked east on Kentucky Avenue toward the courts with a renewed sense of calm, feeling that he had nothing to fear—that it was the man he was meeting who should be afraid. After all, it was that person who had started the cascade that had led them to the current showdown.

As he pulled back the sleeve of his Windbreaker to check his watch, he realized that it was already ten minutes past seven. He thought about making a phone call to see if the other man had backed out, but before he could reach for his cell phone, he saw someone step out from behind the court's north-facing backboard support.

"SOB showed," he muttered.

The person awaiting him was a small wisp of a white man with thinning hair, bulging eyes, and the vaguest hint of a mustache. He was dressed in a rumpled light-beige summer-weight suit with an unmistakable mustard stain just above the buttonhole of the right lapel. The most remarkable thing about the man, at least in Shandell's eyes, was the fact that he was wearing, as was his custom, not dress shoes but black high-top "old-school" Chuck Taylor Converse All Star sneakers.

"Shandell, my man," the man called out, moving away from the backboard support and walking toward center court, "always good to see you."

Shandell slipped his right hand into the back pocket of his warm-ups as the man approached. His response, continued silence and a nod, was the only acknowledgment Shandell offered as, now standing less than ten feet away, he adjusted the snub-nosed .38 in his right hand until the barrel was aimed directly at the man's belly.

The person watching Shandell and the man in the Converse All Stars converge at center court stood eighty yards away, peering down on them from behind a three-foot-high concrete wall rimming the third level of the garage in which Murray Motor Imports, Denver's oldest Mercedes-Benz and BMW dealer, housed its new cars. A .30-06 rested on the concrete floor inches from the wall. The north- and east-facing third-floor level of the garage, which stood catty-corner from the Glendale Post Office and across the street from the Glendale police station, had unobstructed views of the basketball courts.

It hadn't been difficult for the rifle-toter to gain access to the garage. An easily scaled rickety wooden fence had been the only impediment. It had been simpler still to walk up the garage's north-east stairwell from ground level to the third floor. The only remaining problem had been the gathering darkness, which would have interfered with the assignment if the rain hadn't stopped, leaving a picture-perfect twilight.

The spectator watched Shandell and the other man move closer to one another before extracting a pair of form-fitting athletic gloves from a back pocket, dusting them off, slipping them on, kneeling, and reaching for the rifle. The words *like ducks in a pond* wove their way through the shooter's head as the barrel of the .30-06 peeked over the wall.

"I'd put that toy away if I were you," the small man demanded, looking more annoyed than intimidated by the gun in Shandell's right hand. "Unless of course you intend to use it. And you know what? I don't think you have the guts." The man stared at the gun, unfazed.

"Don't fool yourself," Shandell said with a sneer. "You've chipped away at me long enough. I'm done with your threats and your shakedowns. More important, I don't give a shit about any more muckraking you got planned. So go fuck yourself!"

"I see." The man smiled. "Well, it is what it is, Mr. Blackbird. You're the one who made your bed—time to lie in it. But just for the record, I think you're making a real bad choice."

Shandell raised the barrel of the .38 and took point-blank aim at the man's chest.

The man continued to smile. "You ain't got the balls."

Shandell flashed a broad grin. "Watch me."

A split second later, a loud crack echoed in the background and Shandell's grin turned into a contorted look of pain as the bullet from the .30-06 penetrated his left temporal bone.

The man in the high-tops barely had time to open his mouth and scream, "What the . . ." before a second bullet pierced his left eye socket.

Shandell dropped to one knee as the .38 he'd been holding skated across the court. He reached for his head in agony as the man in the high-tops urinated on himself before sprawling dead on the playing surface. As Shandell slumped forward onto the court, gasping for air, gurgling his final breath through a mouth that was filled with blood, the last thing he saw was the center-court stripe. The strip appeared to him to suddenly float above the playing surface on a sea of moist late-summer air before disappearing, just like his killer, into the Mile High City twilight.

Chapter 4

The coroner's wagon carrying the bodies of Shandell Bird and the other Glendale court murder victim drove off into the foggy darkness two and a half hours to the minute after the double homicide had occurred. Aretha Bird had arrived on the murder scene hysterical and disheveled less than forty-five minutes after two seventh graders, eager to hone their basketball skills on the same courts a future NBA superstar played on, had found the two dead men. Aretha had been watching TV when a news reporter on scene had broken the story before the Glendale police could notify her that her son had been murdered. In the hour since she'd arrived, she'd calmed down to the point that she could carry on a conversation without shaking violently, but she was clearly on the brink of collapse. Her eyes, swollen almost shut from crying, were dark, puffy, silver-dollar-sized circles, and her nose wouldn't stop running.

Moments after the coroner's wagon had pulled away, a Glendale detective escorted Aretha into one of the police station's interrogation rooms, along with Damion and Connie Eastland, who'd arrived fifteen minutes after Aretha's frantic call to them. The displeased-looking Detective Sergeant Will Townsend, a bony man with curly brown hair and angular features, sat across from Aretha in the room that had the ground-in-sweat smell of a gymnasium. Townsend sucked a stream of air between the gap in his front teeth, sat back in his chair, and looked directly at Damion, who seemed to him to be in as much pain as the victim's mother and girlfriend.

Damion and Townsend had crossed swords earlier, just as Connie Eastland was arriving. When Damion had pleaded for a look at Shandell's lifeless body, having been told what had happened by a boyish-looking cop guarding the crime scene, Townsend had shunted Damion away, saying simply, "Nope, can't okay that." Damion had watched two crime-scene technicians from the Denver County coroner's office struggle to load Shandell's body into the back of their vehicle, telling himself, *This has to be a dream*. But he knew it wasn't. Connie had cried until she couldn't cry any longer, but she hadn't reached the near catatonic state that Aretha Bird was in. Now, after temporarily swallowing his emotions in an attempt to remain at least outwardly calm in the face of his overwhelming grief, Damion was utterly numb.

Glancing from Damion to Connie and finally Aretha, Townsend, a twenty-two-year veteran of the Glendale force, sucked another stream of air between his teeth. "So all of you are in agreement? Shandell had no real enemies?"

Only Damion looked up at him.

"You got a different take, Madrid?" Townsend asked.

"No enemies to speak of, but I do know of one person who was, how can I put this, well ... upset with him."

Damion's answer caused Connie to raise her head and look at him, but Aretha remained silent and motionless with her head bowed.

"And who was that?"

"A man named Theo Wilhite. But he's an old man who's spent most of his life complaining."

"There ain't any age restrictions when it comes to murder, son. What was Wilhite's beef with Shandell?"

Damion hesitated before answering, uncertain whether Aretha and Connie were aware of Wilhite's complaint.

"Spit it out, son. We're dealing with a double homicide here."

Choosing his words carefully, Damion said, "Wilhite claims to have lost ten thousand dollars wagering on the NCAA championship game last spring, and he thinks Blackbird and I had something to do with him losing that money, Shandell in particular. He thinks Shandell may have missed what would have been the game-winning shot on purpose."

"So he thinks you or Bird were shaving points?"

"Something like that."

"Either you were or you weren't."

"We weren't!"

Townsend began entering the name *Theo Wilhite* into a Black-Berry that sat in front of him on the conference table. "Wilhite with one L?"

When Damion nodded, Townsend asked, "Do you know where Wilhite lives?"

"Somewhere in Five Points. I don't know his address."

Entering "pull address" into his BlackBerry, Townsend asked, "Anybody else you think might have had a grudge against your friend?"

When Damion shrugged and said, "No," Townsend eyed Connie and then Aretha.

Too grief-stricken to answer, Aretha continued to stare at the floor. Connie simply shook her head.

Deciding to change the direction of his questioning, Townsend asked, "Did your boyfriend generally carry large amounts of money on him, Ms. Eastland?"

"No."

"That's strange. My crime-scene boys found a little over three thousand dollars in a pocket of his sweatpants." Failing to mention that they'd also found a snub-nosed .38 inches from Shandell's right hand, Townsend stroked his chin thoughtfully and entered the words "three grand" into the BlackBerry before asking, "Any of you know the other victim, Paul Grimes?"

Damion and Connie shook their heads.

"Mrs. Bird?"

When Aretha Bird failed to answer, Townsend, his tone suddenly insistent, asked, "Mrs. Bird, did you know the other victim?"

Aretha Bird's response was a barely audible, confused-sounding "No."

"Who was he?" asked Damion, attempting to run interference for Aretha.

Townsend paused briefly before answering, as if trying to determine whether or not Damion deserved an answer. Deciding that revealing a little about the second murder victim might help his investigation in the long run, he said, "His name was Paul Grimes. He was an investigative reporter for the *Rocky Mountain News*. Had a real bulldog hell-bound-for-glory kind of rep. Could be he wanted to talk to Shandell about the same thing your Mr. Wilhite was interested in." Townsend eyed Damion and Connie, looking for any hint that one or both of them might have known Grimes. But all he got were looks of surprise. "And Grimes never had occasion to talk to any of the three of you?" Townsend asked, hoping to get a response out of Aretha. As Connie and Damion shook their heads in unison and Aretha remained silent, Townsend said to Damion, "So Grimes never hit you up with accusations of point-shaving similar to Wilhite's?"

Having been raised by a mother who was a criminal defense attorney and schooled by her and CJ Floyd in the ways of inquisitive cops, Damion recognized that Townsend had just asked him the same question in three slightly different ways. Deciding it was time to bring that line of questioning to an end, he said, "We've told you, Sergeant, none of us knew Grimes. Want to move on?"

Townsend smiled, aware that he was being challenged by someone who understood the game he was playing. Telling himself he needed to check out Damion's background more carefully, he said, "A little touchy, aren't you, Madrid?"

With his competitive nature suddenly on the rise and ignoring the question, Damion asked, "Do you plan to keep us here much longer, Sergeant? We've told you everything we know. The two ladies and I would like to leave."

"I see," Townsend said, taken aback. "And by any chance are you their lawyer?"

"No, but if any of us ever needs an attorney, we have access to the very best." Damion flashed the startled detective a wry smile.

Townsend's eyes narrowed until they were a determined squint. "Let me clue you in on something, hotshot. I've got a double homicide here, and my victims happen to be the NBA's number-two draft choice and a well-known investigative reporter. Two high-profile types who just happened to buy it on a basketball court at twilight a mere stone's throw from a damn police station. So here's a news bulletin for you, sonny." Townsend's voice rose to a crescendo that caused Aretha Bird to momentarily glance up. "Somebody with the 'nads to kill two people less than fifty yards from a police station probably wouldn't hesitate to settle up with you too, my friend. So if you're lying to me about knowing Grimes or holding something back that I should know about, especially as it relates to what your Mr. Wilhite seems bent on proving, I'd recommend you 'fess up now."

"I've got nothing to 'fess up about, Sergeant. And neither do they." Damion locked arms with Connie and Aretha and drew them to their feet. "Now, if you're done with us, we'd like to leave."

Townsend slipped his BlackBerry into his shirt pocket. Satisfied that he had everyone's contact information and at least one significant lead in his latest murder investigation, the determined sergeant decided to try to get inside Damion Madrid's head one last time. "So what do you do, Madrid? For a living, I mean, now that you're out of college and on the streets?" There was a hint of sarcasm in his tone.

"I'm a medical student. At least, I'll be one in a couple of weeks."

"So there was no pro basketball in your future like your friend Shandell's?"

"No."

Townsend stroked his chin. "Strange. Missing out on the pros while your best friend hits it big could make a person real jealous, don't you think?"

"It could if they were small-minded enough to think like a cop," Damion said, unfazed.

Thinking, *Touché,* Townsend smiled and sucked a new stream of air through the gap between his front teeth. "Get out of here, Madrid." Looking at Connie and then Aretha, he said, "You're free to leave, but I'll be in touch—count on it." As he watched Damion drape his arms over Connie's and Aretha Bird's shoulders and walk them toward the door, the seasoned detective found himself wondering not only if he'd asked all the right questions but, more importantly, whether the Madrid kid was half as tough or half as caring as he appeared.

Forty minutes later Townsend stood next to his lead crime-scene technician on the third floor of the Murray Motor Imports garage, a step away from a $140,000 Mercedes-Benz. Staring down through the moonlit darkness toward the Glendale basketball courts, the technician, who'd been pretty much silent up to that moment, said, "No question, Sarge, I'd say the shooter was positioned somewhere in this garage. I would've chosen this floor myself, but the second floor would've probably worked just as well. Same stem-wall opportunity, same duck-blind setup, same easy access and quick escape route. There's no other building around here that would have worked as well. I've checked them out."

"What about the post office roof?" asked Townsend.

"I'll check," the technician said with a shrug. "And I'll recheck the apartment building next door. But come daylight you're gonna see it my way."

"Same wager as always?" asked Townsend, who favored the post office rooftop.

"Same one." The technician smiled. "I can smell the aroma of those Cubans you're gonna have to fork over right now."

"Don't count your chickens too fast, Willis," Townsend said with a smirk as he stepped away from the Mercedes and over to the stem wall. "Any evidence that someone fired shots over this wall?" he asked, glancing around a forty-by-forty-square-foot area that had been cordoned off with crime-scene tape.

"Nope, nothing. Clean as a whistle."

"A pro?" asked Townsend.

"No question," said the technician. "At least, not in my mind. Two shots from a high-powered rifle and bang, bang, just like JFK in Dallas, you're dead."

"Smart-ass kid," muttered Townsend, running a latex-gloved finger along the top of the wall.

"What's that?"

"Nothing. Just thinking about that kid I interviewed, Damion Madrid, Blackbird's best friend. A real cocky sort, but in a strange, self-assured, un-pampered-jock kinda way."

"Yeah, I heard from Barney that you came away from talking to him shaking your head. Did you know he was the small forward on that CSU team that went to the NCAA championship game last March? The one they lost to UCLA in the final seconds?"

"Didn't know you followed college basketball that close, Willis. And yeah, I knew."

"I don't, but my kid does. He was a freshman up at CSU last year."

"Did he happen to know Bird or Madrid?"

"I doubt it. He would've mentioned it to me for sure. But I'll ask. Why?"

"Got a couple of real good reasons for wanting to get a better picture of those two. First off, I'm convinced that CSU basketball team is key to what happened here tonight, and so's last year's NCAA championship game. And second, if we are dealing with a professional triggerman here, the Madrid kid seemed stubborn enough to end up doing something stupid enough to get him killed. Maybe your boy has some campus-life insights about Madrid that'll help."

"How's that?"

Townsend smiled and stared out into the blackness. "Can't really put my finger on the pulse of it, Willis, but I've got the strangest feeling that somehow, way down deep, Madrid might just be cocky enough to think he can do our job."

The one-bedroom apartment in Denver's Montclair neighborhood that Damion had leased two months earlier, after he and Shandell had moved out of the apartment they'd shared in Fort Collins, was pin-drop quiet. Except for two streams of light arcing down from a partially activated bank of track lights in the small alcove just off the living room that Damion had set up to be his study center, the apartment was dark. Emotionally spent, Damion sat in the alcove's semidarkness.

Slumped in an oversized wingback leather chair that Mavis and CJ had given him as a college graduation gift, he'd been trying for the past half hour to make sense of what had happened. Six hours earlier he'd been on the cusp of living his dream. Now he wondered if four years of sacrifice, endless nights without sleep, and a career in medicine would be worth it. That same kind of long-term sacrifice hadn't benefited Shandell, who'd spent most of his life honing athletic skills that would never be used. It seemed as if they'd both sacrificed a large part of their youth for absolutely nothing. Glancing toward two largely empty bookcases, Damion rose from his chair. Staring at the empty shelves and thinking, *Why the hell should I even fill them?* he walked over to a half-open window, stared out into the darkness, and shouted, "Shit!"

He had planned to spend the night at his mother's, secluded in the Washington Park home where he'd spent his late teens growing up. He'd wanted to be there with Aretha Bird, Connie, and his mother. But after an hour of pacing the rambling Tudor's echoing hardwood floors, watching Connie cry and Aretha continue to simply stare into space while his mother tried her best to comfort them, he'd decided to come back to his apartment. Aware of Damion's penchant for dealing only too privately with things that troubled him,

Julie had tried unsuccessfully to get him to stay, but she knew arguing with him would be pointless, so she'd finally let him go home.

It wasn't until he was halfway home, driving north on Downing Street at ten miles under the speed limit, that he'd finally broken down and cried. For hours he'd held off crying, maintaining his composure in front of cops, coroner's assistants, Connie, Aretha, and his mother, but when he'd stopped at a red light at the corner of Alameda and Downing, motionless under the glare of a corner streetlight, he'd broken down and cried like a baby. Cried so hard he'd finally had to pull into a nearby gas station and shut down his engine until he could regain his composure.

When he'd finally reached home, he'd realized that his whole rib cage hurt. After taking two aspirin to curb a throbbing headache and calling his girlfriend to tell her the whole story, he'd plopped down in the leather chair and barely moved until this moment.

Turning away from the window, he found himself softly reciting, "Blackbird and Blood! Blackbird and Blood!" It was a chant that hungry basketball fans across the Rocky Mountain region had coined just months earlier during March Madness.

Walking slowly back to the center of the alcove, he stood in the faint glare from the two lights, hurting and feeling hollow inside. As he stood there looking lost and confused, the courtside play-by-play call of the final moments of Colorado State's NCAA championship game against UCLA began to weave its way through his head, working its way slowly along the roots of his subconscious as it had scores of times before.

Fifteen seconds left until we crown a new NCAA champion, folks. Woodson brings the ball upcourt on a high dribble into double-team back-court pressure. But he's a smooth one. He's out of trouble and across the center stripe. No question, Woodson's looking for Bird. Bird's caught in heavy traffic in the right corner. Wait a second—Woodson got the ball to Madrid. How'd he do that? Eleven seconds left. Madrid dribbles out to just beyond the right key. He's double-teamed! He's tied up! Nope. Can you believe it? Somehow Madrid got the ball out to Bird in the corner. It's been Bird's favorite spot all tourney. Six seconds left. Bird's in the air with that corner jumper. This is the ball game, folks! The ball's off the rim. Blackbird missed! UCLA wins! UCLA wins!

Damion had heard that play-by-play so many times that he knew the announcer's inflections by heart. But for some reason right then, at three in the morning, with his best friend dead and his grief all consuming, the announcer's game-ending call seemed to resonate more than ever. Suddenly the call became entangled with Theo Wilhite's unmistakable voice: *The ball's off the rim—tell that to my ten grand—Blackbird missed—maybe you had some incentive to screw up? UCLA wins! UCLA wins!*

Feeling as if he'd just had the wind knocked out of him, Damion dropped back into his seat. Adjusting himself in the chair, he looked across the room and fixed his gaze on a twelve-by-twelve-inch engraved marble plaque on the wall above his desk. That plaque, the only decoration besides his CSU diploma, was slightly cockeyed. Rising from the chair, he walked over to the desk, slipped the plaque off the wall, and stared at it pensively. The words *Denver Police Junior Activities League Basketball Champions, 1998, Rosie's Garage* were engraved on the face of the plaque. A faded gold ribbon was taped to the bottom edge. A single line of type in the middle of the ribbon read, *Shandell Bird, MVP.*

The year they had started high school, Shandell had given the MVP ribbon to Damion, saying he was the one who had really deserved it all those years before. The next year Damion had given it back to him, only to end up with the ribbon the next year. Over the years the issue of who was most deserving of the ribbon had become a standing joke among the two lifelong friends, both of whom had long ago realized that their on-court successes came not from any single effort but from a joint one. The cops, as it were, had simply made a mistake by giving the ribbon to Shandell. "But this time there will be no mistake," Damion told himself, readjusting the plaque on the wall and straightening the ribbon. He'd find out who killed his best friend, and he'd find out why.

"I'll settle up," he muttered, using the same three words he and Shandell had never failed to say to one another whenever one of them made a miscue on the court. "I'll settle up," he whispered, making a final adjustment to the plaque before turning out the alcove lights and heading for bed.

Chapter 5

Connie Eastland wasn't certain if Damion had picked up on the fact that she'd been a lot more nervous than distraught during their interrogation by Sergeant Townsend three and a half hours earlier, and she wasn't sure, given the gravity of the situation, whether she'd given off the proper vibes. She was, however, certain about one thing. She never should have let Shandell Bird become her little black lapdog. They had, after all, been from two vastly different worlds—worlds as different from one another as night from day. Shandell had been an inner-city poor black kid, and in her estimation an amazingly insecure one for a man who was a world-class athlete. She, on the other hand, was a five-foot-four, blue-eyed, blonde-haired beauty with pixieish features and flawless skin from a background that was, although a long way from wealthy, unadulterated middle-class suburban Phoenix cheerleading white bread. She'd rarely seen black people, much less interacted with them, before coming to CSU. But she'd adapted to college diversity quickly, and, after a series of dalliances with other athletes, Shandell had become her ticket to ride.

She and Shandell had been oddly dissimilar in scores of other ways. He'd been her intellectual inferior, and even at twenty, with the benefit of two and a half years of college under his belt when they'd met, he'd remained rough around the edges, morbidly introspective, and far too dependent. In contrast, she had always been an assertive self-starter. In spite of their differences, they'd latched on to one another for reasons known only to them, and for the fourteen months before Shandell's death they'd been campus social darlings.

Now all that Shandell had promised her was gone. There would be no trips around the world or Bentleys or California mansions in her future. But just as certainly, there'd be no more arguments or second-guessing herself—no more behind-the-back snickers or *go-for-it-girl* pats on the back from acquaintances and friends. Shandell was dead. All she had now was a sociology degree and the life of a social worker staring her in the face. But at least she could go her own way now without having to worry about appearances or pleasing people who couldn't be pleased, including her unaccepting parents. Most of all, she no longer had to be an insecure black man's sounding board.

She hoped Damion hadn't been able to see through her during their interrogation by Sergeant Townsend. Damion had been so distraught, so flat-out dumbstruck and racked with pain, that he couldn't see the fact that the man the world had called Blackbird had been little more than a booster rocket to the good life for her.

It was a quarter past midnight and a completely new day, she reminded herself, eyeing her watch. A day that would unfortunately require her to play a part and follow through on being the person everyone thought she was. She had a feeling that the next seventy-two hours would tell her what she was made of. She'd have to walk the walk and talk the talk—never step out of character for even one second. She'd have to let Aretha Bird lean on her and to be the Rock of Gibraltar for a bevy of college classmates, hangers-on, and most of all friends. She'd have to contend with Damion, pretend to him that she was hurting deeply, encourage the man who'd been closest to Shandell to believe that her sense of loss was equal to his.

She'd dug herself a hole, and she knew it. But even at the unsoured age of twenty-one, she'd faced similar situations before, and like an enterprising rabbit she had more than one hole to escape from. Feeling suddenly philosophical, she rose from her chair and walked from the cluttered living room of her Fort Collins condo that sat at the still largely rural northern edge of the city, down a hallway, and into an oversized bedroom that was filled with exercise equipment. The condo, or at least the down payment on it, had been a college graduation gift from her parents, intended as an incentive to get her into the job market and away from Shandell.

Dressed in running shorts and the loose-fitting T-shirt of a pre-Shandell boyfriend, she glanced out the room's only window before mounting a stationary bicycle for what she hoped would be a stress-reducing workout. She found herself quickly pedaling at an eighteen-miles-per-hour clip as she tried her best not to think about Shandell or the cops, Damion Madrid, or murder. She'd settled into a twenty-miles-per-hour pace when a cell phone clipped to the bike's handlebars rang. When a number she immediately recognized flashed on the caller ID screen, she frowned, stopped pedaling, flipped the phone open, and said bitterly, "Yes."

"You sound out of breath."

"I'm working out."

"At this time of night? Now, that's dedication."

"What do you want?"

"Wanta know if you had anything to do with that killin' took place over in Glendale tonight. It's all over the news, you know."

"I should be asking you the same question, don't you think?"

"Maybe, but I wouldn't even think for one second 'bout answerin' you." The caller snickered. "Looks like I'm gonna come into some money."

"Blood money."

"Don't bother me. As long as it spends. Think I better let things calm down a little before I cash in, though."

"You know, you're sickening, Leon."

"And you're a money-grabbing little bitch. A manipulative little white wench who's got no conscience. But like the Good Book says, let us forgive each other our shortcomings. Have to, or you and me wouldn't be talkin'."

"We're talking because you stuck your nose in where it didn't belong, Leon."

"Oh, believe me, little girl, it belonged. And for the record, I prefer being called 'Mr. Bird' when it comes to conversations with little white sluts. So get this, missy. My nose is gonna stay stuck right up your tight little ass for as long as it has to. Don't think that with Shandell outta the way you're gonna be free of me for one minute. I'm here to stay, your little sweetness. You know where to find me. Even better, I know where to find you."

Connie felt the muscles in her throat tighten. A second later, a corkscrew of pain shot through her left shoulder. Feeling that if the conversation continued, she might actually end up suffocating, she said, "Go climb into your drainage pipe, Leon, with the rest of the vermin." Turning pink, she snapped her cell phone shut and let out a long sigh of relief. A rivulet of spittle clung to the corner of her mouth, wedged there in apparent defiance, as if to remind her that her problems were far from solved. Leon would call back. She knew that. But for the moment she was free of him. Free of his threats and intrusion and intimidation, and free of his lecherous surveillance and campy 1960s-style slang.

Staring out the window and into the darkness, she tossed her cell phone onto a nearby floor cushion and once again began pedaling. Soon she was back in rhythm, cruising along at a twenty-miles-per-hour clip and thinking to herself as she settled into her ride that her caller and Shandell's father, Leon Bird, was probably far more deserving of a toe tag and cold morgue slab than his son.

It wasn't at all like the old newspaper days for Wordell Epps. Those days were forever gone. Nor was it like more recent days, when he and Paul Grimes and John Dunning and other Denver newspaper hounds had still been given time to work up a story. Nowadays, things were decidedly different. There was no time to excavate a story's roots, examine its moorings, and determine if its legs were buried in bedrock or quicksand. Nowadays the news was instantaneous and superfluous—nothing more than some talking head's fifteen seconds of "flash and trash."

Wordell had gotten the call telling him that his longtime friend and Pulitzer Prize–winning partner, Paul Grimes, had been murdered from their editor at the *Rocky Mountain News* a little before nine in the evening. After a few words of condolence, he'd been told by the editor to find out what had happened and have a story ready for the next morning's edition. Meeting that deadline meant he would have to dump the story to his editor by midnight. Now, after a couple of hours of running the story down, the way he had in the old days, and verifying his facts and his sources, he was hunched in darkness over his keyboard, locked in the glare from the computer screen.

As a seasoned *Rocky Mountain News* investigative reporter, he'd had the contacts to get at the heart of what had happened to Paul Grimes and Shandell Bird a lot more quickly than most. It was those contacts that TV media pip-squeaks and new age journalists—flashes in the pan, to his way of thinking—would always lack. He knew cops and crime-scene technicians, morgue assistants, and coroners, not to mention a few politicians who owed him their careers. He knew aging mobsters and two-bit criminals, strip-club pole dancers, and his share of flat-out whores. And although there were no longer any Linotype machines to line up each letter of his story in molten metal, the ponytail-wearing Wordell Epps, as flaky-looking and as brilliant as ever, would have his story. The framework of the piece would run a full two columns in the *Rocky* the next morning, but he knew that the truth of what had happened to his friend Paul Grimes and the kid known as Blackbird would keep mushrooming up for days.

He'd rush what he had, incomplete as it was, to some wet-noodle higher-up at the *Rocky* for now. He'd meet his obligation to belch out a morning-edition teaser story. The story would hint that his friend Paulie and a black basketball star named Blackbird had been blinded by gambling and greed.

Glancing down at his high-top Converse sneakers—sneakers identical to the kind preferred by his friend Paul Grimes—Epps smiled and punched the *send* command on the computer, instantly forwarding his story to his editor.

"There'll be more," he muttered, shutting down the computer. "There'll be more," he repeated as the light from his computer screen faded and the room he sat in went black.

Chapter 6

Denver's Bail Bondsman's Row is a block-long assemblage of six aging turn-of-the-century Victorian buildings affectionately known as "painted ladies." This unlikely but enduring cluster of once proud houses lines the west side of the 1200 block of Delaware Street as it knifes its way toward downtown Denver. Darkness never descends on Bondsman's Row, where always-lit neon signs jut from the ornate fascia above weathered wraparound Victorian porches, yelling freedom to the accused before their day in court. Blue, red, yellow, and green neon tubes shaped to spell OPEN 24 HOURS, BAIL BONDS ANYTIME, and NEVER CLOSED flash gaudy promises of at least temporary liberty to those hoping for freedom as well as their families and friends.

CJ Floyd had come home to work on the Row in 1971, freshly separated from two tours of Vietnam and three years in the navy. He'd spent his first three months on the Row working for his uncle as a runner and the next three and a half decades traveling the seamier side of Denver's streets, most of that time as a one-man band. A few years earlier he'd sold a half-interest in the bail-bonding business his uncle had left him to former marine intelligence operative, Persian Gulf War and Operation Desert Storm veteran Flora Jean Benson, who, like Julie Madrid before her, had begun her tenure in CJ's employ as a secretarial temp.

The morning after Shandell Bird's murder, Flora Jean had arrived at the office at a few minutes past seven, as was her custom. Seated at her desk and beaming from ear to ear, she'd just wrapped up a phone call to a florist who had promised to have a bouquet of thirty-seven roses delivered to CJ and his new bride by 8 a.m. Hawaii time. There was a rose for every post–Vietnam War year Mavis had had to put up with CJ's matrimonial foot-dragging. Pleased with herself for coming up with what she considered the perfect gift, Flora Jean hung up the phone to the accompanying jingle of the eight authentic Zulu tribal bracelets that encircled her left wrist.

Chagrined that Mavis and CJ had run off to Hawaii to get married, causing her to miss the wedding, she rose and walked over to the niche at the rear of her office to see if the coffee she'd started before her phone call had finished brewing.

A tad over six feet tall, the statuesque Flora Jean, who'd recently turned forty-one, could instantly turn a roomful of heads. Her cocoa-brown skin, wiry, closely cropped hair, and undeniably Nubian good looks might have announced African queen on another continent, but in America, until the U.S. Marine Corps had intervened, she'd simply been another case-hardened sister, the often adrift daughter of a drugged-out East St. Louis prostitute. But the corps and then a war had intervened, and by the end of her six-year tour with the marines, she'd become not only a soldier but the very essence of a woman. During her Marine Corps stint she'd also fallen in love— and not with just any man but with another soldier who happened to be an intelligence operative just like her, an officer, and white. During her time in the Persian Gulf, she and Major General Alden Grace had had a not-so-secret affair that would have singed the pages of the Uniform Code of Military Justice. Their seventeen-year-long, on-again, off-again romance had reached its zenith a few months earlier when the now retired general had slipped an engagement ring on the reluctant Flora Jean's finger, with CJ standing in Flora Jean's office looking on, and announced that his "reluctant-to-marry-a-white-man future wife" had better work on getting her thinking in sync with that of the new century and forget about her East St. Louis upbringing.

Smiling and admiring the one-carat diamond on her finger, Flora Jean lifted the fresh pot of coffee off the burner. She'd started to pour herself a cup of the steaming Kona brew when her office door banged against the wall and Damion Madrid, looking haggard, stepped into the room.

Puzzled, Flora Jean placed the coffee pot back on the burner, set her cup down, shook her head, and said, "Damn, sugar, you look like you been out on an all-night bender."

When Damion didn't respond, she realized that the mostly straight-arrow, athletically gifted kid whom she'd babysat while his mother attended law school at night was in serious trouble.

"What's wrong, Damion?"

Damion's words came out in a rush. "Blackbird was murdered last night." Choking back tears, he added, "Over at the Glendale courts."

Every muscle in Flora Jean's face seemed to slump. "No!"

"I called you last night, but I couldn't get you."

"I had my cell phone turned off, sweetie. I was down in Colorado Springs at Alden's. What happened?"

Damion shrugged. "I don't know, really. All I know is that someone shot him and some newspaper reporter. They're both dead."

Aware of what it was like to lose a best friend—she'd lost one during Desert Storm—Flora Jean walked across the room and hugged Damion. Holding him reassuringly, in much the same way Julie had the previous evening, she took in the look of desperation on his face.

"What can I do to help, sugar?"

Stepping out of her embrace, Damion said, "You can help me find out who killed Shandell."

"Don't you think that's a job for the cops?"

Aware that the former marine sergeant was also a karate black belt who during her bail-bonding career had been known to knock 200-pound bond-skipping men off their feet, Damion said, "The cops can't do what *we* can do, Flora Jean."

Recognizing where Damion was headed, Flora Jean said, "I think what *we* need to do, sugar, is think the problem through a little better. Talk things over with your mother, maybe give CJ a call in Hawaii."

Damion shook his head in protest. "No way. I know what they'd say."

"Like I said, Damion, it's a job for the cops."

"I'll do it with or without you, Flora Jean."

"Would you hold your damn horses, Damion Madrid? You're on your way to becomin' a doctor, not some CJ Floyd clone. Believe me, ain't no part of life down here on the Row the kinda life for you."

"It wasn't the life for my mother either, but it played a big part in defining who she is. You know as well as I do that most of her clients start their journey right down here. And it's not the life for CJ," Damion said with a chuckle. "The man even claims to be an antiques dealer nowadays, for God's sake, when in fact anyone in the know realizes that he still does bounty hunting on the side. Call it what you will, Flora Jean, but whether you call yourself a lawyer, an antiques dealer, or a marine, there's always going to be a piece of you that was forged down here. I won't let this thing with Shandell go, no matter what, and I need your help."

Flora Jean shook her head, well aware that Damion meant what he said. When he was a teenager she'd watched him practice dribbling and shooting jump shots in his driveway, hour after hour, until his hands were swollen and dehydration seemed just seconds away. She'd seen him study geometry and calculus and French, which he'd hated, late into the night, hunkered down in the conference room just beyond her office door while Julie sat across from him plowing through reams of classroom notes and stacks of law books. She'd seen him at sixteen walk into CJ's office with a bloody, swollen lower lip and a goose egg on his forehead, only to announce to CJ that although two Latino-hating skinheads had gotten their licks in on him, they were both now hooked up to IVs in the emergency room at Denver General Hospital. But as far as she was concerned, the kicker when it came to measuring Damion Madrid's heart had come a year earlier when, after insinuating himself into one of CJ's cases, he'd outfoxed a rifle-toting hit man who'd stalked him to the desolate Pawnee National Grassland east of Fort Collins, hoping to eliminate him from the case, only to have Damion come close to eliminating him.

Deep down, in spite of her earlier comment, Flora Jean knew Damion had the right stuff to make it in her world, or in the world of medicine or sports, or in whatever world he chose. What he lacked when it came to investigating a murder was seasoning and the kind of experience necessary to work the Denver streets she knew so well.

Still shaking her head, Flora Jean said, "Let me think about things for just a bit, sugar." She wanted to take the words back as soon as she'd uttered them.

"You think long, you think wrong," Damion offered with a smile, tossing one of Flora Jean's favorite sayings at her.

"Why don't you tell me everything you know about what happened yesterday, boots on to boots off, and anything else you think I might need to know about Shandell and that reporter who was killed. And Damion, don't leave nothin' out, no matter how unimportant you think it is."

Sensing that he'd made some headway, Damion said, "Okay. But it'll take a while."

"Don't matter none to me, sugar." Flora Jean glanced over her shoulder toward the coffee niche. "We got ourselves all mornin' long and a fresh pot of coffee. Might as well start from the start."

It wasn't the way CJ Floyd would've initiated a murder investigation or, left to her own devices, the way Flora Jean would have either. But one hour and a full pot of coffee later, Flora Jean had mapped out what she considered to be a nonintrusive, low-risk investigative strategy for Damion to follow.

She now knew about the clearly out-of-sync four or five hours that had preceded Shandell's murder, including Shandell's unfocused efforts at the Glendale courts and the awkward dinner he and Damion had shared at Mae's. Damion had also told her about his midday confrontation with Theo Wilhite. They'd spent close to twenty minutes scouring the pages of the *Rocky Mountain News* and *Denver Post*, assessing each paper's take on the double homicide in the hope of ferreting out a connection between Shandell and Paul Grimes. They'd come up with one nugget of information: Grimes and Shandell had clearly known one another in spite of what Aretha Bird had claimed the previous evening, and for a good long while it seemed according to the *Rocky Mountain News* story.

The only other information they'd been able to glean had come from a TV news piece that had aired while they'd been perusing the two newspapers. The story claimed that autopsies on both victims were pending; although the Glendale police had apparently tried to keep all information about the cases close to the vest, word had leaked out that both men had been felled by bullets from a .30-06.

Flora Jean decided with serious trepidation to lay out a division of labor that would separate her investigative efforts from Damion's. She would obtain autopsy findings from Vernon Lowe, chief morgue attendant at Denver Health and Hospital's city morgue and a life-long friend of CJ, dig up everything she could on Paul Grimes, and handle Theo Wilhite. Damion would head up to Fort Collins to see if any of his former teammates, trainers, or coaches could verify Wilhite's claim that Shandell had purposely blown the winning shot in last season's NCAA title game and then get back to her before the Glendale cops had a chance to do the same thing.

Damion knew that his job was to try to determine whether Shandell might've been involved in transgressions that could have cost him his life—things like point-shaving, illicit drug use, or straight-out betting on games. Although he knew, or at least thought he knew, that Shandell would never have gotten involved in such things, he understood very well that Shandell had had one powerful weakness. Notwithstanding his fourteen-month relationship with Connie Eastland, Shandell had had a legendary weakness for women—mostly white women. He'd had a reputation for going through pretty women like a sweet freak working his way through a box of candy. Although Damion wasn't aware of any rifle-toting, sharpshooting disgruntled boyfriends who might have been out for Shandell's hide, he couldn't discount the fact that there might be one.

Armed with what Flora Jean and CJ liked to call a job ticket, he left Flora Jean's office, hastily scribbled notes in hand, on a caffeine high, hoping that by the time he got back to Denver, Flora Jean would've teased out the link between Grimes and Shandell, and maybe even have determined whether Theo Wilhite might be linked to the double murder.

As he sped north on I-25, pinned for the moment between an oil tanker and a wobbling semi hauling a load of cattle, he had the sense that although he and Flora Jean had mapped out a logical investigative strategy, he might not have the time to follow it all the way through. He was due to start medical school on September 5, and that gave him less than two weeks to find Shandell's killer. Ten days, in fact, to play the part of CJ Floyd and find out along the way whether he had what it took to be more than simply a onetime basketball star and would-be doctor.

Moments after stepping out of his customary late-morning, twenty-five-minute shower, Jackie "Happy Jack" Woodson got the phone call from his hGH supplier in Denver, Leotis Hawkins, warning him to keep his mouth shut about anything he knew, suspected he might know, or dreamed he might know about the Shandell Bird murder. The glib, self-anointed ladies' man was toweling himself off and admiring his reflection in a mirror, not paying much attention to Hawkins, until he heard the words "Mouth off, you little rodent, and count on it, you're in for the same treatment as Bird."

Jackie had gotten the word about Shandell's murder early that morning from a friend of Connie Eastland, a woman whose sexual favors he enjoyed whenever the need arose, and he'd laughed. He'd told the woman afterward that at first he'd thought the call was a Blackbird-inspired practical joke.

Shandell, despite his penchant for playing the loner, had been something of a practical jokester, and Jackie had been the butt of those jokes more frequently than any of Shandell's other teammates. Jackie, a vegetarian who was fond of soup and gargantuan leafy salads, disdained the red meat typically served at the team's training table and enjoyed reminding his meat-loving teammates that when cholesterol eventually clogged their arteries and blew their aortas, he'd respect their memories and say good things about them at their funerals. When Jackie found a tree frog swimming in his soup one day in the midst of the team's NCAA championship run, he had no trouble fingering the culprit. But when he confronted Shandell, Shandell swore that he'd had nothing to do with it. Unconvinced, the five-foot-nine-inch point guard with the clean-shaven head that seemed to always gleam with sweat launched into a courtroom-quality cross-examination. Shandell, unfazed by Jackie's accusations, stood his ground through four minutes of unabated grilling until Jackie, hearing his teammates' snickers in the background, gave up, grumbling as he left the training table in a huff, "I know you did it, Blackbird, and sooner or later I'll prove it."

Later, when Damion asked Shandell how he'd been able to keep from caving in to Jackie's full-court press, Shandell simply smiled and said, "Hell, Blood. You know I ain't had nothin' but pressure pushin' down on me all my life. When you're a six-foot-five, doofus-lookin' sixth grader, busy trippin' over two left feet and scared to death of your classmates' finger-pointin', you get good at actin', even better at denyin'. Shit, man, for me, it's pretty much an art."

It was that training-table incident that Jackie found himself thinking of when Hawkins, steaming on the other end of the line, said, "You listenin' to me, Happy Jack?"

"Yeah, yeah. I'm listenin'."

"Good, 'cause if anybody asks, especially the cops, here's a script I want you to memorize and spit back. You don't know why Shandell was murdered. Short and sweet. You got it?"

"Yeah."

"You know any other words besides *yeah*, asshole?"

Bristling, Jackie fired back, "I know Damion Madrid's headed up here from Denver to talk to me about Blackbird. He called a little over an hour ago. I'm thinkin' you need to know that."

"Why didn't you tell me that straight off, you fuckin' flake? And why the shit didn't you tell him to save his visit for later?"

"Are you crazy? He was Blackbird's best friend. Besides, we were teammates for three years. He would've been suspicious."

"Why's he wanta talk to you?"

"Maybe he's just lookin' for a comforting ear."

"Well, support him, then. Let him cry and lean all over you if need be. Just keep quiet about any of our dealin's."

"I won't let anything slip. But just so you know, Blood's real smart. And I don't mean just book smart. He'll spot any bullshit I start tossin' around real quick. His mother's one of those high-priced criminal lawyers. Think maybe he gets his inquisitiveness from her."

Hawkins laughed. "Inquisitiveness, my ass. He's just another wet-behind-the-ears college kid like you. The only thing you oversexed cum drippers are any good at at your age is sniffin' out pussy. Just follow the script, Jackie. Got it?"

"And if I don't?"

"Don't get fresh with me, kid. It don't become you. Now, are we set?" When Jackie didn't answer, Hawkins repeated, "I asked you, are we set?"

"Yeah," Jackie said softly.

"Now, that's the Jackie I know and love. The accommodatin', angle-chasin' Jackie." Hawkins paused as if forcing a smile. "By the way, sorry about the NBA draft passin' on you. But who knows? You could end up smokin' up the courts this year and earn yourself a real high draft choice. You'll hear from me soon. 'Til then, pleasant thoughts, my boy."

Mystified, Jackie found himself listening to a dial tone and standing in a water slick next to his shower. When the oversized towel that had been loosely knotted around his waist dropped to the floor, he found himself naked and trembling, too scared for the moment to move.

Damion and Jackie met a little before noon at the Johnson's Corner truck stop twenty-three miles south of the CSU campus and just off I-25. It was a place where for three years Damion, Blackbird, and Jackie had strategized about games, griped about classwork, bitched about their girl problems, and fantasized about what it would be like in the pros. It had been their place to get away from the rigors of practice and the sameness of campus life. But this time things were different. There was no Blackbird to tell Jackie he was NBA material despite his size, no Blackbird to bemoan being in the spotlight, and no Blackbird to remind Damion that it was okay to choose medical school over the NBA.

The fifteen-acre truck stop's restaurant, known from coast to coast for its mouth-watering cinnamon rolls, sat on a rise just before I-25 took a jog to the east to begin its run to Denver. Noonday customers filled every booth and table as Jackie and Damion, seated in a booth in the far northwest corner, talked quietly.

Eyeing a barely touched glass of orange juice and his half-eaten cinnamon roll, Damion leaned back in his seat and shook his head. "What you're saying doesn't make sense, Jackie. I grew up with Shandell, roomed with him our whole time at CSU. We were closer than brothers. There's no way he'd do drugs."

"I didn't say he was usin' 'em, Blood. You and I both know the man would've never done somethin' like that to his body. What I'm sayin' is he was peddlin' the stuff to kids back down in Five Points. Performance-enhancin' shit. Not coke or H or weed. Nothin' like that."

Damion shook his head again as if he somehow expected the gesture to make the ugly picture that Jackie had been painting for the past ten minutes disappear. "Shandell wouldn't have done something like that!"

Jackie, who had lauded Shandell, Brutus-praising-Caesar fashion, for the first fifteen minutes of their lunch, picked up a fork and aimed the business end at Damion. "Maybe you didn't know Blackbird as well as you thought. We both know how quirky and standoffish the brother could be."

Damion nodded, aware that Jackie's assessment wasn't that far off target. Shandell had always been a secretive sort. During high school he'd even kept the names of most of his girlfriends a secret. It was only after meeting Connie Eastland during his junior year at CSU, after he'd run through a string of jock-worshipping women as a freshman and sophomore, that Shandell had seemed to Damion to have found someone right for him. Except where Damion was concerned, he'd been just as secretive about his study habits, taste in movies, and favorite foods.

Aware that Shandell had been wired a little differently, Damion asked, "Where'd you get your info about the drugs?"

"A good source."

"Where, Jackie?" Damion demanded, annoyed by Jackie's attempt to sidestep the question.

"Where's not important, Blood. What's important is that Blackbird was pushin' performance-enhancin' drugs to kids from his very own neighborhood, kids who wanted to grow up to be just like him. You ask me, that's what got him killed."

Damion stroked his chin thoughtfully as he eyed his arrogant, intelligent, but intellectually lazy former teammate and wondered how Jackie might fit into the Blackbird murder equation. Aware that Jackie would never have stooped to hang out in Five Points, or for that matter have concerned himself with what Shandell was doing when he was back home, he wondered how Jackie had suddenly become so knowledgeable about Shandell's off-campus activities. The idea that Shandell could have been selling performance-enhancing drugs to Five Points kids without someone in Five Points knowing it and blowing the whistle seemed ludicrous.

"You're lying, Jackie," Damion said boldly.

"No, I'm not. Your boy was selling steroids, hGH, and lots of other shit."

Damion leaned across the table until his face was inches from Jackie's. Flashing the same stern, unforgiving look he'd given Jackie scores of times on the basketball court when, because of lack of concentration, the smaller man had made a mistake, Damion said, "I want a straight answer, Jackie. Who's your source?"

"Okay, okay. I got it from Sandy, and the info didn't just bubble up today. Sandy's known about what Shandell was doin' for a long time," said Jackie, hoping to hold Damion at bay with a half-truth and never mentioning Leotis Hawkins's name.

Rodney Sands, the CSU basketball team's longtime trainer, known affectionately to players and the coaching staff simply as "Sandy," had been close friends with Shandell. Knowing that Sandy had been the one largely responsible for keeping the six-foot-eight-inch giant running the court and his temperamental body clicking on all cylinders for four years without serious injury, Damion asked, "When did he tell you all this?"

"Damn, Blood. You sound like a cop."

"When, Jackie?" Damion slammed an open palm down on the table loud enough for the elderly couple in the next booth to react with a start.

"This mornin', right after I told him Shandell had been murdered down in Denver."

"Did he seem surprised?"

Jackie shrugged. "Not really."

Running his tongue along the inside of his lower lip the same way he had since childhood whenever he was stumped, Damion leaned back and checked his watch. "It's almost one. I'm thinking Sandy's in the weight room working out freshmen and red shirts about now."

"That would be my guess too," Jackie said with a nod. "You gonna drop in on him?"

"Sure am."

"He'll tell you the same thing he told me, Blood."

"So I'll hear it a second time. You got a problem with that?"

"Nope." Jackie sat back in his seat and swallowed hard.

Sensing that Jackie was nervous, Damion said, "Strange that somebody with millions of dollars in hand and millions more on the horizon would have risked it all by selling performance-enhancing drugs to kids. Stranger still that I wouldn't have known about it." Damion shot Jackie a look that said, *You better not be lying*, before he slipped out of the booth.

"Sometimes you don't know as much about people as you think," Jackie said, following Damion out of the booth.

Damion nodded. "Maybe." However, the look on Damion's face was meant to make Jackie Woodson realize that he was thinking not about knowing Blackbird but about knowing him.

Chapter 7

The two Colorado State University freshman basketball players pumping iron in a weight room that smelled of sweat and mildewed towels had no idea who Damion was, especially since he was dressed in street clothes and had a full head of hair instead of the shaved head he'd sported throughout the NCAA tournament. As far as they were concerned, he was just another earringless, tattooless, wannabe jock there to ogle. The player who was standing, counting out reps to his workout partner, was black. He had long, knife-edged sideburns, and although he was about Damion's height, he was decidedly more muscular. As Damion stopped to watch the workout, he couldn't help but think that a year earlier he and Shandell had been the ones pumping iron—the ones pushing themselves to the physical brink, hoping to get an edge on the competition.

Suddenly he found himself thinking not about the camaraderie and the exhilaration of winning but about the chastisement he'd received from teammates for not putting an exclamation mark on his dunks and for choosing to fly beneath the sports-hoopla radar. Some in the inner circle of college sports had accused him of being haughty and above it all, claiming that he didn't have what it took to handle the rigors of the NBA.

Shandell had never been forced to suffer the same kind of criticism. Although standoffish to a fault, he'd had the tattoos, three, in fact, the earrings, one at least, and the bling. Although Shandell's college-period bling consisted of no more than a couple of cheap gold rings, purchased from a local pawn shop, and a fake Rolex watch, he'd had no trouble fitting the superjock mold expected of him by fans, his coaches, and his peers. Shandell had understood what it took to sell himself to the public, while Damion didn't really care.

As Damion stood drinking in the familiar surroundings, the dark-skinned freshman stopped counting and watched his teammate set aside his weights before asking Damion, "Help you with something, homes?"

"Nope, just looking for Sandy."

The fact that someone who looked as if he didn't belong in their inner sanctum, even though he was six-foot-five, knew enough to call Rodney Sands by his nickname caught the iron-pumping freshman by surprise. "He was here a little bit ago. Whatta you want with him?"

"Just need to ask him something."

Annoyed that his workout had been interrupted, the ballplayer who'd been pumping iron said, "Hey, man, you need game tickets, this ain't the place. Try Ticketmaster." Eyeing his teammate, he punctuated the remark with a snicker and a hand slap.

Damion, more in tune with jock-fraternity protocol than the two novices guarding the frat-house door could have expected, said, "Seen Coach Horse around? I was hoping to catch him too."

Stunned that the intruder would have the nerve to refer to their coach by the nickname affectionately bestowed on him by players because of his long face, wide-set eyes, and flaring nostrils—a name that only a team captain or a player on his way to the NBA dared utter—the weight lifter took a step back. "He's in his office. Just got back from a recruiting trip back East."

"That where the two of you are from?" Damion asked. There was a clear implication in the way he phrased the question that perhaps it was the two of them, not he, who didn't belong.

"Hey, man, I think you better…"

Before the rep counter could finish his sentence, a pasty-faced blond man with piercing blue eyes and a crew cut came jogging across the room toward them. With each step, he called out, "Blood, Blood," louder and louder until he was on top of Damion and the two freshmen. Looking unrested and shaking his head as if he couldn't believe his eyes, Rodney Sands, half a foot shorter than Damion, grabbed him in a bear hug. "I had a feeling you'd show up. Poor Bird. What a tragedy. The whole damn athletic department's flyin' at half mast."

The two freshmen stepped back almost in unison as the suddenly glassy-eyed Damion slipped out of Sandy's bear hug and patted the longtime CSU trainer on the back.

Realizing that the two freshmen had to be wondering who the hell the foreigner in their midst was, Sandy winked at the two young ballplayers and said, "The man you're looking at here, my boys, all dressed up in street clothes, with a full head of hair, and on his way to medical school, could fire the pill like nobody else. Meet Damion Madrid, the 'Blood' in last year's Blood-and-Blackbird front-court combination that took us to the NCAA championship game. If you didn't meet him during one of your recruiting visits to campus last year, you should have. But then maybe you missed him because you were busy gawking at Blackbird while Blood here was probably in chemistry class."

Looking unimpressed but with a sudden hint of recognition in his eyes, the player who'd been lifting weights said, "Yeah, the guy who passed on bein' picked fourth in the NBA draft this year. We heard about him." Nodding at his teammate, he added, "Dumb-as-hell move if you ask me."

Ignoring the comment and recognizing that he was yesterday's news, Damion eyed Sandy. "Shandell was the reason we went to the finals. No need to hype me."

"Yeah, Blackbird was the reason all right," the iron-pumping freshman said. "Hear he got hisself killed last night. Shame."

"Shit, man. What a waste," added his teammate. "Never got a chance to spend one penny of them millions of his."

Remaining silent and biting back his anger, Damion seemed to stare straight through the young ballplayer. Sensing what Damion was thinking and hoping to keep the two freshmen from making any more stupid remarks, Sandy said, "Madrid here chalked himself up a CSU triple-double record that won't be matched in fifty years. Averaged twenty-two bones a game, eleven rebounds, and ten assists. Trust me. Half a century from now nobody'll eclipse that."

Aware that the two freshmen were barely paying attention, Damion smiled and said, "You got a little time to talk, Sandy?"

"Yeah, sure." Sandy checked his watch. "But we gotta make it fast. I'm sorta swamped."

"Let's go outside. The fresh air might make us feel good."

"Yeah, okay," Sandy said, sounding a bit out of sync. As he and Damion headed toward the exit, Sandy turned back and called out to the two freshmen, "Twenty more minutes of incremental reps and add forty pounds on the half mark." Winking at Damion, he said, "That should keep 'em busy."

Looking displeased, the rep counter called back, "Forty?"

"Yeah," said Sandy, smiling at the two disgruntled-looking ballplayers. "Coach's orders. Horse wants you both chasing that triple-double record I just told you about."

Sunlight arced from between puffy banks of scattered clouds as Sandy and Damion made their way from the weight room and across a grassy knoll to a weathered picnic table and rickety bench that languished beneath a hundred-year-old cottonwood. As they approached the spot where Damion and Shandell had spent untold hours talking basketball strategy during their college careers, Sandy, sensing that they were walking on hallowed ground, asked, "So when's the funeral?"

"Don't know yet, a couple of days probably," said Damion, trying his best to gauge the genuineness of Sandy's concern.

Sandy nodded and stared at the ground. The better part of a minute passed before Damion spoke again. "Need to ask you something about Shandell. Something Jackie Woodson told me about him." Damion took a seat on the bench.

"When did you talk to Jackie?"

"Before I came over to the weight room."

"So what's the something you need to ask me about?" Sandy asked as he also sat down.

"Jackie claims that Shandell was pushing performance-enhancers to kids back in Denver—down in Five Points. He said you knew all about it."

"And you believe him?"

"You see me here asking, don't you? Now, was he or wasn't he?"

A vein running along Sandy's right temple began to pulsate. Staring down at the grass, he said, "Yeah."

"Mind giving me the lowdown?" Damion's tone was calm but insistent.

"Didn't Jackie do that?"

Damion shook his head, deciding it might be best to keep the rest of what Jackie had told him to himself.

"Okay. Here's what I know," said Sandy, slightly red-faced. "During your last year here at CSU, Blackbird was making himself a little extra money selling performance-boosters down in Denver."

"You positive?"

"Sure am. Even know the guy he used as his supplier. A three-hundred-pound Jabba-the-Hutt-sized brother out of Five Points named Leotis Hawkins."

"Don't recognize the name. Mind telling me how you found out what Blackbird was doing?"

When Sandy didn't answer, Damion leaned into Sandy's space until he and the now thoroughly red-faced trainer were almost face to face. "Wanta answer me, Sandy?"

Squeaking his words out, Sandy said, "Jackie knew because he was using the stuff, and . . ."

"And you were in it with him, weren't you, Sandy?" Damion said, contemplating Sandy's unfinished sentence and smiling insightfully. He was well aware that Jackie and Sandy, who'd become thicker than thieves during Blackbird's senior year at CSU, had barely been on speaking terms prior to that. Looking at Sandy as if he might pick him up and shake him, Damion rose from his seat to tower over the suddenly pathetic-looking trainer. "So you recruited Shandell to peddle your garbage to a bunch of hungry-for-fame Five Points kids you knew idolized him."

"I didn't have to push too hard," Sandy said defiantly.

"I don't believe you. Shandell wouldn't have bought into something like that. Besides, I would have known about it."

Sandy sat back and smiled. "Bullshit. When you weren't on the court, you had your head buried in some book, and if you weren't studying, you were back home in Denver either hanging on to your mama's skirt or following that bail bondsman friend of yours around like a lapdog. Hell, the whole team and coaching staff knew it. You and Blackbird were roommates, all right, but you didn't really know him like you thought. If you had, you would've helped him steer clear of the mess he got himself into."

Damion took a deep breath as the bottom suddenly dropped out of his stomach. First Jackie Woodson and now Sandy, of all people, had accused him of not really knowing Shandell. He was on the verge of telling Sandy to fuck off when he remembered something his mother had once told him about searching out the truth right after CSU had suffered a disappointing loss to archrival Wyoming and the team was going through a period of dissension about who was to blame. She'd said that as a team captain he had the responsibility of never losing his cool, never resorting to finger-pointing, and never calling out a teammate in public. "Save it for the locker room," she'd said. "And try your best to act like a lawyer in front of a jury. Trust me, I've learned over the years that any other behavior is bad for business, and it speaks volumes about your skills to the rest of the world."

With Julie's words resonating in his mind, Damion suppressed his anger and in as calm a voice as he could muster said, "What was in it for you, Sandy?" When Sandy didn't answer, he said, "Don't test me, Sandy. You might find out I'm not the mama's boy you've always thought I was."

"What else? Money."

"How much did you make?"

"About ten grand."

Damion shook his head. "That's all Shandell's life was worth?"

"Hey, I didn't have anything to do with Blackbird's murder! And besides, what makes you think he was killed because of our deal? Could be something else Blackbird was into that got him shot."

In light of the fact that an investigative newspaper reporter had also been killed, Damion realized that Sandy might be right, but with frustration setting in, he decided to run a quick bluff. "Sure hope you're giving me the straight scoop here, Sandy, because you know that old Italian guy who always came to our games? The one who liked to boast that he was my godfather? Well, as it turns out, he's the kind of godfather Hollywood loves making movies about. The kind that can make someone insignificant like you disappear."

Uncertain whether Damion was feeding him a line, Sandy nonetheless understood that the man Damion was talking about, Mario Satoni, a onetime mafia don and a longtime friend of Damion's extended family, probably did have the juice to have him killed. He knew that Satoni and Blackbird had also been thicker than thieves. Trying his best to mask any fear, he said, "Are you crazy, man? I told you, I didn't have anything to do with Blackbird buying it."

"What about Jackie?"

In a suddenly quivering voice, Sandy said, "Can't speak for him."

Recognizing that his bluff had paid at least a partial dividend, Damion broke into a half smile and shrugged. "Guess I'll have to go back and talk to Jackie again. But before I do, how about giving me a Denver address for that supplier contact of yours, Leotis Hawkins?"

"Don't have one. I always hooked up with him at the Twenty-ninth and Welton light-rail stop in Five Points."

"What about a phone number?"

"He always called me."

"I see." Damion cocked a suspicious eyebrow. "Is Hawkins still operating down on the Points?"

"As far as I know, yeah."

"You still doing business with him?"

"No way. I got out of the business the day Blackbird played his last game. High risk and not enough reward. I wouldn't be telling you about it right now if I wasn't sure the cops aren't but a few steps behind you. No skin off my teeth giving you a head start. I liked Blackbird, and when word leaks out about what we were doing, I'll probably lose my job anyway."

Damion stroked his chin thoughtfully as he tried to determine his next move. "Guess what?" he said, his eyes lighting up. "You're back in business—and Sandy, I'm thinking you do have a phone number for Hawkins. I want you to call him and say you need to talk to him about what happened to Shandell. Tell him you're nervous about the possibility of being linked to a murder and that the two of you need to meet face to face."

"No way!"

Damion smiled. "You can talk to Hawkins or talk to Mario Satoni. Your choice, Sandy."

Sandy flashed Damion a dumbfounded, deer-in-the-headlights look. "You wouldn't sic a mobster on me, Blood. Come on."

Aware that his featherweight bluff now had the weight of an anchor, Damion said, "You know, Sandy, you're right. I wouldn't. Besides, Mario wouldn't dirty his hands with the likes of you. He'd send one of his people. Bottom line is, one way or another, you'd be dealt with."

Forced to decide between suffering the consequences of rolling on a third-rate drug pusher or possibly having a real-life mobster to deal with, Sandy said, "And then you'll leave me alone?"

"Depends on what I find out. If it turns out you were involved in Shandell's murder, believe me, we'll settle up."

"I told you I wasn't!"

"So you did." Damion's face was suddenly expressionless. It was a look Sandy knew well, a look Damion had never failed to summon when it was crunch time and the game was on the line. "Now, how about calling Hawkins and telling him you'll meet him at the usual spot in Five Points tonight at eight-thirty."

"Right now?"

"Time's a-wastin'."

Sandy hesitated for several seconds before unclipping his cell phone from his belt and punching in a phone number. Moments later, with Damion staring down his throat, Sandy responded to the gruff-sounding voice of Leotis Hawkins. "Leotis, it's Sands up at CSU."

"Long time no see," said Hawkins as Damion, taking in Sandy's side of the conversation, rolled his index finger in a tight director-style circle that called for action.

"Been busy," said Sandy. "Suppose you've heard about what happened to Blackbird."

Hawkins's response was an unsympathetic "Yep."

"Any chance we can get together this evening? Same place as always. We need to talk before the cops start snooping around. Synchronize our stories, if you know what I mean."

"Might not be a bad idea, Sands. Got a time in mind?"

With Damion hanging on his every word, Sandy said, "How about eight-thirty?"

"Works for me. And you're right about one thing, homes, we do need to talk."

"Eight-thirty, then," Sandy said, looking relieved.

"I'll be there." Without another word, Hawkins ended the conversation.

Gripping his cell phone tightly in a left hand that was shaking, Sandy said, "All set. You're on for eight-thirty."

"Good."

"Maybe not. I don't know a whole lot about Hawkins, but I do know from what Jackie's told me that he's done time in Canon City. Twice!"

Damion smiled. "Maybe he enjoys the amenities of our state pen."

"Might not be so funny if he slits your throat, Madrid. He's the kind that prefers knives to guns. I know that for a fact. I've seen what he carries."

"Appreciate the heads-up. Now here's one for you. Don't call Hawkins back to tell him we're trading places tonight. If you do, the people I'll send to deal with you won't be drug-pushing punks—they'll be pros."

Uncertain whether Damion was bluffing but deciding it was in his best interest to steer clear of the Denver mob, Sandy wiped away a rivulet of sweat that had worked its way down his sideburn. "Do you think Hawkins might've killed Shandell? Blackmail gone bad, maybe?"

"Seems like a possible reason to me," said Damion.

"But why kill your golden goose?"

"Maybe no more golden eggs were forthcoming."

"Bad shit any way you slice it," said Sandy with a shake of the head.

"Real bad, and it's gonna get worse once the cops show up on your doorstep, my friend. Happy trails." Damion rose from his seat and offered the shrunken, pitiful-looking trainer a final parting comment.

"I'll find out who killed Shandell, Sandy. Even if it means that you get to end up in the same place as him. So keep your stories straight when the cops show up, because I'll have Mario watching. And while you're at it, don't let those freshman recruits wear you down. Later."

It was several minutes before Rodney Sands summoned up the mental energy to head back to the athletic training facilities. For half that time he simply sat at the old picnic table, staring blankly up at the sun and thinking about where he had been and where he was going.

He'd spent the past eight years on the athletic department staff at CSU after coming home from four years of service as an army paratrooper. Two of those years had been spent suffering through brain-numbing winters at an outpost in Korea. He'd ultimately earned a degree in kinesiology, scored the CSU job, and worked his way up from wiping the noses of pampered jocks to his present lead trainer's position. During his tenure at CSU, he'd doctored the records of out-of-control athletes, wiped out their DUIs, helped get half-a-dozen date-rape accusations dropped, steered his charges to Mickey Mouse courses that a third grader could have passed, and on rare occasions even taken their tests for them. He'd kissed the asses of coaches, played gofer for a string of ego-inflated athletic directors, manipulated unsympathetic, jock-hating tutors into seeing things his way, and even held the hands of heartbroken coeds who'd discovered all too late that they weren't the only one. In all that time, he'd rarely missed when it came to judging who would go along to get along. He'd seriously miscalculated, however, when it had come to Shandell Bird, misjudging Shandell's stoic, soft-spoken, introverted persona for weakness when in fact it had been his strength.

He'd simply been looking for a short-term drug-hauling mule when Shandell, in need of money before his NBA ship came in, had signed up for the job. That choice, he could now see, had been a bad one. One that could end up costing him his job. He had high-level administrative connections and a cadre of admirers among students, faculty, and staff, but if Damion Madrid kept pressing—or even worse, showed back up on his doorstep with a new set of questions—or if he was forced to square off with some eager-beaver cop, he wasn't certain what he'd do. It all seemed somehow unfair since he'd never used or distributed the steroids, the uppers, or the hGH he'd given Shandell to take down to Denver. He'd simply been a middleman, effectively uniting supplier and buyer. He'd hooked up Blackbird and Leotis Hawkins, and that had been it. If the cops or Madrid needed to finger someone, Leotis Hawkins was their man. He'd have no problem rolling on Hawkins if it meant saving his own hide. But for the moment, he'd keep his head down and wait for the clouds to clear, and when everything was said and done, at least he'd still have a head. That was more than he suspected Hawkins would leave Damion Madrid when the two of them met that evening.

Leotis Hawkins's intimidating tone had the desired effect on Jackie Woodson, who now sat shaking in the front seat of his car as he listened to Leotis over his cell phone. "You fuckin' sawed-off little turd. No wonder the NBA didn't want you after your junior year. You've got the brains of a pissant. First you talk to Madrid about things you shouldn't, and then you sic him on that clueless white bread of a weak sister, Sands. When I talked to you this morning, I thought we came away with an understanding. It's a good thing Sandy can understand English a whole lot better than you."

"We do have an understanding." Jackie's response was a near whisper.

"My ass we do. And speak up, you fuckin' wimp. I just talked to Sands. I'm sure that blond-headed piece of shit would roll on me in a second if he didn't figure I'd drive up there to Fort Collins and kick his ass or slit his throat. Now, before I head up there and kick yours, and maybe break a few bones and rip apart a few knee ligaments that'll keep you out of the NBA for good, we need to get us a better understandin'. What's your trainer boy Sands up to, and why does he suddenly wanta see me down in Five Points tonight?"

"I'm guessin' he talked to Madrid and he wants you both on the same page."

"And you spoke party line like we agreed on earlier?"

"Yes."

"You better not be lyin' to me, you little fucker."

"I've got no reason to," Jackie said, knowing that on the contrary, he had a very important, career-dependent reason to lie to anyone he talked to about the Shandell Bird and Paul Grimes murders, including Hawkins.

Hawkins shook his head, unconvinced. "I don't know why in the hell I ever got in bed with a retard like you, Jackie. I should've known better than to hook up with some paratrooper throwback outta some northern Indiana rust bucket. Don't matter, though. I'll just have to make a minor adjustment this evenin'."

"What's up, then?"

"Nothin' you need to know about, dumbass. How close are Madrid and Sands anyway?"

"Not close, really."

"Think they'd try and come down here to Denver and tag-team me?"

Jackie smiled, aware that things couldn't have lined up any better for him. He had Hawkins nervous about both Damion and Sandy. "Maybe."

"Yeah, I think you're right. Think maybe they would. Especially with Madrid bein' all college educated and thinkin' he's slick, and Sands scared shitless. But I'll have somethin' for 'em if they do. Trust me. The same thing I told Blackbird I'd have for him if he ever fucked up. And the same thing I got for you if you mouth off to the cops. You with me?"

"Yeah."

"Good. 'Cause we're floatin' in the same boat here, Jackie."

"Yeah, we sure are," Jackie said with a grin as he tried to imagine what Hawkins might have in store for Damion and perhaps even Sands.

"And since you're insinuatin' it was Sands and not you who tipped off Madrid to me, I'm thinkin' you won't need to be checkin' the rearview mirror nearly as much as Sands. Right?"

"Right." Before Jackie had a chance to say another word, the phone went dead. Concerned that he hadn't completely dropped his Leotis Hawkins problem on Sandy's doorstep, he muttered, "Shit!" and glanced into his rearview mirror, thinking that he now had not one but two potentially life-threatening problems to contend with.

Chapter 8

The seventy-mile drive south down I-25 to Denver gave Damion plenty of time to reflect on where he'd head next with what Flora Jean would surely have referred to as a "snoop and probe" job. Before leaving the CSU campus, he'd gone back by Jackie Woodson's apartment in the hope of getting more information about Leotis Hawkins. Having no luck there, or later at two of the mouthy point guard's favorite campus haunts, he'd swung by the athletic offices and talked briefly to his clearly shaken former coach, Russ Haroldson.

The normally buoyant fireplug of a man was having a difficult time dealing with the fact that the greatest player he'd ever coached had been murdered and after a strained fifteen-minute conversation, Damion had left Haroldson the way he'd found him, looking despondent. Never once had he mentioned what Sandy had told him about Shandell, and he'd promised to keep Haroldson abreast of funeral arrangements. Since Haroldson had helped Shandell navigate the rigors of college as much as Damion had, making certain Shandell went to class, stayed out of girl trouble, and showed up at endless sessions with tutors, Damion reasoned that the man who'd played the role of a father figure to Shandell didn't deserve to have a bombshell dropped on him right then.

Cruising along at 75 and shoving thoughts of insipid trainers, mouthy point guards, and performance-enhancing-drug dealers aside, Damion watched the High Plains landscape roll by. When he suddenly found himself thinking about the very first time he and Shandell had taken a trip up north to the "cow country" and CSU, he found himself smiling. At the time they'd both been heavily recruited by colleges across the country, and he'd pretty much settled on going to North Carolina to become part of that school's legendary basketball program and strong academics. Shandell, however, who'd never felt comfortable much beyond the boundaries of the Mile High City, much less Colorado, had wanted no part of Chapel Hill.

When he'd pushed for Shandell to take a look at North Carolina, insisting that he needed to broaden his horizons, Shandell had responded, "No way." Punctuating the comment with a tinge of anger, he'd added, "Ain't goin' nowhere I ain't wanted. It's the goddamn South, Damion, are you crazy? I don't want no pretentious, syrupy-soundin' Southern belles in my face for four long years, and I don't wanta see no rebel flags flappin' in the breeze neither. The one thing you ain't never been and ain't never gonna be, Damion Madrid, is black. So you can save your North Carolina for NASCAR nuts and rednecks."

In the end, they'd both landed at CSU after Damion, on the strength of a 1525 SAT score and a 25-points-per-game high school scoring average, garnered both full-ride academic and athletic scholarships—something no other institution, including North Carolina, was willing to pony up. Shandell, a first-team *Parade* magazine high school All-American, on the heels of four full-court-press recruiting visits from Coach Haroldson and the encouragement of his mother, announced in a long-awaited *Denver Post* exclusive, "It's CSU for me. I'm stayin' home." A week after the two of them signed letters of intent in front of flashing cameras at the Pepsi Center, home to the Denver Nuggets, sports pages across the region were touting the fact that CSU had unbelievably, and some claimed inexplicably, corralled two of the best prep players in the country.

That all seemed a lifetime ago as Damion, teary-eyed and with his head bent in sorrow, accelerated past an empty cattle trailer wobbling its way toward Denver. As he watched the semi jiggle, he recalled what CJ had once told him about the despondency he'd had to suffer through after coming home from two navy tours as an aft-deck patrol-boat machine gunner in Vietnam. He suspected that like CJ, he'd have to contend for a while with some dark, unsettling times.

As he neared the interstate's Dacono exit, where the highway widened from two lanes to three, he heard the blare of a horn. Realizing that while lost in reflection he'd slowed to less than 55, he moved into the far-right-hand lane to let a gravel-hauling semi rumble by. As the truck pulled away he found himself thinking about Jackie Woodson and wondering whether Jackie could possibly have killed Shandell.

Jackie had arrived on campus the year Damion and Shandell were sophomores, soaring onto the scene as a highly touted, slightly overweight, deadly perimeter shooter but a surprisingly poor defender. A loudmouthed, womanizing, directionless kid full of braggadocio, Jackie had come from a dying Midwestern steel-mill town with less than five dollars to his name and only two changes of clothes. To some extent he'd matured, but in many ways, in spite of the benefits of three years of college and Coach Haroldson's wisdom and tutelage, Jackie remained the same unpolished East Chicago, Indiana, wannabe street thug he'd been when he'd first come to CSU.

During Jackie's first semester he'd done nothing but attend basketball practice and play cards. It had been Shandell who'd convinced him to stop spending his free time trying to be a hustler and

Shandell who'd ultimately sold him on the fact that he had an NBA future. It was that fact that had Damion confused about how things now seemed to have been turned on their heads so that the teacher had somehow become the student and Shandell had ended up playing Jackie's game.

He couldn't understand how someone like Jackie Woodson, a onetime East Chicago gang-banger who spent half his off-court time on the hustle for either an extra dollar or some exquisite piece of ass, could've sucked someone who was destined to become an instant millionaire into a drug-dealing and possibly even a point-shaving scam, or how fast-talking former paratrooper Rodney Sands could've convinced Shandell to be part of such stupidity.

Perplexed that not only Jackie but Rodney Sands had been able to turn the tables on Shandell, Damion realized he'd have to do a lot more digging if he expected to sort things out and pin the tail on Shandell's killer before the cops. He'd have to find out why, if in fact Sandy was telling the truth, Shandell had risked everything—his reputation, his career, and ultimately his life—for what in the long run would have been mere pocket change to him. It seemed as nonsensical as the fact that Shandell was dead, or that ignoring Flora Jean's explicit instructions to him to simply gather facts, later that evening he was going to hook up alone with Leotis Hawkins. Concerned that a desire for revenge, fueled by his often blind competitiveness—something his mother had always claimed would be his undoing if he didn't learn to control it—might in fact be overshadowing his reasoning, Damion suddenly found himself thinking about what he had to lose. At least for the moment, it seemed that, just like Blackbird, he had it all. Medical school was in the offing, he'd had a storybook college basketball career, and he had a supportive family that included everyone from a mother who cherished him to a powerful, once high-profile gangster who constantly bragged about him as if they were related by blood. Even so, he knew there was something missing—something he, CJ Floyd, and Shandell, all men who'd grown up in fatherless households, had discussed more than once. It was the same thing that had driven Shandell and him to master a child's game until they were the very kings of it. The same thing that had pushed him to cram his head full of often useless information in the pursuit of sterling grades and admission to medical school. And the same thing that had made CJ Floyd chase bond skippers, wife beaters, and dope dealers across the Rockies for thirty-five years. When you came right down to it, he suspected that the thing they were all chasing was self-worth. They needed it so much because something essential was missing from their lives, and no matter how well they might appear to have adjusted to its absence, he knew that when you netted it all out, as Flora Jean was fond of saying, what they were each saying in their own way was "Look at me—fatherless or not, I'm a man."

As he exited I-25 and headed east onto I-70 for Aretha Bird's house, he had the feeling that in his haste to once again scream, "I'm a man!" he'd taken the wrong tack with Rodney Sands. Manipulation, not intimidation, was the strategy he suspected he should have employed. Shaking his head and thinking, *You make mistakes at any game when you're a novice,* he slowed down for the York Street exit that would take him into the heart of Five Points. Cruising through neighborhoods that were now all black, he found himself thinking about concepts that his mother had once told him couldn't be measured, concepts such as good and evil, life and death. Less than two blocks from Aretha's house, with those thoughts still filling his head, he remembered something CJ had once told him about the killing machine that was war. "Sometimes when I lost a friend on the battlefield, I wanted to kill everything in sight—not just the VC but the trees, the grass, even the dirt under my feet," CJ had said. "But in time it passed. It had to or I'd've ended up closer to being a wild animal than a human being."

As Damion cruised to a stop in front of Aretha's meticulously maintained Queen Anne home and stepped out into the dry air and bright mile-high sunshine, CJ's words kept ringing in his head. He hoped those words would help him get through the grief he was facing, but more importantly, he hoped they'd help him toe the mark when it came to remaining a human being.

Aretha Bird's bright gray, deep-set eyes had lost their light, and the woman who would normally have greeted Damion with a loving hug barely looked able to stand when she met him at her front door. Glancing back toward the Cadillac Coupe de Ville with Illinois temporary tags that he had parked behind, Damion found himself wondering who else had dropped by to pay their respects. Draping an arm over Aretha's shoulders and hugging her affectionately, he said, "How are you holding up, Mrs. B?"

"Barely, just barely, baby. But I'm still standin', so the Lord must have a need for me to remain upright. How 'bout you?" Her voice descended to a delicate wheeze.

"I just had the two worst days of my life. But I'm standing too." Clasping Aretha's right hand in his, Damion stepped into the familiar musty-smelling, plant-filled entryway and walked with her down a short hallway that led to the living room.

Aretha tried to force a smile that wouldn't come. "Can I get you a drink, sweetie? Maybe one of them room-temperature Coca-Colas in the little bottles that you and my baby always liked so much?" Her eyes began to water the instant she mentioned Shandell.

"Yeah, that would be great," Damion said, stepping down into a cluttered, overly furnished but warmly hospitable living room.

"I'll get you one from the kitchen, baby." Aretha looked over her shoulder as she headed for an archway that led to the kitchen. "It's a good thing you're here. There's somebody I want you to meet." Before disappearing into the kitchen, she called out toward one of the two small bedrooms in the back of the house, "Leon, come up front. Need you to meet somebody."

Damion stood briefly in the center of the living room, biting nervously at his lower lip before walking over to a pedestal table that sat just inside the west-facing bay window. A ten-by-twelve-inch color photograph of Shandell and him, with two basketball nets that had been cut from their hoops after CSU's NCAA Midwest regional finals victory over Kentucky hung around their necks, sat on the table. A beaming Coach Haroldson, kneeling in front of them with his head goose-necked toward the camera, dominated the photograph's foreground. A dust-covered basketball with the game's final score—CSU 88, Kentucky 84—and the letters "B & B" stenciled half-a-dozen times in white along its equator rested like a headstone at the foot of the pedestal.

"Leon, you comin'?" Aretha Bird called out as she reappeared with an uncapped vintage eight-ounce Coca-Cola bottle in one hand and a bowl of potato chips in the other. "I got you some chips too, Damion. Figured you'd like some, just like always." Wiping a lingering tear from her cheek, she handed the bottle and chips to Damion.

Damion swallowed hard, fighting back his own tears. "Thanks."

He took a swig of Coke before placing the untouched bowl of potato chips on the pedestal table.

Searching for something to say, Aretha muttered, "I talked to your mom twice today. Haven't seen her, though. She was in court all day. Said she'd drop by on her way to the airport before flying out to San Francisco for that trial lawyers' meeting she mentioned last night. Flora Jean stopped by with Alden, who's still lookin' every bit the dapper general, to pay her respects early this morning, and so did Mario Satoni." She shook her head before continuing, "Mario didn't look so good, Damion. Somethin' the matter with him?"

Aware that the eighty-four-year-old former don turned antiques dealer had been having recent gallstone problems, Damion said, "He's been a little under the weather with a gall-bladder problem, Mrs. B."

Aretha nodded. "Oh." The room briefly fell silent except for the rhythmic ticking of an antique mantel clock. "And yeah, CJ and Mavis called from Hawaii. I was on the phone with 'em for a good fifteen minutes. Told 'em both there was no need to come back home and spoil their honeymoon with no funeral." Looking at Damion as if she'd suddenly discovered the answer to a long-pondered question, she said, "I been wonderin' where you were all day."

Unprepared for the question and not wanting to tell the woman who'd been as much a surrogate mother to him as Flora Jean while his own mother had spent three years going to law school at night that he'd spent most of the day laying the groundwork for finding Shandell's killer, he said, "I went up to CSU to see Coach Haroldson and Jackie Woodson. Figured it might help for the three of us to prop each other up."

Aretha nodded understandingly. "Funeral's set for the day after tomorrow. Figured there was no need to string out the hurt."

With his eyes locked sympathetically on Aretha's, Damion was about to respond when a booming male voice erupted from the archway that led to the kitchen.

"And we woulda shot for tomorrow if it hadn'ta been for the cops pesterin' us all day and the damn coroner holdin' back my boy's release on account of some autopsy." The man speaking was Damion's height, perhaps a half-inch taller. The hint of a goatee trickled from his chin as his darting green eyes pinballed their way around the room. Although obviously black, he was a shade or two lighter than Aretha, and even from across the room Damion could see that his coffee-colored skin was badly pockmarked. Diamond stud earrings penetrated both of his earlobes, and he sported sideburns that were 1950s-vintage muttonchops. As the man stepped across the room with one arm outstretched, Damion had the sense that he was about to shake hands with someone who represented more pain than comfort for Aretha Bird.

Before the man, who was wearing a designer Nike sweatsuit and a pair of Shandell's prototype Nike sneakers, had a chance to utter another word, Aretha said, "Damion, I'd like you to meet Shandell's father, Leon."

Looking startled, Damion said, "Pleasure." As he moved to shake the hand of a man Shandell had always told him he hated, a man who'd deserted Shandell and Aretha, refusing for sixteen years to acknowledge their existence, Damion's stomach began churning. He'd heard during his senior year at CSU that Leon Bird, the man Shandell derogatorily referred to as "Leech-on," had been hovering at the periphery of Shandell's and Aretha's lives. But he'd never met him.

When Leon was rumored to have shown up at the NCAA Sweet Sixteen finals in Kansas City the previous March, Shandell had lost his game focus. Shooting a miserable 2 for 11 from the field during the first half of their semifinal game against Louisville, he'd been charged with three quick fouls near the end of the half and had been forced to spend most of the third quarter on the bench.

He'd reentered the game a minute into the fourth quarter to lead CSU to a come-from-behind victory only after Damion, who'd suspected what might be eating at his best friend, had whispered to him during a time-out, "No need for us all to come down with pneumonia because you've caught a cold, Shandell. You need to focus if we're gonna stay afloat in this damn thing."

Shandell's 24-point performance in what remained of the fourth quarter quickly became NCAA highlight-reel legend, and although he didn't speak to Damion about it for the rest of that night, or the next day, for that matter, from that point forward, whenever there was any hint that his father might be lingering in the wings, Shandell solved the problem on his own before it could taint the rest of his world.

As Leon continued to pump his arm, Damion found himself wondering whether the man who'd deserted his wife and son sixteen years earlier had had anything to do with Shandell's death.

"You're taller than you look from the stands, Blood, and more solid-lookin' too," Leon said, finally releasing his grip. "If I was you I woulda gone on to the pros."

Damion forced a smile and nodded, taking in the expression on Leon Bird's face. Leon clearly wasn't puffy-eyed from crying. In fact, he looked almost excited and casually dapper with his hair slicked back with pomade, 1950s heart-of-the-hood style.

Realizing that Damion was reading his expression, Leon said, "This here's a sad, sad situation for us all." He glanced sympathetically toward

Aretha. "For me and Aretha. You know, Blackbird and me were close to a full reconciliation." His words had a noticeable air of insincerity.

Damion took a long sip of Coke before looking at Aretha, who remained stoically silent.

"You got any idea what mighta pushed somebody to wanta kill my boy?" Leon asked, watching Damion clutch the nearly empty Coke bottle tightly.

"I don't know." Damion's response was aimed at Aretha rather than Leon.

"Well, you knew him best, so I figured I'd ask," Leon said, his tone pointedly defensive. "Could be he was havin' girl problems, or problems with his agent, or maybe he was battlin' with folks who were jealous of his fame."

"Leon, please!" Aretha said, fighting back tears.

"I wanta know who killed my boy, Aretha," Leon said forcefully.

You mean your newfound meal ticket? Damion thought. But rather than voice his concern, he said, "We're working on that."

"What?" Aretha said, looking puzzled.

"Flora Jean and me, we're running down a few angles—trying to figure out exactly what happened."

"Shouldn't you leave that to the police, Damion?"

"Probably. But I'm not."

"You can't get involved in this, Damion. I've already lost Shandell."

"No worry, Mrs. B. I'm only doing the light work. Flora Jean's doing the heavy lifting."

"Who's Flora Jean, and what's she got to do with my boy dyin'?" Leon interjected.

"She's a bail bondsman, or bondsperson if you're into political correctness," said Damion.

"A woman?" Leon asked, frowning.

"She's also an ex-marine, a onetime marine intelligence op. Did a tour in Desert Storm."

"She's still a woman," Leon countered.

On the verge of saying, *And she's the kind who just might kick your ass if you push her to it,* Damion bit his tongue and proceeded to polish off the last of his Coke. Setting the empty bottle aside, he turned to Aretha. "Do you have a set of keys to Shandell's condo, Mrs. B? Flora Jean wants to get in and have a look around."

Aretha shook her head. "Sure don't, baby. You know how protective Shandell was about his privacy. Matter of fact, that cop who corralled us last evenin' came by here earlier today and asked me the very same thing. Don't know why; I'm sure the cops have Shandell's keys. I think he was just testin' me, tryin' to see if I'd tell him the truth about havin' access to Shandell's place."

"Could be," said Damion. "But Flora Jean'll figure out how to get in."

"You two need me to help?" Leon asked.

"Nope." Damion's response was as quick as it was blunt.

"Damion, please don't do nothin' to bring no more hurt on me than I got right now," Aretha pleaded.

"I won't, Mrs. B. I just need to ask you one last thing before I go," he said, preparing to ask a question he knew he should've asked both Rodney Sands and Jackie Woodson. "That reporter who was killed—had you ever seen him before?"

"I never met him before, but I recognized his name once that detective Townsend started askin' me questions again today. I think he's a reporter who mighta interviewed Shandell about signin' with the Nuggets somewhere along the way."

"There's a whole nine yards about him in today's paper," Leon blurted out. "Almost as much about him as there was about Shandell."

Damion nodded, locking eyes with Leon. "How about you? Did you know the guy?"

"'Course not. But the paper says he was one of them investigative types. The kind that dig up dirt on people."

"Wonder what he was investigating?" asked Damion, eyeing Leon as if expecting an answer.

"Beats me," Leon said with a shrug.

"Guess we'll have to find out," Damion said, moving to leave. "Call me if you need me, Mrs. B." He planted a kiss on Aretha's forehead before walking across the room. "Oh, and when my mom shows up, tell her I said have a safe trip to the coast and that I'm headed to CJ's office to talk to Flora Jean, then over to Mae's to grab a bite to eat."

"Okay," said Aretha. "Just be sure that's all you're gonna do."

"Sure will," said Damion, casting a final pensive look in Leon Bird's direction. "Nice meeting you," he said with a nod before stepping up from the living room to the entry alcove and heading for the door.

"My pleasure," Leon said loudly.

Damion was nearly back to his Jeep when Leon turned to Aretha, who was once again crying, and said, "Strange kid."

When Aretha choked out, "He's gonna be a doctor," Leon Bird, who'd spent two years behind the walls of the state prison in Michigan City, Indiana, said knowingly, "Funny. Sorta struck me more like a cop."

Chapter 9

The man standing at arm's length from Flora Jean, leaning back against his desk and eyeing her as if he wanted to strip off every stitch of her clothing so he could have a good, hard look at the treasures beneath, was anything but the suave lady-killer and dogged journalist he'd once been.

Fifty-seven, overweight, balding, and with teeth yellowed from years of chain-smoking, Arnett Triplett was on the downside of his writing and womanizing career.

Owner and publisher of Denver's only black-owned newspaper, the *Denver Metro Weekly*, Triplett had once played for the Atlanta Falcons. His status as a former professional football player, his gift for gab, and a nest egg left over from his playing days had enabled him to buy the struggling *Denver Metro Weekly* from its founder eight years earlier.

He'd known Flora Jean for just over half of those years, and for most of that time, whenever they'd run into one another, he'd tried his best to persuade her to share his bed, a motel-room bed, the back seat of his car, a picnic blanket, or anything remotely similar, hoping to add another notch to the butt of his sexual-conquests gun.

Winking and licking his lips, Triplett widened his stance and grinned. "I'm telling you, Flora Jean, your boyfriend the general wouldn't have to know a thing. We'd do our thing—real, as you marines like to say, uh, covertly—and then ease on down the road."

"Sorry, sugar. But Alden would kill you, and neither one of us would want that," said Flora Jean, who'd come to Triplett's York Street office in midtown Denver to seek information about Paul Grimes. She was well aware that whether her visit lasted ten minutes or ten hours, she'd have to contend with Triplett's sexual propositions.

Triplett looked unfazed, even though he understood that if pressed, the decorated, no-nonsense former general very likely could have him killed. He had it on good account, although Alden Grace claimed to be retired, that the general still occasionally worked the U.S. intelligence beat from his home base sixty miles south of Denver under the protective umbrella of the North American Aerospace Defense Command in Colorado Springs.

Looking disappointed, Triplett shook his head knowingly. "Never will be able to figure out why you hooked up with a white boy, fine as you are, girl—especially with all us appreciative and dutiful brothers out here. Must be love."

"Must be," Flora Jean agreed, determined not to travel a road she and Triplett had traveled many times before. "Now, sugar, if you're done with your antics for the day, can we get back to why I'm here?"

"Yeah, yeah. The Bird and Grimes murders. I heard you when you walked in."

"So why don't you tell me what you know about those killin's, and I'll be outta your hair so you can quit your fantasizin'?"

Triplett looked hurt. "Like what?"

"For starters, how well did they know one another? Blackbird and Grimes, I mean? There was a *Rocky Mountain News* story this morning claimin' they did."

"Haven't read the story; been too busy here. Who wrote it?"

Flora Jean fished into the pocket of her form-fitting jeans and slipped out the neatly folded *Rocky Mountain News* story that had been penned by a man named Wordell Epps. Surprised that Triplett hadn't read the story, she unfolded it and handed it to him. "You really should keep up with the news, sugar, bein' a newspaperman and all."

"Yeah, yeah," said Triplett, scanning the story. "Why don't you have a seat, beautiful." He walked around his desk and pulled up his chair. His left knee popped loudly enough to be heard across the room as he sat down. "Too many years on the gridiron," he said, shaking his head.

Nope, too many years chasin' tail, you crooked-toothed cockhound, Flora Jean thought. "Know the writer?"

"Sure do. I'm in the newspaper business, remember?" He flattened the clipping on the desktop. "Wordell Epps. Squirrelly little white boy, straight outta the '60s. Been around Denver most of his life."

"Hm. Did Epps have any ties to Grimes?"

"Sure did. Twenty years or so back, they won a Pulitzer together. Sort of the Woodward and Bernstein of the Rockies, and both of 'em as weird as Waco whiskey. But unlike black folks, white folks can weird out on you all day long and still take home the bacon."

"Weird how?"

"Both of 'em were left over from the Age of Aquarius," Triplett said, smiling. "You ever talk to Epps, you'll see what I mean."

"Oh, I'll talk to him. Count on it."

"Then I hope you catch him on one of his coherent days. And when you do, here's a heads-up for you. That Pulitzer he and Grimes won was for an eight-part *Rocky Mountain News* piece they did on Denver's old-time crime families. Sorta laid out in detail the role those families played in helping to set up Vegas. Some folks in the news business, including me, think the whole thing was a piece of fluff served up to a Pulitzer committee that was being paid off to provide a bunch of mobsters with a coat of touchy-feely civic-minded gloss. No question about it, both Grimes and Epps had friends who were mobbed up. But why am I telling you all this when you and CJ Floyd have your own top-tier connections to organized crime? How's Mario Satoni doing, anyway?" Triplett flashed Flora Jean his best "gotcha" grin. He and CJ had never gotten along.

"He's doing just fine."

"Good to hear," Triplett said sarcastically. "But mob connections aside, if you're lookin' to run down why Grimes and the Bird kid were murdered, I'd say you're almost sure to have to look west to Vegas. And I'm thinkin' that your boy Mario's connections are way too rusty to help with that, especially if some Nevada desert rat gets his nose out of joint."

"Then I'll tread lightly."

"Do that. 'Cause I sure wouldn't want any part of that exquisite body of yours to end up gettin' bruised." Triplett licked his lips sensuously.

"Got another question for you," said Flora Jean, ignoring the comment. "You've always had your finger on the pulse of what goes down in Five Points. What have you heard about Theo Wilhite losin' a bundle on last spring's NCAA championship game?"

Triplett poked out his lower lip and eyed her thoughtfully. "You thinkin' that maybe Blackbird was murdered over some kinda gambling scam gone bad?"

"It's crossed my mind."

Triplett sat back in his chair and massaged the cleft in his chin. "Yeah, I've heard about Wilhite losin' ten big ones last spring. Who the hell hasn't, big as that man's mouth is? But I don't think Wilhite would go after Shandell because of that. We both know Theo's a lot more mouth than action."

"Yeah, you and I know that. But what if some of the people Grimes and Epps wrote about in that dusty old Pulitzer piece didn't like the idea that Wilhite was runnin' around Denver mouthin' off that he'd lost his ten grand on a game they fixed? Wouldn't make 'em look real civic-minded."

"Possible. But the people you're talkin' about have bigger fish to fry than the likes of Theo Wilhite. My guess is that if Theo was crampin' their style, they'd have taken care of him long ago."

"Then maybe Wilhite's tongue-waggin' got some lesser underworld types with ties to the gamblin' world thinkin' real hard about keepin' Shandell quiet. Not the kind of biggies who set the odds, or your high rollers, but the kinda folks who lost a nice little nest egg—maybe ten, fifteen, or twenty grand, like him. Could be they wanted to settle up with the guy who was doin' the point-shavin' that cost 'em."

"Could be," Triplett said with a respectful nod. "But why would they wait from last April until now to settle up with Shandell and kill Grimes, and still let Theo Wilhite walk?"

Flora Jean shrugged. "Don't have an answer for the Theo question. But as for Grimes, maybe he was just in the wrong place at the wrong time."

"Unlikely."

"Yeah, you're probably right. Here's a final question for you."

Pouting, Triplett said, "You're gonna make me cry, Flora Jean. Why you gotta sail outta here so fast? I was hopin' to sit here and feast my eyes on you for the rest of the day."

"Sorry, sugar. Guess you'll just have to spend that time dreamin' about somethin' else. So here's my question. If there were some point-shavin' shenanigans involved in last spring's NCAA final, who do you think Theo used to steer him to the right bookie?"

"Afraid you'll have to ask him that. But I can tell you who was probably handling the money at the top around here. Garrett Asalon."

"Yeah, I sorta figured that. Guess I'll have to get Mario to give me the current skinny on Asalon."

"What do you need to know besides the fact that for the past twenty years he's been Colorado's gamblin' kingpin? And Wyoming and New Mexico's, as far as that goes."

Flora Jean gave Triplett a quick wink. "Always pays to know more than less about infected alley cats, sugar. Helps you keep from gettin' scratched. Guess I'll have to talk to Theo Wilhite myself and see if he was usin' a middleman or goin' straight to Asalon with his bettin'. Tell you this, though: Theo's one slippery little bugger. I've already missed catchin' up with him at his place twice today. But like my mama used to say, sooner or later, even night owls and mourning doves gotta come home."

"Smart lady," said Triplett with a grin. "Now, as for home, you're always welcome to spend the night here."

"Sorry, but I've already got a home. Besides, I'm afraid I'd never feel real comfortable around here."

"Why's that?"

"Because I'd never know when another bluebird might fly in and wanta fill my nest."

"You're hurtful, girl," Triplett said, looking wounded.

"Just callin' things the way they are."

"That's your right, I guess. But if you ever overcome your sense of loyalty and dump the good general, remember, I'm here for the takin'."

"Good to know," said Flora Jean, rising from her chair and heading for the door. "Always important to know which trapdoors to shy away from. Thanks for the info, sugar." Glancing over her shoulder, she gave Triplett a seductive parting wink. It was the kind of wink that said, *Wear your eyeballs out all you want, sugar. But don't you dare ever touch.*

Wordell Epps seemed cordial enough a half hour later when Flora Jean called him at his *Rocky Mountains News* office and asked to meet with him. He sounded almost giddy, in fact, like some high school sophomore who'd just scored a date for the big dance. He agreed to meet her at 5:30 at his place in the Capitol Hill section of Denver and announced, thinking she might be unfamiliar with the neighborhood, "The building's a block and a half south of Colfax, on Pearl, just up the street from Argonaut Liquors," before hanging up.

As she stood across the street, trying to figure out why a Pulitzer Prize–winning journalist like Epps was living on the fourth floor of a dilapidated building that looked as if it had been intentionally constructed to look run-down and was probably largely inhabited by transients, she had the sense that Arnett Triplett had been right on the money in his assessment of Wordell Epps.

On guard as she approached the building, she stepped inside a dimly lit five-story atrium that echoed with the noises of crying children and blaring TVs. Thinking as the smells of the place engulfed her, *I've been here before—lived here before,* she headed for a darkened set of stairs, unwilling to ride the elevator. It reminded her far too much of elevator rides from her youth when men with liquor on their breath and coins jangling in their pockets would ride up with her and her mother to their East St. Louis apartment, then pay her a quarter or half-dollar to keep riding the elevator for a while before disappearing inside the apartment with her mother.

By the time she reached the door to Epps's apartment, her ears were ringing, something that hadn't happened since she'd attended her heroin-addicted mother's funeral fifteen years earlier. As she stood at the door trying to decide whether to knock or push the filthy doorbell that had electrical tape and loose wire poking from beneath it, she remembered what Arnett Triplett had said about Epps's disjointedness and wondered whether Epps might be suffering from the aftermath of the same kind of dysfunctional childhood she'd endured.

After several firm knocks, no one answered, so she reluctantly rang the doorbell.

"Coming," someone inside yelled.

"About time," she muttered.

Moments later, a skinny, glassy-eyed white man appeared at the door. He had a ponytail, an unruly mop of silver hair, and a meticulously groomed jet-black and quite obviously dyed Vandyke jutting from his chin. Taken aback by the man's look of dishevelment, Flora Jean almost said, "I'll be damned." Instead she asked, "Wordell Epps?"

"In the flesh." Epps flashed Flora Jean a toothy grin. "And if I'm guessing right, you'd be Ms. Benson. Come on in."

"Thank you." Flora Jean walked down a narrow hall and into a boxy looking twenty-five-by-twenty-five-foot room that was carpeted wall to wall with filthy gold shag carpet, a relic of the early 1970s. Bamboo curtains hung unevenly at the two windows, and a couple of late-'60s college-dorm-room-style smoked-glass coffee-table tops with cinder blocks for legs sat in the center of the room. The makeshift tables were surrounded by a ring of four well-used, cracked vinyl beanbag chairs.

As she waited for her eyes to adjust to the smoky dimness, Flora Jean realized that the place reeked of marijuana.

In a voice brimming with an extended flower-child welcome, Epps said, "Offer you a joint?"

"No, thanks," she said, aware now of at least one reason why the Pulitzer Prize–winning journalist lived the way he did.

"It's good shit. Sure you wanta pass?"

"I'm sure," Flora Jean said with a hint of sadness as she recalled a time during the Persian Gulf War when she'd watched her captain stick the barrel of his .45 into the ear of a mission-endangering fellow marine who'd been high on marijuana just minutes before a mission and announce in the calmest of voices, *I'd kill ya right now, son, if I wasn't the one who had to write home to your mama and say you got yourself killed in action.* After watching her mother die and seeing friends flush their lives and military careers down the tube because of drugs, she'd long ago become unable to tolerate drug use.

"Okay by me. I try not to judge people on the basis of their skin color or recreational habits," Epps said in a tone meant to let Flora Jean know he expected the same attitude from her. He took a toke of his joint. "So we're here for our meeting, just like you asked, Ms. Benson, and since you're the one who called the meeting, you might as well be the one to get the first shot in."

"Yeah, sure," said Flora Jean, shaking off a flood of bad memories. "Like I told you on the phone, I'm lookin' into the deaths of Shandell Bird and Paul Grimes."

"Why and for whom?" Epps's response was quick and surprisingly reporter-like.

Aware that no matter how dulled by drugs Epps might seem, she was still matching wits with a dirt-digging Pulitzer Prize–winning journalist, Flora Jean said, "The why's easy, sugar. I'm lookin' for a murderer. Who I'm workin' for, now, I'm afraid that's my business."

"I see. I'm guessing you're not new at this—looking into murder and those kinds of things."

"And neither are you. So now that we've sniffed each other's undies, can we move on down the road to business?"

"Touché." Epps took another long toke off his joint and seemed to suck in every surrounding molecule of air. "How well did you know Shandell Bird?" he asked, exhaling slowly.

"Pretty well. But I'm guessin' you knew Paul Grimes a whole lot better."

"You'd be guessing right," Epps said boastfully. "I knew him from the time we started out as cub reporters at the *Rocky*. I knew him when we were both graveyard-shift police-beat reporters, begging for something important to happen so we could write about it. Knew him when he was up. Knew him when he was down. I kept him from sinking into the abyss when his wife left him for another woman and shored him up when his baby boy died from pneumonia."

Epps paused, as if he needed to get his bearings, and Flora Jean realized that he'd become misty-eyed.

"He kept me afloat too," Epps said, sounding suddenly defensive. "Like when I got temporarily fired from the *Rocky* years ago because of on-the-job drug use. Paulie was the one who convinced the ass-hole higher-ups to take me back. Said he'd leave on the spot and walk out the door with our newly minted Pulitzer if they didn't. And when I screwed up a second time, he stood in there with me again. He's the one who got me this apartment. The one who made me go to work every day. Bottom line is, Ms. Benson, dead or alive, I owe the man."

"And your plan to repay him is?"

"Direct and to the point. Sure you've never been a journalist?"

Flora Jean shook her head.

"No secret," Epps said with a toss of his head. "I plan to find out who killed Paulie and to make sure they pay."

"Nothin' wrong with that. Sorta coincides with the mission I'm on."

Epps looked surprised. "Mission? You sound like a soldier."

"Was one once."

"I see. So what do you do now to get your kicks?"

"I'm a bond surety agent."

"A bail bondsman! Damn, never would've guessed that. Private eye perhaps, or maybe a onetime cop or even an insurance fraud investigator. But a bail bondsman! No way."

"Well, now you know."

"So I do. And why, if you don't mind me asking, all the interest in the murder of some NBA player? You know, when you come right down to it, most of them are nothing more than dopers just like me." Epps flashed Flora Jean a sly, knowing smile. "Different drugs, that's all. Trust me, I know."

Flora Jean shook her head. "Shandell wasn't the doper kind. I knew the boy from the time he was ten. Drugs woulda never have been in the cards for him."

Epps took a final chest-expanding drag off what was left of his fat boy, shook his head, and tossed the still-lit joint onto the carpet. Noticing the look of concern on Flora Jean's face, he said, "Stuff's not but three ninety-nine a yard at the carpet-remnant store. And it's fire retardant." He ground the joint into the carpet with the ball of his foot. "Now, as for Bird, I know this for a fact. Paulie was working on a story about him. Had been for some time."

"Do you know what the story was gonna be about?"

"Not for certain, but it involved drug use among college athletes, and I know Paulie intended it to be a blockbuster. He expected it to be a big enough piece to get him back into the Pulitzer game. I also know that Bird and Paulie didn't exactly see eye to eye. Paulie told me so himself."

"How bad was the friction between them?"

"Bad enough for Paulie to think about getting himself some kind of protection. The kind that shoots bullets."

Epps suddenly began bobbing and weaving like a punch-drunk boxer. Recognizing that he had slipped into his own special euphoric comfort zone, Flora Jean said, "One last question for you. Why so hard on the cops in your piece in the *Rocky* this morning? I read between the lines. You insinuated that they weren't givin' Grimes's killin' the same kinda priority as Bird's."

"I got no use for cops, that's why. Most of 'em are assholes." Epps's words were as loud as they were slurred.

"I take it you've had some problems with the boys in blue."

Epps laughed. "That's for me to know and you to find out, Ms. Benson. We about done here?"

"Pretty much. Except for this. Could your friend Grimes also have been workin' on a story about Shandell or any of his teammates shavin' points during last spring's NCAA tournament?"

"Could've been." Epps let out a loud burp.

Realizing from the size of his pupils and his increasing unsteadiness that Epps had to have been enjoying the chronic habit long before she'd arrived, Flora Jean simply shook her head.

Reacting with a smile, Epps said, "Or maybe he was workin' on a story about our next manned space flight to the moon, or the definitive piece on global warming. You never knew when it came to Paulie. He was a Pulitzer Prize winner, you know."

"So I've heard." Flora Jean rose from her chair and started toward the door, realizing that she had reached the point of diminishing returns when it came to Epps.

"Sorry you have to leave, Ms. Benson," said Epps, looking lost in a fog. "You find out who killed your man, and I'll find out who killed mine. Fair enough?" he called out as Flora Jean reached the front door.

"Fair enough," Flora Jean called back, closing the door behind her before gulping a mouthful of stale but far less intoxicating air.

Chapter 10

She was the kind of person who demanded that everything have its time, that everything be in its place. So when Wordell Epps appeared as she left her daily health-club workout at a club halfway between Denver and Fort Collins, looking disheveled and glassy-eyed and reeking of marijuana, pouncing on her with an intrusive "Excuse me" as she came out of the club's inner sanctum into its reception area, it was all Alicia Phillips could do to keep from screaming and punching him. And she would have if the young woman looking on from behind the club's wide-arching reception desk hadn't been in her adult psychology class at CSU the previous semester. Phillips didn't think it would seem quite proper to deck a homeless-looking person in front of a former student, no matter how appropriate the circumstances.

Although she'd been immersed for years in the trappings of academe, in spite of an endowed professorship and a national reputation as a sports psychologist, she'd never had much difficulty reverting to her Montana-cowgirl self. That self had mucked horse stalls, broken up river ice for cattle in 20-below-zero weather, and pulled calves on her parents' five-thousand-acre ranch outside Billings on too many mornings at 3 a.m. She'd done those things from the time she'd been old enough to walk, it seemed, until she'd left for college at Montana State a few weeks past turning seventeen.

Her ranching days seemed like a lifetime ago to her now. She often longed for those days of lost innocence now that she was a forty-five-year-old professor whose rise to national prominence in the sports psychology community had been meteoric. The days, the times, and even the smells of the ranch had never left her, and although she realized that she could never go back to being Miss Montana Junior Rodeo Queen or spending days trailing cattle, that independent spirit still coursed through her veins.

Sensing that he'd be sorry if he took another step toward the stocky five-foot-eight woman with closely cropped sun-bleached hair and deeply tanned, leathery skin, Wordell Epps took a step back, shook off the marijuana-induced cobwebs that nowadays always seemed to fill his brain, and said, "Aahhh . . . Dr. Phillips? I think we need to talk."

Alicia once again eyed the girl behind the reception desk, trying to gauge the level of her interest. Realizing that her former student had turned her attention to an overhead television to the left of her desk, she authoritatively said to Epps, "And you are?"

"Wordell Epps. I'm . . . I was a friend of Paul Grimes. His best friend, in fact, when you come right down to it. We won the Pulitzer together. He told me this is where you worked out most days after work. I raced all the way up here from Denver hoping to catch you."

Alicia surveyed the disoriented-looking man who now stood within arm's length of her and frowned. Looking weary and concerned that he knew far too much about her, she asked, "So why do we need to talk?"

Epps looked surprised. "Because my friend's dead, and I need your help and you need mine."

Alicia Phillips looked puzzled. "I have in fact heard about your friend, Mr. Epps. Terrible. The whole CSU family lost someone dear to them as well. But I'm not certain how I can help you. And I'm certain you can't help me."

"Come on, now. Paulie claimed you were writing a book about the soaring Mr. Blackbird. A smoking-gun, tell-all kind of book." Epps flashed Alicia a broad, toothy grin.

"I'm afraid your friend may have deluded you, Mr. Epps."

"Oh. I see." Epps turned stone-faced. "Now, why would he wanta do that?"

"I wouldn't know his reasons, Mr. Epps."

"Maybe you'd do better at coughing up a reason if I was a cop."

"You're pushing the envelope here, Mr. Epps."

"Hope so. Because that Pulitzer me and Paulie won was for what nowadays they call investigative journalism. Paulie claimed you were working on something that would put a less-than-pretty face on Shandell Bird. True?"

"You've overstayed your welcome, Mr. Epps."

"And you sound a little fidgety, Doctor. Any reason?"

"I've no reason to discuss anything I might have been doing concerning Shandell Bird with you, sir." Flashing Epps an icy stare, Alicia turned and walked away.

"Nope. I guess you don't. No need to discuss the likes of some potential NBA superstar's college point-shaving or his possible drug dealing with me. I was just feeling you out, Dr. Phillips, and you flunked. But I'm not passing out grades. At least not this time around. Like I said though, the boys in blue will be and that'll be a whole different story."

"We're done," said Phillips, pushing her way through the club's revolving front door without another word as a laughing Wordell

Epps called after her, "There's done and really done, Dr. Phillips, and we're nowhere near finished with either."

Looking frustrated and feeling violated, Alicia Phillips slipped behind the wheel of her expensive BMW SUV and watched Wordell Epps walk across the parking lot of her club, hands stuffed in his pockets, whistling.

Incensed that he'd been able to invade her world, she drummed her fingers on the steering wheel and found herself doing something she'd rarely done since her Montana Junior Rodeo Queen days—grinding her teeth. She'd had concerns about taking on Shandell Bird's problems and his significant psychological baggage from the first moment he'd come to her for help. But as the CSU basketball team's sports psychologist, and the most prominent in the Rocky Mountain West, she couldn't very well have brushed him off. Her job was to teach and nurture and listen and help. She'd helped kids who'd come to college with eighth grade reading skills—kids who sometimes barely understood the need for a knife and fork, kids who too often found themselves stumbling across a cultural and educational terrain they simply weren't meant for.

She'd counseled sexual predators about not making babies and sociopaths about the art of choosing friends. She'd lectured to egotistical athletes about how to avoid the hundreds of things that could drag them down into the angry underbelly of an adoring but also often jealous society. She'd taught near illiterates how to look and talk and act in front of TV cameras, and she'd turned oafs into virtual Wheaties-box stars.

But, in spite of her successes, she'd also failed. Failed so frequently at fitting square pegs into round holes, and turning young men and

women with amazing athletic skills and not much else into productive human beings, that she'd reached the point that she wanted out
of the limelight and the image-making rat race.

She'd been there herself. She'd seen and felt what it was like to
lose your dreams. She'd watched her father lose his ranch and his
way of life. She'd felt the sting of not really understanding or appre-
ciating who you really are. She'd never intended to become a psychologist in the first place, and certainly not a psychologist to a
bunch of pampered jocks. She had always expected to do what her
father and mother and their fathers and mothers had done. But like
the athletes she counseled, especially the ones who fell off the
pedestal as they stood looking down, she no longer rode horseback
beneath the crystal-blue Montana skies. Instead she wrote books
and graded papers and gave lectures and talked to people about their
feelings in the wake of losing their dreams. Sometimes she had the
sense that she should start telling the athletic dreamers of the world
the bold-faced truth and let them in on the fact that their moment
in the sun would be brief. She wanted to flat-out tell them that the
chance they would capture their dream for the most part was exactly
that, a dream. That they weren't going to make it to the NBA or
the NFL. That gymnastics, no matter how glorified it seemed to a
pint-sized pixie who weighed barely eighty pounds, couldn't sustain
one past that elusive Olympic gold. But for the most part, she didn't
speak the truth, preferring instead to write books and scholarly papers
about those dreamers.

It had been that way with Shandell Bird. His story was an academic sports psychologist's ultimate dream. When she'd stumbled
upon it, she'd readily admitted to herself that publishing it could
only enhance her reputation and career. It was a story she'd dealt

with delicately and discreetly, with the eye of a teacher and scholar and mentor, until Paul Grimes had intervened. And now all she'd worked on for years was about to unravel. Wordell Epps was there to pull her down to the level of Grimes, not to mention the police. She could handle the cops—after all, she was a psychologist. But she wasn't certain she could handle the likes of Garrett Asalon or Leon Bird or the always overly optimistic coach, Russ Haroldson. These were people who were likely to start asking questions after all the sadness and tragedy went away. Questions like why she had in effect strung Shandell along. And more importantly, why she had pages and pages of notes about him.

She'd weather the storm. She always had. And in the end she'd chisel and waggle and serpentine herself out of harm's way. After all, she had overcome the stigma and the pain of watching the Yellowstone County sheriff oversee the packing-up of her family's one-hundred-year-old ranch. She'd find her way to safety. But for now, what she needed was to think things through. Think and reflect and then call Connie Eastland and tell her about Wordell Epps so they could put their heads together and she could muster some sort of damage control.

Nodding and thinking, *Yes, that's what I need to do,* she glanced up from drumming her fingers on the steering wheel and looked around for any signs of Wordell Epps, but there weren't any to be seen. No marijuana smell lingering in his wake, no echoing accusations, no innuendoes or threats. Just an empty parking lot and the realization that Epps was someone who could end up wrecking her dreams, as she'd so often seen happen to the athletes she counseled.

Chapter 11

The smell of marijuana still clung to her clothes as Flora Jean sat curbside in her SUV nearly an hour and a half after leaving Wordell Epps's place, eyeing Theo Wilhite's post–World War II, squat, boxy, blond-brick, cookie-cutter bungalow at 1652 Ivanhoe Street, in the heart of Denver's racially mixed Park Hill neighborhood. She was certain after two failed attempts to catch up with Wilhite at home and one attempt to find him at his favorite bar in Five Points that the cigar-smoking windbag was dodging her.

She had already walked the perimeter of his house, looked in most of the windows, and even tried to jimmy the front door, but just like the antebellum South, Wilhite seemed to be gone with the wind. His car wasn't anywhere to be found, his drapes were all closed, and his house, complete with a pile of newspapers on the lawn, looked deserted. Leaning back in her seat, staring at the bungalow's sagging front porch and feeling frustrated, Flora Jean didn't realize until he was almost on top of her that a boy who'd earlier zoomed his way up the street on a skateboard was now standing just beyond her front bumper. The chubby-faced boy, who looked to be about ten, was undeniably Hispanic. A Colorado Rockies baseball cap was cocked sideways on a large oval-shaped head that the rest of his body hadn't quite caught up to, and his mustard-stained dingy white T-shirt matched the color of the baggy hip-hop-style shorts that stopped several inches below his knees.

Flashing Flora Jean a look that said, *Whatta you doin' in my terri-tory, lady?* the boy stepped off his skateboard. With the toe of his right sneaker, he popped the skateboard up into the crook of his left arm. "You lookin' for Mr. Wilhite?"

"Yes."

"He's gone. Packed up and went fishin' this morning. I helped him with his gear," the boy announced proudly. "Whatta you want with him?"

Smiling at her pint-sized interrogator, Flora Jean propped her elbow on the window ledge and leaned out. "Nothin' I can tell you about, sugar."

The boy poked out his lower lip and stroked it thoughtfully several times with a thumb. "You an undercover cop?"

"Nope. Military intelligence," Flora Jean said with a grin. Uncertain why she was stringing the boy along, other than the fact that she'd learned long ago to never pass up a lead, she bent down, slipped her right hand beneath the seat, pulled out her old U.S. Marine Corps ID, and flashed it at the startled boy.

With eyes that were suddenly the size of half-dollars, the boy asked, "Is old man Wilhite a terrorist?"

"No," Flora Jean said, straight-faced, wondering if the boy might know how to locate Wilhite. "But I need to talk to him. Know when he's comin' back?"

"Tomorrow. He went up to Lake Granby. Told me not to tell nobody. Promised to bring me and my mama back a mess of trout."

Flora Jean nodded and flashed the boy an appreciative grin. "Well, if you see him before I do, would you tell him that Sergeant Flora Jean Benson of the U.S. Marine Corps is lookin' for him? Can you remember that?"

"I sure can, Sergeant." The boy's response was a near salute.

Still smiling, Flora Jean asked, "You live around here?"

"Yeah, right over there." The boy pointed catty-corner across the street toward a house with badly weathered clapboard siding. "You know what, Sergeant? Somebody else was with Mr. Wilhite when I helped him pack up this morning. Seen him around here with Mr. Wilhite a lot. Could be he's a terrorist. Even looked like one. He's got a beard, and he wears one of them terrorist turbans on his head. And come to think of it, I've never seen him when he wasn't wearing sunglasses."

Sitting up in her seat and drinking in the boy's every word, Flora Jean thought, *Damn, ten years old and already programmed to profile.* "Any chance the man mighta had a big chunk of his nose missin'?" she asked, thinking that after missing Wilhite so many times, she might have finally caught a break.

The boy looked surprised. "Yeah. How'd you know that?"

"It's my business to know those kinds of things, sugar." Trying her best to keep a straight face, she asked, "Did the man leave with Wilhite?"

"No, he left in his own car."

Flora Jean nodded. "Guess I'm gonna have to talk to him too."

"You know who he is?"

"Oh, yeah. Like I said, it's my business to know."

"Think he might be a terrorist?"

Uncertain why the boy seemed to have a major case of terrorist on the brain, Flora Jean said, "Nope," well aware that the boy's description fit small-time Five Points bookie, numbers runner, and occasional fence Marshad Lovell to a T. "He's just a street hustler."

The boy looked suddenly at ease. "Hey, I know lots of them."

"I bet you do," said Flora Jean. "Got anything else for me that might be helpful?"

"Don't think so."

"Then I better go chase down that guy with the missing hunk of nose," Flora Jean said, cranking the SUV's engine, eager now to chase down Lovell. With one last friendly smile, she said, "Thanks for your help. What's your name?"

The boy shook his head. "I don't give out that kinda information, lady. Especially not to somebody who just might turn out to be CIA."

"Smart." Flora Jean watched the boy drop his skateboard to the pavement, plant his right foot on it firmly, and skate away.

The boy had disappeared by the time she reached Twenty-third Avenue to head west for Five Points, but she couldn't help but think that he had the stuff to make a good marine. As she turned onto Twenty-third, she flipped her cell phone open and punched in Damion's number.

Damion was at home and in the midst of wolfing down a ham sandwich when he answered, "Damion."

"That you, sugar?" Flora Jean asked in response to the nearly unintelligible salutation.

Responding to Flora Jean's signature use of the word *sugar,* Damion said, "Yeah, Flora Jean. Eating something—sorry."

"Well, set it aside and tell me if you dug anything up at CSU."

"I struck a little gold. How about you? Did you find anything out from Wilhite or that reporter who did the piece in the *Rocky?*"

"A little. Why don't we meet at my office around seven thirty? We can compare notes then," said Flora Jean, schooled in the intelligence game and wary of discussing business on the phone.

"Come on, Flora Jean. Toss me a bone."

"Okay. I'm on my way to talk to Wilhite's bookie. A little weasel of a brother who got religion a few years back and converted to Islam. Name's Marshad Lovell. You know him?"

"No. Where are you gonna meet him?"

"At the den. He spends a couple'a nights a week there hustlin' business. Usually shows up about six before Rosie's real action starts, takes in a few side bets for the big boys up in North Denver and Louisville, talks sports, and takes off with his money. Rosie's been pissed about him skimmin' business for years, but he's never done anything about it 'cause Marshad is pretty much a circus barker who brings people in. Just hopin' Marshad's there tonight."

"Damn. Do you think Shandell might've really been tied into some kind of gambling scam?"

"I'm not sure, but if he was, I'm guessin' that Wilhite's right, and point-shavin' woulda been the angle. What I can't figure out is the why and the how. I'm hopin' you can help me there, Damion, 'cause I'm havin' trouble seein' how something as big as an NCAA basketball fix could be linked to a small-time hood like Marshad. Be at the office on time, Damion. I gotta run down to Colorado Springs to meet Alden by nine, and you know how he is about folks being late."

"I'll be there at seven thirty sharp," said Damion, wondering as he closed his cell phone and retrieved his sandwich if, besides dealing drugs and possibly shaving points in games, there were other things about his best friend that he hadn't known.

Flora Jean knew there was little chance that she'd miss hooking up with Marshad Lovell if he showed up that evening at the den. He never missed the chance to bounce around and show himself off, hoping to suck up as much pregaming cash from Rosie as he could. He generally popped up outside Rosie's Garage on Tuesday and Friday evenings to pay out on bets before collecting the new lay-downs, and since luckily for her it was a Friday, she expected him to make an appearance.

On Fridays Marshad's routine was to handle all the bets he could for the upcoming weekend's sporting events, taking in money on everything from off-track greyhound racing to his biggest money-maker each fall: college and NFL football. When the real football season rolled around, he could assure himself of making $600 to $900 a week, but currently he was mired in the football preseason and NASCAR race doldrums, and since most of the folks who frequented the den happened to be black, with no interest in NASCAR, business was always slow during August unless Tiger Woods ended up playing in a season-ending golf tournament.

As she drove up, Flora Jean spotted Marshad, true to form, hovering around one of the garage bays talking to Rosie, punctuating whatever point he was making with sweeping tomahawk hand gestures. She parked in a spot reserved from nine to five for Rosie's wife, Etta Lee, and thought, *Bingo*. She was barely out of her vehicle when Reggie Daniels, one of Rosie's high school employees, who she knew had his heart set on going to CSU to play basketball and follow in Shandell's and Damion's footsteps, walked up to her and, with his eyes cast sadly downward, asked, "Wash your ride, Ms. Benson?"

"Yeah, go on and give it a bath, Reggie," she said, homing in on his obvious pain.

"You heard about Blackbird, didn't ya?" he asked, taking her keys.

"Yes."

"Brother can't get a break," he said, shaking his head.

"You gotta make your own breaks in life, Reggie. Time you learned that. You still plannin' on playin' ball for CSU next year, aren't you?"

"I guess."

"I'd lose the *guess* if I was you, sugar. Makes you sound too wishy-washy, and that's not the face you wanta show the basketball world if you're a point guard," she said, aware that Damion had long been the boy's idol. "Tell you what. Suppose I get Blood himself to come by and talk to you. He's hurtin' real bad right now too. Talkin' to one another might help you both."

"You think he'd do that?" The boy's eyes sparkled.

"I guarantee it," said Flora Jean, watching the sadness on the boy's face momentarily wane. "Leave your phone number with Rosie and I'll have Damion get in touch with you."

"Thanks."

"And remember, words like *I guess* and *coulda*, *shoulda*, and *woulda* don't never hold a candle to *I am*, *I will*, and *I did*. You got that?"

Reggie nodded and stooped to slip his six-foot-one-inch beanpole of a body behind the wheel of Flora Jean's vehicle. Pleased with herself, she watched him drive off before heading to where Rosie still stood talking with Marshad, complete with turban and sunglasses and badly scarred nose. She was nearly on top of them before Marshad, arms still gyrating as he spoke, looked up.

"Don't stop yakkin' 'cause of me," she said, acknowledging Marshad with a nod and giving Rosie a hug. "If you're talkin' business I can go watch Reggie wash my car 'til you're done."

"No business goin' on here. Just talkin' about the Shandell Bird murder," said Rosie.

"We're done here anyway," said Marshad, his tone acquiescent. "You and Rosie need to talk, go at it."

Flora Jean eyed Marshad, trying her best not to stare at what was left of his pinched-off, scarred right nostril. The wound had been his reward for once welshing on a bet with the wrong person—a male scrub nurse, and courtesy of a surgical scalpel, no less. "Done? Well, you coulda surprised the East St. Louis shit out of me. For somebody who was doin' their best tomahawk chop when I walked up, I woulda thought you had a lot left to say about Blackbird's murder."

"Well, we weren't totally done," said Rosie. "Marshad was tryin' to convince me that Shandell might've been selling drugs to kids down here on the Points and that it was his drug pushin' that got him killed. And I was tellin' him he's crazy."

Flora Jean frowned and shook her head. "The kinds of stories they conjure up about you when you're dead. Ain't it terrible? Seems I've heard just about everything you could make up about poor Blackbird today. From folks sayin' he was a doper to others claimin' he was shavin' points durin' games." She took a step toward Marshad. "I know drugs aren't part of your line of work, Marshad, but point-shavin' and gamblin'—now, those things, sugar, would be a whole different story."

"Wouldn't know anything about Blackbird being involved with either one of 'em."

"Come off it, Marshad. You're among friends. Besides, I know you had a long talk with Theo Wilhite this morning before he went fishin'."

Marshad's eyes widened as, taken by surprise, he squeaked, "So?"

"So what did you and Theo talk about? Whether he expected to catch more rainbows or browns up at Lake Granby?"

"You talked to Theo?"

"Like I said, I've talked to lots of people."

"So I talked to Theo this morning. He's still boiling over losing his money last March."

"Upset enough to kill Shandell?"

"No way."

"Then why'd he take off for the mountains right on the heels of Shandell gettin' killed?"

"Yeah, why?" Rosie asked in a booming voice that seemed to unsettle the small-time, turban-wearing bookie.

When Marshad still didn't answer, Flora Jean said, "You know, Marshad, we can always call the cops."

Rosie shook his head in protest. "Ahhh . . . let's not do that. Least not while we're standin' here in the doorway of my establishment, Flora Jean."

"Sorry." Flora Jean locked eyes with Marshad. "You still haven't answered my question, and remember, we're talkin' about murder here, Marshad."

"I'd answer her if I was you," said Rosie. "The prison time they dole out for gamblin' and book-makin' ain't nothin' but a little chump change compared with the time you'd get for murder. Especially if all you and Wilhite were doin' was gettin' Shandell to shave a few points in a basketball game."

"Wait a minute! We weren't gettin' Shandell to do nothin'. All I did was take Theo's ten grand to somebody who could deal with that kind of money. It was too big a chunka change for me to handle."

"Wanta give me a name?" asked Flora Jean.

"Nope."

"Come on now, Marshad. You can't really think I'm blind to the world you work in, sugar. Wilhite bets ten thousand bucks on a game that's too big for you to handle, and suddenly you find yourself with

a whole lot more ducats than you're used to. Ain't but a few places you coulda funneled that kinda cash around here in Denver, and you can bet your headdress that when I call Mario Satoni and ask him to find out who was handlin' the serious NCAA tournament money locally last spring, I'll come up with a name. So you can give the info up now or give it up later, 'cause any way you slice it, when whoever was handlin' the serious action shows up with their nose bent outta joint over me outin' 'em, you can be sure I'll tell 'em my source was you." Flora Jean flashed Marshad a sly smile.

"Bitch!"

"Now, now, now, no need for any ugliness here." Flora Jean nodded for Rosie, who'd taken a protective step toward Marshad, to stay put.

"He'll kill me," Marshad protested.

"That's your problem, sugar. Time's a-wastin'. And remember, it won't matter in the end whether you tell me or not. I'll swear on the Good Book that you did."

Marshad flashed Flora Jean an angry stare before almost whispering, "Garrett Asalon took the bet. Nobody else around here on the Points had that kinda backup money."

Rosie responded before Flora Jean could answer. "Sorta figured that's the name you'd cough up, especially since nobody in the know around here would screw around with that kinda money from the likes of a bigmouth like Theo Wilhite. Now, Asalon—he'd just be cocky enough to cover that kinda lay-down."

Unlike Rosie, Flora Jean knew Garrett Asalon by reputation only—a reputation that had long established him as the closest thing the Rocky Mountain region had to a real live Las Vegas–type gambling magnate and fixer. What she did know was that Asalon had an MBA from a high-profile Ivy League school back East and that although he was mob-connected, he preferred playing the role of a loner. She had heard that on occasion he'd had the balls to stiff the boys in Vegas and a few well-heeled clients—and although no one could prove it, he'd also supposedly had people killed.

"Looks like you chose yourself a real cobra to sleep with, Marshad," Flora Jean said, shaking her head.

When Marshad didn't answer, Rosie asked, "So did Asalon fix that NCAA championship game?"

"I don't know. All I know is that Theo lost the ten grand I funneled to him."

Rosie looked unfazed. "Losin' ten thousand dollars of Theo's? Shit, that's piss-in-the-wind kinda cash for Asalon. I'm bettin' he was sittin' on fifty times that. Theo was just on the wrong side of the action. And if he's complained to Asalon, I'm surprised he's still breathin'."

"That's not the issue here, Rosie," Flora Jean said, looking puzzled as she tried to regain control of the conversation. "Shandell is. The question is, why would Asalon come back five months later and kill his point-shaver?"

"You blind, girl?" Marshad asked. "Or maybe you missed hearing about that newspaper reporter who was also killed. I'm guessing Shandell was about to talk."

"Nope, I'm not." Flora Jean grabbed Marshad beneath the armpits and lifted him onto his tiptoes until their eyes met. "And if you call me 'girl' or 'bitch' ever again, whatever beef Asalon might have with you won't matter." She shoved the much smaller, startled 155-pound street hustler toward Rosie, who grabbed him and kept him from falling. Turning to Rosie, she asked, "Whatta you think, Rosie? You're in the gamin' business."

"I'm not sure. All I know is that when they played that championship game, nobody came to me clamorin' to put no money on UCLA. Everything I handled, small as it was, went down on CSU."

"That's what I figured, and that's what's got me puzzled. Wouldn't you'a thought, no matter how small the piece of the pie mighta been for you here at the den, that since Shandell grew up right here on the Points and at some time probably rubbed shoulders with mosta the people who woulda been layin' down their hard-earned money, somebody would've sniffed out a rat? Maybe even picked up on the fact that Shandell was either gonna shave a few points off the game or flat-out throw it, and put their money on UCLA?"

"Could be," said Rosie. "But like I said, I didn't get much of a sniff. So what's your point, Flora Jean?"

"Just this. Maybe there was some point-shavin' goin' on, and maybe that's why Theo and who knows how many other folks lost their money, but who's to say that Shandell was the one shavin' the points."

"Yeah," Marshad chimed in. "Somebody else could've been the one shaving points. Maybe Shandell was about to roll on them and tell his story to that dead reporter."

"I'm thinkin' that's a real possibility," said Flora Jean.

"So how do we find out the truth?" asked Rosie.

Flora Jean flashed Rosie the sly grin of someone with inside knowledge. "Why, Mr. Weeks, how can you possibly ask that? We have an inside straight, in case you've forgotten. We've got Damion."

"Think Damion would really know if a teammate of his was shavin' points?"

"He might if he sits down, dissects all the pieces, and faces the possibility that his best friend in life, and maybe even a few other teammates, mighta been into somethin' he never woulda expected."

Marshad took a step back from Flora Jean, expecting that what he was about to say might cost him a second clean and jerk off his feet. "And what if the Madrid kid was in on it? Could be he was the one doing the point-shaving."

"Are you crazy?" Rosie looked at Flora Jean for a response before realizing as their eyes met that, as far-fetched as it might sound, Marshad had a point.

"Well? You gonna talk to Madrid?" Marshad demanded.

"Sure am," said Flora Jean. "In less than half an hour."

"Well, when you do, let Mr. All-American Everything know that maybe he's the one got his best friend in life killed."

"Get outta here, Marshad," said Flora Jean. "Leave. Before I get back to thinkin' about your name-callin'. There's no way Damion woulda gotten himself involved in a mess like that."

"No way, my ass. You can bet that your Mr. Goody Two-shoes likes money just as much as any of the rest of us." Smiling until the tension on his scarred nose made him look grotesque, Marshad turned to leave. He was halfway to the open garage door when Rosie said to Flora Jean, "Think he'll tell Theo Wilhite about our little chat?"

"Absolutely," she said with a wink.

"What about Asalon? Think he'll tell him?"

"I'm countin' on it," Flora Jean said with the wryest of smiles.

Rosie frowned. "You know Asalon has killed people, don't you?"

"So I've heard. But remember, I've got a few friends who kill people too."

The high-gloss shine on Garrett Asalon's $900 imported Italian loafers had him beaming from ear to ear. That morning he'd flown to Dallas to pick up the shoes. Six and a half hours later, he was back.

Perched in a shoeshine booth alcove above the rush of humanity scurrying down Concourse B of Denver International Airport, he tried to make out his reflection in each shoe. Unable to do so but nonetheless pleased, the husky fifty-four-year-old former college lacrosse star with perfectly coiffed blond hair sprang from his seat to the floor. His leap startled the woman who'd shined his shoes while he'd talked casually on his cell phone. She dropped her shoeshine brush when he hit the floor.

"How much?" asked Asalon, eyeing the woman apologetically.

The woman took a step back. "Five dollars."

Asalon reached for his wallet, but instead of slipping it out of his back pocket, he glanced at the man who'd stood and watched with genuine interest while his shoes had been shined. "Craigy, please give the lady a twenty."

Used to following orders, Lemar Craig Theisman, known in the circles he and Asalon ran in simply as "Craigy," fished into a pants pocket, extracted a money clip, peeled off a twenty, and handed it to the woman. "See you again soon," Asalon said politely as he and Theisman headed for escalators that would take them down to the train and baggage claim.

"Who were you on the phone with?" Theisman asked as he stepped onto the escalator ahead of Asalon. "You looked a little caught off guard."

"Astute, Craigy. Real astute," Asalon said, careful not to scuff his new shoes. "I was a little blindsided. But Marshad has a tendency to do that—tweak your nervous system when you least expect it."

Theisman frowned. "That fuckin' dumbass nigger. What the hell did he want?"

Asalon looked down toward Theisman and flashed the bushy-eyebrowed, slack-jowled Irishman who'd been his bodyguard for the past ten years a disappointed frown. "You know how much I dislike the use of racial slurs, Craigy. It's the mark of a poor upbringing and all too often the sign of marginal intelligence. Save your slurs for when I'm not around." Asalon's no-nonsense expression told the beer-bellied man from the bowels of South Boston that he meant it.

Looking like a dog who'd been cuffed as they headed across a marble-tiled staging area to board the train for baggage claim, Theisman said, "So what's Marshad's problem?"

"Seems he had a visit today from someone who's looking into the Shandell Bird killing, and he's feeling pressured. A woman, no less."

"I thought you covered all your bases first thing this morning when you talked to Marshad and Jackie Woodson."

"I thought I did too," Asalon said disappointedly.

"Well, did Marshad feed that nosy woman the party line? Stick with the script you told him and Jackie to follow about the doping angle?"

"No, I'm afraid he didn't. On the contrary, he told her to come have a chat with me."

"That dumb nig—" Theisman caught himself midsentence.

"Very good, Craigy. After all these years, you're learning."

"So who's the woman who's doing the sniffing?" Theisman asked, upset at having had to bite his tongue.

"Her name's Flora Jean Benson, and believe it or not, she's a bail bondsman—or should I say, bonds*woman*. According to Marshad, she's a longtime friend of Shandell Bird and his family."

"Think she'll spell trouble?"

"No more than usual. But she also knows Theo Wilhite, and the old man's loquaciousness could present us with a problem."

"Should I have him tended to?"

"No. It's much too early in the game for that. Besides, I think I might enjoy meeting Ms. Benson. Marshad claims she's a showstopper. I might even learn a thing or two of importance from her."

"Like what?" asked Craigy, watching a train pull into the station.

"Like just how much Jackie Woodson might have been mouthing off, and whether I've been missing out on a component of sexual fulfillment all these years by not seeking out the favors of an African American."

"So you're just gonna wait for her to come to you?" asked Theisman, flashing Asalon a look of surprise as they boarded the train.

Asalon smiled. "Sure am. I'm going to wait for her to come running into the station just like this train. You never know; she just might take me for an informative and very satisfying multicultural ride."

Chapter 12

Damion didn't know how long he could stonewall. In truth, he didn't fully understand why for the past half hour he'd been holding back on telling Flora Jean exactly what he'd learned on his trip to CSU. Perhaps his reluctance was related to the fact that after learning things he'd never known about his best friend, he felt guilty for not recognizing the jam Shandell had gotten himself into and failing to help him. Or his reticence, he told himself as he watched Flora Jean jot notes on a legal pad at her desk, could simply be attributed to his desire to play Superman, track down Shandell's killer on his own, and be a campus hero once again.

When CJ Floyd's voice suddenly echoed in his head with a resounding *Boy, have you gone crazy? You'd better own up to what you know,* it was all he could do to keep from spilling his guts to Flora Jean right then. CJ had always been his sounding board when he found himself in untenable situations, like the fiasco he'd stumbled into the previous summer. He'd almost been killed by a mafia hit man only to have his bacon saved at CJ's behest by Pinkie Niedemeyer, Mario Satoni's one-time personal hit man.

Watching Flora Jean scrutinize her notes, he realized he couldn't evade her questions forever. Sooner or later he'd have to come clean about Shandell's connection to Leotis Hawkins.

"So here's what we've got," Flora Jean said, looking like someone who was struggling to get all the pieces of a puzzle to fit. "First off, we've got ourselves that ex-teammate of yours, Jackie Woodson, claimin' Shandell was sellin' drugs."

"Performance-enhancing drugs," Damion said defensively.

"Don't matter. They're still drugs, sugar. And they're illegal. Now, you gonna hear me out or play at bein' a defense attorney?"

"I'm listening."

"Good. So we've got Shandell dealin' drugs—and as it turns out, on the word of two people. Your boy Woodson and that trainer you told me about, the blond boy with the crew cut . . ."

"Rodney Sands."

"You sure that's everything you could dig up?"

"That's it," said Damion, hoping the look on his face didn't telegraph the fact that he was lying.

"Okay," said Flora Jean, concerned that although she couldn't quite put her finger on the why of it, she had the feeling that the kid she'd babysat all those years ago wasn't exactly being straight with her. "So what about your coach? Think he could've been involved in either the drug angle in all this or Theo Wilhite's point-shavin' claim?"

"No way. Coach Horse was the closest thing Shandell had to a father. No way on earth he would've been involved in either of those things."

"Just covering all the bases, sugar."

"Well, if that's what we're doing, how about taking a look at Shandell's real father, Leon? See what he was up to when Shandell was killed? I told you earlier that he rubbed me the wrong way the instant I met him. Popping up out of the blue and sitting in Shandell's house all comfy with Mrs. B the instant Shandell's gone. Seems premeditated, if you ask me."

"Oh, I'll check on him, sweetie. Don't worry."

"And you'll follow up on that mobster, Asalon?"

"I told you I would a few minutes ago, didn't I? Something the matter you ain't tellin' me, Damion?"

"No," Damion said sheepishly.

Flora Jean knew the headstrong young man believed deep down that no matter what the circumstances, things would always eventually go his way, but it suddenly occurred to her that he might be in over his head this time. "We're not dealin' with controllin' the outcome of a basketball game here, Damion, or about studyin' your ass off and makin' straight As in order to get into medical school. In case you've missed it, we're investigatin' a murder here, sugar. And no matter how hard you might wanta control the end game, or keep from dredgin' up things you don't like, sooner or later the truth's gonna come out. And on top of all that, in case you're somehow thinkin' otherwise, you best remember that the cops don't take kindly to folks like us stickin' our noses into their business, and for that matter, neither does the mob. You ready if either one of 'em starts pullin' on our coattails?"

"I'm ready."

"Then I need you to remember somethin' about teamwork, and I'm not referrin' to the kinda sports-games teamwork you're used to, Damion. I'm talkin' about the kind that's expected outta you when you're carryin' a rifle and the scared-shitless grunt next to you has your life in his hands. I gotta tell you, I was more than a little bit nervous about startin' down this road in the first place, and so far I ain't run across nothin' to calm my nerves. So we act together on this thing, no matter which way it goes and no matter what. You got me?"

"Yes," said Damion, sensing that he was no longer talking to the caring woman who'd help his mother raise him but instead to war-hardened Sergeant Major Flora Jean Benson.

"Fine. So now that I've said my piece, unless you've got a new lead for us to follow here right this very second, I'm thinkin' we're done for the day." Flora Jean checked her watch. "It's about time I headed down to Colorado Springs to hook up with Alden. We'll get back at it tomorrow." She shoved her legal pad across her desk as if to punctuate the statement. "Where're you headed?"

"Thought I'd go over to Niki's and see if I can't talk her into making me some chili and see how Connie Eastland's holding up. Connie was there most of the day, and according to Niki, she's a real basket case."

Flora Jean looked surprised. "Never realized that Connie and Shandell were all that tight. Sorta figured she was just the latest notch in Blackbird's six-gun."

"Surprised me at first too. But I guess they were getting serious. She's gotta be hurting."

"Well, give them two beauty queens my best, and tell Connie I said to hang in there."

"Will do." Damion rose to leave. He was halfway to the door when Flora Jean called out, "And remember what I said about teamwork, sugar."

"I will." Flashing her a thumbs-up, he stepped out into the hallway and headed for the echoing Victorian's front door. The door of the stately old building had barely closed behind him when Flora Jean picked up the phone and dialed CJ. When a cheerful hotel operator patched her through to CJ and Mavis's room, she couldn't help but smile at the thought that after all these years, CJ and Mavis were actually honeymooning.

"It's me, sugar," she said in response to CJ's trademark "Floyd here," "and I think I've bought myself a problem." CJ didn't interrupt as for the next seven minutes she filled him in on the people and the point-shaving and drug-dealing issues that had surfaced in the early stages of her investigation of Shandell Bird's murder. Sounding peeved as she wrapped up her summary, she said, "Damion's holdin' back on me, CJ. I've known that boy since he was ten. He knows somethin' he ain't sharin' with me. I know it."

CJ glanced out from his suite at the Mauna Lanai Hotel to a west-facing balcony where Mavis sat enjoying the sun and reading a book. "Damn, Flora Jean—sounds messy."

At almost fifty-five, he was no longer the imposing 235-pound, six-foot-three, win-at-any-cost bail bondsman and bounty hunter he'd been for the past thirty-five years. His wiry hair was salt-and-pepper now, and although he still cut an impressive figure, outfitted as he was in loose-fitting swim trunks and a muscle shirt, the muscles didn't respond the way they used to. He'd only recently come to understand that his days as Denver's lead-dog bail bondsman were clearly numbered. That was part of the reason that he'd brought in Flora Jean as his partner several years earlier.

Stroking his chin, he said, "You should've let the cops handle things instead of trying to play private eye and surrogate mother. But what's done is done. Where'd you say Damion was headed when he left the office?"

"Over to Niki's."

"Better check with her. If Damion wasn't being straight with you, I'm betting you'll find out from her pretty quick. I'll call Mario and Pinkie Niedemeyer and give them a heads-up. Maybe they can help."

"Pinkie? CJ, are you sure?" Flora Jean asked, puzzled as to why CJ would call in a hit man like Pinkie Niedemeyer.

"Dead sure. For some reason, Pinkie and Damion have an understanding. And believe me, I don't get it. Why two men as different as sunup and sundown would be on the same wavelength beats the hell outta me. But ever since Pinkie saved Damion's behind last summer up at the Pawnee grasslands when Damion got himself all tangled up in that Eisenhower Tunnel murder case I was working, they've been as tight as Dick's hatband. You know Pinkie showed up at every one of Damion's CSU home games last year, don't you? And that Julie almost peed her pants and tripped over her tongue when he showed up at Damion's graduation party to toast Damion's future along with several well-placed judges?"

"Come to think of it, I do recall Julie lookin' a little flustered, and I remember Pinkie lurkin' in the background like the killer snake he is at some of them home games too. You don't think he woulda had anything to do with Shandell's murder, do you?"

"No way. And remember, for what it's worth, that he's *our* killer snake, Flora Jean. If anyone can worm his way into Garrett Asalon's world besides Mario, who's been out of that loop for over four decades, it would be Pinkie. Don't shrug Pinkie off. You might need him."

"Okay. But I'm tellin' you, CJ, I've got a feelin' that Damion's out there about to bite off more than he can chew."

"You can't hold his hand forever, Flora Jean. He's grown. Funny, I told Julie the very same thing just recently. Let's just hope that if Damion's out there on his own, sticking his nose into a dirty business like murder, he has enough sense to know when to either back off or call for help."

"Think I should tell Julie what I think he's up to?"

"Not right now. No need upsetting her over a hunch. Sit back for just a little bit. In the meantime, I'll make those calls to Mario and Pinkie."

"Guess you better." There was a sense of urgency in Flora Jean's tone that hadn't been there when the conversation started. "I'm headin' down to Colorado Springs to Alden's. If you need me I'll be there." Hoping to end the conversation on a lighter note, she said, "And remember, you've got yourself a whole lifetime left to treat Mavis like a queen."

"Always have. Talk to you later," said CJ, glancing toward Mavis with a smile before hanging up.

After making phone calls to Mario Satoni and Pinkie Niedemeyer, expressing Flora Jean's concerns and requesting that they keep tabs on young would-be Dr. Madrid, CJ sat back in his chair and teased a cheroot out of a flip-top box on a nearby coffee table.

"Not in here, CJ Floyd," Mavis admonished, stepping in from the balcony. "Besides, you promised to work on not making me an early widow, remember?" She slipped the cheroot from between his lips, tossed it aside, and kissed him gently. "Who were you talking to on the phone?"

"Flora Jean." CJ eyed his brown-skinned, green-eyed bride of three days, thinking that she filled out her swimsuit like a woman in her midtwenties, not her midforties. He couldn't resist patting her on the behind.

"Anything up in Denver?" Mavis asked, slapping his hand.

"Only the price of gas," said CJ, rising from his chair.

Realizing that CJ's flippant response was meant to end the conversation, Mavis remained silent. Normally she would have probed further, delved a little deeper. But she was on her honeymoon, and at least temporarily planted in paradise. When CJ wrapped his arms around her and kissed so passionately that she could only conjure an endless Polynesian bliss, she found herself suddenly thinking, *Denver be damned.*

Damion felt sick to his stomach over lying to Flora Jean, but he'd followed his instincts, and now, as he stood alone on the Twenty-ninth and Welton Street light-rail station platform in the center of Five Points, waiting impatiently to meet a very-late-arriving Leotis Hawkins, he had the sense that Flora Jean probably knew he'd been less than truthful with her about what he'd found during his trip to CSU.

He found himself wondering whether either Jackie Woodson or Rodney Sands had set him up for a kill. He knew Jackie wasn't about to let anything stand in the way of his fast track to an NBA career. Not a drug-dealing or point-shaving scam, for certain. He couldn't be so sure about Rodney, but he suspected that anyone who prided himself on being the ultimate manipulator, even referring to himself on occasion as "the floor manager," might just be egotistical enough to think he could outsmart anyone, including the cops and the American judicial system, and in the end get away with murder.

An unexpected cold front had eased its way into the Mile High City, and in the half hour since he'd left Flora Jean's office the temperature had dropped from balmy T-shirt-and-shorts weather to a chilly 56 degrees. Damion stood there shivering, dressed only in a CSU sweatshirt with cut-off sleeves and a baggy pair of unlined basketball warmups, upset at not having slipped on the Windbreaker he kept in the glove compartment of his Jeep before striking out to meet Hawkins. He stared down a nearly deserted Welton Street toward downtown, wondering what Five Points and the jazz it had been famous for had really been like during the now struggling community's post–World War II heyday. He'd heard stories from Mario Satoni, a seasoned jazz aficionado, and on more than one occasion he'd listened to the boastful ramblings of Theo Wilhite. But there were no latter-day accounts, he told himself, imagining the excitement and the music that would have emanated from the now boarded-up Rossonian Club two blocks away. The club had once jumped with headliners like Duke Ellington, Ella Fitzgerald, Count Basie, and Louie Armstrong, but the times had changed, and in the sixty years since its heyday, a community that had once been working class and exclusively black had transitioned into a yuppie-bound high-dollar oasis, replete with expensive condos, renovated Queen Annes, and remodeled bungalows owned by upwardly mobile whites.

Aware that no amount of wishing or daydreaming could bring back the past, Damion eyed his watch, shook his head, and turned to walk off the deserted platform, thinking that his meeting with Hawkins, now almost twenty minutes past the scheduled time, was a scrub. He'd half expected Hawkins to be a no-show, so he wasn't surprised. Kicking at an empty McDonald's Happy Meal bag and a half-empty old-fashioned twelve-ounce glass Coke bottle that had been left on the platform, he started down the wheelchair access ramp that ran down to the sidewalk. He was halfway down when someone standing at the bottom of the ramp called up to him, "You lookin' for somebody, homes?"

"I am if you're Leotis Hawkins," the startled Damion said in as calm a voice as he could muster. Holding his ground, he stared down toward a hooded-sweatshirt-wearing, 300-pound black man with the most massive, rectangular-looking head he'd ever seen.

"I'm him. But you don't look nothin' like Rodney Sands to me, bro. Not a blond hair nowhere I can see, and you're lookin' way too Latin." Hawkins burst into laughter. "Mind tellin' me why you'd be standin' here in Rodney's place?"

Damion glanced up and down an all-but-empty Welton Street and found himself suddenly wishing that it was 1946, when the street would have been bustling with workaday people instead of curled up on itself and all but dead just a few hours after rush hour. "Thought I'd try and get an answer to some questions," Damion said finally.

"About what?"

"About Shandell Bird supposedly doing a little drug pushing for you."

"Oh, that." Hawkins smiled, showing off a set of perfectly aligned white teeth. Cutting the smile off, he looked around to make certain he and Damion were alone. "No big deal. Just helpin' a future sports superstar make hisself a little extra college spendin' money."

"Hard to believe." As he continued to stare down at Hawkins, Damion realized that the sweatshirt the big man was wearing failed miserably at hiding his massive forearms and protruding belly.

"Just as hard as it is for me to believe that you would be dumb enough to come down here on my turf and stick your nose into my shit, Madrid. Always heard you were the smart one in that hyped-up Bird-and-Blood combo folks around here still ramble on about so much. But it sure don't seem like it to me."

"You got any proof that Shandell was selling drugs for you?" asked Damion, his tone insistent.

"Shit, you are a hardhead, aren't you, Madrid?" Hawkins shook his head in disbelief. "No, but I got this." Again flashing his teeth in a smile, he slipped a bowie knife with a gleaming four-inch-long blade out of the hand-warmer pocket of his sweatshirt. "What me and your boy Shandell were doin' don't matter so much, really. He's dead." Clutching the knife in his left hand and extending the blade low and out in front of him, prepared for an upsweep, Hawkins glanced around one more time to make sure no one was around before starting up the wheelchair ramp.

Damion glanced over his shoulder and gauged the height of the safety railing that skirted the light-rail platform. Thinking he'd have to leap the three-and-a-half-foot railing and drop seven or eight feet to the sidewalk, he looked for a good purchase point.

"You look scared, Madrid," Hawkins said, closing in slowly.

"And you look real stupid, fat boy," Damion yelled back, aware that just as in the world of sports, a properly placed insult in the heat of battle could be just the thing to keep an opponent off balance. "Is that how you got Shandell and Rodney Sands to do your bidding? Scared the shit out of them with a knife, blubber belly?"

"You fuckin' asshole. I'll teach you somethin' about fear. And wasn't nobody scared in all this but your buddy Blackbird. Scared of losin' his fuckin' reputation. But he ain't got that to worry about no more, does he?"

"What did you have on him?" Damion called out as Hawkins suddenly bull-rushed him, screaming "Yahee!" as he charged. Sidestepping, leaping back onto the station platform, and realizing that Hawkins would surely cut him before he had time to clear the guardrail and jump, he looked around for a weapon, finally grabbing the half-empty Coke bottle that he'd kicked at earlier. Holding the bottle aloft as its syrupy mixture of Coca-Cola and cigarette butts dribbled down his arm, he yelled, "You as good with a gun as you are with a knife, blubber boy?"

Hawkins let out a loud whoop and, surprising Damion with his agility, swung the blade of the knife from knee height up and around in a wide half circle, catching Damion in the middle of his left biceps.

Yelling, "Ahhhhh," Damion jumped back, uncertain how badly he'd been cut until he saw blood streaming down his arm.

Buoyed by the success of his second lunge, Hawkins moved in for the kill. With spittle streaming from one corner of his mouth, grunting and wheezing, he attacked again. In midlunge, Damion slammed the nearly empty, solid-as-a-rock Coke bottle into Hawkins's temple. The mammoth-headed Hawkins barely had time to look dazed before dropping to his knees. Looking like a man in the first stage of what would later become a full-blown grade-2 concussion, Hawkins fell face first onto the platform.

Uncertain what to do next and with a light-rail train suddenly bearing down on the station, Damion scooped up the knife, leaped over the platform's south-facing railing, and dropped down to the sidewalk. Racing up Welton Street into the darkness, he sped across a vacant lot that led to the alley between Welton and Champa Streets with blood oozing down his left arm.

He'd parked his car on Twenty-eighth Street just at the east end of that alley. Lightheaded, gasping for air, and hoping as he raced down the alley that he wouldn't bleed to death, he found himself thinking less about his own safety and more about whether he'd just killed a man. By the time he reached his vehicle, he was floating on pure adrenaline.

As he slipped into the Jeep, gripped by the feeling that he'd somehow just torched his life, he recognized that he was close to being in shock. Shivering and trying his best to remain calm, he popped the glove compartment, slipped his Windbreaker out, looped the sleeves around his bleeding arm, and tied them into a tight knot above the lengthy gash in his arm as he tried to fathom what to do next.

Flora Jean was in Colorado Springs, so she couldn't help. CJ was in Hawaii, and Damion's girlfriend, Niki Estaban, who for the last six weeks had been working evenings on a behind-schedule high-rise architectural project, probably wasn't even home yet. He couldn't run to his mother's house, tail tucked between his legs; she was in San Francisco. He knew he had only two choices. He could head for Denver Health and Hospital's emergency room, where sooner or later he could expect to be grilled by the cops and where very likely, as a felon on the run, he would see his medical-school dreams evaporate, or he could head for Mario Satoni's. In the euphoric state of quasi-shock he was unable to think clearly, and the choice seemed simple.

As he nosed the Jeep away from the curb, running temporarily without headlights and headed for Mario's house in a mostly Italian neighborhood in North Denver, he kept telling himself, *Just let me make it, God. Just let me make it.*

Chapter 13

Andrus "Pinkie" Niedemeyer had lost all his front teeth, top to bottom, eyetooth to eyetooth, and the pinkie finger of his left hand during a New Year's Eve firefight outside the village of Song Ve three days before he was scheduled to come home from a year-long tour of duty in Vietnam. He'd received a Purple Heart and earned himself a nickname for doing his duty that day. In the years since Vietnam, he'd worked his way up a killing ladder to become not what he'd always dreamed of being, a butcher, but a first-tier mafia hit man. He liked to remind those rare, insightful people who knew he was a hit man that he was anything but full-blooded Sicilian; that, in fact, he was half Jewish, and as a kid he'd wanted to be a butcher and own a little neighborhood specialty-meats store with an adjoining pastry shop.

But things hadn't turned out that way for him, and for the past thirty-six years he'd simply been a killer for hire.

Slightly built, edgy, and a man of few words except when he was among friends, Pinkie liked to refer to himself as a "settlement agent," as if he were somehow in the insurance or brokerage business. But people in the know understood his play on words very well—and so, unfortunately, did a handful of enemies.

Pinkie's time as top dog of his profession had come after Mario Satoni's days at the helm of the Rocky Mountain region's mob-based activities in the early 1960s and a few short years after Mario had left the mountaintop when his wife, Angie, had been diagnosed with terminal breast cancer. For years, however, despite the thirty-year difference in their ages, the two men had been friends. More importantly, they both had longtime links to CJ Floyd. Mario's connection to CJ stemmed from the fact that jazz-lover that he was, he'd been fast friends with CJ's late Uncle Ike, the man who had raised CJ, taught him the bail-bonding business, and introduced him to jazz. Ike had also once saved Mario's life as they'd left a Five Points jazz club back in 1948 by clobbering a would-be assassin with what Mario still liked to boast was the meanest clench-fisted, two-armed uppercut he'd ever seen. Ike's actions that night had given him and his only family, CJ, a lifetime protective pass in Mario's world. Pinkie's link to CJ was the fact that he and CJ had shared the same Southeast Asian war.

Pinkie had arrived at Mario's North Denver home twenty minutes earlier, and for most of that time they'd been sitting in Mario's den, the room where the eighty-four-year-old former don now spent most of his time watching his beloved LA Dodgers, discussing the phone calls they'd each recently gotten from CJ. After a lengthy explanation, CJ had asked them both to look out for Damion. Mario's response had been an eager *okay*. Pinkie's response had been more reluctant, but since he owed Mario in much the same way that Mario had owed Ike, he had no choice but to agree to look out for Damion as well.

Mario's house, dimly lit whether day or night, had the ever-present smell of garlic and vinegar, and after a visit, no matter the length of the stay, the odor always seemed to linger in Pinkie's nostrils for days. Leaning back in a wine-colored simulated-leather La-Z-Boy recliner, a twin to the one in which Mario was seated a few feet away, Pinkie tried his best to ignore the smell and to get comfortable.

Smiling at the skinny hit man's inability to relax, Mario said, "I've told you before, Pinkie. These babies are meant for men of substance and girth, not for stringbeans like you." Silver-haired, with barely a wrinkle in his face, the frail looking octogenarian rose, walked over to Pinkie's chair, dropped to one knee, and, with Pinkie looking down on the top of his head, began manipulating the seatback adjustment. "See, you just gotta get . . ."

The sound of someone pounding on his front door stopped Mario in midsentence. When the pounding intensified, he rose and headed across the room to retrieve the 457 he kept in the top drawer of an antique breakfront. He had the drawer half open when Pinkie pulled a 9-mm Glock out of the pocket of the jacket he'd earlier draped across the arm of his La-Z-Boy. "Stay put," Pinkie said softly, bringing an index finger to his lips and waving Mario off. Rising from his chair and heading down the hallway toward the front door, Pinkie called out, "Who is it?" with his weapon aimed chest high at the door.

"Damion," came the barely audible response.

Pinkie glanced back at Mario. "It's Damion."

"Well, let him in, for God's sake, and put away that damn piece!"

With his gun still drawn and at the ready, Pinkie peeked through the door's peephole, realized that it actually was Damion standing outside, and swung the door open.

Glassy-eyed, wobbly, and with the sleeves of his blood-soaked Windbreaker still tied loosely around his left arm, Damion stumbled in.

"Shit!" Pinkie jammed the Glock into a pants pocket, catching Damion in full collapse in his arms.

"What in God's name?" yelled Mario, rushing across the room.

"Got myself cut," Damion wheezed, somehow managing to look embarrassed.

"Get him into the den," Mario ordered.

Struggling to keep someone who outweighed him by sixty pounds upright, Pinkie helped Damion down the short stub of hallway into the den.

"Sit him in my chair," said Mario, as Damion, barely able to keep his feet, plopped down in the chair.

Rushing for a wall phone in the kitchen, Mario called back, "Fill him full of water and try to stop the bleeding. I'll get Doc Bottone here pronto."

No time for water, Pinkie thought, aware that blood loss was Damion's immediate problem. He'd been a combat infantryman during Vietnam, not a medic, but he'd managed his share of battlefield casualties. Taking in Damion's shrunken pupils, he asked, "You got anything left in your tank, Blood?" Before Damion could respond, he undid the barely adequate tourniquet and tossed it aside. He stripped off his own shirt, ripped off the left sleeve at the seam, and knotted it around Damion's arm.

"Think I'm pretty close to empty right now." Damion tried unsuccessfully to mount a smile.

"We'll get you back up and running here pretty quick. Mario's callin' for help."

"Better move fast." Damion's chin slumped onto his chest as Pinkie examined the three-quarter-inch-deep, ten-inch long, crescent-shaped gouge running down his left biceps.

Realizing that the source of the bleeding was a small vessel just below Damion's shoulder blade, Pinkie shouted, "Mario, you got any tweezers?"

"I'll have to look. I'm still on the phone, tryin' to get Bottone to get his ass in gear. Since it ain't like he's comin' to tend to his usual clientele, he's bein' a little stubborn. Think I got a pair of tweezers in a medicine cabinet in the john. I'll go look."

"Bring 'em fast if you do," yelled Pinkie.

Moments later, Mario stood at Pinkie's side with a pair of tweezers in his right hand. "Doc's on his way," he said, handing the tweezers to Pinkie and looking at Damion, whose head had rolled over onto his right shoulder. "I think he passed out," Mario said, dropping to one knee and running two fingers along the inside of Damion's right wrist to check his pulse. "Pretty weak," Mario commented. As he watched Pinkie dab the gash in Damion's arm dry with his own shirttail before jamming the tweezers deep into Damion's deltoid muscle, Mario began to sweat. After fishing around briefly with the tweezers, Pinkie shouted, "Got it." Seconds later, with the tweezers squeezed together tightly on the bleeding vessel, the bleeding stopped. "How long before Doc gets here?" asked Pinkie through gritted teeth as he suddenly found himself thinking about the humid jungles and twisted waterways of a long-forgotten place called Vietnam.

"He said to give him ten minutes," Mario said, gently lifting Damion's head to check his breathing. When he whispered, "Hang in there, Blood," there was no response.

There wasn't any light on in the room for good reason, because light—streetlights, light from the headlights of a car, even the subdued light of a low-wattage bulb—made Leotis Hawkins's head scream with pain. After stumbling home in a daze on the heels of his head-bashing encounter with Damion Madrid, he'd drawn the sagging window blinds in the bedroom of his one-bedroom apartment in Denver's Curtis Park neighborhood, settled into bed with three pillows behind his head for support, and, with his head feeling as if it wanted to split, cursed himself for letting Madrid get the better of him.

He wasn't as dizzy as when he'd first come home, but he understood that he had a serious concussion. If he tried to drink water, his head hurt. If he moved too quickly, his head hurt. If he breathed too deeply, it throbbed. Touching his right temple gently and hoping not to trigger a bolus of pain, he whispered, "If you're not dead already, Madrid, I'll kill you yet, you wetback fucker."

He was afraid of going to sleep. He'd heard stories about people with concussions going to sleep and never waking up. But he wasn't about to go see a doctor. Doctors, in his experience, talked too much, and they asked far too many questions. Those questions all too often led to visits from cops, and if Madrid had bled to death in some back alley with a bowie knife on him that had Hawkins's fingerprints on it, cops would mean trouble.

Although his thoughts remained clouded, some very important ones remained crystal clear. Like the fact that Rodney Sands and Jackie Woodson had better keep their mouths shut about what they knew about his drug enterprise—and, if Madrid turned up dead, what they knew about his Welton Street meeting with Madrid. He'd also have to make sure Leon Bird didn't suddenly get the spirit and decide to spill his guts about the relationship they'd developed. All in all, it wouldn't really be that difficult to handle his problems, he told himself. That was, if he made it through the night without falling asleep and drifting permanently into dreamland.

As he adjusted his head on the pillows and tried his best to get comfortable, he had the sudden feeling that he was floating, but the throbbing pain behind his eyes wouldn't allow him to enjoy the fantasy for long. It was going to be a long night, and if Madrid was still alive, he hoped it would be just as long for him.

Sixty-five-year-old Denver society-pages doctor Carlo Bottone was anything but what Damion had expected after Mario had assured him as he drifted in and out of consciousness that medical help was on the way. Far from being some Hollywood B-movie version of a mob doctor, or an alcoholic who'd lost his license after nearly killing someone he'd treated while drunk, Bottone was steady-handed, clear-eyed, skilled, and reassuring, and he smelled to Damion more like someone who'd just bathed in expensive French bath oils than the silver screen's version of a sawbones down-and-outer whose pores reeked of cigar smoke and cheap liquor.

As he placed the finishing touches on a perfectly aligned row of sutures, tucking the last subcutaneous stitch in with the skill of what he'd been for the past thirty years—a high-profile Denver plastic surgeon—Bottone glanced briefly and silently up at Mario, who hadn't moved since he'd delivered the prominent Denver doctor to Damion's side twenty-five minutes earlier.

Thanks to an IV that had carried a liter and a half of lactated Ringer's solution into his sagging vascular system and a twelve-ounce glass of orange juice, Damion now sat stabilized, albeit still a bit light-headed, in Mario's La-Z-Boy. Pinkie sat across the room flipping through a battered copy of *Sports Illustrated* that featured the LA Dodgers on the cover.

"There," said Bottone, leaning over from the ottoman he'd sat on while performing an arterial tie-off and looking pleased. Dusting off his hands, he extracted a roll of sterile gauze from the oversized doctor's valise at his feet. "Let me dress that puppy for you, and we're done." As he rolled the gauze skillfully around Damion's arm, Damion had the urge to ask how he'd managed to clamp the bleeder, tie it off in nothing flat, and turn what had been a bloody mess into a neatly sutured wound. More importantly, he wanted to know why the good doctor was walking around with a dispensary's worth of hospital supplies tucked inside the oversized turn-of-the-twentieth-century-style black valise at his feet. But he didn't. He knew Bottone was there at the behest of Mario and that some questions would simply have to remain unanswered.

"You could really benefit from a unit of blood, young fellow," Bottone said, checking the dressing one last time. "But I'm afraid from what Mario tells me that you'll just have to do without that for right now. So here's my advice. Early to bed and late to rise. A good night's sleep, half-a-day's rest tomorrow, and a steak-and-egg breakfast when you finally get up should do you just fine." Smiling and nodding, he checked the line on Damion's IV. "You should be all dripped out in another ten minutes." He glanced briefly at Pinkie. The look the two men gave one another told Damion that they'd met under similar circumstances before. Thumping the Ringer's bag with his middle finger, Bottone eyed the sling he'd made from one of Mario's oversized bath towels. "After that, Pinkie can drive you home."

"Nope," said Mario. "He's stayin' here tonight."

"No, I'm not, Mario. We've been through that," Damion protested. "I'm going to Niki's. If anything, ah . . . bad surfaces out of this problem I created, I don't want your name or Pinkie's linked to it. I may have killed a man, remember?" He looked at Pinkie, whom he somehow expected to understand his predicament, for a response, but Pinkie remained silent.

"I doubt you killed anyone, Damion," said Bottone. "Although from what you said happened, I expect your assailant probably has one hell of a headache. I wouldn't fret over it. Remember, the man tried to kill you."

Surprised by Bottone's response, which he would've expected from Pinkie or maybe even Mario but never a physician, Damion said, "I need to know that Hawkins is alive."

Bottone flashed Pinkie a look that said, *This is your territory; want to take over?* Shaking his head, Pinkie said, "I'll check on your Jabba the Hutt with the knife tomorrow. Meanwhile, here's a news bulletin for you, Blood." The way Pinkie said his nickname, as if the word was suddenly lethal, caused Damion's eyes to widen. "You don't go lookin' to tuck somebody in beddy-bye who's tried to kill you. Don't you ever forget that."

Damion looked even more surprised as he watched Mario and Doc Bottone nod in agreement.

Realizing that Damion was a raw green recruit in the world he'd stepped into and hoping to take the edge off the conversation, Bottone asked, "So when's medical school start?"

"In a couple of weeks."

"You'll be good to go by then," said Bottone, who'd long ago run the race Damion was about to start. "Use the sling and take the Levaquin I gave you for the next seven days, every last pill. No telling where the blade of the knife that opened your arm up might have been, and there's no need to help an infection along. So take the pills." Dusting off his hands, Bottone assembled every instrument he'd used along with every piece of unused gauze, suture material, and a small bottle of Betadine into a pile before methodically placing them into several small plastic Ziploc hazardous-material bags and slipping them back into his old doctor's valise. When he realized Damion was staring, he said, "It belonged to my father. Not many calls for these contraptions anymore." Looking at Mario, he smiled, snapped the valise shut, and said, "Looks like I'm all done here."

"You're a savior." Mario hugged Bottone affectionately.

Bottone continued smiling as he returned the hug. Looking at Pinkie, he said, "Andrus, stay well."

"Will do," said Pinkie as Bottone, valise in hand, headed for the front door. Halfway to the door, Bottone looked back at Damion. "Good luck in med school. That first year's a rough one."

"So everybody tells me."

"You won't have any problem," Bottone said, swinging the front door open and giving Damion a wink. "You've got the mental tenacity it takes. I've seen you play ball."

Half an hour later, as Pinkie pulled his gleaming silver-and-black three-quarter-ton pickup to a stop in front of Niki Estaban's house, Damion found himself still wondering about the doctor who'd very likely saved his life. Deciding to ask Pinkie later about Bottone's background, Damion cleared his throat, adjusted the sling holding his left arm, and said in response to Pinkie's assertion that Shandell's murder looked to be the work of a professional, "You sure it's not a problem for you to nose around and see whether Blackbird's murder might've been the work of a pro?"

Pinkie, who'd never liked being asked the same question twice, frowned. "I said it wouldn't be a problem, Damion. I'll check out Garrett Asalon's place up in Louisville and see if he or that bodyguard he keeps around had their fingers in any kinda point-shavin' scam. In the meantime, why don't you go along with Doc Bottone's orders?

Get yourself a good long couple of days' rest and worry about what it's gonna take to get you through that first year of medical school."

"And what about Leotis Hawkins? If he's not dead already, what the hell do I do about him?" Damion realized the instant the words left his mouth that he'd asked a question he shouldn't have. The look on Pinkie's face verified as much.

Pinkie took a deep breath, hoping to take the edge off what he was about to say. "You stepped your foot into a world you really don't belong in tonight, Damion. So here's a nugget to take to bed with you. Unlike Doc Bottone, you're fortunate. You ain't got no blood coursin' through your veins that binds you to a way of life forever, no matter what." Realizing that Damion looked a bit confused, he added, "Let me spell it out a little bit better for you. What did you think of Doc Bottone?"

"He knows his stuff."

"No question. But he's got one foot in a world he can't never leave. A world you don't want no part of. So here's the juice. I'll nose around and see if I can't help figure out who killed your best friend. But once we know the answer, you need to put the likes of Leotis Hawkins and Garrett Asalon behind you."

Realizing that the man who'd probably saved his life that evening was for some reason tied to the mob forever, Damion asked in the meekest of voices, "So what's Bottone's inside connection?"

Pinkie smiled. "You know that sweet angel Mario prays to every night before he hits the sack?"

"Yeah, sure, Angie; we all know that," said Damion, referring to Mario Satoni's late wife and the woman the once-powerful Denver don still talked to on a daily basis, without the least hint of embarrassment.

"Well, Doc Bottone, plastic surgeon to most of Denver's blue-bloods, is Angie's kid brother. Blood's thicker than water," Pinkie said, watching a look of astonishment spread across Damion's face. "When you get called, you get called no matter what. Always remember that. Keep both feet in one world, Damion. Trust me, it's a whole lot healthier." Glancing toward Niki's house and the light streaming from a front bay window, Pinkie leaned across Damion to open the front door. "Now, how about it, Blood? Why don't you go get yourself some rest?"

"Okay, but give me a few minutes to get my story together."

Smiling, Pinkie, who'd been forced to knit more than a few stories together over the years, said, "Take all the time you need."

Chapter 14

Aretha Bird eyed her former husband disdainfully and gritted her teeth. "You're despicable, Leon. A piss bump on the ass of humanity. I'm gonna bury my baby tomorrow, and you've got the nerve to ask me about some damn insurance policy. You're foot rot, Leon."

Leon Bird glanced back over his shoulder at the cooing Hispanic couple sitting in the restaurant booth behind them and motioned for Aretha to tone it down. For the past hour they'd been drinking margaritas and snacking on tortilla chips at the Satire Lounge, a Tex-Mex restaurant in midtown Denver. Unperturbed, the other couple, more concerned with how soon they could find a bed than with the raised voices in the next booth, barely looked up.

"Hey, I'm just looking out for us, baby," said Leon.

"Don't *baby* me, you effing loser. I should've known when you showed up out of the pitch-black darkness last winter that you wouldn't bring me and Shandell nothin' but pain."

"I brought you luck," Leon said defensively. "Or have you forgotten that you're the main beneficiary of Shandell's estate? Baby, you're worth millions."

When Aretha drew back her arm to slap the linebacker-sized longtime bunco artist and petty thief, Leon said, his voice full of anger, "Don't be no fool, girl."

Having felt the sting from Leon's hand more often than she cared to remember, Aretha dropped her hand into her lap, upset with herself for even talking to her abusive ex-husband, who for the past two days had overcome her defenses and fueled her hope by saying that he might have a line on who'd killed Shandell.

"Let's say we get back to that insurance policy instead of throwing punches, Aretha. And trust me, I know there's a policy. Shandell told me there was. Face value of two hundred and fifty grand. I'm the beneficiary, and I know you've stashed it. I want my money, girl. You understand me?"

"Oh, I understand, Leon. Just like I understood the kind of scum you were when you left me and Shandell to fend for ourselves all them years ago."

Unable to contain his frustration any longer, Leon said, "I'll kick your ass, bitch."

Unfazed by the threat, Aretha broke into a broad, toothy grin. "No, you won't. At least, not here you won't." She glanced across the room toward the bar and the sleepy-eyed bartender, a skinny, long-faced greyhound of a man wearing a yellow, black, and green African skullcap. A single gold earring hung from his right ear. Up close it would've been easy to see the sea of pockmarks peppering his forehead, but from fifteen feet away he simply looked lean and hungry.

"Friend of yours?" Leon asked.

"No, he was more of a friend to Shandell. But if I tell him you're bothering me, he's real likely to come over here and kick your teeth in. He finished high school with Shandell four years ago, and he lived on the streets for a couple of years afterward. He's a good kid, really, but he's a tad bit slow. I wouldn't want to test his hair-trigger temper if I was you. Somehow during high school, Shandell seemed to be the only one able to help him stay calm. Even helped him get the job behind that bar over there after he left the streets. He'll be one of the pallbearers at Shandell's funeral tomorrow, and he don't like to see big people pickin' on little ones."

"You think I'd run scared'a some kid?" Leon said with a snort. "You crazy, woman? You the one needs to be runnin' scared. And you the one needs to be diggin' up that insurance policy." Looking as if he'd suddenly hit on the solution to a problem, he added, "I really don't need them papers when you come right down to it. Insurance companies keep records of beneficiaries, you know. All I really need to do is make a phone call and tell 'em who I am."

"Tell who?" Aretha tried not to snicker. "You might as well start with the As under insurance companies in the yellow pages. I'm sure that in this age of identity theft, they'll all be chompin' at the bit to help you."

"Then I'll get myself a lawyer. Won't take one of them sharks more'n a day or two to dig up the right company."

"Then get with it, and be sure to tell your lawyer that in addition to you bein' the policy's beneficiary, you're also a suspect in the policy holder's murder."

"Bullshit!"

"The cops say otherwise. And I know for sure they've talked to you. Sergeant Townsend told me."

Leon frowned as he recalled the lengthy talk he'd had with Townsend earlier that day. Townsend, who'd located him after finding his cell-phone number among Shandell's effects, had indeed pegged him as a murder suspect. "Then why the hell are you here talkin' to me, woman, if you know so much?"

"Because I think you know more about Shandell's murder than you're lettin' on."

"There you go, workin' all the angles again. That's one of the reasons I left your black ass all them years ago. You think too much. I oughta whip your ass right here and now."

Leon had finally pressed the wrong button. Looking violated, Aretha sat forward in her seat and motioned for the bartender to come over. Moments later Jo Jo Lawson was standing a few feet from their booth. Smiling up at him, Aretha said, "Jo Jo, I want you to meet Leon, Shandell's father. He just offered to whip my ass."

With his eyes locked sternly on Leon and in the slowest of Western drawls, Jo Jo said, "Don't think you should say things like that to Mrs. B, mister."

"Why don't you get the fuck outta here, son?" Before Leon could utter another word, Jo Jo had yanked him out of his seat and wrapped his left arm around Leon's neck in an airway-obstructing choke hold.

"You need to leave, mister," Jo Jo said calmly as Leon struggled to free himself. "I'll cut off all your air, you don't stop resistin'." When Leon continued struggling, Jo Jo said, "Don't make me have to go back over to the bar and get my friend Johnny." He looked at Aretha for further instruction.

Aware that the slow-talking barkeep wasn't as quick mentally as most people, and suddenly looking horrified, Aretha said, "Just show him the door, Jo Jo. No need turnin' this into a free-for-all."

With both arms flailing and gasping for air, Leon sank to his knees. The lusting couple in the next booth looked up briefly but barely paid the commotion any attention as a determined-looking Jo Jo helped Leon to his feet and ushered him toward the front door.

"I'll get my money, woman. One way or another," Leon yelled back, his voice raspy.

Aretha remained silent as the marginally retarded boy Shandell had befriended in high school escorted her ex-husband, still gasping for air, out the door.

She'd known when Leon had called her from his motel room and asked to meet her to discuss the insurance policy that things were likely to escalate to the level they had. That was why she'd been careful to choose the Satire Lounge for their meeting and to make certain that Jo Jo Lawson would be tending bar. But she also knew she couldn't pick and choose where or how or when she'd meet up with Leon forever. Sooner or later he might make good on his threat, drag her into some alley, and beat her senseless.

She'd been stupid to let someone who'd once abused her back into her life, even momentarily. But he'd pleaded with her, almost to the point of groveling, and during those first twenty-four hours after Shandell's death, she'd been a ball of Silly Putty in his hands. Now that she was thinking more clearly, she could see Leon in all his natural, evil, living color. A repulsive human being who wanted only the spoils his dead son had left him.

He'd spent months insinuating himself into Shandell's life, chipping away at her precious baby's psyche, and although Shandell had tried his best to keep it from her, she knew that Leon somehow had been able to convince Shandell that the boy owed him. The life insurance policy had been a way for Shandell to either pay him back or pay him off. She and Shandell had argued about his budding relationship with his father, and although she wanted to believe in her heart of hearts that Shandell hadn't paid Leon off in other ways, like possibly shaving points in basketball games, the way Sergeant Townsend had claimed, she couldn't be certain that he hadn't.

Townsend had spent nearly an hour with her earlier that day, pressing her for information about Shandell's insurance policy and insinuating that Shandell might have been involved in a game-fixing, point-shaving scam that could rock college basketball. He'd chipped away at her little by little, all the while sucking air between the gap in his front teeth, until she'd broken down and cried, regressing to nearly the state she'd been in the first time they'd met.

She realized now that she should've called Julie Madrid the instant Leon had shown up on her doorstep and that she should've refused to talk to Townsend without her lawyer. But she hadn't. She'd been too grief-stricken. Too busy trying to play the part of Shandell Bird's tough-love mother. But now she was through playing cat-and-mouse with ex-husbands and gap-toothed cops. From now on she'd let Julie Madrid do her talking.

"Whatta you mean you don't know why you called me, doctor? You know very well why." Wordell Epps broke into a sly grin, adjusted the phone receiver to his ear, and toying with the draw string on his pajamas, sat up in bed. "Like I told you before, there's done and really done, Dr. Phillips."

"So you did." Second-guessing herself, Alicia Phillips pondered why on the heels of an earlier phone call from a very nervous and unsettled Connie Eastland who'd informed her that she'd just received a threatening phone call from Leon Bird, she'd decided to track Epps down. The reason in fact was quite simple. She couldn't take the chance that Epps might end up doing the same thing to her that Leon Bird was doing to Connie. Nonetheless, she questioned whether she was doing the right thing.

"You're awful quiet there, doctor. Any reason?" asked Epps.

"No. Just thinking."

"About that book you're writing?"

"No. I was thinking about whether I can trust you or not."

Epps snickered. "Guess you'll just have to try me and find out."

"When can we talk at length?" asked Phillips.

"Anytime. You pick the hour."

"Tomorrow afternoon perhaps."

"Works for me."

"I'll be in touch," Alicia said, feeling inexplicably out of breath.

"I'll be waiting." Epps cradled the phone and reclined back in bed, thinking to himself that perhaps Alicia Phillips would be the one to take his investigative probe where it really needed to go.

Denver's North Cherry Creek neighborhood, once filled with plain-Jane blond-brick bungalows and scattered apartment buildings, had over the past fifteen years become an assemblage of expensive homes, brand-new duplexes, and trendy condos.

Damion's girlfriend, Niki Estaban, lived in a recently constructed Mediterranean-style duplex at the corner of Third Avenue and Cook Street, on the eastern edge of the trendy Cherry Creek shopping district that abutted her neighborhood.

Niki and Damion, who'd been nearly inseparable during their final two years of college, had drifted slightly apart in the three months since their graduations. Armed with a degree in architecture, Niki now worked for the largest architectural firm in Denver. The second child of a socially and politically prominent South American family, the long-legged, hazel-eyed, exotically beautiful Venezuelan had modeled her way through high school and her first two years of college, and she'd traveled most of the world by the time she was twenty. It was that upbringing and the diversity of her life experience that had caused the two of them to start to feel their differences.

Damion had come up with and from nothing, and although his mother, who'd been CJ Floyd's secretary during his formative years, was now a prominent Denver attorney, Damion remained, at least in his head, simply a poor kid from Five Points with the luck to have a sports skill that had gotten him the education to put him in line to become a doctor. He'd never seen the world and frankly didn't much care to, and while Niki wanted to discover the farthest corners of the globe, his world consisted of Denver and the surrounding wilderness of Colorado, New Mexico, and Wyoming. Whenever the pressures of living or dying with basketball had become too much, he'd generally disappeared for a few days to hike or hunt or fish. In the past three months, since leaving the protective umbrella of college behind, Niki and Damion had slowly begun to recognize the fact that although they were obviously in love, they were markedly different.

Now, as he stood at Niki's front door with his left arm in a sling and Pinkie Niedemeyer standing next to him nervously looking from side to side, Damion wasn't certain what kind of reception he'd get from Niki. He'd tried to reach her earlier by phone without any luck—not surprising considering her busy postmodeling career and her disdain for both answering machines and cell phones.

Niki's response to Damion's light rapping was to stroll leisurely to the front door, glance through the peephole, and immediately swing the door open, staring in disbelief.

Taking in Damion's meek expression, the dark circles under his eyes, the sling, his blood-splattered shirt, and finally Pinkie, she said softly in her Spanish accent, "Come in." She gave Pinkie, whom she'd come to know during Damion's and CSU's run for the Final Four, a look that said, *Are you responsible for this?* before draping an arm around Damion and ushering them both inside. Touching

Damion's arm ever so gently as she headed for her living room, she asked, "What happened?"

"I ran into a problem tonight over in Five Points."

Looking dumbfounded, she again stared at the circles under Damion's eyes and wondered if she might somehow be partially responsible for them. In her quest to complete the required postbac-calaureate on-the-job architectural experience she needed in order to qualify for a Colorado license, she'd spent most of her time over the past three months at the offices of Barrett, Jenkins, and White, often staying until midnight, trying to absorb every nuance she could about the real world of architecture. If she'd been with Damion earlier that evening, she told herself, she might have been able to prevent what had happened. Looking guilty, she eyed Pinkie and asked what she'd been thinking: "You're not responsible for this, are you?"

"He's not responsible for anything, Niki." Damion slipped her arm from around his shoulders and clasped her right hand in his as they stepped down into a large, brightly lit, sunken living room. The butt of his Glock peeked from beneath the pocket of Pinkie's lightweight jacket as he stepped down into the room behind them.

"I should have been here for you, Damion. I'll cut back at work, I promise."

"No," said Damion, looking around the familiar, sparsely furnished room that his privileged raven-haired girlfriend had furnished with an oversized antique wingback chair, a reading lamp, a massive curved leather couch, a coffee table, and a coffin-style German grandfather clock from the 1860s that she'd bought from the virtual antique store that Mario Satoni and his part-time business partner, CJ Floyd, ran out of Mario's basement.

Pinkie headed for the wingback to sit down. Leaving Damion and

Niki standing in the center of the room staring blankly at the moss-rock fireplace, he recalled what Mario had said to him before he and Damion had left Mario's North Denver home earlier. *The boy don't know what he's in for if he gets to fuckin' around with Asalon. Better stay glued to his ass 'til this is over, Pinkie.*

The room remained silent until Niki slipped her hand out of Damion's and took a seat on the couch. "Penny for your thoughts," she said, patting the cushion next to her and nodding for Damion to join her. "I've got soda or juice for anybody who wants some, or I can make coffee," Niki added, trying her best to look calm.

"Nothing for me," said Pinkie, his eyes on alert as they darted between the room's two windows.

"Me either," Damion said, drinking in the look of concern on Niki's face as he took a seat.

"Are you sure you're okay, Damion?"

"Yeah. I'll tell you the whole story about the arm later. But for now I need you to help me with something that might help me pin the tail on Shandell's killer."

The muscles in Niki's face slumped, and for the briefest of seconds her exquisite beauty faded. "Damion, I thought we agreed after that grilling from Sergeant Townsend the other night that you'd let the police handle the case."

Damion looked at Pinkie for support, but the skinny hit man eyed the floor and remained silent. "I am. I'm just probing around the edges."

Niki's voice rose nearly an octave. "I can't believe it. I wish I had a tape recorder. You sound just like CJ."

"Shandell was my best friend, Niki."

"And he was just as dear to me," Niki said defensively, sitting back in her seat and shaking her head. "Look at you. You come in here with blood splattered all over your shirt, your arm bandaged and in a sling, and with a hit . . . Pinkie . . . at your side. In two weeks you're supposed to start medical school, Damion. Do you plan to do that on the side while you play at being CJ Floyd and continue to scare me to death?"

"I'll wrap things up before then, Niki. I promise. Now, can we get back on track?"

Niki frowned and said, "Yes, let's get back on track." Her tone was at once acquiescent and dismissive.

Concerned that he might have just turned a corner with Niki that he really hadn't intended to, Damion asked, "Did you ever hear about Shandell being involved with drugs while we were at CSU?"

"No. Is someone claiming that he was?"

"Rodney Sands and Jackie Woodson both told me that while we were in school, Shandell was selling performance-enhancing drugs to Five Points kids down here in Denver."

"No way."

"I said the same thing. But they insisted he was. Even gave me the name of his drug contact in Five Points. A guy named Leotis Hawkins."

"Hawkins is the one responsible for Damion's arm being in a sling," said Pinkie, hoping to garner Damion a few sympathy points by passing along the information. The look of alarm on Niki's face told him that he'd probably only made matters worse.

Except for the ticking grandfather clock, the room again fell silent. "You aren't going to leave this alone, are you, Damion?" Niki asked, breaking the silence.

"No." Damion's response was quick and absolute.

Sensing that Damion's mind was made up and that no matter how hard she tried, there was no way she was going to get him to change it, Niki asked, "Have you talked to Connie Eastland?"

"Not since last night."

"If anybody would've known about Shandell being involved with selling drugs, it would've been her. And maybe Dr. Phillips."

Damion looked surprised, unable to fathom how either woman could possibly have known something about Shandell that he hadn't. Dr. Alicia Phillips, who'd built a reputation as tutor-queen to the CSU jocks, was nothing less than a gem in his eyes, but he couldn't imagine why Shandell would have gone to her with his problems. "Why would Shandell have talked to Dr. Phillips? I always helped him with the classes he was having trouble in."

"You helped him with the academic things, Damion. Not the psychological side of his problems. For most of our senior year, Shandell went to Dr. Phillips for help a lot. Even I knew it."

"What kind of help?"

"I'm not sure. You'll have to ask Connie. All I know is that she hinted to me while she was here last night that when Shandell was down in the dumps, he usually went to see Dr. Phillips."

Damion shook his head. Once again, he'd been out of the loop. Out of the loop when it came to Shandell's involvement with selling illicit drugs, out of the loop when it came to Shandell's father, Leon, and now out of the loop when it came to helping his lifelong friend when he'd apparently been despondent. Suddenly he found himself thinking that he hadn't been much of a friend. He looked down at his arm, eyed the splotches of dried blood on his shirt, and wondered if they weren't merely the physical evidence that served to prove his point. Something tangible that could scream, *I wasn't there when you needed me, Blackbird, but see, I'm here for you now.*

Sensing from the look on Damion's face that he was trying to quell the deeply hurtful feelings swirling inside him, Niki asked, "What's wrong, Damion?"

"Nothing," he said stoically. "Just wondering about friendship."

Niki eyed Pinkie, who seemed equally puzzled. "Think I'll brew some coffee," she said as the wily hit man offered an affirmative nod. "I've got your favorite. Up for some Kona brew, Damion?" When Damion, looking lost in a fog, didn't answer, she rose from her seat and headed for the kitchen to make coffee and call Flora Jean.

As Damion watched her head from the room, he found himself thinking not about his arm or Shandell's involvement with illicit drugs or point-shaving, or Leotis Hawkins, or even Garrett Asalon, Leon Bird, Jackie Woodson, or Theo Wilhite. What he found himself thinking about was what he was going to say to Connie Eastland when he talked to her the next morning at Shandell's funeral and what he would ask Dr. Phillips about why she had become the sounding board for Shandell's troubles.

Chapter 15

Pinkie Niedemeyer and Garrett Asalon had history. The kind of piss-in-your-face, country-cousin-versus-city-cousin history that had made for deep-seated distrust and long-standing acrimony. They were in effect members of the same club, but Asalon had always been quick to ignore the fact that he was no more than a highly educated criminal, describing himself instead as a successful businessman. The two men had once been close friends, but that friendship, reduced now to a festering wound, had ended years earlier.

A woman had been at the heart of their differences. She had chosen a skinny, fearless high school dropout of a hit man with a wry sense of humor and loyalty to a fault over an educated, unprincipled, underworld mover and shaker with a Princeton MBA. That woman, who'd succumbed at the age of thirty-five to a heart attack precipitated by smoking, alcohol abuse, and a long family history of heart disease, had been Mario Satoni's niece, and although her autopsy report had stated unequivocally that she'd died from coronary artery occlusion and a myocardial infarction, Pinkie and Mario still clung to the belief that Janet Stevens's life had ended all too early because of the scorned Asalon's relentless stalking and unending threats.

It had taken Pinkie the better part of thirty minutes to convince a skeptical, concerned, and clearly disappointed Flora Jean, who'd arrived at Niki's duplex a little before midnight following Niki's frantic call to her, that although she might be fully capable of going after

Asalon, her investigation and Pinkie's psyche would be better served if he was the one who made the trip to Louisville, a onetime mining town twenty miles northwest of Denver where Asalon housed and operated his businesses.

Flora Jean had been reluctant to buy in, but after sharing his story about Janet, leaving Niki misty-eyed and Flora Jean speechless, Pinkie received Flora Jean's blessing and a three-point assignment. He was to find out whether Shandell and possibly Jackie Woodson had shaved points at Asalon's behest, ferret out anything Asalon might know about Shandell's involvement in the sale and distribution of performance-enhancing drugs, and most importantly determine whether Asalon or one of his associates might have killed Shandell.

Pinkie had left Denver for his meeting with Asalon with an additional agenda item on his mind, one that wouldn't help him find Shandell's killer but, no matter what else he might find out, would make his unannounced 1 a.m. visit to Asalon's office an unmitigated success. He planned to make the egotistical mobster squirm, reminding him, as he did whenever their paths crossed, that when it came to the one thing in life that had mattered to him as much as power and money, Asalon had come in second best.

The air was heavy with mist when Pinkie reached the southern edge of Louisville. As he cruised past the weather sign on the First-Bank building, he was surprised to see that the temperature had dipped to a chilly 51 degrees. Aware that Asalon was a highly predictable creature of habit and that the cash that was generated each day by his gambling interests, liquor stores, knockoff product sales, and money-laundering scams made its way to Louisville on a nightly basis to be counted and batched for redistribution under Asalon's watchful eye, Pinkie had little reason to expect that the other man would be a no-show. If for some reason things didn't run true to form, he'd come back the next night.

The single-story, bunker-style, cinder-block building where Asalon closed out his business dealings each evening occupied an otherwise vacant triangular five-acre lot two miles east of Highway 36, which connected Denver and Boulder. The building had belonged to a band of Gypsy card sharks and bunco artists, Cold War immigrants from Czechoslovakia, during the late 1950s. In the mid-'60s they'd sold the building and the land to Asalon's father, who hadn't realized until after the deal was closed that the building was on someone else's land. When Tony Asalon and two of his associates had threatened to castrate two of the Gypsies and serve them their jewels for dinner if they didn't come up with title to the land, the Gypsies had disappeared. In the more than forty years since the land swindle had occurred, neither the county assessor's office nor the true landowner, both aware of the Asalon family reputation for having things go their way, had ever mentioned the issue of encroachment.

Pinkie parked his pickup a quarter of a mile from the building, deciding that the element of surprise, a lesson he had learned in Vietnam and in most of his business dealings since, would serve him well.

Patting the 9-mm Glock in his jacket pocket and thinking, *Here we go again*, he moved in a half crouch across a field of three-foot-high timothy until his pants legs were soaked with dew. He wanted to think that Janet would have been proud of him for taking one more opportunity to stick it to Asalon—wanted to believe that whenever the pompous, wannabe blueblood began to think he was finally free from the sting of Janet's rejection, Andrus Niedemeyer would be there to remind him that he wasn't. But deep down, he knew that neither of those things were true. Janet's advice to him had always been to steer clear of Asalon, a man who had been labeled by medical people whom she trusted as a pathological narcissist. Her mantra for Pinkie, if she had lived, would no doubt have been, *Please, please, please, baby, stay away.*

But Janet wasn't there, and the dark-gray building that at first had been only a low, rectangular shape in the distance was now just a few yards away. He'd been inside the building a handful of times, but always as an escort for Mario Satoni, and never this late. As he stopped to get his bearings, he realized that the building reminded him of a thatch-roofed Vietcong bunker he'd once torched with a flamethrower seconds before his squad leader, a reluctant draftee and stateside chemical engineer, had taken out two fleeing VC with half a clip from his M-16. Memories of Vietnam and of Janet caused him to hesitate and suddenly take a step backward.

As he stood motionless, as if expecting a supportive word from Janet or an order from his squad leader, a low-pitched, gravelly voice erupted behind him. "Don't take another step, cocksucker." Clicking on the flashlight in his left hand and adjusting the .357 in his right, Craigy Theisman looked Pinkie up and down. "What the fuck are you doing out here, numbnuts?"

When Pinkie didn't answer, Theisman yelled, "Hands on your head and turn the fuck around."

Clamping his hands on his head and smiling, aware that he very likely now had a way into the building, Pinkie pivoted to find himself face to face with the thick-bodied Theisman.

"Well, mother of mercy." Theisman's voice rose a full two octaves. "Take myself a smoke break and look what I find! A killer rat out on the prowl! Damn! Hand over whatever you're carryin', Niedemeyer.

Or then again, maybe you don't want to." Theisman smiled and fingered the trigger of the .357.

Aware that Theisman would love an excuse to shoot him on the spot, Pinkie reached into his pocket and handed over the Glock. Theisman tucked the flashlight under his arm, took the gun, and jammed it into the left-hand pocket of his bulky, grease-stained jacket. "If I'd'a known who you were when I first spotted you, I'd'a put one in your temple, real sweet and easy."

"You wouldn't have done shit, Craigy. Except for what you're doin' right now—talkin' to hear yourself talk. Your puppet strings are showin', lardass, and they're singin' the same song as always: *Don't do nothin' without an okay from Garrett, especially not somethin' as stupid as offin' somebody on the front doorstep.*"

Incensed, Theisman flipped the beam of his flashlight back toward himself, cupped the lamp in his hand, and jammed the foot-long handle into Pinkie's midsection. Gasping for air, Pinkie dropped to his knees. Theisman patted the flashlight handle and burst into laughter. "Guess you never played football and had the wind knocked outta you, Niedemeyer. You'll be okay shortly. Feels like you're gonna die right now, though, don't it?" He watched Pinkie continue to catch his breath before twirling the flashlight around baton-style and clamping it to his belt. Nudging the muzzle of his .357 into the flesh beneath Pinkie's chin, he whispered, "Time to get up, sucker. We're goin' inside to have a talk with Garrett. He'll wanta know why the hell you were out here nosin' around. Hell, maybe you were huntin' frogs or somethin'. There is a frog pond just north of here." He pointed into the darkness. "But who's to know? Could be you were just out here beatin' off. Dreamin' that woman they say you snookered Garrett out of was givin' you a hummer."

Choking back his rage as he rose to his feet, Pinkie remained silent. All he could think of as Theisman gave him a hard shove in the direction of the building was that he owed the cocky, beer-bellied, South Boston Irishman a lesson.

A pleasant, fruity smell greeted the two men as they entered the surprisingly cold Asalon Enterprises building and walked its dimly lit length, past roulette wheels, gaming tables, cases of liquor stacked six feet high, and half-a-dozen slot machines. The gaming and liquor inventory ended abruptly near the far end of the building, a four-hundred-square-foot area that was lit up like a Christmas tree. Except for a couple of old leather chairs near one wall and a wrought-iron table that sat between them, the area was empty.

Dressed in tailored Italian slacks, a black silk shirt, and a light-weight cashmere car coat, Asalon stood a few feet from the table rubbing his hands together to warm them. He was busy talking to a square-headed midget of a man with a massive forehead, bulging frog eyes, and a nose that looked as if it had been flattened a lot more than once in a boxing ring. When Asalon glanced up from the conversation to see Pinkie and Theisman, his head shot back. "Well, I'll be."

"Found him snoopin' around outside when I went out for a smoke break," Theisman said proudly, bringing Pinkie to a halt just in front of Asalon. "I watched him for a good little while before I moved in. Strange, he was startin' to back away from the building when I swooped. I'm thinkin' maybe old Andrus here mighta suddenly been gettin' cold feet."

"Nope," Pinkie said with a chuckle. "I was just movin' downwind from that cancer stick you were puffin' on, Craigy. I knew you were there all the time, dumbass. Just needed a way in here that would keep me from gettin' my head blown off." He looked at the suddenly slack-jawed Theisman and smiled. "And you know what? You proved to be the perfect escort." Nodding at Asalon and the midget he'd been talking to, a well-known Motor City hit man Pinkie had known for years, Pinkie said, "Garrett. Aloysius."

"Bullshit," yelled Theisman.

"Would you tone it down please, Craigy?" Asalon said, looking displeased. "You're always so visceral. One day you're going to overreact and rupture a vessel." Asalon eyed the midget. "I think we're done here, Allie."

Aloysius Slocum glanced at Pinkie before turning to leave. "Hope you're not here on any kind of official business, Pinkie."

"Not the kind I expect you are," Pinkie said, puzzled as to why a high-profile rifleman like Slocum would be in this neck of the woods.

Poker-faced, Slocum said to Asalon, "Talk to you later," before waddling toward the exit.

Asalon watched the pint-sized hit man disappear through the self-locking front door before turning back to Theisman. "You can put the gun away, Craigy. I don't think Andrus represents much of a threat."

Looking disappointed, Theisman slipped the .357 into his jacket pocket.

"So what brings you up our way, Pinkie?" For the first time Asalon sounded noticeably peeved.

"A killin'."

"I always thought killing people was your side of the street."

"That and hangin' out with dried-up old dons and bail-bonding niggers," said Theisman.

Ignoring Theisman's description of Mario Satoni and CJ Floyd, Pinkie squared up to face Asalon. "Are you up on the news about the Shandell Bird killin'?"

"Yes. Heard he was murdered down your way the other night. Shameful what a peaceful little cow town like Denver has come to these days."

"Did you have anything to do with it?" Pinkie asked pointedly.

"Straightforward these days, aren't we, Pinkie? Not even a little bit of hemming and hawing. Well, for the record, do you think I'd tell you if I did?"

"Probably not. But I'm thinkin' you had a reason. I've got it on good authority that Bird might've been tied into a college basketball point-shavin' scam you were ramroddin'. Could be Bird was fillin' in that reporter who was killed along with him, so you decided to shut them both up."

"Pinkie, Pinkie, Pinkie. Do I look that unschooled? Take a look around you. I'm not into speculative forms of making money. Never have been. I prefer to stick with things that are weighted in my favor. The kind that these days are pretty much legal everywhere. Now, why on earth would I risk a sure thing for involvement in some kind of basketball point-shaving scam that could easily have brought the wrath of sports lovers across the country, and maybe even the feds, down on me?"

"Money, Garrett. Money. I understand you handled a nice-sized piece of change that Theo Wilhite laid down on the UCLA–Colorado State game last March. Wilhite claims the game was fixed."

Before Asalon could respond, Theisman said, "That bald-headed, cigar-smokin' nigger's got a mouth that's way too big for him."

Asalon flashed Theisman a look of pure disappointment. "You don't seem to ever learn, do you, Craigy? Guess I'll have to wash your mouth out with soap later." Turning to Pinkie, he said, "Yes, I handled Wilhite's money. Seems that when it comes to gambling, the poor man loses an awful lot, and when he does, he's always so disgruntled. Perhaps he should invest some time in attending Gamblers Anonymous."

"Maybe he should, but let's say we get back to the Shandell Bird killin'. How's this scenario work for you? Shandell sees his NBA future suddenly in jeopardy, and he's primed to talk to a reporter about his past point-shavin' transgressions, so you kill him—or have him killed," said Pinkie, recalling Aloysius Slocum's hasty retreat.

"You're in outer space, Pinkie. Why are you so interested in the Bird murder anyway?"

Pinkie eyed Asalon thoughtfully. "I'm interested because I've got friends who are interested."

"They lose money too?" Theisman asked.

"No. They lost a friend, and they're grievin'. It's an emotion you wouldn't understand, Craigy. One that's common to humans."

Theisman let out a snort, rolled his eyes, and flashed Asalon a look that said, *Please let me kill him.* Asalon ignored him.

Pleased that he had Theisman close to foaming at the mouth, Pinkie said, "Here's another question for you, Garrett. Any word leak down your way that mighta had Blackbird peddlin' sports-dopin' drugs? Steroids, hGH, beta-blockers, that kinda stuff?"

"You really are out there in the ionosphere on this, aren't you? Drugs aren't in my lineup. They're for amateurs. You know that, Pinkie."

"But money is. And like I said, you love the smell of it."

"Not enough to get involved in what you and I both know is poor folks' territory," Asalon said, enjoying the verbal joust. "Now, here's a question for you. Who pointed you my direction? Those same friends you mentioned earlier?"

"Never known you to be that worried about friendships, Garrett," Pinkie said smugly. "Why the question?"

"Cuts both ways, Andrus." Realizing that he and Pinkie were about to head down a road they'd traveled many times before, and that if they continued, Janet Stevens's name was bound to come up and he'd very likely lose his well-bred cool, Asalon said, "I think we're done here, Craigy. Why don't you escort Andrus out."

"No need. I can find my way."

"Of course you can. But my way's better." Asalon nodded for an eager-looking Theisman to walk Pinkie to the door. "And Andrus, when you get back to Denver and speak with those friends of yours who are so intent on finding out what happened to your Shandell Bird, be sure to let them know that you were issued a just-expired, free one-night pass onto the premises. There'll be no more passes handed out. Should they decide to pay Asalon Enterprises a visit, I'm afraid Craigy might have to meet the intrusion with deadly force."

Pinkie offered Asalon a silent half-nod as Theisman grabbed him by the arm.

"No need for that, Craigy. Just show the man out," ordered Asalon. With Pinkie and Theisman headed safely toward the exit, he walked across the room toward a 1950s-style rotary telephone. Pinkie was already back out in the damp night air when Asalon dialed Leotis Hawkins's number, thinking to himself that it was high time to get everyone on the same page.

The sound of a telephone ringing caused Leotis Hawkins's already splitting headache to seek painful new heights. Grumbling obscenities and rolling over in bed, he shoved a bank of four pillows aside and picked up the receiver. "Yeah." Startled to recognize Garrett

Asalon's voice on the other end of the line, he sat up in bed and leaned against the headboard, prepared to listen.

Asalon's tone was intimidating and authoritative. "I had a surprise visit from someone I thoroughly despise tonight, Leotis, and he asked me some very uncomfortable questions. Questions that lead back to you. Did I know whether Shandell Bird was in the drug-peddling business, for instance."

"Was your visitor cut real bad and bleedin'?"

Looking surprised, Asalon said, "No, he wasn't. Why?"

"Nothin', really. I had a problem with some asshole over in Five Points earlier tonight. Thought it mighta been the same person."

"Well, your problems and mine do seem to be mounting, don't they? It doesn't do my sense of security or well-being a lot of good to know that there are people out there primed to push my buttons, Leotis. We need to talk, and not by telephone. I want you to get up here to my place in Louisville right now."

Hawkins eyed his alarm clock. "It's two in the mornin' and I got a headache that won't quit. Can't it wait 'til tomorrow?"

"I'm afraid not. I want you here within the hour. Do you understand?" The threatening undercurrent in Asalon's tone made Hawkins shiver.

"Yeah, I'm comin'," Hawkins said with a groan.

"Good. I'll see you in an hour." Asalon cradled the receiver, and glanced up to realize that Theisman had returned. As he picked the receiver back up to dial Jackie Woodson's number, his only thought was, *You'd better be there, kid.*

Seconds later the diminutive point guard responded with a groggy "Hello."

"This is Asalon. I want you here at my place in an hour and a half."

"What?"

"Be here, Jackie." Asalon handed the phone to Theisman. "I think our wonder boy needs a little push, Craigy."

Smiling, Theisman said, "Craigy here, nigger boy. You heard the man. Have your black ass here in an hour and a half. That is, if you wanta keep that dick you're so proud of stickin' in every white woman on campus still swingin'."

Drawing an approving nod from Asalon, Craigy hung up, aware that when push came to shove, Asalon understood full well that racial slurs could have a purpose.

Chapter 16

A half-dozen notepads sporting the Holiday Inn Express logo were spread out on the bed in Leon Bird's motel room. Only the first page of each notepad had anything written on it. Four of those pages had the names and phone numbers of the half-dozen prominent insurance companies he'd called jotted below the logo, just above the names and addresses of several Denver attorneys. He'd placed a star next to the names of the insurance companies and lawyers he planned to call.

A bottle of Old Crow, the contents nearly drained, sat on a nightstand next to the bed. Looking exasperated, Leon moved several of the notepads around three-card-monte style before rising from the edge of the bed to massage the cramp in his left calf. Thinking that he'd come all the way from his home of East Chicago, Indiana, to Denver to prime a pump that could no longer give water, he mumbled, "Shit," and kicked at several wadded-up scraps of paper he'd tossed to the floor. Realizing now that he should have acted faster to set Shandell up and guarantee his pot of gold, he staggered over to a desk in a far corner of the room.

The desktop was covered with NCAA basketball tournament mementos and sports memorabilia, including a half-dozen scorecards, an equal number of game programs, a host of key chains and money clips sporting the CSU seal, and a passport wallet emblazoned with the words "NCAA Sweet Sixteen." Some of the items Leon had purchased as part of his effort to get in good with Shandell; others had been given to him by Shandell, Shandell's coaches, or other members of the team.

The odd item out, which had always puzzled him, was a book that Shandell had given him, A Morning at the Office. It was a thin paperback written by some Caribbean writer, a book Shandell had told Leon was one of his favorites. Leon had always told himself that one day he would read the book, and earlier that day he'd even thumbed through the pages, briefly fascinated by the stylized drawing of a typewriter on the front cover. He didn't expect the book or any of the rest of the junk piled high on the desktop to help him secure the $250,000 in insurance money that was rightfully his, but he wasn't about to discount anything that might end up being part of a road map to his money. So the book and everything else would stay.

Retrieving the book from the pile, he smiled and thought about the time he'd found three crisp new hundred-dollar bills tucked inside an old calendar that had been sitting on the kitchen countertop in a South Side Chicago home he'd robbed. But when he held A Morning at the Office up by the spine and gave it a shake to ruffle the pages, nothing fell out.

Still angry with himself for letting Aretha Bird's bartending friend from the Satire Lounge get the drop on him, he glanced back at the clock on the nightstand and realized it was 3 a.m. Time didn't matter, really. He wasn't planning to leave Denver until the insurance deal was settled. For the moment, he was flush. The thousand dollars Shandell had given him the day before he'd been murdered would hold him for a while. He could wait things out. He didn't like the idea of having to attend Shandell's funeral in what was now less than seven hours. That would be risky. But he'd put on his best grieving face and a dark suit of sadness and work at pretending the best he could.

Deciding he needed a nightcap and a breath of fresh air before calling it a night, he tossed *A Morning at the Office* back toward the desk. The book landed on a bed of old Las Vegas betting slips as he slipped an unopened bottle of Old Crow out of the nightstand drawer, uncapped it, and poured a finger of whiskey into a glass sticky with barbecue sauce.

As he rolled the liquor around in the glass, his cell phone rang. Surprised that anyone would be calling him at that hour and fuzzy-headed from too much Old Crow, he fumbled with the phone. Finally bringing the receiver up to his left ear, he slurred, "Hello."

The caller's voice sounded as if it were coming from inside a tunnel. "Leon?"

"Yeah."

Speaking directly into the wadded-up handkerchief covering the phone's mouthpiece, the caller said, "We need to talk."

"Who's this?"

"Someone with the answer to your problems."

"Asalon?"

The caller didn't answer.

"What the hell do you want? Jackie? Connie? Aretha? It better not be one of you."

"I'm outside. Below your balcony. Like I said, we need to talk."

"Yeah, yeah, sure." Leon steadied himself against the nightstand. "And I've got a direct pipeline to Jesus Christ." He pulled the nightstand drawer open, slipped out a long-barreled .38, and tucked the gun under his belt. "If you got somethin' to tell me that'll get me the money I'm owed, I'll hear you out. Otherwise, shove off."

"I do."

"Okay. Just hope you ain't up to nothin' funny, friend, 'cause I got somethin' here for you if you do."

"I'm not."

"Smart. Fuck with me and you'll regret it." Leon staggered over to the room's sliding glass doors, pulled back the drapes, and peered out into the moonlit darkness. "I don't see you," he said, wishing he'd enjoyed a little less Old Crow.

"You wanta know how to get your money or not?"

Concerned that he was being set up, Leon asked, "Why don't you just come on up to my room?"

"Afraid not. What's the matter, Leon, afraid?"

"Afraid my ass." Cautiously sliding the door open, Leon stepped out onto the second-floor balcony and into the glow of a full moon. In the distance he could hear the whine of jet engines. His motel, a dot in a hay meadow in the middle of unincorporated nowhere, was six miles from Denver International Airport.

Eyeing the moon and thinking about what $250,000 might buy—a new car, a quick trip to Vegas, cases full of whiskey—he slipped the .38 from his belt. "You out there?"

He was about to ask a second time when a shot rang out. The shot wasn't all that loud, or all that quiet, but at a little past 3 a.m., there was nobody around to hear it. The bullet that pierced Leon Bird's neck and severed his windpipe to ultimately lodge in his second cervical vertebra felled the forty-four-year-old bunco artist as quickly and as permanently as the bullet that had killed his son.

When his .38 thumped to the balcony floor, there was no one above or below him to hear it, and when he crashed face first onto the concrete, fracturing his lower jaw in the midline, no one came to help. Seconds after Leon's last breath, his killer stopped a pickup on an access road that led to Pena Boulevard, the main thoroughfare to Denver International Airport, to stash a set of night-vision goggles and a .30.06 with a night scope behind the seat. As the killer drove away, never looking back, the only sound penetrating the 3 a.m. silence was the high-pitched whine of a DC-10 cargo jet's engines.

The frightened-looking Guatemalan cleaning woman who had discovered Leon Bird's body at 7:30 a.m., lifeless, cold, and working its way toward rigidity, spoke almost no English. In the hour since she'd found Leon lying face down on the concrete balcony, his head in a congealing layer of blood, a haze common in the low-lying former hay meadow had engulfed the motel.

The lanky homicide detective who'd taken the woman's statement after finally calming her down had taped off the murder scene, called in a team of crime-scene technicians, and phoned his colleague and Police Activities League friend Detective Sergeant Will Townsend to inform him that, pending final confirmation, the father of the victim in the high-profile case he'd heard Townsend was working had been found shot to death on a motel balcony a few miles west of DIA.

Townsend, who'd just taken his initial sip of the second of his absolutely mandatory morning vanilla lattes at a trendy Cherry Creek Starbucks when the call had reached him, had arrived at the murder scene just as the distraught cleaning woman was being escorted away by a female officer.

"So what have you got for me here, Cookie?" Townsend asked, ducking beneath crime-scene tape that spanned the motel-room doorway and striding across the room to shake hands with Richard Cook, a twenty-year police force veteran.

"Not much more than I told you earlier. Except that we've had a pass at the victim's car. Illinois registration, no insurance papers, and an expired registration sticker. But he's your boy Blackbird's father, all right. I've got a whole shitpot full of photos, trinkets, and signed 'To Leon from Shandell' game programs sitting over there on the desk to prove it." Cook shook his head. "He was packing a .38 long-barrel. A lot of good it did him."

"Two Birds with clipped wings in a space of thirty-six hours. Looks like somebody's got it in for folks with that last name."

"Seems so."

"Any leads on the murder weapon?" Townsend eyed an all-but-empty Old Crow bottle on the nightstand.

"Are you serious? I've spent the last thirty minutes trying to keep a hysterical cleaning woman from popping a gasket. That'll teach me to learn Spanish."

"Did she see anything?"

"No. He'd probably been dead three or four hours when she found him. From the looks of it, he took a single round to the neck from a high-powered rifle. Entry wound says so anyway."

"Think it was from the same weapon that took out his son?"

"If I were a betting man, I'd lean that way," said Cook. "But the bullet's still stuck in him somewhere. Got no exit wound. The crime-scene boys say it's probably lodged in his spine."

Townsend nodded and scanned the room. "Nothing in the human anatomy stops a bullet like a good solid piece of bone."

"No question. Speaking of betting, got something to show you." He motioned for Townsend to follow him over to the room's desk.

Eyeing the desktop, Townsend said, "Looks like Bird the elder was a collector of things." He studied the assemblage of trinkets, key chains, scorecards, and programs.

"And he collected a lot more than souvenir bottle openers and scorecards. I counted up a dozen Vegas betting slips in that pile. Looks as if the senior Mr. Bird liked to gamble."

"Interesting fodder from my investigation. I spent almost an hour yesterday evening talking to a sawed-off Five Points blowhard named Theo Wilhite who swears that Blackbird was shaving points during games. A little later I had a talk with a friend of that reporter who bought it the same time as Shandell. The friend turned out to be a zonked-out, over-the-hill hippie named Wordell Epps. He's convinced there was point-shaving going on too."

"Think maybe Shandell was giving his old pappy a little inside dope? Telling him exactly when to spend his sports-pick dough?"

"More likely than not," said Townsend.

"But why pop the reporter too?"

"Could be Mr. Grimes was getting too close to the truth."

"Ties things up real nice and neat," said Cook. "Now all we've got to do is find ourselves a murderer."

"Or two," said Townsend. Stepping away from the desk, he extracted a couple of latex gloves from a box on the bed and slipped them on. "Mind if I sort through that stuff on the desk?"

"Be my guest. Looking for anything in particular?"

"No, just trolling." Townsend shoved several game programs aside before casually flipping through a stack of betting slips. "Run of the mill," he said, eyeing the collection of money clips and key chains. "What's the book doing here?" he asked, picking up the copy of *A Morning at the Office*.

"Beats me. I asked the same thing when I saw it."

"A book right here all by its lonesome among throwaway favors, trinkets, scorecards, and betting trash. I'd say it's out of its element."

"Could be Mr. Bird liked to read."

"Maybe." Townsend flipped through the book's pages. "But it's more likely that Shandell did," he said with a wry smile.

"How's that?"

"Take a look at the inside of the back cover. It's inscribed." Townsend handed the book over.

Shaking his head as he read the inscription, *To Leon from Shandell. Like I've told you . . . everyone likes to fit in,* Cook said, "Afraid I missed it."

"Easy to miss, an inscription on the back cover like that. In my experience, authors and gift-givers tend to sign their names in the front of a book."

"Think it has any meaning?"

"Who knows? But I'm thinking I should ask around about books and betting fathers and such. Turns out I've got the perfect place to start."

"Where's that?"

"At Shandell Bird's funeral an hour or so from now. You never know, I might learn something about your murder from the folks who show up."

"Are they expecting a big turnout?"

"More than likely. We're talking a celebrity death, you know."

"Funny, but I don't think old Leon here will end up getting the same kind of send-off."

"You're right about that." Townsend eyed the hodgepodge spread across the desktop. Placing *A Morning at the Office* back on the pile, he said with a shake of the head, "Never like to see things turn out like this. But sometimes, as they say, like father, like son."

Chapter 17

The bright 11 a.m. Mile High City sun could do little to mask the sadness of the graveside service or brighten the tiny plot of land that was now Shandell Bird's. Most of the lofty things that could be said about the twenty-two-year-old college basketball phenom had been said to an overflowing crowd of more than six hundred people back at Mount Gilead Baptist Church. The crowd had now dwindled by half.

Aretha Bird stood at the head of Shandell's casket, intermittently shivering as she shook the hands of departing mourners. Five of the six pallbearers, including Damion, his left arm still in a sling, Jackie Woodson, Coach Russ Haroldson, Jo Jo Lawson, and Shandell's sports agent, Colin McGee, remained next to the coffin, looking somber.

Connie Eastland and Dr. Alicia Phillips stood talking quietly to Rodney Sands at the foot of the coffin as Flora Jean stood several yards away, next to a towering sugar maple, arms behind her back, hands clasped together, talking to Niki and Mario Satoni and watching the crowd disperse. She was still disappointed in Damion for not telling her the truth the previous evening about the Five Points meeting he'd set up with Leotis Hawkins.

No one among those three groups of friends and family or in the throng of departing, teary-eyed mourners noticed that Sergeant Townsend was in their midst until Townsend appeared a few steps away from Aretha and said, "Mrs. Bird? I'd like to speak with you."

When several people looked at Damion rather than Aretha for some explanation as to why a skinny, gap-toothed white man was suddenly in their midst, Damion mouthed the word, "Cop."

"Sorry to have to show up right now," Townsend said, aiming his words at Aretha before he briefly locked eyes with each person flanking the coffin. "But I'm afraid it goes with the job. I'm certain you're not aware of it, but your former husband, Leon, was found shot to death earlier this morning."

Aretha's reaction was a nod. "Don't surprise me at all."

Before she could say anything else, Damion stepped up and draped an arm over her shoulders. The remaining pallbearers stared at Townsend, dumbfounded. Damion waved for Flora Jean, Niki, and Mario to join them. "You picked a bad time to do your job, Sergeant. In case you missed it, this is a funeral."

"Afraid I don't get to pick the perfect time or place to do my work, Madrid," answered Townsend, eyeing Damion's injured arm.

Slipping out of Damion's embrace and suddenly looking every bit as unintimidated as she had the previous night at the Satire Lounge, Aretha said, "No need to run interference for me, Damion. Worse comes to worst legal-wise, I can always get your mama to do that." She locked eyes with Townsend. "Wasn't no way Leon could ever come to anything but a bad end, Sergeant. But if you're thinkin' I had anything to do with him gettin' murdered, you're thinkin' wrong." She took a half step toward the casket as Flora Jean and Mario eased up beside her.

Realizing that he was now all but surrounded by nine people, including five husky pallbearers, Townsend said, "Is there somewhere we can talk that's a little more private, Mrs. Bird?"

"Nope. We're headed for a repast. You really need to talk to me, you can do it there."

"Can't it wait?" Flora Jean asked, staring down at the much shorter Townsend.

Aretha shook her head in protest. "No need puttin' bad off for worse, Flora Jean. For the next couple of hours, we're gonna be celebratin' my baby's life, Sergeant. Like I said, you can ask your questions there if you wanta. Unless of course you've got a reason to arrest me right now."

Eyeing Townsend with the kind of disdain she reserved for the worst kind of social misfits, Alicia Phillips said, "Aretha, are you sure you want him to come to the repast? Whether you want to admit it or not, you're more than a little fragile right now."

Aretha capped her response with a smile. "I'd have to agree with you, Doc. But you also gotta remember, I'm not one of them pampered jocks you counsel or some depressed kid who's just been told he's gonna have to ride the bench the rest of the season. No disrespect intended, but right now I don't need no head-shrinkin'." Slipping her arm into Damion's, Aretha eyed Townsend. "We're headed for the Five Points Recreation Center, Sergeant. You're welcome to come if you want."

Townsend glanced around at the nine sets of eyes glaring at him. Looking embarrassed, he said, "Lead the way."

As the two lead mortuary limousines filled with family members and close friends left Fairmont Cemetery, two cars lingered: the fifteen-year-old mud-brown Honda Civic with 165,000 miles on it, which Wordell Epps prized nearly as much as his Pulitzer, and a sleek, black, late-model Corvette belonging to Leotis Hawkins. Neither man knew or recognized the other as, slouched down in their front seats eight car lengths apart, each with his windows rolled up, they considered what it was they now needed to do about their problem.

Sweating and gripping the Honda's steering wheel, Epps, seasoned journalist that he was, reasoned that sooner or later he'd figure out the answer to his. Leotis Hawkins, his head still throbbing, expected that the .357 lying on the seat next to him would be his most important problem solving tool.

The Five Points Recreation Center was a boxy, drafty, echoing two-story brick building that had served as everything from a shelter for the homeless to a polling place, dance hall, and gymnasium during its forty-year lifetime. African art and scores of black-and-white photos depicting the history of Five Points adorned every first-floor wall. The repast for Shandell was being held in a giant room with sixteen-foot vaulted ceilings. The room was hot, muggy, thick with people, and rich with the smells of black folks' cooking. Half of the crowd had come to support Aretha and pay their respects, most of the others had come for the food, and a handful had simply wandered in.

Sergeant Townsend's presence curtailed Pinkie's and Mario Satoni's stay. They left with Styrofoam containers piled high with fried chicken, greens, cornbread, butter beans, and coleslaw. As they moved to leave, Mario pulled Flora Jean aside to let her know he had Pinkie covering Damion's overeager and very unschooled rear. Advising her not to be too hard on Damion for not telling her the truth about his rendezvous with Hawkins, he offered some advice. "Damion's new to the game, Flora Jean. And he's thinking that just like in college, through sheer force of will, he can move things his way and on his own. Hopefully that ten-inch-long knife wound running down his arm will remind him for the rest of his life that he probably can't."

With Pinkie trailing behind him, casting a final glance in Townsend's direction, Mario gave Flora Jean a parting reminder. "Now

that Pinkie's given us all the lowdown on Asalon's possible part in all this, we've got a leg up on the cops. But remember, you've got Damion helpin' you, not CJ. If you need backup, let me know." Winking at Flora Jean, Mario caught a glimpse of Townsend staring at him, as if trying his best to place the face, before he headed down the sidewalk to his car.

For thirty minutes after that, Townsend made his rounds, talking briefly to everyone he thought might be able to help him with his investigation into the Shandell Bird and Leon Bird killings. Now, as he sat at a long folding table that was draped in grease-stained, waxed butcher paper, staring at Damion, he had the sense that he was just a few questions away from leaving. Bookended by Alicia Phillips and Connie Eastland to his left and Flora Jean and Jackie Woodson to his right, Damion found himself nervously rubbing his wounded arm, thinking about Shandell, and eyeing Aretha who was seated across from him. Suddenly Townsend asked, "Are any of you familiar with that book I mentioned? The one Shandell signed for his father?"

Connie Eastland's response was a forceful "No." Everyone else either shook their head or shrugged.

"I see." Turning to Aretha, Townsend asked, "Was your ex-husban much of a gambler?"

"Afraid I don't know, Sergeant. Until last year we'd pretty mu lost contact with each other."

"What about Shandell? Did he gamble?"

"We went through all that when you came by my house ye day. I told you, my boy didn't gamble. Why you so intent on p a gamblin' monkey on my dead baby's back?"

"Yeah, why?" asked Damion.

Avoiding any mention of his conversation with Theo Wil

the fact that he'd found a dozen gambling slips in Leon Bird's motel room, Townsend said, "Point-shaving is in the air here, folks. No need pretending. I think we all know that."

"There wasn't any point-shaving going on on our team," Damion said, looking at Jackie for support.

"No way," Jackie chimed in.

"I'd have to agree, Sergeant," Alicia Phillips said indignantly. "The psychological makeup of the team wouldn't have allowed for that."

"Oh, I see," Townsend said sarcastically. "So I take it you've got a crystal ball that allows you to look deep inside people's heads, Dr. Phillips?"

Alicia Phillips's face turned pink with embarrassment as, gritting her teeth, she lowered her eyes to the table.

Realizing that he'd worn out his welcome, Townsend said, "We're not adversaries here. We all want the same thing—to find Shandell's and his father's killer."

"Or killers," said Flora Jean, eager to send Townsend on his way. "You've said your piece, Sergeant, and we've all sat here and listened. Time you take your show on the road."

"Are you threatening me, Ms. Benson?"

"Nope, just searching for that one drop of humanity I know you must have somewhere inside you."

Townsend stared at the sad, unforgiving faces at the table. Thinking to himself that there'd be other days, other times, and other places, he rose. "Okay. I'm leaving. But trust me, we'll talk some more." He slipped his BlackBerry out of his pocket, turned it on, and scrolled down the list of phone numbers he'd taken from the people seated around him. "I can reach you at 970-221-3795, right, Mr. Woodson? And Madrid, 303-722-9669?"

Looking nervous, Jackie Woodson nodded. Damion's response was a defiant stare.

"Like I said, we'll all be talking later." As he moved to leave, Townsend cast a final glance at Damion's injured arm. "Must be one nasty wound you're carrying around under that dressing, Madrid. Still intent on keeping what happened to yourself?"

"Sure am, Sergeant."

"Fine." Townsend broke into an all-knowing smile. "Sure hope your injury isn't tied to my case. Take heed, Madrid, especially since you're headed off to medical school. Doctors and hospitals keep records. If push comes to shove, I can find out about that arm."

Damion returned the smile as he recalled the very calm and collected Dr. Carlo Bottone. "I'm well aware of that, Sergeant, but I might be out of medical school by then," he said with a grin, knowing Townsend would never be able to determine how he'd gotten injured. "Have a nice rest of the day, and while you're at it, don't trip over the paperwork."

Chapter 18

Sergeant Townsend had been gone for close to half an hour, and the crowd at the repast had dwindled to a hardcore group of twenty people, when Jackie Woodson, feeling pressured by Damion's incessant questioning, looked defiantly at Damion and said, "I told you six ways from Sunday, Blood. I wasn't shavin' no points."

Rodney Sands, who had joined Damion and Jackie at the table when all the women save Niki had left to go to the bathroom, quickly came to Jackie's defense. "There wasn't any point-shavin' goin' on, Damion. Lighten up."

"Yeah, just like you said there wasn't any drug dealing going on, Sandy." Damion glanced briefly at Niki, trying to gauge how long she'd indulge his CJ Floyd impersonation, then fixed his gaze back on Jackie and Sandy. "One of you primed Leotis Hawkins to take me out last night. Who's feeling confessional?"

"Wasn't me," said Sands. "All I did was set up the meeting." He eyed Damion's injured arm. "Besides, I warned you that Hawkins was into knives."

"Me either," said Jackie.

"So a little birdie did it, then." With mounting frustration evident in his voice, Damion said, "No matter. I'll find out, and then we'll talk. And so you both appreciate the gravity of the situation, I'll bring along somebody from Mario Satoni's shop with me when we do." He glanced at Niki for her reaction to his threat. The look on her face told him he'd pushed things to the limit. Sensing that she was right, Damion asked, "Either of you know anything about that book, A Morning at the Office, that Townsend claimed he found Shandell's signature in?"

"Never heard of it," Sandy and Jackie said a half beat apart.

"It's a book about a group of office workers in Trinidad and what their daily lives are like, as I recall," Niki said, surprising all three men.

"You've read it?" asked Damion.

"Yes. In high school. I'm originally from Venezuela, in case you've forgotten." She flashed him a quick wink. "The Caribbean's not that far away."

"So why didn't you tell Townsend you'd read the book when he asked?"

"Because that's not what he asked. What he asked was whether any of us was familiar with the book he'd found." Niki smiled. "I wasn't. I'd never seen that particular book before."

Damion burst into laughter. "If I didn't know better, I'd swear you've been taking witness-coaching lessons from my mother."

"I haven't. But don't forget I've got family members who are lawyers too."

Aware that Niki's father and older brother were attorneys in Venezuela, Damion said, "Touché. Looks like I've got some reading to do in addition to looking at game film."

"I told you, you won't find nothin' in those films, Blood," Jackie said, slapping his palm down on the table to hammer home the point.

"Maybe not, but since you and Sandy insist there wasn't any point-shaving going on, I thought I'd have a look just to make sure. Especially since I've never looked at those tapes with the idea of point-shaving in mind."

"I told you, I wasn't shavin' nothin'," Jackie said defensively.

"And I heard you. But you never know. Maybe somebody else was."

"Besides Shandell, you mean?" Sandy asked with surprise.

Jackie locked eyes with Damion and said, "Yeah. Who's to say it wasn't you who was shavin' points, Blood? Could be you're the one who got Blackbird killed, and you're tryin' to point fingers to cover your tracks."

Damion scooted over to Jackie and draped an arm over his former teammate's shoulders. "Just be certain when all's said and done that my finger isn't pointing at you." Glancing at Sandy, he smiled and said, "Ditto," just as Alicia Phillips and Connie Eastland walked back up to the table.

"Real chummy there, aren't we?" asked Connie. "What did we miss?"

"Not much. Just reminiscing." Damion moved away from Jackie and turned his attention to Alicia. "Have you had time to think about what I asked you on the limo ride from the cemetery?"

"I've thought about it. But I'm not sure I can share some things with you. Most of it is privileged, and I'm afraid neither the university nor the state board of clinical psychologists would look very favorably on my discussing Shandell's case notes with you."

"But Shandell's dead."

"That doesn't matter. There are rules. What I can tell you is that Shandell had his share of problems last year."

"Problems related to what?"

Alicia took a deep breath and sighed. "Most of the issues I helped him with centered around his relationship with his father. That's all I can tell you."

"Why on earth did he let Leon slip back into his life in the first place?"

"I can't answer that. I can tell you, however, that he and his father were trying to work things out."

Damion glanced up at Connie, who stood next to Alicia, nervously rocking from side to side. "Did Shandell say anything to you about the problems he was having with his father?"

"Not really. But I knew Leon was stringing him along, trying to make him feel as if Shandell was in part responsible for their estrangement."

Damion lowered his eyes and shook his head. Once again he had the feeling that everyone had known more about what had made his best friend tick than he had. It was almost as if Shandell had purposely tried to keep him as far away as possible from any dark side he may have had, and from his problems. Problems that had apparently involved not only point-shaving and drug dealing but an estranged, conniving father. Somehow he had the feeling that even those weighty issues represented less than the whole story. There had to be something else, something so overwhelming that it had cost a father and son their lives.

Feeling dejected, Damion had the sense that for the first time in his life, he had no one to lean on. CJ was in Hawaii enjoying a honeymoon that should have come twenty years earlier. His mother was in San Francisco at a national trial lawyers' convention, and Flora Jean, the person he should have been counting on the most, was still upset with him.

Warding off the sudden feeling of self-pity, he glanced at the people around him and realized that they'd all lost something too. Connie had lost her lover. Jock-sniffing Rodney Sands had lost his opportunity to rub shoulders with celebrity and fame. Jackie Woodson would more than likely lose his scholarship and a spot on the team once all the issues surrounding performance-enhancing drug use surfaced, and Dr. Phillips, who'd likely missed the mark with Shandell and underestimated the gravity of his personal problems, stood to have her reputation tarnished. In the end, nobody could possibly come out a winner.

Sensing that Damion was as confused as he was hurting, Niki took his hand and squeezed it. "I think it's time we go," she said, watching a member of the catering crew remove the butcher paper from the next table.

"Think you're right," Damion said softly.

"I'm headed home too," said Connie. "You and Damion are welcome to come by if you like."

"No, thanks," said Niki. "Think we'll just rest."

"I'm headed back up to CSU," Dr. Phillips said, patting the despondent-looking Damion reassuringly on the shoulder. "If you need me, Damion, don't hesitate to give me a call."

"I will," Damion said as Jackie and Sandy stood, tapped fists all around, and offered their good-byes.

"Take care of that arm," Sandy said, walking away, leaving Damion and Niki staring pensively at one another.

"What now, my love?" asked Niki, hoping the question might help get Damion back on track.

"Don't know, babe. Right now I'm running on fumes."

"I've got a suggestion. What say we head up to the cabin? It'll be peaceful up there."

Damion flashed Niki a guilt-ridden smile. In compiling his list of people who had something to lose because of Shandell's death, he'd somehow excluded her, completely overlooking the woman who'd first convinced him, a bookish, basketball-crazed kid from Five Points, that there was a world beyond his neighborhood. In an attempt to suppress his grief and prove to himself with some silly list that he was on top of things, he'd discounted the person who was his rock. Suddenly he found himself thinking about something CJ had said to him a few days before he and Mavis had left for Hawaii. "Hang on to Niki for dear life, Blood. Nothing trumps the love of a good woman—trust me." Realizing that he hadn't responded to Niki's question about going up to the mountain cabin in Nederland that her uncle, a University of Colorado engineering professor, used as a retreat, he said, "I'm game, but you better call your uncle and see if he's using the place."

"No need. He's in Barcelona on sabbatical until the first of the year, and I've got the keys."

Damion forced a smile, recalling the three days that he and Niki had spent at the cabin the previous Thanksgiving. Their time there had been perfect save for the fact that at the last minute Connie and Shandell had begged off joining them. "I'll get some wine," Damion said with a reluctant smile.

"You're thinking my kind of thoughts." Pleased that she'd forced a brief smile out of Damion, Niki said, "I'll have to run by my place and get some things." Looking up, she watched a very solemn-looking Aretha Bird approach the table.

"Yeah, so will I." Damion scooted down the bench to make room for Aretha.

"We got through it," said Aretha, tearing up. "Did my baby proud. I'm headin' out of here pretty quick. You two are welcome to come by the house if you want. Flora Jean's comin' by."

"Thanks, but we're going up to Nederland for the night," said Niki. "Unless you need us to spend the night with you."

"No, no. Go on up to Nederland. Should be nice and peaceful up there in the pines. Flora Jean's gonna stay with me this evenin'. And just for the record, Damion, she's a little disappointed in you for not tellin' her about that face-off I understand you had last night over at the light-rail station in Five Points."

"I know."

"Well, don't you be holdin' out on her or me no more. You got me?" The way Aretha said, *You got me?* reminded Damion of the hundreds of times she'd said the same thing to Shandell and him when one or both of them were failing to toe the line as teenagers.

"I've got you."

"Good," Aretha said, forcing back tears.

Hugging Aretha tightly, Damion said, "I know it's hard, Mrs. B."

"And I'm afraid it's gonna be hard the rest of my life, baby." Wiping away tears, Aretha eyed Niki. "Don't let this boy get away, Ms. Universe," she said, calling the statuesque, dark-haired Venezuelan by the nickname she'd given her at their first meeting four years earlier. "Trust me, won't never be nothin' out there better."

"I'm hanging on for dear life, Mrs. B."

"Okay. So now that we've settled that, I'm thinkin' I need to clear up a little somethin' else. We may have booted that Sergeant Townsend outta here real quick-like today, but he'll have reason to come back—no question."

"Why?" asked Damion, looking puzzled.

"'Cause sooner or later he's gonna find out that Leon was the beneficiary of a two hundred and fifty thousand dollar life insurance policy Shandell had on hisself."

From the way Aretha uttered the words *sooner or later,* as if doomsday were somehow imminent, Damion had the feeling she'd left something unsaid. "I'm taking it there's more, Mrs. B."

"'Fraid there is. Turns out I'm the secondary beneficiary, and Coach Horse is the third." Aretha shook her head. "Makes a good motive for murder, don't it?"

"It could. But since you and Coach Horse didn't kill Leon, it doesn't matter."

"I know that, but since the cops and the law can sometimes twist things around to their likin', I figured I should tell you."

"It's good you did because I know someone who's pretty good at massaging the judicial system too. Think it's time I gave her a call."

"You sure?"

"Yes," said Damion, thinking about how long a telephone call it was going to take to bring his mother, Julie, up to speed.

Looking up to see Jo Jo Lawson strolling across the room toward them, Aretha said, "Appreciate it. Just don't bother your momma too much on my account. Where you been, Jo Jo?" Aretha asked as Jo Jo took a seat and slapped hands with Damion.

"Out walkin'. Tryin' to clear my head."

"Did you get enough to eat?" asked Aretha.

"'Fraid I never got around to it."

"Come on with me and I'll get the caterers to make you up somethin' to take home." Waving for Damion and Niki to leave, Aretha said, "You and Niki go on, get on outta here."

"Are you sure, Mrs. B?"

"Yeah. Now, the two of you scoot. And call me after you talk to your mama."

"Will do," said Damion, watching Aretha and Jo Jo head toward the kitchen.

"Think she'll be all right?" Niki asked.

"In the short run, yes, but she's going to need our support."

"I'm here to help."

"I know you are." Damion kissed Niki on the cheek. "Ready to head out of here?"

"Yes."

"Okay. I'll drop you at home and pick you back up in an hour."

"Why so long?"

"Got an errand to run."

"Mind letting me in on it?"

"You'll see once we get to the cabin." Damion draped an arm over Niki's shoulders and headed for the exit.

"Is it that big of a secret?"

"No. In fact, it involves something you've seen before."

"Is it bigger than a breadbox?" Niki asked, smiling broadly as she quoted the classic line from the 1950s American TV classic *What's My Line?* It was a line she used on Damion whenever she felt the need to poke fun at American tastes and habits.

Smiling back, Damion said, "Believe it or not, my leggy Venezuelan sexpot, the damn thing is a perfect breadbox size."

The forty-six-mile trip from Denver through Boulder Canyon, gateway to Nederland and Colorado's majestic northern Rockies, was punctuated by Damion and Niki's unusual silence. It was a trip Damion had first taken a dozen years earlier when CJ Floyd, cruising along with the top down on his '57 Bel Air convertible, had taken him on his first fly-fishing excursion.

As they started up the canyon and he turned on the Jeep's radio, Niki hoped Damion was primed to shed a layer of sadness. Ten miles up the canyon, Damion nosed his Jeep into a stretch of highway that cut a swath through a nearly sunless, half-mile-long fern and aspen glade. Tapping him playfully on the shoulder and watching the Jeep's shadow follow one of the canyon walls, Niki asked, "Have you ever really seen a breadbox, Señor?"

"As a matter of fact, I have," said Damion, knowing the question was meant to comfort him. "At Mario's once. At least, I think it was a breadbox. Hard to tell. Mario had the thing stuffed full of antique clay pot miniatures."

Just over a year earlier, Damion had helped Mario and CJ organize and catalog the inventory that made up the virtual antique store that Mario, with CJ's help when he wasn't busy writing bail bonds, operated out of Mario's basement.

Niki said, "I still don't think you have. Otherwise you'd know that most breadboxes are quite a bit taller than that VCR you brought along."

"And I'd know they can't play tapes of last year's NCAA tournament games," said Damion, who had gathered a half-dozen CSU game tapes he had at home, packed them into a cardboard box along with a VCR and the hundred-year-old Colt Peacemaker that CJ had given him as a college graduation present, and slipped everything into the back of the Jeep. "I should've looked at the game tapes before I ran all half-cocked up to CSU the other day."

"No need to beat yourself up. You had no idea there might have been point-shaving going on."

"No, but I knew Theo Wilhite had been spouting off about that championship game being rigged for months. I should've suspected something. If I had, it might have saved Shandell."

Sensing that any steps that Damion might take toward conquering his sorrow could only be impeded by further debate, Niki said, "I brought something along for you to have a look at too." She reached into the leather purse between her feet. "I dropped by the Hermitage Bookshop while you were digging up your breadbox." Smiling, she extracted a well-used paperback copy of *A Morning at the Office* and placed it on the console between them. "It's the only copy they had. It's long out of print and difficult to find. Set me back a whole twenty bucks."

Damion eyed the stylized image of a typewriter on the book's front cover and below it the author's name, Edgar Mittelhölzer. Surprising Niki and ignoring the fact that he still had limited use of his left arm, he picked the book up and opened it to a middle page with his right hand.

"Get your hand back on the wheel, Damion Madrid!"

"Sorry. Just found myself wondering how heavy a book that could lead us to a killer might be."

"No heavier than a breadbox," Niki said, hoping the breadbox reference might assuage Damion's sorrow. Instead of a laugh or a smile, the look on Damion's face turned pensive. Tightening his grip on the wheel and heading into a new set of curves, he simply said, "Yeah."

Leotis Hawkins's Corvette handled the hairpin curves of Boulder Canyon with far greater ease than Damion's Jeep—so effortlessly, in fact, that it was all he could do to keep from running up the Jeep's rear. To keep from being seen on the trip from Denver to Boulder, he'd squeezed between a moving van and a half-empty car transport. There were no such oversized vehicles to hide behind on the trip up the canyon, so he'd been forced to use the curves of the road for cover.

The hint of a headache surfaced each time the canyon opened up to let in a canopy of sunlight, reminding him that he had a concussion. Eyeing the monogrammed towel that covered the box of ammo on the seat next to him, a towel he'd pilfered from a Four Seasons hotel in Los Angeles, he smiled and began to hum. Drumming his fingers on the steering wheel, he interrupted his humming and slipped a compact disc into the car's CD player. Seconds later Smokey Robinson's melodic falsetto voice oozed the initial words to the 1960s Motown classic "What's So Good About Goodbye." Tapping one foot, Hawkins sang along with Smokey. Halfway through the song, he reached over and pushed the stereo's mute button. With his thumb cocked and index finger aimed six-gun style at the back of Damion's SUV, he crooned the now silent Smokey Robinson's words: "All it does is make you cry."

Chapter 19

The smell of freshly baked donuts and French-roast coffee filled the LaMar's Donuts shop that had long anchored a small strip mall at the busy intersection of Kalamath Street and Sixth Avenue. Wordell Epps had picked the sparsely furnished donut shop for his meeting with Connie Eastland after they'd talked by cell phone following the Shandell Bird repast because, sweet-tooth fanatic that he was, he had a genuine weakness for the Kansas City–based chain's glazed donuts.

The droopy-eyed woman who'd brought Connie and Epps their coffee and donut orders had quickly disappeared into the back of the shop to check on her freshly baked inventory, leaving her only two patrons staring stand-off style across a Formica-topped, 1950s-era malt-shop table at one another.

Biting into the second of the three glazed donuts he'd ordered, Epps smiled, set the pastry aside, and licked his three middle fingers. "Now, these are donuts."

"Are we here on business or to tape a commercial?" Connie asked, sipping lukewarm coffee.

"Both, I'm afraid, my dear Ms. Eastland." Epps took another bite and rubbed his belly. "To market, to market, to buy a fat pig, home again, home again, jiggety jig." The smile on his face disappeared as he wiped a thin line of sugar from one corner of his mouth. "I know who you are, Ms. Eastland—know how hard you planned—know where you so desperately wanted to go. But your ticket to ride got himself killed. Who knows? Maybe even by you. And now, my dear, you're on your own. As we both know, in the fractured world we live in, no tickie, no laundry." Epps burst into laughter.

"You're a brain-dead pothead freak, Epps!"

"You know, you might be right. But I'm still alive and kicking. That's more than we can say for your late boyfriend, or sadly for my friend Paulie Grimes. And what's inside my freaky head keeps telling me that either you or that prissy professor you were following around like a puppy dog at your dead sugar daddy's graveside ceremony have inside info on what I understand from the news are now three mur-ders. I was in the crowd at the church and at the cemetery, Ms. East-land. I saw you act. Isn't it fantastic how crowds can run interference for you when you don't want to be seen?"

"I don't know what you're talking about."

"Strange. Dr. Phillips gave me pretty much the same song and dance when I talked to her yesterday. But I suspect the two of you have probably already commiserated about that visit. Could be that's the reason you're here, in fact. You're running the traps for Dr. Egghead."

"We haven't commiserated about anything, jerk. I only agreed to meet you because you threatened me."

"Now, how could that be? I simply informed you in a very brief phone call, on what can only be described as one of the saddest days in Colorado sports history, that you could talk to me about the book I understand Dr. Phillips is writing, or you could talk to the cops. How on earth could that be perceived as a threat?"

"I'm not aware that Dr. Phillips is writing a book."

The muscles around Epps's eyes tightened as he squinted in anger and chomped off another piece of donut. "Stonewall all you want, Ms. Eastland, but know this. I investigate things for a living, and trust me, I've worked my way to the bottom of things a lot more convoluted than the mess we have here."

"Then I'd suggest you start your dirt-digging with someone other than me."

Deciding to shift gears, Epps stroked his chin thoughtfully. "Do you know anything about Shandell either using or selling performance-enhancing drugs?"

"No."

"Know anything about him shaving points during games or about him using a bookie named Garrett Asalon to bet on games for him?" Epps leaned back in his seat, pleased that he'd tossed Asalon's name onto the table. "Like I said, Ms. Eastland, I've done some digging."

"No."

"I think you're lying."

Trying her best to remain calm in spite of the fact that her knees were shaking, Connie took a long sip of coffee, smiled, and stood. "Good-bye, Mr. Epps. I hope you drop dead." Giving him the finger, she turned and walked briskly toward the door.

"Run, little chicken. Run, run, run," Epps called after her as their server reappeared from the back. Puzzled by Connie's hasty exit and Epps's loud voice, the woman asked, "Is there a problem, Señor?"

"Oh, no. No problem. As it turns out, the lady prefers Krispy Kremes." Epps broke into a snicker that quickly escalated to a booming laugh.

Alicia Phillips's second-floor office in the Wilford Hall annex building on the CSU campus was the only room in the stately hundred-year-old brick building showing any sign of activity. The full-professor types, who occupied the other six large offices in the tree-shaded landmark a block west of College Avenue, had been gone for hours.

To be assigned space in Wilford Hall, a professor had to be at the top of his or her discipline. The anthropologist across the hall, one door down from Phillips, a leading expert on genetic-induced differences in bone-density scans of the world's various ethnic groups, had received a MacArthur Genius Grant two years earlier. The office next to her housed a young geography professor who was executive director of the Frontier Centre for Public Policy, a think tank funded by ecology-minded oil interests, and two doors down was the office of the archaeologist who'd developed the gold standard for post-sand-sediment aging.

Phillips liked to joke that she'd never fully understood why an obscure sports psychologist like her was housed among the university's academic elite. In truth, she did understand why. She too was an academic gem, and like her Wilford Hall colleagues, she was inventive, entrepreneurial, well respected, and blessed with an international reputation in her discipline. During a career that had spanned two decades, she'd been awarded millions of dollars in research funding from the National Institute of Mental Health as well as funds from private foundations to support her investigation of the psychological parameters that affected the attitude, perceptions, and behaviors of athletes involved in modern-day college sports. Her current research included studies designed to calibrate the influence of absent fathers on the performance of elite male and female athletes, with the secondary goal of defining the psychological factors that foster teamwork among athletes.

At that moment, however, as she stood a few feet from Connie

Eastland in the lengthening six o'clock shadows of her office, Alicia Phillips wasn't interested in coming up with answers for research objectives, trying to fit in with the eclectic mix of professors who shared her building, or even something as routine as reading through the stack of term papers that sat on a nearby table. What she and Connie, who was busy feeding papers into a shredder, were interested in was erasing a paper trail that could link them to a murder.

"The damn thing's jammed again," Connie called out in frustration, struggling to extract a half-inch-thick wedge of paper from the shredder.

"Well, unjam it."

Connie flashed Phillips a look that said, *Screw you, bitch.* It was a look that Phillips had seen a half-dozen times in the hour since Connie had arrived from Denver in a state of near hysteria. Smiling calmly, Phillips said, "I know you'd love to smother me if you could right now. But you can't. It's bad form to kill one's mentor."

"Save the psychobabble for another time, Alicia. In case you've forgotten, unlike the rest of your charges, I never played sports. Mentors don't mean a damn thing to me."

"Oh, I'm aware of that—except of course for the bedroom kind."

Gritting her teeth, Connie yanked the papers from the mouth of the shredder, clearing the jam. "You're a witch. A vile, uncaring, egotistical witch. I should've steered clear of you from day one."

"But you didn't, sweetie. You like the smell of money too much. You reap what you sow in this world, your highness. From now on, you should try to remember that."

"Insightful words, and from the ultimate manipulative money grubber. Come now, Alicia."

"Well, if I am, I'd suggest that from now on you follow my example to a T. That is, if you don't want that cop who's working Shandell's murder case breathing fire after you."

"That man has a name," Connie said, noting how adept Alicia was at either forgetting or ignoring the names of people she deemed unimportant. "Have you forgotten it?"

"It's slipped my mind, I'm afraid."

"Of course it has. And has Wordell Epps's name slipped your mind too?" Connie asked, wondering how Alicia planned to deal with the man who'd sent her scurrying up to Fort Collins in fear.

"On the contrary, I've been thinking about him ever since you burst in here demanding that I help shake him off your leg," Alicia said, failing to mention that she and Epps had talked twice since he'd ambushed her at her health club the previous day.

"And your solution is?"

"I'll have one before you leave."

"Good, because Epps has me scared." Connie picked up another sheaf of papers and began feeding pages into the shredder.

"You scare too easily, darling. Epps will be no problem. No problem at all."

Connie glanced at the woman who'd first introduced her to the world of superjock sports, a world ripe with money, power, out-of-control egos, and prestige. And a world filled with liars, cheaters, sex, and drugs. She realized now that in terms of their sensibilities, upbringing, cunning, and intellect, she and Alicia were miles apart. She should have known that someone who'd come from the primitive, raw, ranching world of eastern Montana, someone who talked with pleasure about stalking and trapping wolves and shooting them as they tried to wriggle free, a person who laughed about putting a bullet in the head of a lame horse, would have no trouble dealing with someone like Epps. "So I should forget about Epps, then?"

"Yes. Just like you should forget about the papers we're shredding and the money you've earned."

"And what do you plan to forget about, Alicia?"

Phillips tapped the papers she was holding together on the desktop. "I plan to forget about being someone I never intended to be. To forget about having to nuzzle up to lamebrain athletes, lecherous coaches, blind-eyed athletic directors, and provosts and presidents with half my brain. But most of all, I hope to forget about losing an opportunity that will probably never come around again."

"We never should've picked Shandell."

"And Lincoln never should have gone to the play. Life's a learning process, Constance. The key is to never let the same bad things happen to you again. It's the code I live by."

"So since I shouldn't worry about Sergeant Townsend or Wordell Epps, what about Damion Madrid?"

"Now, him I'd be concerned about. In fact, you just shredded half-a-dozen sheets of paper profiling his type. Maybe I should've had you read those pages. In the end, Epps, and even Townsend, will probably simply go away. Damion Madrid won't. Epps's mission is fueled by self-important vengeance and the glimmer of a career that's long since passed. Townsend is just a flatfoot doing his job. Unfortunately for us, Damion's quest is fueled by a mix of principle, grief, guilt, and the genuine need for the answer to who murdered his friend. And that makes him dangerous."

"So how do you expect to rein him in?"

"I'm not certain, but I will."

"Think we might need Asalon?"

"Maybe. But again, that's not really my territory, is it?" An unmistakable look of jealousy spread across Alicia's face.

Connie frowned, looking as if she needed to spit out a bad taste.

"Why the frown, Constance? I only speak the truth." Alicia's tone was mocking. "Asalon's partial to your kind. Large-breasted, tight-waisted, conniving, and above all submissive, especially when he needs them to be. And fortunately, he'll eat out of your hand. I think maybe you should call him, wet your lips, and purr."

"He makes my skin crawl."

"But we need him, dearie. So right now, if I were you, I'd get into a better frame of mind. Call the man and let him sniff it. He'll fall in line. And when he's all hardened up and champing at the bit, remind him that we need a little help with our problem."

"You think he'll listen?"

Alicia fed the remaining sheets of paper in her hand into the shredder. "Of course he will. You're his prime cut of meat. His succulent, thoroughly educated, girl-next-door piece of ass."

Connie called Asalon an hour later at his Boulder home, fully expecting that he'd have gotten there by 6:30 to take his customary two-hour break from the office before he returned to tally the day's receipts. Craigy Theisman answered, and, knowing that to get through to Asalon she had to kiss up to Craigy, she spent a few moments making nice to a man she expected had used and sold heroin and very likely killed people. Asalon ultimately came on the line, sounding eager and virtually cooing into the phone. "So how goes it, beautiful?"

"Not as good as it could be."

"Well, how about telling Daddy what's the matter?"

"Alicia's concerned about this Shandell Bird thing, and so am I. She thought I should give you a call."

"Why all the uneasiness, sweetness? My sources tell me they buried everybody's Mr. All-American this very day."

"Burying him won't stop the murder investigation. Alicia and I spent a good part of the late afternoon purging files, and in case you haven't heard, to make matters worse, Shandell's father was killed this morning."

"As a matter of fact, I did hear. Shame." Asalon drew a deep breath as if he expected somehow to be able to inhale Connie's perfume. "So what can I help you with?"

"I'm worried that Shandell's teammate Damion Madrid and some washed-out hippie who was a friend of that reporter who was killed are going to cause problems for us."

"Wordell Epps, you mean?"

Surprised that Asalon knew Epps by name, Connie said, "Yes."

"Epps has already dropped by. Yesterday, in fact. Quirky little man. He's merely trying to connect dots that can't be connected. I wouldn't worry that beautiful little head of yours over him."

"He scares me, Garrett." Connie's response came out in a near whine.

"Let me handle Epps and Madrid." Asalon eyed Theisman, who stood a couple of feet away looking eager to serve. "Any other problems?"

Connie thought hard before answering. "None other than the fact that although she hides it well, Alicia is close to panic mode over the possibility of losing her reputation and maybe her job because of this Blackbird thing."

"Maybe the good professor should've looked before she leaped."

Recalling Alicia's caustic similar advice to her, Connie said, "She's a country girl from Montana, Garrett. I don't think she was ever really ready for your kind of prime time."

"And you're just a schoolgirl. A schoolgirl with the kind of hidden talents it takes to launch a man's dreams. I want you to come up here to Boulder tonight."

"I can't."

"Sure you can. I'll send Craigy for you."

"I said I can't."

Asalon sounded peeved. "Remember what I've told you about denying me before? You don't want to do that."

Knowing that Asalon always meant what he said, Connie, who'd been sitting on the edge of her bed dressed only in panties and a bra, exhaled slowly and stood. Her response was a weak "Okay."

"Be ready in an hour, and bring your box of sex toys with you. . . . Did you hear me, sweetness?" Asalon asked when she didn't immediately answer.

"Yes."

"Good. Because I need a good fuck. The kind I would expect to get from an NBA superstar's woman," Asalon said sarcastically, cradling the phone.

Feeling sorry for herself, Connie walked across her bedroom and stepped into the massive walk-in closet. That closet had been the principal reason she'd leased the condo. It was a closet that she'd expected to fill with clothes—a superstar's woman's clothes. She and Shandell had even talked about how, after he began playing pro ball, she'd have the perfect outfit in which to be seen with him morning, noon, and night. Now that possibility was gone. She wasn't even certain how she'd pay the next month's rent. Her salary at the PR firm she'd been working at for less than two months certainly wouldn't cover it, and she couldn't ask Asalon for the money, although he'd offered. That would make her a common whore.

Glancing at herself in the closet's door-mounted, full-length mirror, she shook her head and muttered, "Hell," as she thought how inexplicably naive she'd been to let Alicia Phillips talk her into latching on to Shandell. It had been Alicia who'd convinced her to relax, set aside her inhibitions, and have the courage to do "a black thing." Alicia who'd conned her into thinking it would be healthy for her "suburban white-bread" psyche. And Alicia who'd urged her to hang in there with the game plan when Shandell had become so paranoid and fearful of things crashing down on him that he'd talked about killing himself. Alicia was the one whose pants got wet whenever she set foot near a black man, the one who'd had affairs with black athletes during truncated stints at two other universities, and the one the CSU administration had had to warn about purported unhealthy relationships with student athletes.

Studying her reflection in the mirror, Connie shook her head. She'd let her beauty and her body do the talking for her for most of her life, and what had it gotten her? A life that was now lost, an unwanted affair with a mobster who very likely had had a hand in killing at least one and maybe even two men, alienation from her family, and a boatload of guilt. *Nowhere to run, nowhere to hide,* she thought as she turned to search for something to wear that would please Asalon. As always, she knew it would be painful to acquiesce to him, but in the end she had to look out for herself.

Chapter 20

The fire Niki had started in the massive river-rock fireplace in the great room of her uncle's mountain cabin was largely uncalled for, given outside temperatures in the mid-40s. Nonetheless, a fire was part of the ritual she and Damion enjoyed whenever they visited the cabin, and since it had been a chilly 57 degrees inside when they'd arrived following a brief detour to nearby Brainard Lake, a fire was roaring.

Niki thought the side trip to the nearby mountain lake, where Damion and Shandell had honed their fly-fishing skills under the tutelage of CJ Floyd and his friend Billy DeLong, a legendary Wyoming cowboy, had seemed to temporarily soothe Damion's spirit and quiet his grief.

Barefoot, down on one knee, and dressed in form-fitting jeans and one of Damion's faded CSU athletic department sweatshirts, Niki stabbed at the fire with an antique poker that her uncle had brought with him from Nicaragua twenty years earlier. Spikes of flame rose from a bank of four aromatic piñon logs as Damion, shoeless, dressed in sweatpants and a ratty-looking wool sweater, and seated on a foot-stool a few feet from Niki, eyed the leggy woman in front of him and wondered how on earth he'd been the one to capture her heart. Rubbing his injured arm, he tapped Niki's thigh with his foot. "Ever thought life is preordained?" he asked as Niki scooted over to him and began massaging the foot.

"No."

"Not even a little?"

"Not even."

"Then you subscribe to the theory that shit just happens?"

"No. Generally we make shit happen."

"Do you think Shandell was responsible for what happened to him?"

"To answer you honestly, I think he has to bear some of the responsibility."

"Why?"

Niki shook her head. "Sometimes I think you were purposely blind to Shandell's idiosyncrasies, and vice versa. His standoffishness, his absolute love affair with secrecy, his inability to blend in. It's as if the two of you were trying your best to play Butch Cassidy and the Sundance Kid—Blood and Blackbird against the rest of the evil world, and loving every moment of it."

"Could be," Damion said matter-of-factly. "So what's your take on whether Shandell was actually shaving points and selling drugs?"

"It hasn't changed since the last time you asked me, Damion. I think there's a good chance he was."

"Okay, okay." There was agitated disbelief in Damion's response. "Let's say he was. Why? There had to be a reason, and it couldn't have been the money."

"That's where I think you're wrong. Just because money isn't the holy grail that motivates you, don't think for one second that it isn't a motivator for others."

"But Shandell was worth millions."

"He wasn't worth millions while the two of you played for CSU. Take off your rose-colored glasses, Damion. How many times did Shandell borrow money from you while we were in school?"

"So you think being poor is what set him up?"

"You're putting words in my mouth, but to answer your question, I think there were lots of things that would have made Shandell vulnerable to the performance-enhancing-drug peddlers and game fixers of the world. His shyness, his dependence on you, his ever-present need to prove himself. It's almost as if, his quirkiness and basketball skills aside, he needed to prove that he was just like everyone else. Didn't you find it strange that someone who couldn't afford a pizza our junior year was buying Connie diamond bracelets the next?"

"Could be some NBA scout helped him out with a loan."

"Damion, please. You know Coach Horse wouldn't have allowed that."

"Yeah." Damion looked disappointed as Niki placed his foot back on the floor. "Any more comets falling from the sky you think I missed when it came to Shandell?"

"Not really. Except that Connie claimed that he wasn't very affectionate. She never elaborated on it, at least not to me."

"Talk about kicking a man when he's down."

"Maybe, but you have to admit that Shandell was a little bit quirky when it came to women. Running through half the girls in the freshman class our first year, pretty much swearing off them altogether the next, and then after our third year settling in with Connie like some suburban insurance salesman with a mortgage, a dog, two kids, and a station wagon."

"It's a little strange, I have to admit. But no stranger than in high school. I don't think that during the first three years he ever had a date. Then our senior year, it was wall-to-wall women." Damion leaned over, kissed Niki softly on the cheek, and teased a hand beneath her sweatshirt. "But what do you expect? It's hard to find Ms. Perfect."

Niki slapped his hand playfully before planting it firmly on his right thigh. "No you don't, Damion Madrid. We're going to air this out once and for all. You're not going to wake me up at three in the morning wanting to talk about Shandell's murder."

Pouting, Damion asked, "Think I should have a talk with Connie, then?"

"I would."

"And I should probably talk to Dr. Phillips too," he added, watching Niki nod in agreement. "When I think back on it, Shandell was in and out of her office a hell of a lot during our NCAA run, and I'm certain that most of their talks dealt with the fact that his father had appeared on the scene out of nowhere. No question, Leon made him uncomfortable. Shandell told me so more than once. Claimed Leon was the kind of person who'd turn on him in a second if it meant a possible payday. Strange that I never met the man face to face until a couple of days ago. I always had the feeling he made certain I didn't."

"Yeah. Makes it seem like Leon was either hiding behind a rock all that time or Shandell was hiding him on purpose. What does Aretha say about her and Leon's relationship?"

"I haven't had a chance to ask her, but Jo Jo Lawson told me at the repast that just last night, Leon and Mrs. B almost came to blows over at the Satire Lounge. Jo Jo said he ended up nearly having to kick Leon's ass."

"Think she would've been angry enough to kill him?"

"If she thought he'd had anything to do with Shandell's murder, absolutely."

"Have you said anything to Flora Jean about what Jo Jo told you?"

"I mentioned it. But Flora Jean's still a little bent out of shape over me running off and trying to play Superman." Damion eyed his injured arm. "She did mention on the limo ride from the church to the cemetery that Paul Grimes, that newspaper reporter who was killed, has a friend, some leftover hippie named Wordell Epps, who wants to find Shandell's killer as badly as I do. According to Flora Jean, Epps claims that Shandell was shaving points."

"Think this guy Epps might've killed Leon?"

"Maybe. But I've been told by both Pinkie and Flora Jean to keep my distance." Looking frustrated, Damion stood and helped Niki up from the floor. "So I am—for the moment. Why don't we take a break? I'm starting to feel like I did a few hours ago."

"That's why we're here, Damion. To try and put a little of the sadness behind us. Think I'll make some hot chocolate to help out." She ran a hand gingerly along the top of Damion's injured arm. "Hurt?"

"Not at all."

"So what's next?"

"We're going to look at some game tapes."

"Do you think they'll help you find out what happened?"

"I'm not sure." Damion stepped over to the fireplace and retrieved the poker, prepared to stoke the fire. "Warm enough for you to take off that sweatshirt yet?"

Niki shook her head. "The word was hot chocolate, not sex, Mr. One-Track Mind. And no, I'm still chilly."

Looking disappointed, Damion turned and stoked the fire until flames were once again leaping. When he turned back around to see Niki, sans sweatshirt and bare-breasted, sitting on the footstool he'd vacated, he couldn't help but smile. "Thought you were cold," he said, moving across the floor toward her on his knees.

"I am. But I've got someone here to warm me up."

"What about the game tapes?"

"Guess they'll have to wait." Niki slipped off the footstool and down onto her knees.

Towering over her and nuzzling her hair, Damion said, "Just remember, I'm injured."

As they kissed and collapsed onto the Navajo rug in front of the fireplace, Niki muttered, "I can fix that." Soon they were making love. There was something, however, about Damion's part in that ritual that seemed to Niki to be tentative, almost unpracticed, and although their bodies melded as always, she could tell Damion's mind was elsewhere. As she sat astride him and slowly worked them both to climax, she knew that the pleasure would quickly take a back seat to Damion's search for his best friend's killer. As she reached her own point of explosion, squeezing her thighs together until they burned, she wanted to stop time, knowing she couldn't. Moments later, as she moved to slip off Damion, experiencing one final deep vaginal postcoital aftershock as she melted into his arms, she wanted to say, "Let's just lie here all night." But she didn't.

They lay in silence, clinging to one another and listening to the crackle of the fire for several more minutes, until Damion whispered, "You own me, Niki."

"Forever?"

"Longer."

"Let's lie a while longer and put everything else on hold. Damion, please."

Damion pulled her to him tightly. "Okay. For a while."

The fire had become a smoldering log and a few glowing embers when Damion slipped his arm from beneath a very contented, half-asleep Niki twenty minutes later. Barely opening her eyes, she said, "Damion, please, just a little longer." The look he gave her let her know that no amount of pleading would keep him from his game tapes any longer. Realizing that the very thing that had driven Damion to become an All-American basketball player was driving him right then, she said, rising from the warmth of the rug, "Everything'll go quicker with that hot chocolate I promised. I'll go make some."

Damion drank in every inch of Niki's naked body as she stood. "You know, you're exquisite."

"Oh, I bet you say that to all the girls, Mr. Madrid," Niki said, blowing Damion a kiss.

"Nope. Just to the ones who've stolen my mind."

Every step she took toward the kitchen made Damion wonder just how much of his mind still belonged to him.

An hour and two cups of hot chocolate later, Damion sat on the king-sized wrought-iron bed in the cabin's master bedroom, with Niki snuggled next to him, staring at a wall-mounted TV screen several feet away. They'd watched CSU dispose of Oregon and UNLV, with Damion attempting to wear out the fast-forward and reverse buttons on the VCR's remote. Now, as they watched the final minutes of the NCAA championship game, Damion jotted notes on what was now the sixth page of the legal pad resting on the muscular thighs that had helped him become a college rebounding phenom.

His notes included comments on the pace of each game, musings on who was doing most of CSU's scoring, who was blocking out, who was rebounding, and who'd run into foul trouble straight out of the gate.

Noting the intensity on Damion's face, Niki asked, "See anything special?"

"Not really," Damion said, shaking his head and looking frustrated. "It's hard to pick up anything that might be construed as point-shaving—even if you know the game and you're looking for it—if you're stuck with nothing but what a damn TV camera can see. But it's what television has conditioned us to do. Follow the ball and focus our attention on one player. Problem is, I can't really appreciate what the players who don't have the ball are doing."

"TV's also conditioned everyone to buy more beer."

Pleased that Niki had cut through the intensity, Damion laughed and kissed her on the cheek. "Hang in there with me, okay? If Shandell or anyone else on the team was shaving points, sooner or later, I'll spot the setup." Leaning forward and refocusing, Damion prepared to watch the final two minutes of the most disheartening game of his life.

As the tape wound down to the game's final critical seconds, he watched Jackie Woodson bring the ball upcourt with his usual high, left-handed dribble. For what seemed like the thousandth time, he saw Jackie get double-teamed. He ran the tape back and forth a half-dozen times as, near the edge of the screen and almost out of camera view, he watched Shandell struggling to get out of defensive traffic. When the ball skyrocketed out of Jackie's hands, not toward Shandell but straight across court to Damion, Damion muttered, "Okay." With the ball now in his hands, Damion froze the tape, telling himself, *Forget about watching the ball, and forget about having the play-by-play announcer's words bounce around in your head one more time. Look at what every other player is doing.* Running the tape back and forth, he tried to account for each player's position. There he was in the process of passing the ball. Shandell, wide-eyed and surprised that he was open, stood eagerly awaiting his pass, and Corky Blake was boxed out in the lane away from the ball. There was no missing Corky's trademark knee-high white socks or Willie Morgan's size 14s caught up in baseline traffic, even with the camera focused elsewhere. "Where the hell's Jackie?" Damion yelled suddenly, startling Niki just as, tape now rolling, Shandell let his final errant shot fly. Leaning back against the wrought-iron headboard, Damion whispered as if Shandell himself might be listening, "Damn, Jackie was free."

"What?" asked Niki, looking puzzled and feeling the muscles in Damion's right arm quiver.

"Jackie was free." Damion ran the tape briefly backward and stopped it. Restarting the tape, he said, "Look, Jackie's two steps inside the free-throw line on the left-hand side of the basket. The camera's only picking up his legs, but it's Jackie all right. There's nobody on Jackie when Shandell goes up to shoot. Nobody! Damn it, Shandell could've gotten him the ball. Shit! I can't believe I've missed it all the times I've run the last few seconds of that game through my head."

"Have you seen this tape before?"

"Only once. Coach Horse had the whole team look at it two days after the game. But hell, back then I wasn't looking for any signs of point-shaving, and neither was anyone else. We were all too devastated. We sleepwalked our way through our standard postgame film review. All this time I've been running the final fifteen seconds of that game through my head, thinking about the damn ball when I should've been looking at who was offering weak side help, who was doubling down in the middle, and who it turns out had lost their man. What an idiot!"

"Damion, come on. You had no idea."

"Well, I should have. We were better than UCLA. Better at every position. There's no way we should've lost that game and no way Shandell should've lost his life." He jotted a note on his tablet and dropped the pen at his side. "Now that I think about it, the evidence was there in the other game tapes too. Everything you'd need to see if you were looking for point-shaving. Shandell coming across the middle just a hair too slow to set his pick. Jackie holding the ball a split second too long on a simple give-and-go or failing to pick up his cutter. And Shandell shooting when he shouldn't have, just like in the championship game's final seconds. Hell, we've all run that cut-for-the-basket play, the one where Jackie breaks free, since the sixth grade. Jackie would've known he'd be the cutter. So he got the ball to me knowing that I'd look for Shandell and that even if he was free, Shandell wouldn't get him the ball." Damion slammed his palm against his forehead. "Shit!"

"So, if you picked up on it, wouldn't Coach Haroldson and the rest of the coaching staff have seen the same thing?"

"Maybe. Maybe not. All three of the games we've just looked at were pressure packed, and they all went down to the wire. You've gotta remember, we were college players, not pros. When you're dealing with amateurs, you've got to leave some margin for pressure-induced errors. If Coach Horse or any of his assistants had picked up on anything, they probably would've chalked it up to us crumbling under pressure. Besides, who would've thought that the top college player in the nation would have purposely missed setting a pick or failed to box out or, most important of all, failed to pass the ball to an open man in the biggest game of his life? Shandell was supposed to take that final shot, and he did. The whole country was preprogrammed to expect it. And if he missed on purpose, no one, including me, would have been the wiser.

"But when you start seeing a recurring theme on the court, a reproducible pattern of missing cutters, failing to box out, and screwing up give-and-gos, you take notice. These tapes say a lot, and what they shout the loudest is that Jackie and Shandell were probably working together, and they were doing it in an unbelievably smooth and calculated fashion. They weren't blowing layups or free throws—nothing that blatant. As the person running the offense, Jackie was simply slowing down the game. Putting a ceiling on the score. And damn it, what Shandell was doing was slapping a governor on his game."

"You've lost me, Damion. Want to explain?"

"Sorry. I'm so upset, I guess I've gotten ahead of myself. What Jackie and Shandell were doing in the subtlest of ways was keeping the rest of us from scoring. If either one of them made a bad pass, failed to fill a lane, missed setting a pick, or failed to cut for the basket when they should've—what they were actually doing was making certain that their error meant the rest of us couldn't score."

"I think I get it. They were keeping the ball out of their other teammates' hands by making errors in order to control the score, and since most of the time you won anyway, no one would have been the wiser."

Damion leaned over and planted a wet kiss on Niki's forehead. "That's it exactly. Their goal was to shave points so that someone betting on the game based not on the outcome but on the gambling point spread would come up a winner. They weren't out to have us lose the game, except with the championship game, where the sky was probably the limit and some smart gambling fixer stood to make the ultimate killing." Damion stroked his chin. "One thing's for sure: Shandell and Jackie never could've done it by themselves. Someone else had to be in on the fix."

"Who?"

"Garrett Asalon, that big-time Vegas-style gambler and fixer Flora Jean sent Pinkie after, may have gotten into Shandell's head. And I know that Pinkie had a talk with Asalon about possible point-shaving but that he came back empty-handed. I had to force the info out of Flora Jean at the repast, but she finally told me."

"So you think Shandell might've gotten himself involved with a mobster?"

"Unfortunately, yes."

"You can't go after somebody like that, Damion."

"You're right, I can't. But Flora Jean can. And if worse comes to worst, there's always Pinkie."

"Damion, do you hear what you're saying? That you're going to sic Flora Jean on some Las Vegas–style mobster who may have killed Shandell, and if that doesn't work, you'll send your own personal hit man after him?" Niki rolled her eyes in disbelief. "The game clock's expired, Damion. You need to let the police handle this. You've already nearly gotten yourself killed, and you've come within a whisker of losing the use of your left arm. Would you please tell Sergeant Townsend what you suspect and give up your vendetta? I'm not interested in being in love with a dead man."

The outrage on Niki's face told Damion that now wasn't the time to debate the issue. They could do that after he found Shandell's killer. As he reached over to embrace her, he had the strange sudden sense that Niki was feeling the very same thing that Mavis Sundee must've felt during all the years she'd struggled to keep CJ from being swallowed by the dark shadows of his world. Recognizing that he was far too much like the man who was his godfather, he said, "Can we talk about it later?"

"There's nothing to talk about, Damion. You know where I stand. I think we should just call it a night, okay?"

"I guess," said Damion. As Niki slipped out of his embrace, he had the feeling that, like Mavis before her, Niki didn't really believe he'd give up his quest to find out who had murdered his best friend. There would be time for debate, and for explanation, if it came to that, but for the moment, he realized that silence was the clear winner.

Chapter 21

Leotis Hawkins was frustrated at having had to wait over three hours for the lights inside the cabin to finally dim. Now, as he hummed the refrain to the old Ray Charles standard "The Night Time Is the Right Time," he moved in for the kill. He'd had plenty of time to think about how to settle up with Madrid, and after passing on the idea of charging in and shooting him and the woman he was with—a risky proposition since he didn't know whether Madrid was armed; picking one or both of them off when they came out for more fire-wood—which never occurred; or driving Madrid's Jeep—a vehicle he could certainly have hotwired—into the cabin's porch, forcing Madrid to come out and investigate, he'd decided on a fourth course of action. He'd smoke the fuckers out.

Dropping to one knee next to the tinder-dry brush he'd piled up and partially jammed beneath the front steps of the porch, he realized that for the first time all day his headache had disappeared. It had taken him a good thirty minutes and half-a-dozen stealthy approaches to assemble the ingredients for his bonfire, and he wasn't quite certain as he lit the pile whether the three-inch-thick Douglas fir steps would actually catch fire. But that didn't matter. The brush fire alone would be enough to get Madrid to forget about the sweet piece of ass he was probably getting and come a-running. He was certain of it.

As the smell of burning piñon and the musty aroma of smoking

Douglas fir filled the air, he knew he'd set up with a game winner. Watching smoke rise, he found himself humming "The Night Time Is the Right Time" once again. Retreating from the fire, he settled in behind a four-foot-high boulder twenty yards away from the steps to wait. He scooped up a couple of baseball-sized rocks, the last of the ingredients in the equation that would get Madrid's attention, and cocked his arm.

Niki smelled smoke seconds before she heard two loud thuds against the front of the cabin. Suspecting that a fireplace log was responsible for the smoke and that a tree limb had likely fallen onto the porch, she sat up in bed and gently nudged the peacefully sleeping Damion.

"What?" Damion sat up, looking disoriented.

"I think the fire's restarted. I smell smoke. And a tree limb may have fallen on the porch. I heard a couple of loud thuds. Better go check."

Looking puzzled, Damion sniffed the air. "I thought I banked that fire." Shaking his head, he slipped out of bed and into the pair of faded CSU warmup sweats at his feet.

Admiring the muscular upper body of the man who'd earlier sent her to new sexual heights, Niki said, "Guess you didn't, Mr. Eagle Scout." She winked and wagged an index finger at him playfully.

Damion pointed back and smiled. "When I get back I'll show what a Boy Scout can do, Ms. Estaban."

"Promise?"

"Count on it." He headed for the bedroom door, inhaling the increasingly strong scent of burning piñon. As he looked back to see Niki buried beneath the covers, he ran his tongue back and forth along the inside of his lower teeth, a nervous habit he'd had since his early teens that seemed to surface whenever he was stumped by something that failed to make sense—like Shandell's murder, fires that mysteriously restarted, and things that went bump in the night.

The aromatic smell filling the air seemed much too strong to be coming from a couple of rekindled logs, and as he walked down the hallway that led to the great room, he wondered whether the cabin, or maybe even the surrounding forest, might be on fire.

Stepping into the great room, he glanced out of one of the room's floor-to-ceiling windows to see flames and a rising plume of smoke perfectly framed by the window. As he turned to run and get a fire extinguisher from an emergency cabinet in the kitchen, he glanced back toward the window and realized that there was no smoke outside the adjacent window. Torn between retrieving the fire extinguisher and determining the fire's source, he raced to the second window and stared out into blackness, thinking all the time that he was wasting precious seconds trying to determine the source of the fire instead of simply putting it out. Mumbling, "Shit," he finally ran to the kitchen, grabbed a fire extinguisher, and headed for the front door. He was about to open the door when Niki screamed behind him, "Damion, the cabin's on fire!"

Looking confused but feeling somehow strangely fortunate that Niki had stopped his mad rush out the front door, Damion stared at the fire again. Nudging Niki to the floor, he whispered, "Shhhh."

"Damion, we're on fire!"

"Yeah, but the fire's acting too much like it's man-made. And that thud you heard earlier—where'd it come from? I want you to go back to the bedroom and lock the door."

"Damion, are you crazy?"

"Go back and lock the bedroom door, Niki! And take one of your uncle's shotguns in there with you."

Niki stood naked and speechless, watching the determined look in Damion's eyes. It was a fearless look she'd seen before. One that said, *I'll take the game-winning shot; just get me the damn ball.*

"Damion, is there someone outside?"

"Now, Niki!"

Shivering, not from cold but from fear, Niki headed for her uncle's gun case. When she glanced back to see Damion taking his antique long-barreled Colt Peacemaker out of the box his game tapes had been in, her heart sank. As he spun the chamber on the hundred-year-old six-shooter with his thumb, she knew that there was nothing she could do to stop him from doing things his way.

Damion headed for the back door of the cabin, reasoning that if someone were waiting out front, he might surprise them with an end-around maneuver. As he prepared to step out into the moonlit darkness, he had the eerie feeling that he'd stood in the exact same place scores of times before. There was no reason to believe that if someone had started the fire to smoke him and Niki out, they couldn't be waiting for him at the back door. Nonetheless, dressed only in sweatpants and with his gun at the ready, he stepped out onto the soft, damp ground. There was no one. For a split second he found himself thinking that maybe he was crazy. That standing there in the cold, half naked, toting a six-gun in one hand and a fire extinguisher in the other, he'd lost his ability to reason. Then he heard it. Not the sound of a crackling fire or the noise made by some forest animal running for cover but the low, muffled sound of what he swore could only be someone humming.

As he moved barefoot and in a crouch toward the sound, protected by the wraparound porch's three-foot-high, ivy-laden river-rock super-structure, he could see that the fire was limited to his side of the porch. What he couldn't determine in the semidarkness was whether the porch, the steps, or simply the pile of brush that he could now clearly make out was burning. He knew for certain, however, that no matter the source, it would be difficult for the fire to consume the heat-treated, fire-retardant, three-inch-thick Douglas fir porch steps and decking, which meant he had some time.

Moving in the direction of the humming, he tried to pinpoint its source, but the competing crackle of the fire made it difficult. Convinced that for the moment at least the cabin was in little danger of going up in flames, and that Niki was armed and safe, he decided to try a ruse that he'd heard CJ and Billy DeLong laugh about for years. They'd used the trick to get a heavily armed band of whacked-out ecoterrorists who had cornered CJ and Billy near a ranch house out-side Baggs, Wyoming, to expose their position.

He smiled as he thought about the oft-told tale's punch line: *If you can't get Moses to come to the mountaintop, then you best bring the mountaintop to him.* With Billy's words ringing in his ears, Damion steadied his gun barrel on the porch decking and, with the Peace-maker aimed squarely at where he thought the humming was coming from, fired off a round. A split second later, half-a-dozen rounds from a semiautomatic rifle came zinging his way.

Losing his grip on the fire extinguisher, Damion dropped to the ground, landing on his injured arm. Brushing a clump of moist dirt off his dressing, he heard someone call out, "See you're outside, fucker. Gutsy move, Madrid. But this time I'm gonna do more than cut you. Or maybe it's your woman doin' the shootin'. No matter. I'll handle her too."

Damion eyed his arm and whispered, "Son of a bitch." There could be no mistaking Leotis Hawkins's voice. Concerned that he'd outthought himself in his rush to emulate Billy and CJ, he remained silent, thinking, *What next?*

Even in the light of the fire, he couldn't determine exactly where Hawkins was hiding, but the best bet seemed to be a lone boulder twenty yards beyond the front steps of the cabin. Deciding to chance another shot in an effort to see if he was right, he fired at the boulder. That shot was met with another half-dozen rounds from Hawkins.

"I know where you're hiding, rabbit," Hawkins called out. "Hope you got more than one hole."

When Damion didn't respond, Hawkins bellowed, "You gonna answer me, cocksucker? Then again, maybe your arm's hurtin' too much to talk." His words were punctuated with an echo of laughter that was cut short by three shotgun blasts from the opposite corner of the porch. The shots peppered the boulder Hawkins had parked himself behind. Niki yelled, "He's behind the boulder, Damion," and followed it up with three more blasts from the Remington 12-gauge over-and-under her uncle kept handy for what he liked to call *coyote spankings*. Damion suddenly found himself smiling.

The second round of shots sent Hawkins ducking for cover as Niki broke into a self-satisfied grin. She had years of experience with firearms. Although her father and brother were lawyers, three of her uncles, including her father's youngest brother, the Nicaraguan-born engineering professor who owned the cabin, had fought shoulder to shoulder with guerrilla freedom fighters in Nicaragua during the Sandinista revolution. It had been that uncle who'd taught his sheltered Venezuelan-born niece during her childhood visits to Nicaragua that the world was filled with unsavory people whose ugly warts sometimes needed shaving. By the time she was twelve, Niki had learned to wield a handgun, a shotgun, and a rifle with equal facility.

"Niki! Are you okay?" Damion called out.

Watching the fire finally get a toehold on the porch's bottom step, Niki yelled, "Yes!" to which an agitated Leotis Hawkins responded with several rounds of fire.

"Stay down," Damion called out the instant the firing stopped. "If we can't see him, he can't see us."

"I've got all night," Hawkins yelled. "And trust me, when that front porch finally catches fire, things out here are gonna light up like the Fourth of July. I'll see you then."

Aware that they'd reached an impasse, Damion pondered whether it would be better to circle around behind the cabin, link up with Niki, and increase their firepower or to stay where he was and keep Hawkins in a crossfire. He'd risen onto a knee when someone behind him whispered, "Tough spot, Blood. Sorta reminds me of bein' in country during 'Nam." Looking remarkably calm, Pinkie Niedemeyer brought a finger up to his lips and pushed aside Damion's gun barrel, now aimed at his gut.

"Pinkie, where'd you come from?" Damion asked, shaking so badly he could barely get the words out.

"Mario said I should stay glued to your ass, so I did. At least until you got to the cabin earlier tonight. I figured you and Niki wouldn't want me droppin' in unexpected and rainin' on your parade. So I drove down to Nederland and got myself somethin' to eat before headin' back up to camp out in my vehicle for the night. Looks like I came back to a mess."

"How'd you get back without Hawkins seeing you?"

"That's for me to know and Mr. Hawkins to find out." Pinkie's eyes narrowed as his face turned expressionless. "Vietnam teaches you a lot about killin', Blood."

"So what do we do?"

"What you're gonna do is circle around the back of this cabin, let Niki know I'm here, tell her to stay put, and then hustle right back here to your post."

"The two of us can take him, Pinkie. I know it."

Pinkie flashed Damion the cold, hard stare of a seasoned warrior. "Do what I say, Damion. You hear me?" His no-nonsense tone sent Damion scurrying. Moments later, out of breath, Damion was at Niki's side. Looking at her, dressed as she was in a lightweight jacket, a pair of her uncle's hunting fatigues, and a Colorado Rockies baseball cap, Damion had the sense that she could easily have fought alongside her uncles in Nicaragua. He hugged her tightly. "I've only got a few seconds, Niki. Pinkie's here, back on the other side of the cabin. He plans to take care of Hawkins on his own."

A look of fear spread across Niki's face. "He'll kill Hawkins, Damion." She slipped out of her jacket and draped it over Damion's bare shoulders.

"He might have to," Damion said, sounding unfazed. "I've gotta get back." Briefly eyeing the fire, he kissed Niki on the cheek and took off. "You stay put, no matter what!"

Niki nodded and thought about her uncle as Damion disappeared back into the darkness. Once when her uncle had been teaching her brother and her how to handle a rifle, insisting that the unrest in Nicaragua had the potential to one day reach her father's doorstep, she'd asked him if he'd ever shot anyone. "Shot them and killed them," he'd quickly answered, letting her know with words unspoken that in times of peril she might have to do the same. Eyeing the fire, which had now made its way up three porch steps, Niki whispered, "Pinkie, hurry."

Leotis Hawkins had it all figured out, or so he thought. He'd wait for the fire to do its job. It had been slow to take hold, and he'd never counted on the cabin's steps and porch being made of three-inch-thick, fire-retardant decking. But he could wait until there was a roaring inferno and a hint of daylight to flush out Madrid and his girlfriend. Wait until his superior firepower gave him the hands-down advantage. Wait in the middle of a forest thicket ten miles from nowhere until the cows came home.

Stepping back from the boulder and leaning his weapon against it, he thought about the fact that he hadn't felt a single twinge of headache pain for hours. Deciding to place a fresh dip in his mouth, he reached for the half-empty pouch of chewing tobacco in his jacket pocket. He'd just pinched out a wad when he heard a swishing noise behind him. As he looked around to pinpoint where the sound had come from, he found himself staring down the muzzle of Pinkie Niedemeyer's 9-mm Beretta, a replacement for the Glock he'd been forced to leave behind at Asalon's. Before Hawkins could reach for his own handgun, Pinkie slammed the butt of the Beretta into Hawkins's temple. The last thing Hawkins thought as he slumped semiconscious to the ground was that his headache was back in spades.

Pinkie called out, "Damion—it's Pinkie. Got things under control over here. How about you two lovebirds gettin' a handle on that fire?"

Within minutes Damion and Niki had emptied the fire extinguisher's contents onto a blaze that had consumed most of her uncle's front porch steps, and as they stood dousing the smoldering steps with separate streams of water from two garden hoses, Niki found herself wondering what she would tell her uncle about what had happened.

She had the feeling, as Pinkie and Damion walked the still dazed Leotis Hawkins past her and up the porch steps for what she knew would be a serious grilling inside, that everything in her life had suddenly swirled out of control. When she asked to come inside to hear what Hawkins had to say, Pinkie and Damion waved her off, insisting that she stay outside and handle damage control. Fearful that Pinkie might still kill Hawkins, she looked at him and said, "Pinkie, please."

Pinkie nodded at an angry-looking Damion and said, "I don't think it's me you've gotta worry about."

Several minutes later, with his head still ringing and with both eyes tearing from a second concussion and the smoke, Hawkins stared across the cabin's great room, struggling to bring the wall nearest him into focus. His hands and feet were bound to the seat and legs of a kitchen chair with the baling wire Damion had found in the emergency cabinet, and a belt was looped around his chest, securing his torso to the chair back. "I can't breathe," Hawkins gasped, looking down at the belt.

"Should've thought about bein' able to breathe before you started that fire," Pinkie said.

"Kiss my ass, you skinny-ass faggot."

Certain that Hawkins had no idea who Pinkie was or what he did for a living, Damion said, "If I were you, I'd choose my words more carefully, Leotis."

"Fuck you too, Madrid, and that goes double for your mama."

As Damion cocked his arm to deliver a blow that would have sent Hawkins flying off to dreamland once again, Pinkie grabbed him by the biceps. Lowering Damion's arm, he looked at Hawkins and said,

"Now, Blood here's asked you a couple of times real nice what you know about Shandell Bird's murder, and all you've done so far is bombard us with obscenities and admit real grudgingly that you know Garrett Asalon. That's real impolite, Leotis. Maybe you and me need to talk to one another without Damion bein' here."

"Then send the wetback Puerto Rican son of a bitch on his way."

Damion shook his head in protest. "No. I'm staying."

Hawkins laughed. "No need shakin' your head for effect, Madrid. Fuck you both. I've played good cop, bad cop before—and with the best of 'em."

"Oh, have you?" Pinkie eyed Damion. "Why don't you go on and step outside, Blood?"

Shaking his head in sudden fear for Hawkins's life, Damion stood his ground. "I'm staying."

"Okay. But if you stay and things don't go down to your likin', remember I told you to leave."

"Screw you both," Hawkins said dismissively. He was about to offer a new obscenity-laced protest when Pinkie reached into his pocket, pulled out his Beretta, and jammed the gun barrel into Hawkins's right ear. "We need to get somethin' straight here, Leotis. I'm not who you think I am. I ain't a cop, a PI, a drug dealer, or a pimp. And just so you know it, I never take prisoners. If Blood and his girlfriend weren't here, I would've capped your ass out by that boulder. Now, since you don't seem one bit worried about who it is that's got the barrel of a 9-millimeter stuck in your ear, I'm gonna give you a chance to find out and maybe change your tune."

Pinkie slipped his cell phone off his belt, flipped it open, punched in a phone number with his thumb, and held the phone up for Hawkins to speak into. "Since the only thing you'll admit to is knowin' Asalon, and for the life of me I can't figure out why you'd even admit that except to have us runnin' off on a wild-goose chase after somebody you think might off us, I've dialed his number for you. If he's not there, ask for Craigy Theisman—could be you know him too—and tell whichever one of 'em you get on the line that Andrus Niedemeyer has you over a barrel and you wanta know what your chances are of walkin' away from the situation."

"Fuck you, asshole."

Pinkie smiled. "Okay, have it your way. Why don't you just ask the question the way you see fit."

Hawkins smiled smugly. When Craigy Theisman answered, "Theisman," Hawkins said, "Leotis here, Craigy. Got a question for you. Who the fuck is Andrus Niedemeyer? Got myself into a situation where I need to know."

Hawkins's face slumped as Theisman chuckled out his answer, with both Damion and Pinkie kneeling and listening in on the conversation. "He's a fuckin' hit man, you dumbass nigger, and don't you ever call me Craigy. It's Mr. Theisman to you, shine. Hope you ain't told him nothin' 'bout your dealin's with Mr. A. You keep your mouth shut, you hear me?"

Hawkins swallowed hard, trying his best not to look at Pinkie.

"Mr. A ain't available, but I'll pass on the message. One of us'll call you later. That is, if Niedemeyer ain't whacked your ass by then." Theisman erupted in a final burst of laughter before slamming down the phone.

Pinkie twisted the gun barrel around as suddenly, looking for an out, Hawkins said, "You won't pop me with Madrid and his girlfriend here."

"Wanta try me?"

When Hawkins didn't respond, Damion said, "You can spare us all a lot of grief by telling us what you know about Shandell's murder."

It was the placid, uncaring look on Pinkie's face rather than Damion's request that caused Hawkins to shiver. "I told you. I don't know nothin' about that killin'." He paused and took a deep breath. "But I do know some things. Things I'm guessin' you'd think are worth knowin'."

His expression not the least bit changed, Pinkie said, "Time you shared them then, brother."

"Or you'll kill me?"

"Count on it."

Hawkins looked at Damion. The pleading look Damion gave Pinkie, a look that said, *Please don't,* told Hawkins that the time had come to tell the truth.

"Okay, so I know some shit. But not about no murder. But before I tell you anything, you're gonna have to get that gun outta my ear and find me some damn aspirin. My head's splittin'."

Damion let out a relieved sigh as Pinkie extracted the gun barrel from Hawkins's ear and slipped the gun back into his jacket pocket just as a determined-looking Niki walked through the front door. "Fire's under control," she said. Watching Pinkie's gun disappear, she exhaled slowly.

"So are things in here," Damion said as the vice-like pressure on his chest dissipated. Realizing that he'd never know for sure whether Pinkie would've killed Hawkins, he understood very well that Hawkins had made the right decision by deciding to talk. Thank God he'd made the right decision for all of them.

Chapter 22

"I hate dressing up like this, Garrett. I'm not a whore." Connie East-land stared at Garrett Asalon, who sat across from her in an over-stuffed chair, drinking in every inch of her nearly nude body.

"Of course you're not, but then again, you're not a virgin." Asalon smiled and waved for her to walk toward him across the teakwood-paneled library of his house in Boulder's historic Mapleton Hill dis-trict. "And this time, try and put a little wiggle in it."

Dressed in fishnet stockings, a purple garter belt, and three-inch-high spiked heels, Connie walked slowly across the room.

"That's it, and show me a little pout. Good, good, good." When she was within arm's reach of the tuxedo-clad, cigar-smoking mobster, Asalon set his cigar aside and pulled her down into his lap. "Now, wiggle that sweet little ass of yours for me until I get it off."

Connie rolled her body into his, letting Asalon fondle her breasts, nibble at her earlobes, and lick the small of her back until he quickly spent himself and his arms dropped to his sides. She'd never under-stood why he liked to play such games, especially since they'd had glorious sex an hour earlier. His explanation for what she viewed as half-baked kinkiness had always been that it was the equivalent of enjoying a sleep-inducing nightcap—icing on the cake, as it were. But to her, it had always seemed freaky. Getting some guy in a tuxedo off by rolling her ass on him was a long way from her sexual cup of tea.

But since Garrett liked and even demanded it, she knew better than to turn him down.

Looking relaxed, Asalon retrieved his cigar and took a long, slow pull off the $200 Cuban. "You're a sweetheart, a real cock-teasing sweetheart. I can never seem to get my fill of you."

Connie flashed him a coy smile as he ran a finger around her right nipple in a slow circle. "So are we on the same page with this Blackbird thing?" she finally asked.

"Yes. And if Epps or the Madrid kid get too close, you're to call me and I'll have Craigy deal with them."

Connie flashed a relieved smile. "And if that Five Points drug peddler, Hawkins, gets a wild hair?"

"No problem. Craigy will deal with him too. Don't worry your tight little body over it."

"I wish I didn't know as much about this as I do, Garrett."

"But you do, princess, and that's what makes us so symbiotic. And since I don't want that relationship to die on the vine, you need to forget about what you know and think more about keeping those wonderful vaginal muscles of yours tight and ready." Asalon nudged Connie off his lap. "Why don't you run and get dressed. I'll have Craigy take you home."

Connie slipped the smock she'd been wearing earlier off the back of Asalon's chair, draped it over her shoulders, and walked toward the double-doored library exit. She swung the door open to find Craigy Theisman standing sentry. His mounting erection became all the more obvious with each step she took down the hall that led to Asalon's bedroom. Theisman took a final wistful look as she disappeared into the bedroom suite before poking his head into the library.

Sounding dismissive, he called across the room, "Hey, boss. I think we might have a problem."

"How many times must I tell you, Craigy? I'm not your boss. I'm your employer. Boss is such an unrefined, primitive-sounding term. Now, what's the problem?"

"Had a call a little bit ago from Leotis Hawkins. Fucker's gotten himself into some kinda scrape with Pinkie Niedemeyer. He wanted to know if Pinkie was the kind of person who'd kill him."

"And what did you tell him?"

"Told him Pinkie would probably enjoy it."

"Did Hawkins say what their dispute was about?"

"No."

"And you didn't ask?"

"Nope."

"Craigy, Craigy, Craigy. Sometimes I wonder about your instincts, if not your wits. Pinkie lands on our doorstep last night peppering us with questions, and now he's jamming Hawkins. Can't you see the red flag? Seems to me that Andrus is into some heavy-duty investigating. The question, Craigy, my boy, is for whom?"

"That Madrid kid. The one Hawkins told you about. Who else? Think maybe Hawkins got himself into a bad enough bind that Pinkie mighta offed him?"

"We can only hope so. Mr. Hawkins, it seems, is becoming more and more of a liability, and you know how I detest liabilities, Craigy." Asalon relaxed back in his chair. "Why don't you keep your ear to the ground and a close watch on Hawkins. If he looks or acts like he's going to crack, you do the cracking first. And if he doesn't, maybe Pinkie will do it for us."

Realizing that he was sticky with semen, Asalon smiled and massaged his limp penis. "And Craigy, as soon as Connie's ready, run her home. Sweet ass on that woman. As sweet as morning clover." His tone was boastful, as if he somehow needed to share his testimonial.

The aspirin Damion had given Leotis Hawkins hadn't put a dent in Hawkins's throbbing headache. Fifteen minutes into Damion and Pinkie's interrogation, Hawkins was still seeing double, both ears continued to ring, and he had the strange feeling that he was being dunked back and forth underwater. Rubbing his bound hands together, he let out a snort and eyed Pinkie and Damion disdainfully. "You could untie my hands."

"Be lucky that you had someone here who insisted we untie your feet," Pinkie said, glancing across the room toward Niki. "Now, finish answerin' the question."

Hawkins looked across the room to where Niki stood, leaning on the back of a leather wingback chair. Realizing from Niki's expression that his attempt at pity had missed its mark, he said, "Like I was tellin' you, it was that woman of Blackbird's who got his life all fucked up. She was the one who introduced us."

"How'd you meet her?" asked Damion.

Hawkins remained silent until Pinkie grabbed him by the cheek and pinched a generous knot of flesh between his thumb and forefinger. "Need an answer, Hawkins."

Yelping and twisting out of Pinkie's grasp, Hawkins said, "Asalon introduced us after one of the CSU basketball games."

"How'd Asalon know Connie?" Damion and Niki asked, almost in unison.

Hawkins rubbed his cheek, trying to return feeling to it. "I'm not sure, but I think her old man mighta known Asalon. Heard tell he was a gambler."

"He was," Niki said, taking a seat in the wingback. "But Connie told me he gave up gambling years ago, after they nearly lost their house."

"Could be she lied," said Pinkie.

"Or maybe he fell off the wagon," Damion said with an insightful nod. "Any way you slice it, it sounds to me like Connie has some explaining to do." He eyed Hawkins. "Was Shandell making any money off your deal?"

"Enough to keep that woman of his in fancy clothes and jewelry and the two of 'em eatin' at them fancy Cherry Creek restaurants. He told me so himself."

"Seems strange, Connie using Shandell like that," said Niki. "She's never struck me as being that way."

"Could be you never looked hard enough," Hawkins said with a smirk. "And maybe you should've looked harder at what made your boy Blackbird tick."

"Maybe. Then again, Asalon may have been offering both Connie and Shandell something they couldn't refuse," said Damion.

"So, when do we talk to Connie?" asked Niki.

"Soon. But not without some help from Flora Jean this time around." Damion eyed Hawkins, then glanced down at his injured arm. "Think I'll look before I leap."

"I can help," said Niki.

Recalling the three shotgun blasts that had sent Leotis Hawkins ducking for cover, Damion eyed the fatigue-wearing beauty, who he knew would someday be his wife, and smiled. "Okay. Tell me how."

Niki glanced at Hawkins. "With him sitting here?"

"Oh, he won't be doin' any talkin'," said Pinkie. "To Asalon or Connie or anyone else."

Looking terrified, Hawkins said, "Keep him off me, Madrid."

Pinkie flashed Hawkins a smile. "Don't worry, Leotis. All I plan to do is send you packin'."

Raising a hand and cutting off the discussion, Damion said to Niki, "So what do you plan to do?"

"Talk to Connie, that's all."

"Things could get real sticky."

"No stickier than they are right now."

"Okay, talk to her. But be careful." He turned to Pinkie. "What do you think about giving Asalon a second tumble? If he knows you've had a chat with Leotis, he might be more cooperative than when you dropped in on him last night."

"Do whatever you want to," Hawkins said before Pinkie could respond. "Just don't have Asalon or that slow-thinkin' pit bull of his, Craigy Theisman, lookin' to take a bite outta my hide. I've told you all I know about Blackbird."

Damion stared Hawkins squarely in the eye, uncertain whether he was lying. "Was Shandell using any of the drugs you were supplying him with?"

"How the hell would I know?" Hawkins said defiantly.

"Maybe you wouldn't have, but my guess is that he wasn't. And that's got me confused," Damion said, eyeing Niki and then Pinkie. "If he wasn't using them and all he was doing was acting as a go-between for Hawkins, it was a dumbass decision, and Shandell was smarter than that. And if he was shaving points and money wasn't his siren call, we still don't know a reason why. Maybe Connie or Asalon had him over a barrel for some other reason."

"Don't matter, Madrid. Your boy Shandell wasn't nothin' but a money-grubbin' golden boy pimpin' drugs. That's the why."

Watching Damion seethe, Pinkie said, "Your mouth's about to get you in trouble again, Hawkins."

"No, Pinkie, let him talk," Damion said, looking suddenly reflective. "You know, Leotis, you could be onto something. But you've got it backward. I'm thinking there were lots of people pimping Shandell. The question is which pimp killed him?" Grabbing Hawkins by the shirt collar and choking the collar down until Hawkins could barely breathe, Damion said, "Just now, when I asked you if Shandell was using performance-enhancers, you got so defensive I thought you might swallow your tongue. It's as if I struck a nerve." Damion flashed Pinkie a look that said, *I'm going to need your help here, Andrus.* "What do you think, Pinkie? Think Leotis here can stand another concussion?" Damion tightened his grip on the collar. "When I was playing ball, the coaches used to tell me that for an elite athlete, three serious concussions pretty much end a career. After that your brain's just way too scrambled. Wonder what three concussions in the span of forty-eight hours would do for you?" Damion watched Pinkie slip his 9-mm out of his jacket pocket.

"We can sure find out," said Pinkie.

Niki rose from her seat as, cocking his arm, Pinkie prepared to slam the butt of the gun into Hawkins's temple. His downswing was swift, causing Hawkins and Niki to scream as the butt of the gun brushed Hawkins's right ear and slammed into a nearby coffee table. Eyeing the gouge in the table, Pinkie said apologetically, "Tell your uncle I'll buy him a new one." He turned to Hawkins. "The next divot comes outta your skull, friend."

"Three's the magic number," said the stern-faced Damion.

"Damion, no!" Niki raced across the room toward Hawkins, pleading, "Tell them, tell them, tell them."

With his head still so foggy that he couldn't think straight, Hawkins decided he'd rather chance Asalon or Craigy Theisman coming after him than suffer a possible life-ending concussion. He said, "Okay, okay. Blackbird was holdin' back a little of the stuff he was supplyin' me with for somebody up at CSU. Never knew whether it was for a teammate, some trainer, a coach, the water boy, or some cheerleader he mighta been screwin'. But he was holdin' back a stash for somebody, I know that. Asalon even let it slip out once. It was like he was braggin'."

"Oh, I'll find out who," said Damion. "Count on it."

Pinkie eyed the gouge in the table and smiled, aware that more often than not, the threat of violence trumps the actual act. "So, looks like we got ourselves a game plan," he said to Damion. "You get to track down whoever it was up at CSU that Shandell was supplyin' with drugs. Niki talks to Connie, and I handle Asalon."

"Works for me," said Damion. "But that still leaves us with that off-the-wall reporter that Flora Jean claims has his nose stuck into this."

"Yeah, I forgot about him."

"Have you ever heard of a guy named Wordell Epps?" Damion asked Hawkins.

"Nope."

"What about Leon Bird? Did you know him?"

"Nope. But I know he's dead. Read about it in the papers," Hawkins said with a grin.

"Sure hope that's how you know," said Pinkie. "I'd hate to think you were dumb enough to kill three people."

Glassy-eyed, slurring his words, and suddenly sounding coura-geous, Hawkins said, "Untie me and you'll find out how dumb I am, hit man." Hawkins balled his still bound fists and threw a two fisted handcuffed haymaker into empty air.

Looking worried, Niki said, "I think he needs to see a doctor, and quick."

Nodding in agreement, Damion said, "Think you can drive him back to Denver in that plastic pig of his we found stashed in the woods, Pinkie? I'll drive your truck, and Niki can drive the Jeep."

Pinkie shook his head. "Bad idea, Damion. Real bad. Nursemaidin' somebody who's tried to kill you is never smart."

"We can't leave him here," Niki said, looking helpless.

"Okay. I'll meet you both halfway. I'll take Hawkins back to Den-ver, hogtied, of course, and drop him wherever he says. His house, Denver General, Shotgun Willie's, or the First Baptist Church—but that's it. He wants a doctor, he's on his own."

"Screw you all," Hawkins mumbled.

Grabbing Hawkins by a hank of hair and ignoring his pained yelp, Pinkie said, "Listen, dumbass, if I didn't think killin' you would come back to bite these two young people here, you'd already be dead. So here's some advice. The next go-round you and me have, Damion and Niki ain't gonna be around to save your bacon. So on our way off this mountain, if I hear so much as a whimper, I'll send you on to your reward. You got enough brain cells still swimmin' around inside your head to understand what I'm sayin'?"

Hawkins nodded without answering.

"Great. That's exactly what I wanta hear all the way back to Den-ver. Silence." Flashing Damion an authoritative look, Pinkie said, "Go check on the fire, make sure it's out, then hose down the porch and the steps some more. Fire's an ugly, sneaky beast, you don't kill it. You got any rope around this place?" he asked Niki.

"I'm sure there's some in the emergency cabinet."

"How about gettin' it for me so I can strap Leotis here down for the count." Pinkie turned to offer Hawkins one final comment. "For the next hour and a half, I want you to think of yourself as a prisoner of war and me as your prison-camp commandant. Stay on your best behavior and you get out of prison. Do anything else and—well, you get the picture." Pinkie eyed Damion. "Now, what about gettin' busy with that water hose, Blood?"

Fifteen minutes later, a Corvette and two other vehicles rolled down the remote cabin's long driveway and onto the winding gravel road that led back to the highway ten miles south. Leotis Hawkins, his knees roped to his neck and his torso strapped to the front seat of the Corvette, listened to Pinkie drum his fingers impatiently on the car's steering wheel as, barely conscious, Leotis tried not to slobber on himself. Damion sat attentive but uneasy behind the wheel of Pinkie's pickup, thinking that when he got home, he'd stay up for as long as it took to do the final thing he'd planned to do at the cabin before Hawkins's arrival on the scene. He'd read *A Morning at the Office* and see if the oddly out-of-place little volume about Caribbean office workers might not shed some light on who Shandell's murderer might be.

Trailing the Corvette in Damion's Jeep, Niki found herself wondering whether the queasiness in the pit of her stomach was the same undulating upset that Mavis Sundee had felt all the years that CJ Floyd had worked the streets of Denver as a bounty hunter and bail bondsman. More importantly, she found herself asking whether

Pinkie really would have killed Hawkins if she and Damion hadn't been there.

Leotis Hawkins thought for certain he was in the first stages of dying. His head was pulsating, and a steady stream of mucus continued to flow from both nostrils. It had been two hours since Pinkie Niede-meyer had left him standing in his driveway in the equivalent of a drunken stupor with a whispered warning: "Call Asalon and warn him that you gave up Connie Eastland, or that you told us anything about any point-shaving scam, and you get to answer to me."

Fearful of who was more likely to kill him, Niedemeyer or Asa-lon, he'd worked himself up to the point of cold, transient shivers. Concerned that he'd be picked up by the cops on any number of out-standing warrants if he marched into some hospital emergency room seeking medical treatment, he'd decided that his best option would be to stay put at home, call Asalon, twist the truth a bit concerning his encounter in Nederland, and pass along some helpful hints that might get Asalon dogging Pinkie and Damion instead of him.

He knew Asalon wouldn't answer his phone at that hour, but he suspected Theisman would. With both hands shaking, he dialed the number he had for Asalon in case of emergencies. When Craigy Theisman answered, his voice groggy with sleep, Hawkins said, try-ing his best not to sound flustered, "This is Leotis. I need to talk to Asalon."

"What the shit do you want this time of night?"

"I need to pass on some info to your boss about that Pinkie Niede-meyer problem I was havin'."

"Save it for tomorrow."

"Can't wait."

"Damn it. This better be good, boy."

Leotis sucked a rope of mucus back up into his nose. "It's good."

"Hang on. I'll get him on the line, and like I said, your shit best be golden."

Moments later Asalon came on the line. His tone was calm. "What have you got for me that can't wait until morning, Leotis?"

"Information about Pinkie Niedemeyer and that Madrid kid who played ball with Blackbird."

"Which is?"

"They know Connie Eastland and you are connected."

"I don't suppose you're the one who gave them that information, are you, Leotis?"

"No. I called Craigy earlier to clue you in, but he said you were busy. It's had me worried, so I figured I better try and get in touch with you again."

Asalon took a deep, thoughtful breath as he tried to determine whether Hawkins was lying. "So how'd they find out about Connie and me?"

Deciding the time was ripe to play his ace, Hawkins said, "Madrid's girlfriend sniffed out the connection. Turns out the girlfriend and Connie are good friends."

"I see. And what exactly do they know about my and Connie's little arrangement?"

"I'm not sure they know anything specific. All I know is that Niedemeyer slapped me around real good tryin' to get me to cave in and give him what I knew, but I didn't. All he knows is that I had Bird mule for me and that you and Connie are connected, nothin' else. I think he's workin' for Madrid."

"You mean Madrid wasn't there when Pinkie roughed you up?"

Hoping that so far nothing in his voice had telegraphed the fact that he was lying, Hawkins said, "No."

"I hope you're telling me the truth, Leotis."

"I am. Just wanted to give you a heads-up in case Madrid or Niedemeyer came snoopin'."

"I appreciate that. Now, why don't you go get some sleep. Sounds to me like you're catching a cold. I'll handle things from here."

"Okay."

"And Leotis, I appreciate the loyalty." Dressed in blaze-orange silk pajamas, one of a dozen pair he'd had handmade in Hong Kong, Asalon slipped off the edge of his bed, left his bedroom, and walked down the hallway to where Craigy Theisman had been listening in on a second phone. Eyeing Theisman, he asked, "Think he was telling the truth?"

"No chance."

"That's my assessment too."

"So whatta we do?"

"We address the issue in the morning, after I've talked to Connie and cooler heads have prevailed. I'm thinking you're likely to be busy tomorrow."

"Gonna need me to shut her up?"

"I'm not sure. We'll see how things shake out in the morning."

"You're damn-sure calm. I'd'a killed that nigger."

"It pays to stay calm, Craigy. Haste makes waste, and lying can be infectious. Too bad Leotis doesn't seem to appreciate that. He should've known better than to lay his reason for giving me up to Pinkie on the doorstep of hearsay from the girlfriend of that Madrid kid. Guess poor Leotis doesn't fully appreciate the parameters of the code adhered to by a settlement agent like Niedemeyer." Asalon smiled. It was the knowing smile of someone with inside dope. "If Pinkie were the only one he'd passed along his information to, poor Leotis would be dead by now. I'm guessing the Madrid kid was there when he coughed up the information, and maybe Madrid's girlfriend too. Witnesses, Craigy, my boy, two witnesses. Leotis had a couple of guardian angels there protecting him without even knowing it. In the future, he'll need a few more."

Chapter 23

Damion had never done well on less than four hours of sleep. Lack of sleep tended to make him irritable and unfocused, and as it stood right then, the day was shaping up terribly blurred. He hadn't finished reading *A Morning at the Office* until 5:30 a.m., and he'd spent the next three hours tossing and turning in bed, trying to fall asleep. When Niki finally couldn't stand it any longer, she'd gotten up, made a pot of coffee, poached herself an egg, and quickly read through *A Morning at the Office*. Fifteen minutes later Damion joined her in the kitchen.

They had already talked over the previous evening's events, rehashing the way they'd watched Leotis Hawkins stumbling into his apartment, fearful that Pinkie might decide to pop him on a last-minute whim. But Pinkie had simply gotten into his pickup and driven off, saying he'd be in touch. They'd even discussed the possibility that Hawkins might have died during the night. The one thing they hadn't talked about was Shandell.

Unshaven, puffy-eyed, and looking like someone with a bad hangover, Damion lumbered across the kitchen, poured a cup of black coffee, and took a sip. Surprised to see *A Morning at the Office* lying on the kitchen counter, he picked it up and shook his head. "This thing sure didn't tell me much, other than the fact that the main character, an office boy named Horace Xavier, didn't seem to fit in with his job—like Shandell."

"I remembered that when I paged through the book. Not much there to go on, really." Looking guilty, Niki said, "Babe, I still have to go to work, and I'm late."

"Okay." Damion took a sip of coffee, shook his head, and once again found himself reflecting on *A Morning at the Office*. "Turns out Horace was too black, too uneducated, too uncultured, and just too plain nappy-headed to fit in. No wonder he walked away from the job of a lifetime in the end. Trinidad—what a place to live."

"And there's never been that kind of racism here in the U.S."

"Of course there has. The question is, how does Horace Xavier's story dovetail half a century later with that of a future NBA superstar worth millions?"

"Maybe Horace Xavier isn't the key. Maybe the key lies with another character."

"Nope. Xavier's the key. I'm missing the hidden tie-in, that's all. Shandell as much as told us about the not-fitting-in part with that inscription he wrote to Leon in the book. I'm just going to have to think things through a little better."

"Then I suggest you think things through by this evening before we pick up your mother, CJ, and Mavis from DIA. I've got a feeling that when they find out about everything that's happened, you won't be doing any more investigating."

"Yeah, I know. That's why I'm going to have Flora Jean help me get to the bottom of everything today."

"Ambitious." There was concern in Niki's tone. "And if Leotis Hawkins or that mobster Asalon comes after you, you'll just wave your magic cape at them and fly off?"

"Niki, please."

"No, Damion. I've just about had enough. I don't appreciate the fact that Hawkins tried to burn down my uncle's cabin or that he tried to kill me last night. I don't like being hunted, which we still probably are, spending my free time hobnobbing with a hit man, or, God forbid, if Leotis Hawkins dies, being an accessory to a murder."

"He's not going to die, Niki. Just hang in there with me a little longer."

Staring intently at Damion, Niki tried to reconcile her emotions with his actions, aware that he'd lost someone as close to him as a brother. She understood and appreciated his pain. What she couldn't comprehend was what was driving him to solve Shandell's murder on his own. Rising from her stool, she slipped behind Damion and massaged his shoulders. "Why do you want to keep after this, Damion?"

"I'm not quite sure. Maybe if I tell you a story, it'll help you understand." Damion cleared his throat and took a sip of coffee. "Shortly after Shandell and I both turned fourteen, we decided to bicycle over to Skyline Park and find a pickup basketball game. We were both big enough and skilled enough to play with kids a lot older than us, and on that day it turned out that everyone there was seventeen or eighteen and they all happened to be black.

"When we chose up sides, I didn't get picked. As I headed over to a bench to have a seat and watch the game, Shandell asked a kid named Rufus Jenkins why no one had picked me. Jenkins laughed and said, 'Because your buddy Madrid is a fuckin' Puerto Rican, Bird.' Shandell said if they were gonna be that way, he wouldn't play, so Jenkins grabbed him by his T-shirt and ripped it down the front. I don't think I ever saw Shandell so enraged. He picked up a four-foot length of quarter-round that was lying on the ground, the kind they use to finish off baseboards, and swung it at Jenkins. A nail happened to be sticking out of the business end of the wood, and it caught

Jenkins right in the side of his neck. Blood shot out of the puncture wound like water from a fire hose.

"When everyone standing around began yelling, Shandell simply walked away. As we left the court Shandell glanced back at Jenkins, who was holding a towel to his neck, and mumbled under his breath, 'Ignorant ass.' I just stared at Shandell in disbelief and said, 'You could've killed him.' I'll never forget Shandell's response: 'You never wanta be the odd man out, Damion. Never. Besides, I know you'da done the same for me.'"

Niki shook her head. "It's not always tit for tat in this world, Damion. You're twenty-two years old now, and that's a long way from fourteen."

"It's still tit for tat until my trip out to DIA tonight. After that I'll leave it alone, okay?"

"Promise?"

"Yes. But until then I plan to go at this full bore, and like it or not, I'm going to need your help."

"How?"

"I need you to call Connie Eastland. Find out everything you can about her and Shandell's relationship. Find out whether they fought when we weren't around. Ask her what kinds of gifts Shandell gave her, how expensive they were, and where she thought the money was coming from to buy them. I'm looking for a link to Garrett Asalon, Niki. There has to be one."

"You're asking me to find out things I doubt Connie will tell me, Damion."

"I need to know, Niki."

"Then perhaps there's another way. One that'll prove more productive than me going one-on-one with Connie."

"What?"

"I can call some of Connie's sorority sisters and ask them about Shandell and Connie's relationship. Trust me, they'll know things you and I wouldn't. And they'll be a lot more candid than Connie; count on it."

"Fine. How many can you round up?"

"A couple, I suspect."

Looking puzzled, Damion asked, "Why would they know things about Shandell and Connie that we wouldn't?"

"Because they're Connie's sorors, Damion. Sisters in a society with arcane oaths and secret handshakes."

"What makes you think they'll talk to you?"

Niki smiled. "There's a chance they won't. But I'll give them my best Oprah Winfrey dish-the-dirt-girl arm-twist. I'm bound to find a nugget. Let me make a few phone calls and get dressed, okay?"

Damion shook his head and chuckled as Niki left the room. He knew that with her brand of dogged determination, there was no way Niki would fail to come up with something.

Damion's four quick calls to Jackie Woodson's and Rodney Sands's apartments and cell phones yielded but one recorded answer: "Rodney's not in. Talk to me, bro." He couldn't be sure if one or both of them were screening their calls. He had the uneasy feeling that they both knew more about Shandell's involvement in point-shaving and about his murder than they were letting on.

When he caught up with them this time, he'd have better control over his emotions, he told himself. He'd learned a valuable lesson about pursuing suspects from his earlier mistakes. Smiling, he recalled something CJ had insisted he master when he was first learning to fly-fish: *"Remember to always cast your line lightly, Damion; otherwise you're bound to spook the fish."*

Niki, it turned out, was more successful in her attempt to track down Connie Eastland's sorority sisters. One of Connie's closest friends during their days at CSU had been a woman Niki had been friendly with as well. She now worked for a software firm in Broomfield, a twenty-minute drive from Niki's office in downtown Denver. The woman had seemed surprised by Niki's early-morning call, but she'd been cordial and even forthcoming after Niki had explained that she was helping Damion try to find Shandell's killer. She'd agreed to meet Niki for lunch at a sandwich shop at the Flatiron Crossing Mall, a few minutes from her Broomfield office. Cradling the phone and rushing back out to the kitchen, where Damion sat practicing mock fly casts, Niki said, "Think I've got something."

"Hope it's better than what I came up with. I'm batting zero."

"I talked to Maria Carpenter. She's the only person I could reach."

"And?" Damion asked, recalling the skinny, serious blonde with knobby knees and a peekaboo boy's haircut who'd followed Connie around like a puppy during most of their time at CSU.

"And for your information, Dr. Madrid, we're having lunch at noon."

Suddenly wide-eyed, Damion planted a kiss on Niki's forehead. "Did she tell you anything that might help us out?"

"Not really. In fact, she seemed a little hesitant to talk. It was almost as if she didn't want to be accused of telling tales out of school."

"Then maybe she knows something."

"Guess we'll simply have to wait and find out."

"It's one more lead than we had, anyway."

Niki eyed the antique school clock on the wall and grabbed her purse. "I'm afraid I have to head for work, Damion."

"Think you're up to working after only four hours' sleep?"

"Three, Mr. Whirling Dervish. And yes." She flashed Damion her best tough-as-nails smile. "So what's next on the agenda?"

"Think I'll call Coach Horse, tell him what I saw on those game tapes, and see if he can't give me his take on what might have been going on. Then I'll head on over to Flora Jean's office and beg for some help."

"She might not be real willing, considering your past lack of candor."

"Yeah." Looking worried, Damon said, "But maybe I can twist her arm."

"If you think so," said Niki, thinking as she moved to leave that very few people, even on their best days, could twist the arm of the no-nonsense six-foot-one former combat marine.

"You wouldn't have the sense to come in out of the rain if someone told you a tidal wave was coming, Sands." Looking thoroughly displeased, Garrett Asalon sat comfortably in a wingback leather chair in his library, clipping his fingernails as he talked to Rodney Sands on the phone. Craigy Theisman stood a few feet away in a half slouch, looking dour and subordinate. Trying to contain his anger, Asalon said, "But I'll take the blame on this. Uninsightful old me. How was I to know you had an entrepreneurial spark bouncing around inside you? I give you one of my best sources for a few performance-enhancers for our boy Jackie Woodson, and you decide to use that information to start your own drug-peddling business down in Five Points, using a dimwit like Leotis Hawkins to push the product and Shandell Bird as your poster boy. Are you there, Sands?" Asalon asked, listening to the silence on the other end of the line.

"Yes."

"Well, get this. You're cut off forever. It wasn't enough for you to simply get the stuff to Jackie so he could put a little icing on his game. You had to cut Bird in on the deal. Dumb move, Sands. Especially since I have a feeling the cops are eventually going to look my way."

"I was only trying to make a few extra bucks."

"And in doing so, you just may have derailed a gaming venture I've been working on for years. You take the cake, Sands. Was Jackie Woodson in on your drug-peddling scam?"

"No. I just gave him his regular monthly supply of hGH, and he was happy."

"Nice to know. I wouldn't want to have to flog the wrong horse." Asalon clipped the nail on his right pinkie and tossed it aside. "I'm thinking you and Jackie are in need of a come-to-Jesus meeting. So I'm going to send an associate of mine up to Fort Collins to have a talk with you both today. I'll put him on the line in a moment, and he'll set up a time. When did you last talk to Woodson, anyway?"

"I haven't talked to him since Shandell Bird's funeral."

"Best run him down and let him know he's got a meeting to attend. Are we clear?"

"Yes."

"Hold on for my associate Mr. Theisman." Asalon covered the receiver with his hand. "I hate to add to your list of things to do, Craigy, but when you talk to Connie and Alicia Phillips I'm going to need you to . . ."

"Yeah. I heard, boss."

"Good. We'll need to talk about how to handle each of our four wayward children if the necessity arises." Asalon handed Theisman the phone.

Theisman quickly made arrangements to meet with Sandy and hopefully Jackie that evening, hung up, and turned to Asalon. "So how should I hit 'em? High or low?"

"High enough to get their attention and low enough for them to worry about their nuts, I suspect."

"And what if one of 'em decides to hit back?"

"It's summertime, Craigy," Asalon said with a smile. "And in the summertime we swat pesky flies."

Frustrated, Damion flipped his cell phone closed and tossed it onto the passenger seat. Gunning the Jeep's engine just to punctuate his upset, he turned off Colorado Boulevard onto First Avenue and sped into surprisingly light midmorning Cherry Creek shopping center traffic toward Flora Jean's office.

He couldn't help but marvel at the fact that, seemingly full of energy, Niki was on her way to work, ready to take on the day. At noon she was going to link up with one of Connie Eastland's old sorority sisters, and maybe even dig up an all-important lead on who might have killed Shandell. And what was he doing? Still batting zero. The one person he'd been able to get in touch with was Coach Haroldson. He'd just hung up after talking with the low-keyed, genial, basketball fundamentals guru and no-nonsense disciplinarian. He'd caught the coach just as he was getting ready for a team shoot-around, and they'd exchanged small talk before Damion had gotten up the nerve to mention his point-shaving suspicions.

Haroldson hadn't seemed particularly surprised; he'd intimated that after reviewing the UCLA game film, he'd also had the feeling that Shandell and Jackie Woodson might have been "altering the flow of the game." He admitted to having had nightmares about that game ever since Shandell's death, although he'd been quick to point out that a single game didn't necessarily prove that there was point-shaving going on.

They'd spent a few more minutes discussing their suspicions, including the fact that, whether the questions came from Damion or the cops, sooner or later Jackie Woodson was going to have some things to explain. When Haroldson, suddenly sounding like a man concerned that his coaching legacy might end up tainted, had ended the conversation, saying he had to go manage the shoot-around, Damion's heart had sunk. Sounding guilty, Haroldson had added that he thought Damion needed to speak directly to Jackie Woodson about his point-shaving suspicions, or better still with the team psychologist, Alicia Phillips, who he was certain could provide more insight into what had been going on inside Shandell's head than he could.

Cruising around a slow-moving Volkswagen whose driver appeared to be looking for an address, Damion told himself that his disjointed investigation of his best friend's death was almost totally out of sync. Coach Horse's abrupt termination of their conversation had made him suspicious. Jackie Woodson and Rodney Sands were nowhere to be found, and suddenly a man without an ounce of nonsense in his bones was touting the team psychologist as the person most likely to have an answer to Shandell's head problems, and maybe even his death. Hopeful that Flora Jean could help him sort things out, he sped up, praying as he eased his foot down on the accelerator that Coach Horse wasn't somehow involved in Shandell's murder.

"I'll help if I can call the shots, Damion." Stern-faced, Flora Jean stared Damion directly in the eye. "That's it. No need for he-saids or she-saids at this point. We're startin' out fresh. No glancin' back over our shoulders lookin' for a sackful of don't-matters."

Eyeing the battle-tested Persian Gulf War veteran, Damion nodded and said, "Okay." For the next twenty minutes he brought Flora Jean up to speed on every facet of his disjointed investigation into Shandell's murder, including all that had happened from the time they'd left Shandell's repast until he'd left Niki's duplex that morning.

Now as he sat in the wobbly chair that CJ's late Uncle Ike, the man who'd taught CJ the bail-bonding business, had reduced three inches in height by sawing off the legs so that any prospective client would be forced to look up at him, Damion had the sense that he was about to learn a few much-needed investigative lessons.

Adjusting herself in her chair, Flora Jean said, "So now that you've painted me the big picture, sugar, whatta you propose doin'? I'll give you my take soon enough, but first I want yours."

Damion eased back in his seat and thought for several seconds before answering. "Since Niki's working on that Connie Eastland angle, I'd say we head back up to CSU and run down Jackie Woodson." He eyed Flora Jean tentatively, uncertain of the correctness of his answer.

Flora Jean nodded and cleared her throat. "Reasonable but unnecessary. At least for the moment. From what you've said about what you saw in those game tapes, Jackie's not goin' anywhere. Nobody's come after him so far. I'm guessin' he may feel a little pinched but not painfully uncomfortable. And since somebody with muscle, Asalon more than likely, owns his butt, I'm thinkin' your friend Happy Jack Woodson is feelin' real protected. He'll be there when we need him. And so will Coach Haroldson. As for Dr. Phillips and Garrett Asalon, they've both got too much at stake to run."

"So what do you say we do first?"

"We go back and look under a rock I didn't turn over completely the first time."

The look of puzzlement on Damion's face, a look that said, *But I've checked out everything already,* caused Flora Jean to smile. "You're lookin' a little confused, there, sugar. I know you've been tryin' real hard, but I got a few more miles on these treads of mine than you've got on yours. Let me wipe your confusion away. First off we're gonna pay a visit to somebody who lost a friend, somebody just like you. That pothead reporter I told you about, Wordell Epps. He knows more than he told me the other day when I talked to him—bet on it. Besides, I saw him hangin' around the cemetery during the inter-ment ceremony. Slouched all down in the front seat of his car thinkin' that somehow he was invisible. Bad way to make a funeral showing, especially around an overly suspicious former intelligence op like me. So we talk to him first, and then we head up to Fort Collins to try and run down Jackie and Sandy."

"What do you think Epps was up to?"

"Beats me, sugar. But we're gonna find out. Just like we're gonna find out if there's things he didn't tell me the other day."

"Where do you think we can find him?"

Flora Jean checked her watch. "At work," she said with a smile. "Where you find most God-fearin' folks this time of day."

Mario Satoni's tone was insistent. "You stay with that boy, Pinkie. You hear me? Asalon'll kill him. We both know that. And Hawkins may decide to come back." Increasingly hard of hearing, the eighty-four-year-old former mafia don pressed the receiver to his ear.

"I've got his back," Pinkie Niedemeyer said, sounding perturbed. "Stop worrying, will ya?"

"I hope you've got his back, and a lot sooner than you did last night."

"I told you, Mario, nobody got hurt up there in Nederland but Hawkins."

"Let's keep it that way. And you keep me posted, you hear?" Mario cradled the phone, leaving Pinkie shaking his head and listening to a dial tone. Tossing aside the *Rocky Mountain News* sports section he'd been reading, Pinkie rose from the 150-year-old rocking chair Mario had given him thirty years earlier on the day after Pinkie and Janet Stevens had announced their engagement, retrieved his shoulder holster and 9-mm from one of the chair's uprights, and thought about the fact that he was probably going to have to have a chat with Leotis Hawkins and Garrett Asalon one more time.

Chapter 24

Damion shook his head in mock disbelief. "You've gotta be kidding. I thought Pulitzer Prize–winning journalists spent their time hobnobbing with the rich and famous, or at least snuggled up to their sources."

"Guess you pegged things wrong," said Flora Jean. Her eyes were glued to the front door of the LaMar's Donuts shop that she and Damion had watched Wordell Epps enter fifteen minutes earlier. Stretching her legs out in the front seat of the ageless Suburban that CJ had used for surveillance work for the past twenty years—a vehicle she'd inherited half ownership in when they'd become business partners five years earlier—she glanced down at the oversized purse between her feet and the barely visible butt of the Browning 9-mm she'd carried since her return from the first Persian Gulf War.

"Think he'd be crazy enough to put up a fuss?" Damion asked, noting Flora Jean's quick glance toward the purse.

"Who knows? I'm hopin' the kinda fusses he likes to make are the ones he makes with words."

"Funny the way his supervisor at the *Rocky Mountain News* didn't hesitate one bit in telling us where Epps would be having lunch. I got the feeling when you told him who you were and why you wanted to talk to Epps that the man enjoyed hearing someone was out there looking to beat Epps at his own game."

"I don't think his newspaper cronies like Epps very much, and I can't say I blame . . . wait a second. Here he comes. Stay put, Damion."

Flora Jean watched Epps walk out of the donut shop and head for a battered, mud-brown Honda, the same car she'd seen him slouched down in at Shandell's interment. In one fluid movement, she grabbed her purse, opened the door, and stepped out onto the crumbling pavement. "Mr. Epps, wanta hold up for a sec?"

Clutching a bag of donuts in his right hand and looking startled, Epps continued toward his car. "What the hell do you want, Benson?"

"Need to talk to you about somethin', sugar."

"I talked to you as much as I intend to the other day."

"Why the brush-off, sugar? I used my roll-on this morning."

"You can dispense with the one-liners, Ms. Benson." Epps stopped next to his car and slipped his keys out of his pocket. "Since we last talked, there's been another murder. Shandell Bird's father, in case you missed it. Besides that, I had a very long and unpleasant visit from a homicide cop who didn't like the idea that I was rooting around in his murder investigation. Now, I don't suppose you're the one who sicced gap-toothed Sergeant Townsend on me, are you?"

"Sure didn't."

"Well, he got wind of what I was up to somehow." Epps extended his right arm as if to drive his index finger into Flora Jean's chest. Flora Jean grabbed the pesky investigative reporter by his hand, bending it backward until Epps screamed in pain.

"No touching, sugar. Cardinal rule of mine."

"Aaaahhhh! Let go!"

"I will. As soon as we come to an understandin'." She adjusted her purse strap on her shoulder.

"Okay, okay."

Strengthening her grip, Flora Jean said, "You mentioned to me the other day that your buddy Paul Grimes was workin' on a book."

"Yeah, he was." Epps let out a grunt.

"Well, since we talked, I've had the strangest feelin' that you know a lot more about that book than you told me. And, book lover that I am, I'm dyin' to have you tell me about it, especially since, unlike the cops, I don't give a rat's ass whether you're withholdin' evidence in a murder case."

"Let go of my hand, would you?"

"Glad to if we're gonna talk."

"Okay. Okay, we'll talk."

"I like your decision-makin', Epps." Flora Jean eased up on her grip and smiled. "Hate to have someone walk by here, see us in this love embrace, and call the cops. So now that you've agreed to talk, let's decide where. My place or yours?"

"Yours."

"Figured you'd say that. Nope, sugar. It's yours."

"Why?"

"'Cause at my place I've got nothin' to hide. Can't be so sure about that at yours. Who knows, you could have a houseful of murder evidence chucked away in your bureau drawers." Renewing the tension on Epps's hand, she turned to face the Suburban. "See that beast of a four-by-four over there?"

"Yeah." Epps winced in pain.

"We're gonna head straight for it, hand in hand, just like young lovers. The young man with me is gonna slip out of the front seat and let you get in while he slips in the back. You with me?"

"Yeah."

"Good." She lowered Epps's arm and, arms swinging, they headed for the Suburban. "Real good. 'Cause I got a 9-millimeter in my purse that says you better be."

Wordell Epps's apartment seemed smaller and darker than Flora Jean remembered. But small and dark or big and bright, the place had the putrid lingering smell of marijuana. On the ride from the donut shop, Epps had barely said a word except to say to Damion after Flora Jean's hasty introduction, "So I finally get to meet a man who turned down a sure million bucks. Funny, you don't look that stupid."

They'd just entered the apartment when Epps, wide-eyed, twitching, and acting like a hardcore junkie, rushed to his kitchen, extracted a bag of joints from a drawer, teased one out, and lit up. Offering the bag to Flora Jean and Damion, he said, "Happy to share." Looking disappointed and shaking his head when they both declined, he tucked the bag back into the drawer. "Feel a little better now." Continuing to inhale like a dying patient on a respirator, he took a donut out of the now grease-stained bag he'd set on a kitchen countertop. "These things are as sweet as sunshine; have one." He aimed the bag at Damion.

"No, thanks."

"Ms. Benson?"

"Nope."

"So what the hell is it the two of you do for fun, kick sick little puppies?"

"We track down murderers," came Damion's quick reply.

"Oh, yeah. I almost forgot. Just like Batman and Robin, except one of you's a woman."

Flora Jean stepped up to Epps, whisked the bag of donuts off the countertop, and handed the bag to Damion. "How many donuts are in there, Damion?"

Opening the bag and peering inside, Damion said, "I count eight."

"Eight. Now, that's a good, round, easy-to-remember number."

She patted Epps softly on the cheek. "That was a love tap, friend." Smiling, she slapped him on the other cheek with enough force to snap his head back and send his joint flying. "You've got a perfectly round eight minutes to give us some answers, Epps. I don't intend to do-si-do with you this time around."

"I don't have any answers," Epps said, retrieving his joint and looking petrified.

"Then I'll ask you a question. Why were you lurking around at Shandell Bird's funeral? You aren't family, and you certainly aren't a friend. And for the record, I know you were there. I saw that rattle-trap of yours and your pumpkin-sized head poking up from behind the steering wheel as I left."

When Epps didn't answer, Flora Jean said, "Seven minutes and ticking."

Uncertain exactly what the woman who, he'd discovered since her first visit, had once been a marine intelligence sergeant would do if he didn't cooperate, Epps said, "Suppose we do this. I give a little, and you give a little." He looked at Damion for support, only to realize from the look on Damion's face that Flora Jean was the lone decision-maker. "Whatta you say, Ms. Benson?" Epps took a quick toke off his joint. "It might be worth your while."

"Okay. Let's give it a try." Flora Jean eyed her watch. "Sing your song, sonny."

Looking relieved, Epps took a long, satisfying drag off his joint. "Paulie was writing a book about the college sports scene that he claimed was going to be a blockbuster."

Flora Jean eyed Epps thoughtfully, trying to determine if he was about to offer a piece of worthless information. "If it was a book about athletes using performance-enhancing drugs, that's yesterday's news."

"Nope. That's not what the book was about." Epps sounded to Flora Jean as if he was trying to determine how much information he could give out and still save his own skin. "What he was writing was a psychological-profile kind of book, a sort of case study. One of those Dr. Phil kind of books the public seems to lap up." He glanced at Damion and smiled. "Matter of fact, you're in the book, Madrid. And quite prominently, I might add," he said, noting the quizzical look on Damion's face. "Don't look so shocked, my man. You spent your college years pretty much playing the part of a public figure. No reason to be surprised that someone decided to write about you."

"So how is it you know so much about the book?" Flora Jean's voice was filled with skepticism. She took a step closer to Epps. "Better still, why didn't you tell me the whole story the other day?" Resting a hand on Epps's shoulder, she pressed her thumb against his collarbone until he winced in pain and jerked away.

"Who knows? Maybe it had something to do with feeling left out of the book thing. Although Paulie had one hell of a nose for news, and most of the time he could write rings around other people, he couldn't spell, punctuate, or use a computer worth a damn. When it came to writing, the man was old-school to a fault. Always wrote longhand on a yellow tablet—that is, when he wasn't at work."

"No computer at all?" Damion asked, looking surprised.

"Computers were heresy to Paulie, although he was forced to use them at work. I think in some ways he was actually afraid of the damn things. Because of his lack of punctuation, spelling, and computer skills, I generally copyedited anything he wrote outside the office. The newsroom secretary covered his ass at work." He eyed Flora Jean and smiled. "That's why I know so much about the book."

"I see. Mind telling me when I can run down and pick up my copy at the book store?" said Flora Jean.

"That I don't know. What I do know is that Paulie was almost done with the book when he was killed. And I know each chapter profiled what Paulie and the professor who was writing the book with him defined as a psychological archetype. He and that professor used personal case histories to drive home their points. They weren't quite done with every case history, including yours, Madrid."

Trying her best to understand Epps's story, Flora Jean asked, "That professor you keep talking about wouldn't happen to be Dr. Alicia Phillips, would it?"

"How'd you know that?" Epps asked, looking surprisingly self-satisfied.

"Turns out that just like you, I investigate things for a living. So now that we're down to the nitty-gritty, tell me, that manuscript you so lovingly copyedited for your friend Grimes—is it handy?"

"Yes, but I'm thinking the person I should be showing it to is that homicide detective working the case, Sergeant Townsend."

"Funny, the first time we talked, I got the impression you didn't particularly like cops. 'Assholes' is the word that comes to mind."

"I don't. But I got myself a little religion when Shandell's father turned up dead. Started to wonder if maybe I'd be next."

"Why would that be?" asked Damion.

"That book we've been talking about. Could be the killer knows I'm the one who pretty much transcribed it for Paulie. Could be the murderer's in the damn thing and doesn't really want to be. Like you, for instance, Madrid."

"Awfully convenient way for you to get us thinkin' you aren't the killer, don't you think?" asked Flora Jean.

"I'm not! If you want to talk to somebody who might've had a reason to kill Bird, talk to his girlfriend. A woman named Connie Eastland. Now, there's a double-dipping murderous shrew for you, at least according to Paulie."

"We've got someone working on that," said Damion, wondering how far Niki was into her luncheon assignment.

"Then it sounds as if you and Ms. Benson have your finger on the pulse of just about everything. The cops, Dr. Phillips, the Eastland woman. Anything the two of you think you missed?"

"We haven't found the murderer yet, but we will. In the meantime, why don't you fill us in on what you know about Connie Eastland." said Flora Jean.

"Sure," Epps said with a shrug. "And I got this straight from Paulie. He said she was milking the shit out of your boy Shandell, or at least she was planning to. And all the time she was doing it, she was also busy jacking off a mobster named Garrett Asalon. Bottom line is Mr. Macho Future NBA Superstar was getting himself used."

"And I'm pretty sure that's part of the reason he was killed," said Damion.

"Real likely. I talked to Eastland recently. Suggested that I knew about Paulie and the Phillips woman's book. Let her know I even had inside dope on her boyfriend Shandell's involvement with drugs." Epps broke into a self-satisfied grin. "For the record, Ms. Benson, I'm capable of doing your kind of investigating too."

"How'd she respond?" Damion asked.

"She got up her hackles. Told me to drop dead."

"We've got ourselves some sideshow goin' here." Flora Jean shook her head. "Tell-all books, gold-diggin' women, game-fixin' mobsters. A real three-ring circus. Might as well toss one more item in the ring." She flashed Epps a look that as much said, *Time to give it up.* "The manuscript, Mr. Epps. Wanta get it?"

"Sure. It's here. I wouldn't think of keeping something that valuable anywhere near the vultures I work with. They told you where to find me today, didn't they? No question the SOBs would steal."

Epps reached for his stash to get another joint, but Flora Jean grabbed the bag out of his hand. "You'll have time for that after we're gone. Right now we're interested in somethin' a little more mind-blowin'."

The 228 pages of Paul Grimes and Alicia Phillips's manuscript were formatted much like the scores of college term papers Damion had written. The text featured separate subject headings, each followed by a detailed discussion. What differed was the fact that the discussions featured profiles of so-called athlete prototypes, and that each discussion was followed by a lengthy case history.

Seated on a lumpy couch in Wordell Epps's living room a few feet from where Flora Jean and Epps stood talking, Damion let out a sigh. He'd just finished reading a rambling eight-page discussion of what Phillips and Grimes defined in broad psychological terms as their profile for the "Self-Reliant Paranoid Introvert." Gritting his teeth, he flipped back to the first paragraph of the discussion and reread it:

Hardworking, efficient, standoffish, officious, often sycophantic, and flattering to the extreme, the paranoid introvert is the perfect example of someone who lives in mortal fear that their day of disaster will surely come and that when it does, they will be required to either escape from the imagined or real gulag they've created for themselves or suffocate. They are fearful that in the end their manufactured identity will be stripped from them and their deepest secrets revealed. One would think that someone as athletically gifted and potentially powerful by virtue of wealth, strength of personality, and charisma as the Self-Reliant Para-noid Introvert would be immune to such fear. But they are not. Although one might expect that the archetypes described in this book, men and women whose words and TV images are so profound as to influence millions, have few detectable flaws, that is not actually the case. CASE HISTORY TO FOLLOW. EXAMPLE: SHANDELL BIRD. TEXTUAL PSEU-DONYM: DARRYL HOWARD.

A handwritten note had been jotted near the bottom of the page: *Consult Connie E. for details and determine if we can use Leon Bird in Shandell's case history. She'll know, $$ could be pricey.*

Shaking his head, Damion slowly flipped through several more pages. He recognized the names of several people he'd known either personally or through the news. There were profiles of NBA play-ers, coaches, and former rivals of his from other schools. Some of the discussions and case histories were complete. Others, like Shandell's, appeared to be works in progress. In every instance the real individ-ual's name had an accompanying pseudonym.

When he reached his own name on page 48, he realized that his hands were sweating. He eyed the subject heading: "Decisive, Self-Assured Perfectionist (Also see 'Self-Assured Perfectionist, Indecisive,' page 83)" and read on:

As noted earlier in this volume, the terms used to describe our sports archetypes are not necessarily standard taxonomy for the profession. Rather, they have been arrived at after years of research in a reasoned attempt to examine the psychology that motivates the gladiator ath-lete. The term "Self-Assured Perfectionist" is thus a research term coined to accurately define an archetype rather than standard taxon-omy of the academy.

The Self-Assured Perfectionist is competitive to a fault, and like many of the athletic types described here, they tend to be natural leaders. This athletic type tends to occasional sullenness and is frequently unable to come to grips with the fact that it is their athletic skill, rather than some other attribute they may see as more significant, that defines them. They sometimes have trouble seeing the forest for the trees, and although they tend to be natural leaders, they prefer to shun the limelight. Frequently, when finished with their athletic careers, they find no place to land. CASE HISTORY TO FOLLOW. EXAMPLE: DAMION MADRID. TEXTUAL PSEUDONYM: CARL LYNART. EVALUATION NOTES FROM DAMION MADRID'S SUMMER SESSION, FRESHMAN YEAR, TO BE TRANSCRIBED HERE.

Noting the look of anguish on Damion's face, Flora Jean said, "So whatta you got, Blood? Found yourself in there yet? And are they singin' your praises?"

"Less than I would've liked." Damion shook the manuscript at Epps. "This thing reads like pop-culture psychobabble."

"Madrid, Madrid. You sound offended. Something in the text touch a nerve? Takes the wind out of your sails to see your reflection in the mirror sometimes, doesn't it? Well, for the record, according to Paulie, the book wasn't intended to have any kind of scientific, scholarly, or academic merit. Quite the opposite. From what I gathered, the intent was to have the book hit all the right best-seller lists so Paulie and Dr. Phillips could make the TV talk-show rounds, dish their dirt, and rake in the money."

"Where the hell were they getting their information? Neither one of them ever interviewed me," Damion said defensively.

"Maybe not, but they sure as hell interviewed your friend Blackbird. And according to Paulie, some of the information they assembled on him was gathered before he even started at CSU."

Damion slammed his fist into the couch. "Damn! I did talk to Dr. Phillips one-on-one the summer before our freshman year, but everyone on the team did. Coach Horse required us to. It was nothing more than a fifteen-minute chat about keeping my nose clean and what to expect from college life, as I remember it."

"Could be you're remembering wrong," said Epps. "But whether you are or aren't, it looks like Dr. Phillips was into finding out what made you tick long before you ever hit the school and the basketball court."

"But I barely talked to her during the next four years after that. Even though Coach Horse sometimes insisted that I should after I'd had a bad game or we came off a tough loss."

"Barely's not the same as never, Madrid. You talked to her, and that's the point." Epps seemed to enjoy his chance to point the finger at Phillips.

Feeling duped, Damion said, "Yeah, I did. So how long had she and Grimes been working on their project?" He tossed the manuscript aside on the couch.

"I'm not sure about Paulie's involvement—a year, maybe two— but he told me Phillips had been working on her premise of showcasing chinks in the armor of her so-called gladiator athletes for a good part of her career. It almost got her canned at another university, according to him. Something to do with inappropriate contact with student athletes by a person in a position of trust and unsanctioned human experimentation."

Flora Jean shook her head. "Sounds like the good doctor was makin' up the rules as she went along."

"Yeah, it does," said Damion. "What I'm wondering is what was in it for her."

"A big fat paycheck, what else?" said Epps, taking a toke off a newly lit joint and eyeing Damion as if he were stupid. "I know they had a contract with a publisher in New York. Paulie never told me exactly what they signed on for, but it was in the high six figures, I know that."

Damion eyed the manuscript and shook his head. "They pay you that kind of money to write that kind of crap?"

"We live in a tell-all, voyeuristic, celebrity-driven society, kid. Maybe you should start taking notice."

"They couldn't possibly have gotten away with it. Someone would've sued them."

"Unlikely," said Epps. "They weren't going to name names. The manuscript you're turning your nose up at is just a draft. No real names would've appeared on publication. Your friend Blackbird would've simply become Joe Dokes and the subject of Case History A. And you, my friend, would have been just another Sam Smith and turned into Case History B. Who knows, in the end, considering the public figure angle involved here, they could have ended up using the real names."

"Yeah, I saw the name changes in the notes. But the information was gathered without our permission, and I'd be willing to bet that Dr. Phillips probably used either federal or state grant funds to generate her data. Even college students know that's a no-no."

"Can you prove that?" Epps asked pointedly. "In case you missed it, we're not talking cancer research here, Madrid. No DNA markers involved, and none of that *CSI* shit. What we're talking about is at best a few tape-recorded sessions, some handwritten notes, fifteen or twenty years' worth of a leading sports psychologist's observations, and a Pulitzer Prize–winning investigative reporter's thoughtful impressions. Have you got any documentation that proves Phillips didn't have permission to use her notes from talking to you before you began your freshman year? Any proof in fact that she talked to you at all? Can you produce any receipts or records, tapes or signed consent forms, to show that she used federal or state or even private research funds to tell you and your teammates any more than what to expect in college?"

Taking in the look of betrayal plastered on Damion's face, Flora Jean said, "Damn, Epps. You're one hell of an operator when it comes to manipulatin' the truth."

Epps smiled and shook his head. "No, Paulie and Alicia Phillips had me beat by a long shot there. I'm simply your run-of-the-mill investigative reporter." He sounded disappointed.

Eyeing Flora Jean and looking confused, Damion asked, "Do you think Dr. Phillips killed Shandell?"

"Maybe. At this point I'm not certain. At least this new information gives us another reason to land on the good doctor's doorstep." She glanced at Epps. "What's your take?"

"I'd say she was a conduit at best. But since you're asking, I'd put my money on that mobster you mentioned on the way over here being the killer—Asalon, I believe you said. Or maybe the coach. He could've been acting as her shill, feeding her a steady diet of available athletes."

"For the record, sugar, the name is Asalon, and I'm less inclined to think he's the killer. The man's a pro, and even if he was involved, he sure wouldn't have been stupid enough to kill Shandell and Grimes himself. He's the kind that has other people do his dirty work."

"Craigy Theisman maybe," said Damion.

"Now you're talkin' my language," said Flora Jean. "Or maybe that hit man out of Detroit. The midget you mentioned that Pinkie told you about last night."

"But why would Asalon want to get rid of Shandell and Grimes?" Damion asked, looking puzzled. "Asalon didn't have anything to do with the stupid book."

Epps responded quickly. "For the same reason you got all bent out of shape just a bit ago when I said something about recognizing yourself in the mirror. The cops have a way of putting a name and ultimately a face on a murderer when quite often they don't start out with anything but a reflection in the mirror. Maybe Shandell's case history pointed a finger at Asalon, and he didn't like it."

Nodding in agreement, sensing they'd gotten what they'd come for and that she and Damion had said enough about where they planned to head with their investigation in front of Epps, Flora Jean said, "Think it's about time we go, Blood. Let's let Mr. Epps do his thing and we'll do ours."

"Okay," Damion said, eyeing Epps with a renewed hint of suspicion. "You sure know a lot about that manuscript."

"Like I told you, I pretty much typed it for Paulie."

"You wouldn't have wanted to steal your friend's thunder, now, would you?" Flora Jean asked.

"Of course not. You're far too jaded, Ms. Benson."

"Comes from dealin' with the what's-in-it-for-me kinda folks I've had to rub shoulders with for so many years." Glancing at Damion, who'd reopened the manuscript to page 48, she said, "Let's go, Blood. See if we can't run down a better class of people."

Chapter 25

Flora Jean had skirted most of downtown Denver's traffic crunch, taking York Street northbound. Satisfied at having erased twelve minutes off the travel time to Fort Collins by cutting through the western edge of what some people considered the 'hood, she and Damion found themselves cruising through the clogged 104th Avenue–I-25 interchange. Pegging the shock-weary Suburban's speedometer at 70, she eyed the ever-encroaching sea of houses, condos, townhomes, and business parks hugging the interstate and thought a little sadly about what had once been open tallgrass prairie.

"So whatta you think about Coach Haroldson tellin' you he's a beneficiary on that insurance policy of Shandell's?" Flora Jean asked as they sped north past mile marker 231. "Think two hundred and fifty grand coulda gotten him thinkin' that one of his former players might've been dispensable?"

"Things are bad enough, Flora Jean. No need to start conjuring stuff up. Coach Horse didn't kill Shandell."

Flora Jean's response was an understanding nod. She understood very well that Damion couldn't fathom someone he revered having such a dark side. She decided not to belabor the point, or to mention cases she'd worked in which brothers had bludgeoned their sisters to death, wives had electrocuted their husbands, and businessmen had pushed their partners to their deaths from ten-story buildings in order to collect on far less lucrative policies.

Two miles south of the always-busy I-25 Dacono exit, Damion's cell phone rang, chirping out the first few bars of the Motown classic "My Girl." "It's Niki," Damion said, snapping the phone off his belt.

"How do you know that?"

"From the ring tone."

Flora Jean shook her head. "Kids."

"What's up, Ms. America?" Damion asked eagerly.

"That's Ms. Venezuela to you, you Yankee dog. Where are you, by the way?" Niki asked, forcing back a laugh.

"Cruising up I-25 in the Suburban with Flora Jean on our way to Fort Collins. How'd your lunch go?"

"Not so good."

"Don't tell me Ms. Blue-Eyed Blonde told you your locks were too black and your skin a tad too cinnamony for her and her sisters to invite you to the pledge party?"

"I wish it were that simple, Damion." Niki's voice trailed off.

"Sounds like you turned something up."

"I did."

"Bad?"

"Depends on how you look at it."

"I took my rose-colored glasses off a long time ago. Might as well lay it on the line."

"Okay. Maria knows a lot. A lot about Connie and her family, and I'm afraid a lot about Shandell."

"And?"

"And she claims Connie was just using Shandell. That he was her one chance at the brass ring—that she only latched on to him for the money."

"Nothing new there. In fact, I sort of suspected it."

"Me too. But some other things came out that I didn't expect. According to Maria, Shandell was using Connie too. Have you got your seatbelt on, Damion?"

"Yes." Looking perplexed, Damion glanced down at his seatbelt. "Sure do."

"Maria said Shandell was gay."

"*What?*"

"That's what she told me—point-blank—right as we were having coffee. I almost spit my coffee out, I was so shocked. She said she's the only other person in the sorority who knew and that Connie swore her to secrecy. She claimed Connie and Shandell had an understanding—he'd take her where she wanted to go socially and financially, and she'd be the ever-present don't-dare-question-my-masculinity drop of feminine sweetness on his arm. Those were Connie's exact words, according to Maria."

"There's no way."

"That's what I said. But there's more. Maria claims Connie started to cash in a few of her chips early, before Shandell ever headed off to the NBA, by hooking Shandell up with that mobster Asalon, the one Pinkie told us about. It was part of a pact Shandell agreed to in order for Connie to keep his secret."

"She's full of it." Damion slammed his fist down on the armrest, startling Flora Jean. "No way in hell Shandell could've been gay!"

"I'm just telling you what I found out, Damion."

"Well, somebody's lying."

"I'm just the messenger, Damion. No need to shoot me."

"Sorry, babe. Let's just drop the issue for the moment and let me get my brainwaves back in sync. Anything else come out of your meeting?"

"Yes. One other thing. It turns out that the blonde-haired tight-bodies of dear old Tri Delt like to dig into your family history when they're considering giving you a key to their kingdom. Maria seemed to know as much about Connie's family as she knew about Connie."

"Got a for-instance for me?"

"Sure do. She said Connie's father spent a lot of money on lawyers a few years back, getting himself out of a mess involving what Maria would only define as a petty white-collar crime. All I could get out of her was that it had something to do with junk bonds, underworld types, and improperly registered securities."

"Interesting. Could be Mr. Eastland found himself in bed with the wrong people. Would you believe the name Garrett Asalon suddenly keeps popping up in my mind?"

"We're on the same page there. That's all I could get out of her besides getting stuck with the lunch tab. Oh, and by the way, hot-shot, as we were leaving Maria asked me if we'd gotten engaged."

"What did you tell her?"

"I told her the truth. That in a lot of ways you were chiseled out of the same piece of noncommittal granite as your godfather, CJ Floyd. That shut the prissy little gossip-monger up."

"I'll be sure to tell CJ that when I pick him and Mavis up tonight at DIA."

"He loves me, Blood. He'll take my side. So what are you and Flora Jean planning on doing while you're in Fort Collins?"

"Talk to everybody with any kind of insight into who might've killed Shandell one more time. We did get a lead from that bong-head, Wordell Epps. It turns out that Alicia Phillips and Paul Grimes, that investigative reporter who was killed, were writing a book about the psychological dark side of college athletes. Shandell was one of their featured players."

"Interesting. Did you make the cut?"

"Sure did."

"And what's your dark side?"

"Don't have one.... At least, I don't think I do," Damion added with an uncustomary air of uncertainty.

Realizing from his tone that she'd struck a nerve, Niki said, "Call me when you get back from Fort Collins, Damion, and please would you try listening to Flora Jean?"

"I will." Damion flipped his cell phone closed. After staring straight ahead down the interstate for the next couple of minutes, mulling over what Niki had said and trying to come to grips with the often ugly and ever-changing nuances of life, he turned to Flora Jean. "So what do you think, Flora Jean? You heard the conversation. Do you think Shandell was gay?"

"Don't really know, Blood. But I can tell you this for sure. Being outta step with the rest of the world, for whatever reason, is sometimes enough to get you killed."

Damion found himself thinking about the takeaway message from *A Morning at the Office: Outsiders aren't welcome here*. Recalling the inscription Shandell had written in Leon's book, a message that only seemed to reiterate that point, he eyed Flora Jean and said, "I guess nobody really enjoys being on the outside looking in."

"You're right there, Blood. Absolutely and positively nobody."

Damion sat, thoughtfully silent for the remaining twenty-minute ride to Fort Collins. He'd never even considered the possibility that Shandell might have been gay, let alone the idea that he might have been killed for reasons tied to his secret. The more he thought about it, the more he realized that blackmail could easily have triggered his best friend's murder. There was no way Shandell would've gotten himself involved in peddling performance-enhancing drugs to kids unless someone had had a gun to his head, and he knew that Shandell wouldn't have let Coach Horse or his teammates down by getting involved in a point-shaving scam unless he was fearful of losing his reputation, his life, or both.

When it came to the elite masculine world of college and professional sports, Damion understood that you'd jump off a bridge before you'd admit to being gay. Drug use, petty larceny, infidelity, spousal abuse, lying, being a flat-out racist, and even committing a felony were problems that could be overcome. But homosexuality was a guaranteed kiss of death. Even whispers about one's sexual orientation in the wide world of sports had the potential to end a career.

Sitting back in his seat and frowning, Damion tried his best to recall any instance in all the years they'd known one another when Shandell might've dropped even a hint that he was gay. He thought about the scores of camping and fishing trips they'd been on with other kids, about school dances and basement parties. Even about their first teenage drinking experiences, when they'd both been at least temporarily uninhibited and adrift in those euphoric, let-your-hair-down, tell-all moments. He reflected on the endless basketball clinics and strength-conditioning camps they'd been to, where participants had often been forced to bunk eight and ten to a room. He racked his brain trying to recall anytime during high school or college when Shandell had gone off on his own to, in effect, do his thing. But no matter how hard he tried, he couldn't recall a single instance when Shandell had acted like anything but the introverted gentle giant he was.

And then it hit him. Paul Grimes and Alicia Phillips had even touched on it in their manuscript, and it appeared, he told himself, that Shandell had honed it to perfection. What Shandell had done was spent his all-too-brief lifetime mastering the art of hiding who he was. And who better to pull off a charade like that than a world-class athlete, someone used to the grueling and repetitive aspects of practice? Someone adept at masking physical and mental pain? If Shandell had been gay, he was one person who could have played his heterosexual part so perfectly that no one, not even his best friend, could've seen beyond the facade.

It would have been easy for someone who was performing such a charade to spend his entire freshman year of college orchestrating a reputation as the ultimate playboy. Tossing coeds aside one by one and never bedding one of them until he could settle down with someone Machiavellian, callous, and cagey enough to go along with the game. And it had worked until Shandell had come up against a ruthless sports psychologist itching to write a book, an investigative reporter looking for his own pot of gold, and perhaps even a long-absent father who wouldn't leave Shandell alone.

The question now, as Damion saw it, was who among all the people Shandell had conned—including teachers, coaches, teammates, gangsters, family members, and friends—had had a reason to kill him.

Glancing at Damion as she took the Fort Collins–bound Prospect Road off-ramp from I-25, Flora Jean said, "You've been too quiet for too long, Blood. Gonna pop a gasket, you don't get your feelin's out real soon."

"I'm okay," Damion said sullenly.

"And I say you aren't. Wanta tell me what you been thinkin' about these past twenty minutes?"

"I've been thinking about Shandell and who might have killed him. And right now, after that latest bombshell, I've gotta admit, I'm pretty confused."

"No need for confusion, sugar. We start where we said we would back at the office. First we run down Rodney Sands and Jackie Woodson. Then we head for a little powwow with Dr. Phillips. Sometimes bein' a good soldier means holin' your position when you're under fire. A lot of times when you think long, you think wrong, Blood. Remember that."

Smiling at the sage advice, Damion said, "I will."

"Be sure you do. You don't wanta end up missin' the forest for the trees."

With Flora Jean's admonition reverberating in his head, Damion relaxed back in his seat, recalling that Alicia Phillips and Paul Grimes had used pretty much the same words to describe his archetype in their manuscript. Sensing that things were about to come to a head, he had the feeling he'd soon find out if they were right.

It was always when she looked at the photograph of her two horses that Alicia Phillips regressed the most. Generally she let the past stay where it was, encased in the same mystical place as the long-lost cattle ranch she'd grown up on and her dead father and mother. Lost forever in a sea of tall grass, meandering trout streams, and alpine timber. But whenever she decided to take a close, hard look at the photograph of her horses, who'd been auctioned off at a sheriff's sale, the enormity of her loss resurfaced.

She'd just turned fourteen when her father had lost their ranch through a combination of bad business decisions, bad management, hostile neighbors, and a city miles away in need of a commodity as precious as gold: their water. The psychological scars that had come with the loss of her five-thousand-acre playground remained, and even though she now had a life that most people would envy, it was a life she'd never fully embraced, or for that matter even wanted.

In the years since the loss of their ranch, she'd battled to re-create her own version of it. Progress had been slow and measured, but real. Ten years earlier she'd purchased a five-acre parcel thirty miles northeast of Fort Collins, and soon after that an adjoining fifteen acres. In the past year she'd bought the 160-acre quarter section that abutted her land directly to the south, and although she realized that the 180 acres she now owned could never replace the five thousand she'd lost, it was a start. Once she finished reassembling her dream, she'd kiss academia and CSU good-bye, turn her back on research proposals, across-the-hall geniuses, and recalcitrant students, and return to where she belonged.

She'd hoped that the book she'd been writing with Paul Grimes was going to put her there more quickly, but for the moment it would have to stay in limbo, forced to take a back seat to the murder of Shandell Bird. But when the crisis passed, she would return to rebuilding her dream.

Glancing out her office window and placing the photograph of her two Swedish warmbloods back on her desk, she decided she'd given the university enough of herself for one day. If she left right then and said to hell with students and research papers and poorly written master's theses, she'd be able to get to her ranch in time to enjoy the smell of the earth, the warmth of the sun, and maybe even a horseback ride at sunset.

She'd turned to lock a file cabinet when a wide-eyed Connie Eastland rushed into her office, looking perturbed. Not at all surprised by the unannounced visit, since like most of her colleagues in the building she reserved Monday afternoon for office hours and student visits, Alicia gave Connie a thoughtful look and said, "You're lucky you caught me. I was just about to leave."

Returning the greeting with half a nod, Connie said breathlessly, "We've got serious problems, Alicia."

Familiar with Connie's emotional ebbs and flows, Alicia said, "So tell me about it."

Connie's words came out in a shower of spittle. "I got a call from one of my college sorority sisters a little bit ago. Someone I'd trust with my life. She said she'd just had lunch with Niki Estaban, Damion Madrid's girlfriend, and that Niki had given her the third degree about me and Shandell's relationship. Asking her questions like how close had we really been, had I really cared about Shandell, and whether I was seeing other men. To top it off, Niki mentioned Garrett Asalon. Damion's getting closer, Alicia. I know it. He's going to figure every-thing out. You've got to do something."

Patting Connie reassuringly on the shoulder, Alicia said, "Take a deep breath, Connie. And for once in your life let your head do your thinking instead of your pocketbook. Damion's not going to figure out anything because there's nothing to figure out."

"What? How can you be so blasé? He'll figure out that I was using his best friend, and sooner or later he's going to figure out that in effect I was pretty much blackmailing Shandell."

"I don't think so. Blackmail involves the extortion of money. Did you ever extort money from Shandell?"

Looking confused, Connie said, "Well, no. You know what I did. I agreed not to out him to the world in exchange for a ticket to the good life. You knew our deal."

"And your deal was for him to give you money for that favor?"

"Not exactly."

"Case closed, then. Shandell made his choice. Just like you and me. He could either tell the world who he really was or continue to dribble a basketball, rake in the money, and have the masses grovel at his feet. He chose the latter."

"And when Damion figures that all out, he'll come after me. I'm not made of cast iron like you are, Alicia. I didn't grow up battling rattlesnakes and coyotes on some hardscrabble ranch. And I didn't have to overcome losing my mother and father to suicide or have to deal with some spinster aunt who beat the hell out of me. And I certainly don't have what it takes to look someone in the eye and ask probing questions about their life, knowing I'm writing a book about that life that could destroy them. I'm not as hardened as you are, Alicia. Let's face it—that's how you and Grimes got your so-call gladiators to cooperate. You looked them sympathetically in the eye, lied to them, and got them to pour out their souls."

For the first time since Connie had rushed in, Alicia looked truly aggravated. "Could be you're right. But then again, where's the proof? We shredded all those counseling session records, remember?"

"Yes. And that might very well get you off the hook. But I'm still the one in the hot seat when it comes to Damion."

"And I'll take care of that. Why don't you run down the hall and get yourself some water before you blow a gasket? I'll make a couple of phone calls that'll short-circuit the would-be doctor. Then we'll head out to the ranch and talk this over more thoroughly. Craigy Theisman called me earlier anyway. Said he wanted to talk to us both. I was going to call you and tell you."

"The ranch? I can't. I've got plans. And what are you going to have that gorilla of a man do to Damion?"

"Nothing that will hurt anything but his ego. What Damion needs is to be wrapped in a nice, neat-fitting homosexuality shroud, just like Shandell. Now, are you going to game-plan with me or not? We'll only be at the ranch for an hour or so."

"Okay," Connie said hesitantly.

"Fine. Let me make those phone calls, and instead of water, why don't you run across the street to Starbucks and get us a couple of lattes? I could use the caffeine jolt." She reached into her purse, extracted a twenty-dollar bill, and handed it to Connie.

Looking relieved, Connie said, "Yes, that might be better."

"Make mine hazelnut. And Connie, try and calm down. We'll be out of this thunderstorm in no time."

"I hope so," Connie said, turning to leave.

"We will. I'd bet the ranch on it, and you know if I wasn't certain of the outcome, I'd never do that."

As a transplant to the Mile High City from Massachusetts, Craigy Theisman had been robbed of his favorite Bay State delicacy for over a decade, forced all that time to eat water-logged Rocky Mountain imitations served on tasteless, often rock-hard buns instead of the signature East Coast Thumann's hot dogs he'd grown up on. That was, until Steve's Snappin' Dogs had debuted on Denver's East Colfax Avenue a few years earlier. Since that time Theisman had never failed to stop by Steve's on any trip that put him within fifteen minutes of the place.

Theisman had taken his time on the trip from Louisville to Fort Collins that morning. Garrett Asalon had told him to take things leisurely. His instructions were to talk to Phillips and an increasingly nervous Connie Eastland, together if at all possible, and remind them that they'd both signed on for the long haul when they'd agreed to use the threat of a tell-all book about his homosexuality to get Shandell Bird to shave a few points in critical basketball games. He also had meetings scheduled with Jackie Woodson and Rodney Sands to remind them that they needed to keep their mouths shut about those point-shaving schemes.

Theisman hadn't heard from Connie, but he had called her condo and left a message, and he expected that before he finally got to the overgrazed, windy patch of cow pasture Alicia Phillips liked to call a ranch, Connie would call him back.

The man who had served Theisman two Jersey dogs—an all-beef hot dog loaded with spicy mustard, relish, caraway sauerkraut, red onions, and bacon—and a basket of skin-on French fries was busy talking with another customer when Theisman waved across the restaurant at him and said, "Snappin' good as usual, Joey."

"We aim to please," Joey Farthing said, cocking his arm and giving Theisman a crisp salute. "Don't want people leaving here on a half-empty stomach. Could be dangerous to their health." Farthing broke into a booming laugh.

"That it could be," said Theisman, patting the 9-mm in his jacket pocket. "A hungry man is a mistake-prone man, and the world's got enough mistakes runnin' around already." Rising from the stool he'd occupied for almost half an hour, Theisman exited the restaurant and walked across the parking lot toward his car to head for Fort Collins. He'd deal with every issue Asalon had assigned him, even if it took until midnight to round up Eastland, Phillips, and Jackie Woodson.

Concerned that Connie might come back any second and interrupt her conversation, Alicia Phillips was thirty seconds into a phone conversation that had her seething. "I want you to be out at my ranch and set up within ninety minutes." Sounding like an infantry officer barking orders at an inept subordinate, she said, "I'll give you directions."

"Why the hell are you so nervous? Calm down, would you?"

Ignoring the directive, she said, "You can set up down by the creek. The spot will be marked for you."

"Are you sure we need to take her out? Maybe we should talk it over first."

"Would I be calling you if I wasn't? She's poison."

"Okay. I'll set up. But you're taking the blame on this if anything goes wrong."

"It won't come to that. Just wait for me to walk her down to the creek and take your shot when she's on the downstream side of the creek bend."

"Okay."

"Gotta get off. I think I hear her coming back. Be ready, okay?"

"Always am." The phone clicked off without another word being said.

Chapter 26

Like most people trying to locate someone who likely didn't want to be found, Damion had never realized how large the so-called sleepy college town of Fort Collins could be. He and Flora Jean had spent an hour and a half trying to find three people, with absolutely no success. No Jackie Woodson and no Rodney Sands in any of the places Damion thought they might be. No returned phone calls, and worst of all, Coach Haroldson turned out to be out of town on a hastily arranged recruiting trip, according to his secretary.

Frustrated at having wasted an hour and a half, Damion glanced across the front seat of the Suburban at Flora Jean and shook his head. "Maybe we should've called earlier, let them all know we wanted to talk to them. Chances are we would've stumbled across at least one of them."

"Probably not, sugar. Folks on the run and folks with somethin' to hide don't sit around waitin' to have tea and crumpets with the people lookin' to pin 'em to the wall."

"Coach Horse isn't running."

"Well, he ain't nowhere to be found, is he?"

"He's on a recruiting trip," Damion protested as Flora Jean pulled the Suburban up to a stoplight at the intersection of College Avenue and Prospect Road.

"Okay, so he's out recruitin' his next Blood-and-Blackbird tandem while Woodson and Sands are at the library crammin' for their

PhDs. Wanta keep an open mind on this, Damion? Nobody gets excluded as a suspect. Even Coach Haroldson."

Recalling their agreement, Damion said, "Yes."

"Okay. Let's say for the moment we move on past Sands and Woodson and the coach and down the road to Dr. Phillips. You good with that?"

"Yeah. I'm pretty sure Mondays are still office-hour days for her. She should be in."

"Know the way to her office?"

"It'll be seven or eight blocks down College Avenue," Damion said, pointing to the right.

"Maybe we'll turn up something solid." Flora Jean turned right onto College, nosing the Suburban due north.

"Hope so," said Damion, sounding almost as frustrated as he had after reading his profile in the Phillips and Grimes manuscript.

The Wilford Hall annex was dark and all but empty when Flora Jean and Damion stepped out of the late-afternoon haze into the building's foyer.

"Strange-lookin' place," said Flora Jean. "Kinda dark and musty. And creaky," she added, as the hundred-year-old hardwood floors creaked beneath their feet.

"It's a landmark. The joke around campus has always been that the handful of professors who have offices here need it dark so they can think. Heavy-duty eggheads and faculty superstars occupy the place for the most part."

"Dr. Phillips ranks that high up the food chain?"

"She's pretty damn smart."

"Let's hope she's smart enough to have stayed late today. Where's her office?"

"Second floor, northwest corner."

"Corner office? Damn! Do it, girl!"

"There's an elevator down at the end of the hall, but the stairs are quicker."

"You got point, Blood." Flora Jean motioned for Damion to lead the way.

The way she'd said *point* had an eerie ring. More than once, Damion had heard CJ utter that very word in absolutely the same way. Always with the same foreboding tone of a war veteran. As they headed for the brass-railed stairway that led to the second floor, he had the sense that after so many miscasts, they were about to finally get a strike.

The second floor was mustier and darker than the first, but its fifteen-foot-wide hallways and twelve-foot ceilings gave it a surprisingly open feel.

"Last office on the left," Damion said a few steps before reaching the door to Alicia Phillips's office. Looking disappointed, he glanced up at the transom above the door. "I don't think she's in. Her transom's closed." Shaking his head and looking dejected, Damion stepped back from the door. He was about to take a second step backward when the office door directly behind him and across the hall swung open and a tall, gaunt man with wrinkled, sun-damaged skin stepped out into the hallway.

"Can I help you?"

"Yes. We're looking for Dr. Phillips," Damion said, pivoting to face the man.

"Why, you're Damion Madrid," the man said, almost in awe. Damion nodded and smiled.

"I saw pretty close to every game you ever played for CSU." The man extended a hand. "I'm Lucas Hogan, and to tell you the truth, I'm surprised we've never met. Guess you didn't require as much of Alicia's hand-holding as most of your fellow athletes. Hear you're headed off to medical school."

"Sure am. In a couple of weeks."

"Medicine's a long way from rocks," Hogan said, pointing to the Geology Department sign next to his door before glancing at Flora Jean.

Smiling, Flora Jean nodded politely and said, "Flora Jean Benson."

"Afraid you just missed Alicia," said Hogan.

"How long has she been gone?" asked Flora Jean.

"No more than fifteen minutes—twenty minutes tops. I'm sure she's headed for her ranch."

"Why so certain?"

The way Flora Jean posed the question, as if he might be mistaken, caused Hogan to hesitate and stroke his chin before answering. "She had her riding boots with her when she left. That usually means she's on her way to her ranch."

"Did you talk to her? Get any kinda confirmation on where she was headed?"

"No. I doubt she even saw me. You sound concerned, Ms. Benson. Is there a problem?"

"No problem. Was she alone?"

"As a matter of fact, she wasn't." Looking as if he'd stumbled onto the answer to a thorny problem, Hogan asked, "Are you and Alicia and Damion here looking into the Shandell Bird murder case?"

Flora Jean responded with a quick "Yes."

"Sorry about your friend," Hogan said sympathetically to Damion.

"Thanks." Damion paused momentarily before asking, "Now, what about that other person who was with Dr. Phillips? Did you know them?"

"No, I didn't, but I can tell you this—she was attractive. Small-ish, short hair, and sort of athletic-looking. And pretty well-endowed, if you know what I mean." He looked at Flora Jean as if hoping he hadn't offended her.

"Go on," said Flora Jean.

"That's it. I'm sure I've seen the young lady here before, but I can't give you a name."

"Think it mighta been Connie Eastland?" Flora Jean asked Damion.

"That would be my guess. The description's right on."

Damion slipped his wallet out of his back pocket, took out a plastic bifold filled with photos, and held one of the photos up for Hogan to look at. "Is that her?" he asked, pointing to Connie in a photograph of her, Niki, himself, and Shandell at the Sweet Sixteen regional NCAA basketball tournament the previous spring.

"Sure is. Looks like you were all having fun."

"We were." Damion's voice, tinged with sadness, trailed off. "So you think they're headed for Dr. Phillips's ranch?"

"I don't know about the young lady, but it's more than a safe bet that Alicia's headed for that ranch just like she does every Monday. If she could live out there full time and never set foot back on this campus, I know she would. And you know what? There's some of her wistfulness in all of us. If I could've, I'd have been a fighter pilot myself."

"I'd be a little wary of them F-16s if I were you, Professor. They've been known to get shot outta the sky," said Flora Jean.

"That's why they make ejection seats," said Hogan, but his look said he wondered what if anything the tall, buxom woman actually knew about F-16s.

Looking the man up and down, Flora Jean found herself thinking, *You know what, maybe you could handle an F-16.* "Do you know how to get to that ranch?" she asked, turning to Damion.

Damion shrugged. "No."

"No problem," said Hogan. "I've been out there half-a-dozen times. I'll be happy to give you directions, but first you've got to tell me if you think that woman in the photo is tied to the Blackbird killing."

"She may be," said Damion.

"Good gracious. Do you think she might harm Alicia? Maybe we should call Alicia and warn her."

Aware that they had offered Hogan too much information, Flora Jean flashed Damion a look that said, *Need you to be quiet for a second here, Blood.* Looking back at Hogan, she said, "Of course not. So can we get those directions?"

Sounding relieved that Alicia apparently wasn't in harm's way, Hogan said, "Yes, I'll write them down for you."

"Appreciate it," said Flora Jean. "And who knows? Keep on dreamin', and one day you just might get your chance to fly that F-16."

The arched entryway to Alicia Phillips's Lazy 2 Lazy U Ranch was nearly identical to the one at the Montana ranch she'd grown up on. Remarkably the same. She'd used the same six-inch-diameter drill-rigger's pipe that her father had used to fashion the uprights and crosspiece. She'd set the uprights in identical four-foot-deep holes and flanked each with a row of three ponderosa pines. The Lazy 2 Lazy U cattle brand, which her family had first registered in Montana 120 years earlier, swung lazily from the middle of the crosspiece in the eastern Colorado plains breeze.

Wind gusts had been kicking up all day, sending dust devils, tumbleweed spores, and a constant mist of pollen into the air. Connie Eastland's hay fever had shot into overdrive the moment she and Alicia had arrived at the ranch. Now, as they sat in matching wicker chairs in the screened-in breezeway that separated the main part of the ranch house from the garage, Connie's eyes were red and puffy.

Sneezing and looking miserable, Connie asked, "Can't we go inside? I'm feeling worse by the minute." She sneezed and finished off the last of a tall glass of lemonade.

"Sure, sure," Alicia said, clearly distracted. "Just let me see if that colt of mine can hold his own with the old broodmare over there in the south pasture." Alicia rose and fixed her gaze on three horses about forty yards away. "I dropped a bucketful of grain into an old tire next to that dead cottonwood in the middle of the pasture." She pointed toward the gnarled old tree. "I want to see if the colt will go up against that mare for the right to it."

Connie wanted to ask Alicia why she'd set the horses up to battle over food, but she didn't. She understood that it was simply Alicia's way. She'd seen Alicia pit animal against animal before, and athlete against athlete. Alicia, she had learned, enjoyed watching man and beast alike struggle to maintain superiority.

"The colt's nosing the old mare off! See it? See it?" Alicia said, her voice charged with excitement. When the colt flicked its head assertively and pawed at the ground with a front hoof, Alicia screamed, "Good boy." As the mare slowly ambled away, she yelled,

"Serves her right. From now on she'll have to wait her turn." She eyed the colt with admiration. "Good boy, Thunder."

Sneezing and rubbing her eyes, Connie asked, "Can we go in now, Alicia?"

Without answering, Alicia stared past the horses and down toward the bend in Little Owl Creek, the quarter-mile-long stretch of stream that more or less cut the ranch in half. Turning to go inside, she glanced back toward the stream, paused in the breezeway door, smiled, and said, "Sure."

Looking up from the vantage point of a perfect location for a kill shot and camouflaged by a clump of creekside cottonwoods, Alicia Phillips's coconspirator smiled and thought about the fact that the time had come for a solution to their thorny problem. A shot to the head or perhaps the chest would do it—plain and simple. A perfect takedown in a sea of grass in a cluster of cottonwoods in the middle of nowhere. The cottonwoods would muffle the sound of the shot, and it would all be over in an instant.

In contrast to Alicia's blasé attitude toward it, killing wasn't something that came naturally to the shooter. But like so many other things in life, it was a learned skill. One that could be perfected, much like dribbling a basketball.

The sound of the breezeway door slamming shut in the wind gave the shooter a start. Glancing down at the barrel of the .30-06 lying on a blanket in the grass a few feet away, the shooter muttered, "Should be easy," and waited.

Chapter 27

Weld County Road 126, narrow, winding, and worn pretty much down to road base, wound its way northeast for fifteen miles into the short-grass plains east of I-25 before taking a straight shot across Little Owl Creek and turning back to the south toward Fort Collins. Bucking a headwind, kicking up a rooster tail of dust, and squeaking out a plea for new shocks, Flora Jean's Suburban was the lone vehicle on a seemingly endless stretch of county road.

Deep in thought, Damion lurched forward in his seat as Flora Jean skirted a prairie-dog hole and said, "I've been thinking about what makes people tick."

"Well, when you figure it out, be sure and let me in on the secret, sugar. Never been able to figure it out myself."

"I'm serious."

"Never said you weren't. So what have you come up with?"

"Now, follow me here, okay?"

"I'm followin'."

"Suppose you had the world by the tail, and everything you'd ever dreamed of was about to be yours. And to top it off, you were idolized and adored and praised at every juncture. Suppose that with all that going for you, you had a deep, dark, potentially dream-scuttling secret. A secret you couldn't tell even your closest lifelong friend for fear that letting it out would destroy you. What would you do?"

"Easy. I'd keep the secret to my damn self."

"Exactly. But suppose you were being blackmailed by someone who knew your secret? Someone who was threatening to broadcast it to the world? What would you do then?"

"I'm not sure, Blood. Maybe I'd just have a long, serious talk with that broadcaster."

"That's an answer. But not the one I'm looking for. The one I'm looking for is what would Shandell have done."

"So whatta you think he'd have done?"

"I think he would've gone to somebody he trusted for help, and since for whatever reason he didn't come to me, I'm thinking perhaps Coach Horse or Dr. Phillips very likely filled the bill. I think he chose Dr. Phillips. And from there I'm thinking things got sticky. He had no way of knowing he was sharing his secret with someone who had her own agenda. Now, what do you suppose Shandell would have done if he'd found out he was being used?"

"He'd have slam-dunked somebody for sure."

"Absolutely. Except that Dr. Phillips and maybe even Coach Horse weren't the only ones who knew his secret. I'm betting that muckraking reporter Grimes and Garrett Asalon and that stooge of his, Theisman, along with Connie Eastland and Wordell Epps, knew Shandell's secret. Especially since, as it turns out, at least one of Connie Eastland's sorority sisters had inside dope. So in the end, Shandell's secret had plenty of potential to take a trip around the world."

"And your point is?" Flora Jean asked, focusing her gaze on a lone farmhouse in the distance.

"My point is that we're missing something here, Flora Jean. Something that's the key to telling us exactly who it was that killed Shandell. Something akin to that forest-and-trees analogy everyone seems to be so fond of reminding me about. We've, or at least I've, spent too much time focusing on gambling and point-shaving and drug dealing, and you know what? I don't think any of that really matters. I'm beginning to think that what matters most is what was going on inside Shandell's head when his world started to crumble. In the end I think he was a lot like that character I mentioned to you on our way up here, from A Morning at the Office. Frustrated enough to say, *To hell with it; go on and tell the world.*"

"So you think he'd reached the point that he was sayin' to himself, *Can't hurt me no more, no matter what?*"

"Yes. Just like Horace Xavier, he'd had enough. Enough of being blackmailed and used and probably even threatened."

"I'd say those are good enough reasons for us to have a real long talk with the lady who was more or less his shrink." Flora Jean nodded toward the now clearly visible ranch house and set of corrals before them. "Pretty little valley. Let's hope Dr. Phillips is in and that she has some answers for us."

Damion stared down the gently sloping county road toward the Lazy 2 Lazy U compound. He could now see that it included not just an alabaster-white ranch house and corrals but a barn, a machine shop, and an implement shed. "Uptown," he muttered. "And she's there. See that black crew-cab pickup parked near the corrals?"

"Sure do, sugar."

"The truck's hers. No question. I've ridden in it before a couple of times with Shandell. Let's go get some answers," Damion said boldly.

"No need charging down San Juan Hill," Flora Jean said, scanning the landscape and letting her military instincts kick in. "Let's pull over and stop right here for a second." She turned off the road and nosed the Suburban toward a stand of cottonwoods. "I'm thinkin' we should probably get the lay of the land first."

"Okay," said Damion, wondering what it was that had Flora Jean spooked. When he noticed the glimmer of something in the cotton-woods that lined the far side of the creek meandering through at least a quarter section of fenced-off property, he understood.

Alicia and Connie strolled leisurely toward the bend in Little Owl Creek, blind to the fact that Flora Jean had a set of navy binoculars trained on them. Looking nervous and a bit unsettled but no longer sneezing, Connie drank in the picturesque creek-bottom landscape. "Sooner or later the police are going to figure things out, Alicia. They're not stupid. And if they don't, Damion will."

"Then let them."

"You don't seem concerned at all."

"I'm not. Things will work out in the end. How's your hay fever?"

"Not as bad as it was when we were sitting in your breezeway." Looking frustrated, Connie said, "Are you listening to me, Alicia?"

"Yes, I am. Just let me check on that head gate that's been giving me fits all summer, and we'll talk this through."

"Why'd you decide to write that book anyway?"

Alicia eyed the wide expanse of rolling hills surrounding them before answering. "See that fence line over there? The one running up along that ridge from the creek bottom?"

"Yes."

"It marks the boundary of my property. It's where I start and stop. And you know what? I don't want to start and stop there. We should never be limited by a fence, or a city's need for water, or some developer's condo dream."

"But your place is beautiful, Alicia. What do you need with more land?"

"When we get down to that head gate, I'll show you. Let you in on why it's so important to never have limits." Alicia glanced toward the stand of cottonwoods that had shaded the bend in the creek for more than a hundred years. For a brief moment she thought she caught a glimpse of something in the sunlight—a flicker of light in the trees, perhaps. She couldn't be certain. It could just as easily have been a low-hanging tree limb swaying in the breeze, or a bird on the wing, or a squirrel scurrying from tree to tree. But she knew one thing for certain. Whatever it had been, it was still there.

Flora Jean adjusted the focus on her field binoculars and leaned out the rolled-down window of the Suburban. "There's somebody down there in the cottonwoods standing a few yards away from a vehicle, Damion. Straight across from that dogleg in the creek."

"Where?" Damion asked excitedly.

"About fifty yards away from us and just off to the right." Tapping the top of the binoculars against the window jamb, she suddenly sounded concerned. "Shit; the SOB's got a rifle, and Connie and Dr. Phillips are headed straight that way."

Flora Jean handed Damion the binoculars. "Look straight at the bend in the creek and a little bit to your right. Whoever it is is decked out in camouflage. The nose of the vehicle's peekin' out of a cluster of willows ten yards or so from where the shooter is." Realizing she needed to do something fast, Flora Jean reached over the seat back and slipped her 9-mm out of her purse.

"Damn, they're perfect targets," Damion said, adjusting the binoculars' focus.

"Yeah, I know." Flora Jean stuck her left arm out the Suburban's window and fired three rounds into the air.

Unsure where the shots had come from, and with Alicia and Connie suddenly sprawled on the ground, the shooter turned and fired two shots in the direction of where the rounds seemed to have come from.

"What's going on?" Connie screamed as Alicia rose and turned to run.

Deciding she was too far away from the two women to do much good, Flora Jean laid her weapon on the center console and put the Suburban into gear. Before she could take off, Damion grabbed the 9-mm. Screaming, "Go after Alicia and Connie!" he jumped out of the truck and charged downhill in an all-out sprint toward the creek. The will and athleticism that had propelled him from fourth grade peewee basketball to the brink of an NBA career soon had him zigzagging his way between cottonwoods and willows, closing the gap between him and the shooter.

The willows and trees were too thick for Flora Jean to follow in the Suburban. Beside herself for having been separated from her weapon, an unconscionable mistake for any marine, she mumbled, "Damn it, Blood," and aimed the nose of the truck straight at Connie and Alicia.

Aware that the shooter's vehicle was more strategically important than anything else right then, Damion worked his way between fallen cottonwoods, through a thicket of willows, and finally past a stand of chokecherry trees toward the shooter. All he could make out as he closed in on the vehicle was a chrome bumper. In the rush and confusion that had followed Flora Jean's shots, he'd never actually seen the shooter, and he wondered whether the shooter had seen him. When two shots, very obviously from a rifle, slammed into the ground a few feet from him, he knew the answer. He dove for cover, aware that his life was on the line and that he'd have hell to pay when Flora Jean finally caught up with him. He realized he'd better not make a mistake.

Convinced that it would be difficult for the shooter to get off an accurate shot in a thicket of downed tree limbs and underbrush, Damion kept as much tree protection between him and the shooter as he could. He was fifteen yards from the vehicle when he heard a car door slam. Telling himself, *Damn the protection; it'll be even harder for the son of a bitch to get off a rifle shot from inside a car,* he burst from his protective cover and raced for the car. He was only yards from the vehicle when he realized that he was closing in on Wordell Epps's Honda.

Unsure what to do next, uncertain where Epps was, and suddenly aware that Epps could have a handgun as well as a rifle barrel aimed at him, Damion knelt behind a cottonwood stump and shouted out the first thing that came to mind. "We've got cops on the way, Epps. Best come out."

Before he could say anything else, two more bullets slammed into the tree stump. Looking up, he realized that the Honda was headed his way, with Epps at the wheel and a rifle barrel poking out the window.

Final game, final second, final shot, was all he could think as he squeezed off four quick shots at the Honda's windshield. The safety glass crumbled as one bullet found its mark, ripping into a howling Epps's shoulder, shattering his collarbone, and clipping off a silver-dollar-sized piece of shoulder blade before lodging in a back-seat armrest. Out of control, the Honda high-centered on the stump just as Damion jumped out of its way, and a .30-06 came flying out the window and hit the ground. Looking terrified as Damion carefully approached the car, Epps moaned in pain, "Don't shoot, Madrid. Don't shoot!"

Two feet from the car, Damion stopped and aimed the gun barrel point-blank at Epps's temple.

"No!" Epps blubbered as his blood pressure plummeted and tears streamed down his face.

"Did you kill Shandell?" Damion asked, fighting back his own tears.

When Epps didn't answer, Damion reached into the car, grabbed Epps by the shirt collar, and yelled, "I asked you! Did you kill my best friend?"

This time Epps couldn't answer. He'd passed out.

Eyeing the pathetic lost soul who sat slumped on the steering wheel and thinking seriously about shooting him right then and there, Damion suddenly remembered something he'd once heard CJ tell his mother, Julie, about killing an enemy soldier during the Vietnam War. *Sometimes just before I drift off to sleep at night, I swear I see that Vietcong soldier's face, Julie. And when I do, I wanta take that shot back. I wanta jam that bullet back in the chamber and buy myself some peace. But I can't. The genie popped out of the jar that day at Quan Tre, and I knew right then and there that I'd never be able to get him back inside.*

Damion looked around, half expecting to see someone who would take the pressure off him. Someone who would tell him what to do. CJ or Flora Jean or Coach Horse or even his mother, Julie. But all he saw was what had become a jungle of grass, a forest of menacing cottonwoods, and a creek bed stained the color of blood. Realizing he'd become briefly lost in another world as he'd contemplated taking a life, he looked up to see the Suburban moving toward him and took a long, deep breath. Only then did he realize where he was.

Lowering his gun and reaching into the car, he ran two fingers down Wordell Epps's neck and felt for a pulse. Epps's pulse was weak and thready. As he looked at the other man's surprisingly placid face, he found himself wondering whether, if he had indeed pulled the trigger, he would, like CJ, have forever seen Epps's face in his dreams. Feeling exhausted, he patted his belt in search of his cell phone.

Locating the phone in his shirt pocket, he flipped it open. It wasn't until the Suburban was almost on top of him that he realized that Alicia Phillips was tied to the rear bumper by her wrists—with a four-foot length of bungee cord, no less. She was shaking with fear or anger, he couldn't tell which, and her jeans were wet nearly up to the waist from having had to ford the creek behind the truck. His mouth agape, Damion dialed 911.

"Once a marine, always a marine," Flora Jean said from behind the wheel as she winked at Damion. "Got me a couple prisoners of war, and the one here in the front seat with me is shakin' like a leaf. I'm thinkin' this is gonna take some real sortin' out, Blood."

Damion bent to get out of the glare of the sun that partially blocked his view of the front seat until he locked eyes with a catatonic-looking Connie Eastland.

"You okay?" Flora Jean asked, staring at the Honda's windshield.

"Yeah. But Wordell Epps is in bad shape," Damion said as the operator asked, "911, what's your emergency?"

"I'm at the Lazy 2 Lazy U Ranch just off Weld County Road 126. We need paramedics and the sheriff out here in a hurry. There's been a shooting."

Chapter 28

Parked on a rise three-quarters of a mile away from Alicia Phillips's ranch house and peering through binoculars, Craigy Theisman scanned the assembly of police cars and flashing lights in the distance. Moments earlier he'd pulled off the road that led to the Lazy 2 Lazy U Ranch and into a willow thicket to make a cell-phone call to Garrett Asalon. "Got trouble out at the Phillips place, boss. Cop cars everywhere," he'd said to an out-of-breath Asalon, who'd just finished a strenuous workout. "There's even a fuckin' police helicopter parked on the front lawn, and the county road's barricaded about two hundred yards up from where I'm sittin'."

"Any sign of Connie or Phillips? You said earlier that Phillips told you they were headed for the ranch after you left that hot-dog stand you're so fond of, right?"

Theisman adjusted the focus on his binoculars. "Yeah. But from the looks of things, I'm thinkin' she likely told somebody else ahead of me. With a perimeter already set up and that chopper being here, no question the cops have been here a while."

"Good thing you weren't there in the middle of whatever went down," Asalon said, sounding relieved.

"Yeah." Thinking that maybe one additional Snappin' Dog had saved his ass, Theisman smiled. "So whatta you want me to do?"

"Get the hell out of there. I don't want anybody knowing I have any connection to Phillips. And I sure don't want the cops nosing around and figuring out that I had Phillips and Connie putting the squeeze on Shandell Bird for me."

"What about Connie?"

"What about her?"

"She knows a hell of a lot."

"That she does, but since I didn't kill anybody, I sort of like my position. With a chopper on site and as many cops as you say you've got up there, I'm guessing there's been either a shooting or a murder. Either way, whatever went down puts the paltry little sports fixing I was doing into perspective, wouldn't you say, Craigy?"

"Sure does."

"Now, get on out of there before you get swept up into the mix."

"I'm leaving now." Theisman cranked the engine on his SUV.

"It's a shame, though, when you come right down to it," said Asalon as an afterthought.

"What is?"

"That in the future I'll probably have to miss out on getting that sweet little piece of Eastland ass I've gotten so used to. But that's the way things go in this world, Craigy. You've got to take the bad with the good."

Weld County Sheriff Lester Sabbott tried to remember the last time he'd been involved even peripherally in investigating the murder of a celebrity. The answer was clearly never. Sabbott had arrived at the Lazy 2 Lazy U Ranch two hours earlier to find a semiconscious gunshot victim with a life-threatening wound in his shoulder, a woman tied to the back of a Suburban with a bungee cord, a second woman who was nearly as hysterical, a nervous-looking former basketball star whose entire college career it turned out Sabbott had followed, and a stoic, clearly undaunted former marine intelligence sergeant calling herself Flora Jean Benson.

The barely stable shooting victim had been rushed to Poudre Valley Hospital in an ambulance that had already been on the scene, and as the ambulance had sped away, sirens wailing, all he'd known for certain was that the victim's name was Wordell Epps and that he'd been shot by the former All-American basketball star Damion Madrid.

When Sabbott realized that he'd plopped right down in the middle of an investigation involving a triad of murders that had been on the front pages of regional newspapers for days, he'd called the homicide officer in charge of the highest-profile killing, the Shandell Bird murder, and asked for help. An hour later a Glendale, Colorado, police helicopter had deposited an only-too-eager-to-assist Will Townsend on Alicia Phillips's front lawn. Sabbott made sure his deputies cordoned off access to the ranch while for the next thirty minutes he and Townsend interrogated people and tried to piece things together.

Now, as Townsend questioned Connie Eastland in the ranch house living room, following up the intense fifteen-minute sessions he'd had with Flora Jean, Alicia, and Damion, Flora Jean and Damion remained in an adjacent heavily guarded bedroom with their feet and hands handcuffed, trying their best to hear what was going on in the living room, while Alicia Phillips sat similarly restrained in the master suite.

"Sure you don't want any water, Ms. Eastland?" asked Townsend, hoping to ingratiate himself with the exceedingly nervous Connie Eastland.

Looking defeated, Connie said, "No."

"Okay, but be sure and let me know if you want any. It might help." Townsend glanced down at notes he'd jotted on a sheet of CSU Department of Psychology letterhead. "Now, let me get this straight. You're claiming that a book Dr. Phillips and Paul Grimes were writing is the reason Shandell Bird was killed?"

"That's right."

"Mind telling me how that's so?"

Connie let out a long, heavy sigh. "Alicia and Grimes were writing what the two of them liked to call a psychological blockbuster. A book about college athletes that featured information Alicia had been gathering on them for years. Accounts of the athletes' unknown darker sides that highlighted their money problems, their sexual preferences, their drinking and gambling habits, their dalliances and infidelities, their insecurities, and their flat-out failures. They were planning to make money off what had started out as a clinical research project by turning Alicia's research into one of those popular tell-all kinds of books."

"How do you know so much about the book?"

Hesitating before she answered and looking guilty, Connie said, "They paid me to give them dirt on Shandell."

"So what went wrong?" asked the mesmerized Sabbott.

"A third person got involved. Too many cooks . . . you know the saying."

"And that third person I take it was Wordell Epps?" asked Townsend.

"Yes. I'm not sure how Epps found out about the book. Could be he peeked at the pages like I did while I was a research assistant for Dr. Phillips. Or maybe Grimes told him. Who knows? What I do know is that Epps wanted in on the action and that he threatened to blow the whistle on what Alicia and Grimes were up to if they didn't comply. Alicia told me so when we were shredding a bunch of her case-history documents one day."

"Sounds like she trusted you."

"She did. I think I made her feel young."

Nodding and failing to mention that both Flora Jean and Damion had told him Epps had admitted actually typing portions of the manuscript, Townsend said, "Could be Epps wanted what all authors want: recognition and money."

"I guess so. What I know for certain is that after Leon Bird was killed, Alicia seemed to get cold feet. She put the brakes on the book, and we started destroying all her records."

"So what did you and Dr. Phillips have on Shandell?"

"I knew Shandell was gay."

"Heavy duty," said Sabbott, sounding astonished.

"And what about Epps and Grimes?" asked Townsend, looking and sounding like someone who'd heard it all before.

"They knew, of course. But I'm not sure how big a deal it was to them. There were thirty or more dark-side profiles in the book. Shandell's was just one of them."

"Even so, it sounds like a lot of people were into blackmailing Shandell Bird," said Sabbott.

"But Epps is the one who killed him," Connie whispered. "And if you ask me, I think Alicia had an inkling Epps was the killer. That's what probably gave her cold feet."

"Well, if she did, she's keeping it to herself. The only thing we've been able to get out of the good Dr. Phillips is 'You'll have to talk to my attorney.' And that, Ms. Eastland, brings us to another question. Why so cooperative?" asked Townsend.

"Because I didn't kill anybody. I'm not about to be a scapegoat, and it looks as though Alicia may have set Epps up to kill me."

"Good instincts, Ms. Eastland. Nonetheless, my instincts tell me you were probably blackmailing Shandell as well. And the law says that's a no-no."

"Did Damion tell you that? Because if he did, here's a scoop for you, Sergeant. There aren't any laws against someone's boyfriend giving her money or buying her gifts."

Townsend smiled. "You're right, Ms. Eastland, but there are plenty against extortion. Now, just suppose that instead of getting someone to shower you with gifts, you got them to instead shave a few points in very important basketball games?"

"You'd have to prove that, Sergeant."

"I'll work on it," Townsend said with a grin. "Who knows? A prosecutor or two I know may even decide to ask for a little assistance from you in that regard. Might help your case. But that's another story," said Townsend, deciding the time wasn't quite ripe to let Connie Eastland know what he'd found out about Garrett Asalon's operation. "Why don't we finish up the current story? Your take is that Wordell Epps killed Shandell Bird and that he also killed Paul Grimes, and perhaps even Leon Bird, because he wanted to hoard the profits from some unpublished manuscript?"

"According to Alicia, yes." Looking up at Sheriff Sabbott as if to say, *I hope you don't want another twenty minutes of my time too,* she asked, "Are we about done here?"

"Close. One last question. Do you know if Alicia Phillips owns a .30-06? It's the kind of rifle you'd need out here on a ranch like this all by yourself."

"No, why?"

"Just wondering." Townsend stroked his chin thoughtfully and stared Connie directly in the eye. "That's about it. Thanks." Ending the interrogation with a smile, he turned, walked to the bedroom where Damion and Flora Jean were being held, nodded for the deputy outside to open the door, and waved to Sheriff Sabbott to follow him into the room. "We're back," he said, greeting Damion and Flora Jean with a broad, toothy grin.

"So does everybody's story fit, Sergeant?" asked Flora Jean, aware that the separate interrogations had been orchestrated so Townsend and Sabbott could see if everyone's story about the Epps shooting meshed.

"Afraid you'll have to ask your lawyer that," said Townsend. "You two do have one, I trust?"

"Sure do." Flora Jean eyed her watch. "And I'm guessin' she's arriving at DIA just about now."

"Then I'd suggest you use that phone call you're entitled to to give her a call. Wouldn't you agree, Sheriff?"

"Absolutely," said Sabbott. "Because for the time being I'm going to have to hold you both."

"On what charge?" Flora Jean demanded. "Damion shot Epps in self-defense, and I sure as hell didn't shoot nobody."

"But you're an accessory," said Sabbott. "And until my people check out the ballistics on that slug they found in the tree stump Madrid claims he ducked behind when Epps tried to kill him, and we check out the rifle found at the scene, you and Madrid are suspects in an attempted murder. Like it or not, the two of you are going to get to spend some very special time with me."

Fearful that his medical career might be in jeopardy, Damion said, "In jail?"

"Afraid so, son." Sabbott turned to Flora Jean. "I'm thinking that in addition to a lawyer, the two of you just might need another bail bondsman like yourself, Ms. Benson."

"Oh, we've got one," Flora Jean said smugly, watching a look of surprise spread across the sheriff's face.

"And where's he? At DIA as well?" asked Sabbott.

"You got it, Cisco," Flora Jean said with a grin. "I'm thinkin' that just about now he's givin' our lawyer a hug and a great big kiss."

Damion had never spent time in jail, but he had no choice but to, as Flora Jean aptly put it as they were being hauled off in handcuffs from the ranch to the Weld County jail, go with the flow. Julie's later frantic phone calls aimed at preventing Flora Jean and Damion from spending the night in jail didn't do a thing to stop Sheriff Sabbott from placing them both on twenty-four-hour hold pending the issuance of a formal charge. And much to Julie's consternation, she, Damion, and Flora Jean had barely had ten minutes to talk before Damion and Flora Jean were led off to separate holding facilities. A fitful night of sleep had Julie thinking early the next morning that somehow she needed to even the score with Sabbott and Townsend.

When she and CJ returned to the Weld County North Jail Complex that morning, Wordell Epps was listed in stable condition at Poudre Valley Hospital. By noon a sheriff's deputy had found a second .30-06 slug in the cottonwood stump Damion had sought refuge behind, and Sergeant Townsend, warrant in hand, had searched Wordell Epps's apartment and found two pristine copies of a manuscript titled *Campus Gladiators: The Dark and Lonely Side of NCAA Sports*.

Sergeant Townsend had spent most of his early morning on the phone pushing people in both the Glendale and Weld County ballistics departments to match the bullets that had killed Shandell, Leon Bird, and Paul Grimes to the .30-06 that had been found next to Epps's Honda. He'd then driven the sixty miles north from Glendale to Sheriff Sabbott's office to take a look at the second tree-stump bullet and the rifle for himself. Done with his business, he stood talking to Sabbott outside Sabbott's office when Flora Jean and Damion, released on a judge's order after a morning of legal maneuvering by Julie, walked down the hallway with CJ and Julie at their sides.

Excusing himself, Townsend called out, "Madrid, Ms. Benson, wait up." Strolling up to a beleaguered-looking Damion and a surly Flora Jean, Townsend eyed CJ, then Julie, and asked, "So who's the lawyer and who's the bail bondsman?" as if hoping that his attempt at levity might somehow erase the fact that Damion and Flora Jean had just spent the night in jail.

Flora Jean flashed Townsend a steely-eyed stare and said to Julie, "The stand-up comic is Sergeant Will Townsend."

"Sorry about the jail time," said Townsend. "Sabbott's call all the way. We're way out of my jurisdiction."

Nodding politely, Julie said, "I doubt that, Sergeant. But be that as it may, I'm Damion and Flora Jean's attorney, Julie Madrid. I'm also Damion's mother." She made no attempt to shake Townsend's extended hand. "The gentleman in the Stetson is CJ Floyd."

"Floyd. Yeah, I've heard of you." Staring up at the deeply tanned, much taller man, Townsend found himself surprised that Damion's attorney was also his mother.

"Hope it's all been good." CJ slipped a cheroot out of his vest pocket and toyed with it.

"Looks like your clients are going to come out of this okay, counselor," said Townsend. "Turns out we've pretty much got Epps dead to rights in the Shandell Bird killing. Got a smoking gun, or a smoking rifle at least, and motives galore. Blackmail, financial gain, a chance at the resurgence of a career and newfound fame."

"And you're telling us this because?" Julie asked, perfectly aware of the reason for Townsend's sudden forthrightness.

"Because I'm thinking we'll very likely need your clients' testimony to help convict Epps."

"My, my, my, Sergeant. From what I hear, you and Sheriff Sabbott weren't nearly so friendly or cooperative yesterday," CJ countered.

"We had a possible murder on our hands, Mr. Floyd."

"Then why didn't you take the Eastland woman's story about what happened into account? According to my clients, she saw everything," CJ said, his voice rising.

Julie smiled and tugged at CJ's vest. "Let me pull your coattails, CJ. The sergeant here, with the blessing of the prosecution, I'm sure, just might have his eyes on a bigger fish than Epps. You see, Connie Eastland's the kind of witness they can use to go after someone else. No need to ruffle her feathers over a mere shooting in the woods. Right, Sergeant? Just for the record, I've been told all about Asalon. And I've got a feeling that instead of asking Connie Eastland for an explanation of what really happened at that ranch, which would've saved my clients the indignity of a night in jail, you were buttering her up. Kissing up to her and hoping she'd be there in the future to roll on one of our state's biggest gaming connected mobsters for you."

"So because of your little charade and what it has cost my son and Ms. Benson, I'm going to let you in on what I plan to do in rebuttal." Julie flashed Townsend her best courtroom *gotcha* smile. "I'm going to have Mr. Floyd here run down everything you've ever done during your twenty-two years on the Glendale force. That's right. Twenty-two years. As you can see, Sergeant, I've already started. And he's going to find out everything about you. From whether you ever took as much as a free stick of gum from anyone for doing them an out-of-bounds favor to whether you've ever yelled at a neighbor's cat. Not to mention your antics yesterday concerning Ms. Eastland. And then I'm going to use what he finds out to make life unpleasant for you. It'll be the kind of unpleasantness that ensures you'll never make lieutenant, Sergeant." Julie's grin broadened. "That is, unless you help me with a problem."

"Which is?" Townsend said defiantly.

"I want you to talk with Sheriff Sabbott and see if you can get Damion's and Ms. Benson's records expunged."

"They were only here on twenty-four-hour hold. There is no arrest record. What's the big deal?"

"You and I know that, Sergeant. But there's no telling what might turn up in some state board of medical examiners' office years down the road. I don't want that risk hanging over Damion's head."

"I'm afraid you'll have to talk to Sheriff Sabbott about that."

"Nope," CJ said, his tone insistent. "You'll have to talk to him." He reached into the back pocket of his jeans, pulled out his wallet, and extracted a check. Unfolding the check, he showed it to Townsend. "The check you're looking at is made out to me from Ms. Madrid's law firm, and as you can see, it's for a thousand dollars. Know what that means, Sergeant? It means I'm being paid right this second to look at you through a microscope, and it means my trip into your little world, as private as you might think it is, is going to be real, real reportable and official. Makes you wanta squirm a little, doesn't it?"

"Don't threaten me, Floyd."

"Oh, I wouldn't think of doing that. But since we're screwing around with careers and futures here, I thought you should know my position."

Townsend stroked his chin and eyed Damion. "When do you start medical school, Madrid?"

"Ten days from now," Damion said, feeling caught in the middle of something he didn't fully comprehend.

Townsend looked back at Julie. "I'll see what I can do."

Julie flashed him an artificial smile. "Now, that's taking a positive look at things, Sergeant. And believe me, we all appreciate that." Eyeing CJ, she said, "Everybody ready to blow this pop stand?"

"Whenever you are, counselor," CJ said, ushering a very amused-looking Flora Jean and a slightly bewildered Damion toward the exit.

Chapter 29

A week after the first rash of newspaper stories appeared, calling the events at the Lazy 2 Lazy U Ranch a modern-day shoot-out at the O.K. Corral, police and prosecutors had assembled just about everything they needed to make what many believed would be a punishable-by-death case against Wordell Epps. They had the weapon that had been used to kill Shandell Bird and Paul Grimes, irrefutable ballistics evidence to support that claim, and Epps's fingerprints and DNA all over the weapon.

In addition, they had a commitment from Connie Eastland that she would testify against both Epps and Alicia Phillips. Prosecutors planned to name Phillips as an accessory to the attempted murder of Damion Madrid and Eastland, and to shore up their claim, they had the revenge-minded Epps willing to point to Phillips, in an attempt to save at least a piece of his hide, as the person who'd suggested he kill Connie Eastland. They had Flora Jean's and Connie Eastland's eyewitness accounts of Epps's attempt on Damion's life. But perhaps the best single piece of evidence they had going for them was the Grimes and Phillips manuscript, the very trigger for the first two killings and a document that prosecutors were claiming the scorned, irrational, marijuana-addicted, onetime Pulitzer Prize winner, who quite likely had intended to kill only Grimes, had seen as a vehicle capable of returning him to his journalistic glory days.

Alicia Phillips, in search of a plea-bargain deal, had willingly given Epps up, telling prosecutors she would gladly testify to the fact that when Epps had realized the career-resurrecting and moneymaking potential of *Gladiators*, he'd insinuated himself into the project and demanded to be made a coauthor. She said the fact that his long-time friend Paul Grimes had denied him that distinction, telling him he would receive only a brief acknowledgment, had sent an enraged Epps over the edge. That was the story the district attorney for the 18th Judicial District and Alicia Phillips were busy constructing, and they were sticking to it.

The rifle that had been used to kill Shandell and Grimes turned out to have been a gift presented to Grimes and Epps by a grateful Colorado cattle rancher whom they'd done a story about years earlier. The rancher had a five-thousand-acre near-century-old family spread outside Aspen that at the time had been suffering under the slings and arrows of heavy-handed ski resort encroachment. He had eventually sold the ranch and moved to Santa Barbara, California, but now he was another potential witness for the prosecution. It turned out he had saved not only newspaper clippings of the Grimes and Epps' *Rocky Mountain News* piece that had told his David-against-Goliath story but also the story's sidebar photograph that showed him presenting the alleged murder weapon to Grimes and Epps. A portion of the incriminating caption below the photo read: *And in further appreciation, Mr. Hicks plans to teach the two investigative reporters "how to shoot the dang thing."*

Whether Hicks had actually taught either Grimes or Epps how to handle the .30-06 was of little consequence to prosecutors, since behind closed doors they were chuckling that the story would not only make for good courtroom theater but also offered them the once-in-a-lifetime opportunity to introduce into evidence a photograph of the ultimate smoking gun.

There was, however, something missing from the prosecutors' story. Something that was more than simply a minor glitch in their near-perfect nail-'em-to-the-wall scenario. They had their man, the enraged, murderous, drugged-out, scorned best friend, and they expected corroborating testimony from police psychologists waiting in the wings. The psychologists would claim that Epps had very likely decided to take his vengeance not simply on Grimes but on Shandell as well.

There was only one thing missing from the prosecutors' perfect score, and that was the fact that their smoking gun and ballistics data and eyewitness accounts of Epps's attempted murder of Damion Madrid, and the plea-bargain deals, and all the psychological posturing in the state couldn't explain the fact that the bullet that had killed Leon Bird hadn't come from Wordell Epps's rifle. That single inexplicable finding cast a very definite shadow on their otherwise perfect game. The prosecutors were relatively unconcerned, but the shadow had had "Self-Assured Perfectionist" Damion Madrid searching for answers for over a week.

Damion had spent his last few days before entering medical school, much to the consternation of Niki, his mother, Julie, Flora Jean, and even CJ, trying to tie up that one loose end, which Julie had gotten wind of in her capacity as a trial lawyer. And now, as he sat in CJ's office staring up from his chair at the soles of the run-over Luchesse boots firmly planted on CJ's desktop—boots that had gotten more than their share of stares in Hawaii—Damion found himself confused.

Still a shade darker than when he'd left for Hawaii, CJ continued puffing on his cheroot and blowing smoke rings in the air while he waited for a runner to bring him the paperwork he needed to clear a client's bail. Unable to contain himself any longer and concerned that he hadn't been able to bring the murder of his best friend to complete closure, Damion eyed CJ and said, "This thing's not over yet, CJ."

"Damn, Blood. You're gonna work yourself up to the point that you won't be able to focus on crossing the street, much less get through the first year of medical school. I say leave it alone. For once the law may have got it right."

Damion shook his head. "Mom claims maybe they don't. She says that when the DA and his minions waltz into court claiming they've got Epps dead to rights, the defense is going to pull out that ballistics report on the Leon Bird shooting and argue that another gunman with another rifle could've killed both Shandell and Grimes."

"The DA's not that stupid, Damion. Besides, he's got more than enough to hang two murders on Epps. No need for a third."

"You're right. According to Mom, he's not stupid, just arrogant. And she should know. She went to law school with him. He's up for reelection, and he's looking to score as many points with voters as he can. She says he's egotistical enough to let the ballistics report on the bullet that killed Leon get entered into evidence just to prove that his two bullets, the ones that killed Shandell and Grimes, are from the perfect smoking gun. One he supposedly has a two-decades-old photo of. Mom says he could screw this up, CJ. And like she's so fond of saying, there's nothing more unpredictable than a trial by jury."

"Damn it, Blood. You're starting to sound more and more like some damn attorney and less and less like a doctor."

"Gotta remember, CJ, both professions are analytical."

"Yeah, and one's full of sharks, excluding Julie of course."

"Oh, she can shark when she has to. We both know that." Damion met CJ's acknowledging smile with one of his own.

CJ's smile quickly faded. "So since there seems to be no stopping you from pressing on, you might as well tell me where you're headed with this and I'll see if I can help." CJ wagged an outstretched index finger at Damion. "But Damion, none of that charging-down-San-Juan-Hill-on-your-own shit that you pulled on Flora Jean. I'll thump your ass, you hear me?"

"Yes."

"Okay. Lay out what you're thinking."

Elated that CJ was at least willing to listen, Damion gave a rapid-fire response: "The cops and the prosecutors have it right. The ballistics report on the bullet that killed Leon just might shore up their case against Epps, but that report also tells us where to look for the weapon that killed Leon."

"How?"

"You're not gonna like this, CJ."

"Try me."

"We're gonna need to run over to Shandell's house and talk to Mrs. B."

CJ frowned, and his eyes narrowed into a squint. "You're right, Damion. I don't like it one bit."

"I said you wouldn't." Damion rose from his chair. "But you promised to help."

"So I did," said CJ, slipping his feet off the desktop. "So I did."

A knot of fallen leaves swirled down the middle of the street in the wind as CJ cruised east down Fourteenth Avenue with the top down on his '57 drop-top Chevy Bel Air, headed for Welton Street and the straight shot that would take them to Five Points and Aretha Bird's house.

"Gonna be an early fall," said CJ, watching the leaves dance up over the curb. "Hard to believe that for the first time in years, I won't be watching you play ball."

Damion nodded, swallowed hard, and thought about Shandell. About all the years they'd been best friends, comrades in arms, and teammates. Smiling, he thought about the fact that they'd been actual oath-taking blood brothers—Blood and Blackbird against the world. As a sudden dryness filled the back of his throat, he found himself thinking that it would probably be there forever, whenever he thought about Shandell. Looking at CJ and feeling the warmth of the late-summer breeze on his face, he said, "Why do you think Shandell kept from telling me his secret all those years, CJ? I damn sure wouldn't have told anyone."

"I'm not certain, Damion, and I'm sure no shrink, but I can tell you this. In that macho fishbowl of a sports world the two of you lived in most of your lives, there never was and there never will be room for gays."

"But that's crazy. I can tell you for a fact that I played ball with guys whose sexual orientation I questioned from day one. Hell, I think some of them might've been sleeping with goats."

"Better goats than other men, Damion. We both know that."

"He just should've told me," Damion said, shaking his head in frustration as CJ turned onto Welton Street.

"In some ways he did. And I'm thinking maybe that was Shandell's way of protecting you. His way of keeping you from being tarred with the same brush as him if people ever found out he was gay. It could be that manuscript of Grimes or Alicia Phillips or Epps, or who-ever wrote the damn thing, said it best. They pegged Shandell pretty much right on in that psychological profile of theirs. Standoffish, fear-ful, close-mouthed, and dutifully efficient, as I recall from reading that copy your mama somehow pilfered. I'm thinking his behavior was designed in part to keep the spotlight off him and on you."

"Me?"

"Damn right. Who else do you think they would've been pointing fingers at if it ever came out that Shandell was gay?"

"Get serious, CJ. Nobody's ever questioned my sexual orientation. Besides, I have Niki."

"And Shandell had Connie." CJ watched the expression on Damion's face become a blank stare.

Damion rubbed the cleft in his chin. "Come to think of it, CJ, you could be right. Shandell and I barely hugged during the cutting down of the nets at the Sweet Sixteen and the Elite Eight last year. It was almost as if he was avoiding me on purpose. I thought back then that it was because both of those times he'd had bad final games. But then again, his lack of emotion could've had something to do with the point-shaving issue."

CJ shook his head. "Coulda, woulda, shoulda. Bottom line is, we'll never know, Damion. I've given you my reason for his behavior."

Damion fought back a rush of emotion that had his stomach sud-denly churning. "Yeah, that would've been like him. Be humble and stoic—reflect the glory."

Sensing that if the conversation continued in the same guilt-producing vein, whatever had kept Damion from falling apart emo-tionally for ten solid days might suddenly disappear, CJ said, "We're almost to Aretha's. Time to tell me what we're looking for, Blood."

Without hesitation, Damion said, "We're looking for a rifle. A .30-06, to be exact."

Following a round of hugs, some tears, and a few what-ifs, Damion and CJ settled on Aretha Bird's living room couch as Aretha sank into the room's lone overstuffed chair.

Looking over her reading glasses at Damion, Aretha said, "So, you ready for school, baby?"

"As ready as I'm going to be."

"And CJ, what about you? You down from cloud nine now that you're hitched and back from your honeymoon?"

"Mavis tells me I am. And since I've written two bonds this morning and Mario Satoni called to tell me he sold a nine-hundred-dollar antique steamer trunk out of that virtual antique store he and I own together, I'd say it's starting to look like business as usual."

After a few moments of awkward silence, Aretha took a sip of the limeade that she'd insisted everyone have a glass of, eyed Damion, and said, "You're here for a reason, Damion Madrid. I watched you and Shandell searchin' for wiggle room when you were up to somethin' for too many years. Might as well spit it out."

Hesitating and clearing his throat, Damion glanced at the lengthy healing scar running down his left arm. A scar that he realized would always be there. Eyeing Aretha, he said, "I'm looking to finally bring some closure to a festering wound."

"Might as well tell me about it, sweetie."

Damion let out a lengthy sigh. "You remember that night Leon met you at the Satire Lounge? The night he was killed?"

"Couldn't forget it in a thousand years."

"Well, I've talked to Mom about that night, and she says you told her Leon threatened to beat you."

"He did. Where are you headed with this, Damion?"

"Somewhere I really don't want to go, Mrs. B. Believe me." Damion gnawed briefly at his lower lip. "Who else was there when he made the threat?"

Aretha eyed Damion thoughtfully before looking at CJ to see whether she should answer the question.

"It's okay, Aretha. Go on and tell him," CJ said.

Sitting up in her seat, Aretha said, "A bunch of customers, but I don't think they heard Leon when he made the threat—and Jo Jo Lawson, of course."

"And when Leon threatened you, what did Jo Jo do?"

Frowning, Aretha said, "He nearly choked Leon to death."

"Do you remember him doing anything else?"

"Not really." Looking as if she'd forgotten something, she said, "Oh, he did say he'd get Johnny to help him with Leon if Leon didn't leave."

"Johnny who?" asked Damion.

"Another bartender, I guess."

Damion shook his head. "I don't think so. I've checked. There's no bartender named Johnny working at the Satire."

"Then I don't know who he was going to get to help him. But he did say Johnny. I'm certain of that."

"Yeah, I know." There was a sadness in Damion's eyes that hadn't been there when the conversation had started. As he looked from Aretha to CJ, the sadness seemed to mount. "Would the two of you mind running over to the Satire Lounge with me? I called the manager first thing this morning to ask what time Jo Jo would be in. He told me Jo Jo would be there by ten for sure because it was his day to put up bar stock."

"Okay," said Aretha. "But I'm not sure I understand what's going on here."

"You will, Mrs. B; you will." Damion glanced at CJ as if to ask, *Am I doing okay?* When CJ flashed him a supportive wink, Damion said, "When we get there, everybody just follow my lead."

Jo Jo Lawson's face lit up when he saw Aretha Bird walk into the Satire Lounge. Realizing that CJ and Damion were right behind her, he raced toward them. "Mrs. B, Damion, Mr. Floyd. Happy to see ya!"

CJ, who'd helped Jo Jo out of a few scrapes with the law when the young man had lived on the streets for a couple of years right after high school, shook Jo Jo's hand as Damion high-fived the marginally retarded bartender and gave him a hug. Aretha followed Damion's hug with a motherly kiss on the cheek.

"So how's it going, Jo Jo?" Damion swallowed hard and thought, *Can I do this?*

"Good. Real good, except of course for losin' my best friend." He eyed Aretha and Damion sympathetically.

"We're all hurting that way," said Damion. "You know they got the murderer."

"Yeah. I heard. Been readin' all about it in the paper."

Watching CJ ease his way behind Jo Jo, Damion asked, "So, Jo Jo, got a question for you."

"Shoot, Blood. I'm listenin'."

"Remember when we were in high school and a bunch of the other kids used to pick on you?"

Jo Jo eyed the floor. "Yeah. A bunch of 'em," he said softly.

"Shandell was the one who put a stop to all that, as I remember," said Damion.

"You helped too, Blood. You helped too."

Damion smiled appreciatively. "So would you say that because of that you owed Shandell?"

"Of course. He was like a brother."

"And you owed Mrs. B too," Damion said, eyeing a suddenly glassy-eyed Aretha.

"I owed her, sure," Jo Jo said, looking puzzled.

Hesitant to utter what he knew had to come next, Damion worked his tongue slowly around the inside of his cheek. "I know about Johnny, Jo Jo. Shandell told me all about Johnny a long time ago. It wasn't until last night when I was moping around listening to some old tunes that were popular when we were in high school and thinking about Shandell that I even remembered."

"What did Shandell say about Johnny?"

"Everything, Jo Jo. Everything. Most of it on a road trip when the basketball team went down to play Pueblo East our senior year. We were bumping down I-25 in one of those big yellow buses when he told me the two of you had recently come up with a name for all the vicious and hurtful things people used to keep other people in line. Things like fear and intimidation and abuse. It was a name Shandell said you also reserved for crooked cops and guns and prison and hateful words and hurtful stares. He said it was the name you gave to the razor strap your father used to beat you and your brother Marty with and keep you and your mother in line. He said the name the two of you came up with was a simple, easy one to remember—Johnny."

"Yeah, that's the word we used," said Jo Jo, eyes glued to the floor. "It was somethin' nobody knew about but us. Just me and my friend Shandell. I didn't even think you knew, Damion."

"I wish I didn't."

Wide-eyed and looking childlike, Jo Jo began rocking from side to side. "That razor strap of my daddy's. He almost killed Marty with it one night." Jo Jo's voice became a whisper. "And the whole time he was beatin' Marty he kept sayin' he was gonna turn him into a retard like me. I swore after that I wouldn't never let anybody do that to somebody I cared about again. I threw that strap away that night, and he never found it again."

Jo Jo looked up at the pained expression on Damion's face. "That's pretty much when I decided I needed a Johnny of my own. Shandell and I used to joke about goin' to get Johnny when somebody slighted us or called us a name like stupid retard or dumbass jock. It was our special secret. Only thing is, Shandell never really needed no Johnny like me."

"You're wrong there, Jo Jo. In a lot of ways Shandell needed protection more than anyone." Damion looked Jo Jo squarely in the eye. "And you were forced to use Johnny the other night after Leon and Mrs. B argued in here, right?"

Jo Jo nodded slowly.

"Had to. Just like Daddy, Leon might've ended up killin' Mrs. B."

"So what did you do with the rifle?" CJ asked, stepping up and draping an arm over Jo Jo's shoulder.

Jo Jo eyed the floor and shuffled his feet. "Johnny's over behind the bar where I always keep him. You can go take a look, Mr. Floyd. I ain't gonna run. Wouldn't do nothin' but make matters worse."

Damion let out a sigh as he watched CJ head for the bar. "I think you need to talk to my mom before we go any further with this, Jo Jo." He glanced at Aretha, who nodded in agreement.

"You think I'm really gonna need her help? I was only protectin' Mrs. B."

"Yes, I do," said Damion.

"But why?"

"Because she can give you the kind of protection you're going to need, Jo Jo. A lot like Johnny, only with words."

Epilogue

The rotund, bespectacled anatomy professor standing at the podium in front of the 128 newly enrolled students in the University of Colorado medical school freshman class was a seasoned veteran of the academic wars. In his more than thirty-four years at CU, Donald Venton had taught anatomy to thousands of students, and in the vernacular of academic graybeards like himself, when it came to students, he had seen and heard it all. He'd taught students who were dyslexic, anorexic, and bipolar. He'd infused the spirit of medicine into men and women who weren't quite sure they wanted to be doctors, literally becoming the wind in their sails. He'd watched students excel and flounder and just plain goof off. He'd seen students get married, have kids, get divorced, and even get kicked out of school. Over the years, he'd been there for students who'd had miscarriages or abortions. He'd dealt with the deaths of family members, an amputation, and more than one student who'd turned out to be a cheater. So as he planted his feet and adjusted his ample belly behind the lectern to begin his instruction in anatomy for the first semester of his thirty-fifth year, he had no reason to expect that the new term would offer him any new spins.

Damion was seated in a row near the back of the lecture hall, fumbling with a pen and trying his best to stay focused. The two days leading up to his first actual medical school class following a day and a half of orientation had been hectic. He'd learned just that morning from Mario Satoni that Pinkie Niedemeyer had used a very special form of encouragement to convince Leotis Hawkins that it would be best that he never bother Damion again, and that perhaps in the interest of his own well-being, Leotis should consider leaving town. When Damion had asked Mario what form Pinkie's encouragement had taken, Mario had smiled and said pointedly, "Pinkie promised to kill the bastard if he ever fucked with you again."

The day prior to beginning orientation, Damion had had a visit from a clearly euphoric Sergeant Townsend, who'd informed him that the NCAA, the FBI, and perhaps even Congress would be looking closely into allegations that Garrett Asalon had been involved in a point-shaving scam to fix the outcome of NCAA tournament games, and that an incensed Coach Haroldson and former teammates of Damion's, including the now suspended Jackie Woodson and the recently fired athletic trainer, Rodney Sands, were expected to testify against Asalon.

The case against Wordell Epps hadn't proceeded much further than it had in the days prior to the start of school except that a third murder charge against Epps had been dropped when information about Jo Jo Lawson's involvement in the Leon Bird murder had come to light.

Alicia Phillips had been placed on indefinite administrative leave at CSU, leave that was certain to culminate in her termination once a full investigation of the scale of her inappropriate clinical research was under way. Her lawyer was fighting to keep her salaried, but the fact that she'd been slapped with an accessory-to-murder charge was bound sooner or later to not only squeeze off her salary pipeline but send her to prison.

Fortunately, the same thing couldn't be said for Jo Jo Lawson. Julie

Madrid had mounted an aggressive defense on Jo Jo's behalf, one that was playing out in the local papers and had made its way more than once to the editorial pages of Denver's two dailies. Julie's defense was designed to lead to an outcome that would likely find Jo Jo guilty of killing Leon Bird but on the grounds of mental impairment. She meant to argue that in his limited, almost juvenile vision of the situation, he'd had no choice but to protect Aretha Bird's life against an imminent threat from Leon.

Julie had warned Damion that there was only a fifty-fifty chance that her strategy would work, but she had stacks of case law to support her position, and she and the grateful Aretha intended to stick by Jo Jo to the end.

Clearing his throat and thumping his lapel mike with an index finger in order to get the class's attention, Professor Venton said, "I suspect you've heard about my tradition of asking students what their summer was like, and if you haven't, you have now. I've learned over the years that it helps us to get to know one another better."

A few students near the back of the room snickered.

Unfazed, Venton said, "So, in keeping with that tradition, I'm going to ask three or four of you, just as if you were all sitting rosy-cheeked and fired up to learn in the first grade, to let the whole class in on what you did on your summer vacation. Believe it or not, sometimes we get some pretty wild stories." Venton glanced down at the three pages of color photos of students with their names typed below them and spread the photos out on the lectern. Looking up and then straight ahead, he said, "Ms. Samuels. Why don't we start with you?"

As Venton and the class listened to Amanda Samuels's description of working in a fish-canning factory in Alaska for the months of June and July, Damion thought about what he'd say if called upon.

Deciding that he really didn't have a good response, he slouched down in his seat, trying to remain inconspicuous.

Two more students responded to Professor Venton's question. One, a burly, thick-necked Cleveland native, had worked in a tire factory in Akron, and the other, a prissy-sounding woman from Santa Fe, who Damion could only imagine was going to be four years of trouble, announced that she'd worked in a restaurant in Vail and had hated it.

He was caught off guard when Dr. Venton asked, "And Mr. Madrid, why don't we close out with you before moving into today's topic: the anatomy of the integumentary system?" Eyeing the sea of eager faces, he added, "For the uninformed, and for those of you primed to enjoy the cushy life of a dermatologist, the lecture will be about the skin."

The class erupted in laughter.

"So tell us what you did this summer, Mr. Madrid, and we'll move on."

Almost involuntarily, and in a chilling voice that immediately turned the room silent, Damion said, "I tracked down the murderer of my best friend."